SEX, HAIR & BILLIONAIRES

ADVENTURES OF A CELEBRITY

HAIRSTYLIST

BRANDON MARTINEZ

D0833061

This book is dedicated to every one of my clients.

Without all of you, I would be nothing.

I love and appreciate all of you.

CONTENTS

Introduction

1

SO A STRAIGHT MAN

2

3

4

5

6

THIS IS FOR THE READER!

I want to start by saying that I appreciate you buying this book and taking the time to read it. I am so happy and blessed to have gone through these experiences as I don't know another hair stylist who had it like I did, or I should say as I do, since I'm still doing hair!

Since I've been a hair stylist in Hollywood, I have been compared to Warren Beatty's character, George, from the movie Shampoo. I'm not trying to brag, but the movie Shampoo has nothing on my career. Warren Beatty's character didn't have the clients that I have and didn't even come close to the experiences I went through!

This book is about billionaires, moguls, celebrities, rock stars, crazy rich women, sex, money and, of course, hair! It's also a love story. A love story between two people from completely different backgrounds, growing closer to each other over a 10-year period.

It's *Romeo & Juliet* without the suicides. It's *Scarface* without the cocaine! It's hair that brings these two people together in search for true love because we all know you can't find love through money!

That said, I am going to save you from having to listen to me go on about my childhood or anything like that because at the end of the day, my life didn't start until I began doing hair.

When I first became a hair stylist, I had no idea that I would go through the experiences that were coming to me. It was like the universe was confirming that I was on the right path in my career as a Hollywood hair stylist.

The reason I wrote this book is because when you do hair, being able to make great conversation is 90 percent of your job description. Hair stylists who are silent usually have no business. As I was experiencing these situations, my clients, to whom I would tell these stories, would constantly tell me: "Brandon, you have to write these things down! You could write a book for sure!"

Now, I'm sure a lot of people in my shoes are told that all the time. However, because I am a straight male in a predominantly gay- and female-heavy industry, this made my experiences that much more interesting. I have been and always will be a 'fish out of water' in this business.

As I contemplated writing a book, I had personally never really written anything. I am a damn good storyteller but most of my storytelling happens while I'm behind the chair cutting and coloring someone's hair, hopped up on shit tons of coffee!

I'm naturally an animated person, which always makes any story more exciting! Writing an actual book is really an unknown medium for me. Would I be able to convey my stories on paper the same way I convey them in person?

Fortunately, it's in my personality to be fearless and take risks, so I figured, fuck it! What have I got to lose? As an artist, I've been able to translate my artistic qualities into other fields including photography, drawing, guitar playing and, obviously, cutting hair. Writing is just another art form.

The people that I talk about in this book are so famous and powerful and the situations I got to see them in were fucking priceless! From a dying rock star's wife trying to molest me every chance she got, to being flown to a private island just to do hair, to crazy rich women who are married to old men throwing temper tantrums left and right, I heard and saw it all!

These stories had to be told! However, the biggest and most important reason I wrote this book is because of love. I fell in love with someone during all this time as a celebrity hair stylist. The person I fell in love with comes from a completely different world than I do. I basically met my dream woman, became her hair stylist, and grew to love her more and more with each passing year.

I have seen this person in a lot of different, emotional situations. I even lived under her roof for a short period of time when I was having difficulties in my own life. This person has been there for me more than once and that ultimately made me love her even more.

I never thought that I would fall in love with a famous socialite from New York City but love has no rules! This woman makes me want to be the 'better me!' That's how I know my feelings for her are true.

In the beginning, she seemed so unattainable because of her immense financial situation, which makes normal, rich people look homeless. For me, I never cared about her money or anyone else's money for that matter, and everyone who really knows me knows this to be true, including her. What I fell in love with was her heart. Her heart has driven me more in my life than anyone could ever compare to.

I really owe this book to her because, if I could, I would write songs about this woman. I would make a movie about this woman. She knows I would do anything for her. That was enough to drive me to do something I had never done before...write a book.

I hope you enjoy what you are about to read because everything in this book is one-hundred percent true. I myself am unable to lie. I've always worn my heart on my sleeve and I always shoot from the hip, even if it's not politically correct.

This book really writes itself and everyone who really knows me also knows this to be true.

* This is a work of creative non-fiction. The events are portrayed to the best of Brandon's memory.

While all the stories in this book are true, some names and identifying details have been changed to protect the privacy of the people involved.

SO A STRAIGHT MAN WALKS INTO A GAY BAR…

I wasn't a hair guy. In fact, I'd never touched anyone else's hair - or even thought about it - until I was 24 years-old. That was the year I walked into beauty school like a deer in headlights.

By nature, I'm a high energy person. I really wanted to do something with movement. Looking back, it's funny how obvious it was that I was meant to do hair. It was the just the ride that I wasn't quite prepared for. But how do you prepare to meet the most famous and powerful people in the world?

Like most men in Hollywood, I spent my early 20s trying to be an actor. To keep the lights on, I worked nights as a bartender at a gay bar in a nightclub. It didn't take long to see a pattern. 'Actor type' guys, boring and vanilla as hell, landing roles that at best were a long shot. 'Straight' bartenders making out with gay men at the end of the night. One thing was clear as fuck: while acting talent could certainly get you real work, there was a fast track.

In Hollywood, it's not just women who get privileges (read as 'used') for their looks. From studio executives to agents, to acting coaches, most of

Hollywood is run by a network of gay men, better known in Hollywood as the Velvet Mafia. If you're a good-looking guy and you're willing to let older, gay, influential entertainment guys blow you or fuck you and you're willing to blow them and fuck them back, you too can be famous! I'm not saying that all famous actors played this game to get ahead. What I'm saying is that if they did, it probably helped them.

I didn't.

I also didn't have an ounce of acting experience but I knew I had way more talent and instinct than many of the guys around me. So, I just went for it. I ended up getting some acting work. I did my acting due diligence, getting headshots and enrolling in acting class.

Cold calling has always been easy for me, so finding an agent wasn't too difficult. I think my pitch was: "You need to see me. All the big agents in town are meeting with me."

I landed an agent in a week. With 300 auditions in two years, I booked four solid acting jobs and got my Screen Actors Guild (SAG) card on my first real job. (A SAG card basically makes or breaks your career. You can't make any real money without it.)

It was my balls that got me those jobs.

The first job ended up being the biggest job I

booked in my short acting career. The movie was *The Debut*, a coming of age story about a Filipino teenager in an American high school. I played one of the kid's American best friends. My character was supposed to be loud, wild and great-looking. I know. it was a stretch for me! I used the Method technique to perfect my performance.

The Filipino kid was played by Dante Basco, who got famous for being the leader of the Lost Boys in *Hook* with Robin Williams. "Wow, I hit the jackpot!" I said to myself when I booked the job. "I'm gonna be so famous from this fucking movie!"

Oh, how green and stupid I was.

I immediately started flaunting a wannabe celebrity attitude. Why not! I was famous (I was not) and I was cast in a million-dollar project (low budget by studio standards). I thought I had to be that way to get respect. I learned later that being a really good actor was the only thing that was important. The director was always professional with me when it was my turn to be on camera, although I'm sure I was a serious frustration and pain in his ass.

Regardless of the budget, I made demands like a diva. Since the budget was small for *The Debut*, no one in the cast had their own honey wagon (on-location trailer), not even the lead actor. Me? I demanded my own and eventually got it. I demanded clean, fresh food instead of the oily, fried crap that they served us. A moment on the lips is a lifetime on the hips. Demand and you will receive!

After it was all said and done, I felt guilty for behaving this way. But when you're 21, you're still trying figure yourself out. And you figure yourself out by being a moron and, if you're lucky and have good people around you, you learn how to eat humble pie.

The first week of filming, we shot from 6pm to 6am - every day for seven days. That sucked the diva right out of me...at least when I was in front of the director; I didn't want my scenes to get cut. I spent a long, hard month on that job. I learned to chill out. I stopped being a nightmare and brought my own goddamn food. And I realized that, even though acting seems exciting and larger than life, it probably wasn't going to stick.

So, while I was hustling to create an acting career, at night I was a straight bartender at a gay nightclub in Hollywood called The Firehouse. I encountered gay men that thought they could turn a straight boy gay. I would let them think what they wanted. I knew how to work it when need be. I was there to get mine, whatever that was. It was the best training for what was to come later in the salon world.

The nightclub business is like the entertainment business. It's all one big fucking show night after night! Three drug-addicted, crazy motherfuckers ran The Firehouse. Not a single one of them could speak clearly by the end of the night. Cocaine and Jagermeister were the culprits. I had never worked for a place where you had to ask for your hourly wage at the end of the week. Like it was a favor or a surprise to them.

You had club owner number one: April. April was an overweight, white woman who treated her cocaine-loving nose like a Dyson vacuum. She was married to a gay man named Otto, who would sometimes work security at the front door. He was Canadian and the first person I ever met named Otto. April married him so he could get his US citizenship. Otto also supplied the club owners with the cocaine and whatever else they could use to get themselves off. The club opened at 9:30pm, give or take. Give or take because if April was opening, you could bet we'd be waiting at least half an hour for her to show up.

April had no idea what personal space meant, especially when she was drinking Jagermeister and snorting coke. At the end of the night, she would talk so close to my face that the smell of the Jager would turn my stomach. It was as if she lost her hearing and would talk to you like you didn't understand English. Tell me you'd be able to concentrate on what someone is saying when they are spraying you with saliva and you're staring at two rings of coke lining the inside of their nostrils.

By the end of the night, her low-cut tops would reveal a nipple or two, depending on how much mingling she did. Of course, because of how insane she was, none of the staff would help her in those departments. I have always been good like that with my friends. If I see a booger in their nose, I would tell them right away. You can't let your friends roll out with shit in their nose or their tits hanging out if they don't know and everyone else does!

Then you had owner number two: Victor. All his friends called him Vicky - good-looking Latin guy from Baldwin Park, California, who - I swear - had multiple personalities. If you don't know where Baldwin Park is, you're not missing anything. It's next to a city called West Covina, which doesn't matter either. Anything east of downtown Los Angeles is non-existent in Hollywood.

Victor, or Vicky, depending on which personality you were getting at that moment, would either be your best buddy, telling you how great you are and what an amazing bartender you are, or, in one hot second, he'd be screaming at the top of his lungs to the beer delivery guy for parking in his personal parking space. Spit flying out of his mouth like he has Tourette's! The poor driver was just delivering the beer that you ordered, dickhead!

People who weren't good looking were screwed. If he didn't think you were cute, he would be really nasty. I guess it was because it was such a burden to look at you and talk at the same time. Obviously, he did the hiring for the bar staff and front door security.

Victor could be such a dick and then turn it around on you and be totally nice in the same conversation. He really knew how to mind-fuck people. Say no to drugs, kids! Victor would make out with more guys in one night than the number of girls I kissed my entire senior year of high school. Every night he would go home with a different guy and was definitely equal-opportunity when it came to his men - as long as they were good looking.

Then you had owner number three: Josh. Josh was the first person I ever met who had AIDS. He looked very sickly and his skin was sort of caved in around his face. Later, I learned that guys who have AIDS could get these sunken-in faces, a purple tint to their skin and round bubble bellies from the medication that's keeping them alive. From what I was told by other gay men, the reason a lot of gay guys were so muscular was because the AIDS virus has a tougher time traveling through muscle than fat. Josh had all these things.

Knowing that Josh had AIDS kind of bugged me out, especially when he would sneeze or cough around me. But to my surprise, as sick as he was, he was the nicest and most sane of all the owners.

My parents thought I was crazy for living in such a wild neighborhood and working at a place like The Firehouse. Not that money is everything, but let me break down the situation for you. I was making $200 to $1,000 in cash a night working a four-hour shift! I was in my early 20s and living the dream.

The Firehouse was this bizarre bunch of bartenders, club promoters, door guys and famous people. Total shit show. The male clientele loved to drink and would tip extremely well. They also loved doing coke, so they wouldn't always feel the effects of the alcohol, which meant they would just keep drinking!

We just always made better money with the guys. One lesbian night, I had a famous lesbian-comedian-turned-daytime- television-host come up to my bar with her girlfriend, who was a famous actress. With them was another actress who was on a sci-fi TV show that was very popular at the time. (The male co-star is now fornicating all over a major cable network with his own show.) Anyway, all three girls rolled up to the bar. The comedian-television host ordered three drinks: three vodka martinis, straight up with twists. I was very happy to serve her because she was famous and I was thinking she was going to tip me well all night. I made the drinks, told her how much - $35 or something like that. She handed me a $100 bill and I gave her the change. She grabbed the cash and walked away, leaving nothing. I was shocked!

Then I thought: "Well, she'll come back for more and leave me a bigger tip at the end of the night, even though she paid cash and not with a credit card." I was giving her the benefit of the doubt. Of course, you couldn't ever say anything, and I never would. I think she came back three times during the night but never tipped once. (Turns out the comedian's girlfriend disappeared one day. Seems like she ran away from home and they found her out near Bakersfield mumbling to herself on some family's lawn out in the middle of fucking nowhere!)

The thing about working in that club, in that type of environment, is that anything goes. It was like Vegas.

What happens in the club stays in the club. I would see totally famous people who I never would have thought were gay. Sure enough, by the end of the night they would be in the bathroom making out with someone of the same sex. It really opened my eyes! Now, when I hear rumors about some celebrity being gay or when things keep happening that point towards that person being gay, like constantly marrying random women who come out of nowhere, I figure that it's true. In Hollywood, especially if you're a leading male actor, you can never really come out. It sinks your career! Comedians are one thing but sex symbol-type leading male actors can never come out. The American public can't handle it. Just look at Rupert Everett. You're like: "Who?" See what I mean? As soon as he came out, game over.

Even though I never saw a fight at the club, we had to have door guys - to check IDs and make sure people stopped drinking by 1:30am. Most of these guys had a pretty tough look about them, like you could imagine them in a motorcycle gang. By the end of the night, they'd be taking it in the pooper, too! I would never judge these guys because I'm sure wherever they came from, looking the way they did, they could never get away with being gay. They had to come to West Hollywood to liberate themselves.

West Hollywood is the first place I ever saw gay cholos. Cholos are Mexican gang members that you would see in rough neighborhoods of Los Angeles. Having grown up in Los Angeles, I was always afraid of them because you never knew if they were going to stab you or shoot you or rob you for your car or something. Never in a million years did I think there were cholos who were gay. They looked like gang members but had this effeminate swish to their walk.

Until I started working in West Hollywood, I had no clue that people like this existed. I know that sounds naïve but I never really knew that there were gay men who looked straight and acted straight but were into men! I always pictured gay men to be really effeminate and girly, not the super muscular, manly gang member-looking guys coming into our establishment. What did I know?

While tending bar, I always kept a straight face and was as nice as possible to everyone because it was all about making the customers happy and getting the best tips. But I'd turn up the Martinez charm a few notches for these cholos. My mind would keep asking: "What's the worst that could happen if I cross them?" Oh, just getting jumped in an alley after work and getting it in the ass!

This world was all so new to me. Even though I grew up seven miles west in Santa Monica, West Hollywood might as well have been a different planet. I've never been homophobic, it's just that the crazy lifestyle hits you like a Mack truck on a deserted highway. My first year was like boot camp. I took it all in with my eyes wide open. Now, looking back, I couldn't possibly imagine living anywhere else in Los Angeles. That's why I stayed in West Hollywood for 20 years.

Either way, for a 21-year-old, good-looking, straight guy, this job was almost too good to be true. And the women, holy shit, the women!

Straight women hit the clubs with their gay guy friends and there we were, the straight bartenders, attracting them like magnets. These girls were my age or older and obviously had more experience than I did. They were super fucking hot and open to some freaky shit. It was like being in a porno without the cameras!

Next door to our club was a bar called The Mother Lode, an old-school gay bar with just gays guys working there. I used to score pot and smoke with a bartender there named Michael. He was older, probably 40-something at the time. Michael used to sell weed to support his meth addiction and to help him come down after three- night meth bending, all-male orgies. Michael really gave me an education. The amount of butt fucking was unprecedented!

One night, Michael brought over this really hot blonde to The Firehouse. This girl (to this day I can't remember her name) had come into my bar earlier and spotted me behind the bar. Later that night she mentioned me to the bartenders at the Mother Lode. Michael chimed in with: "Oh, I know that guy. He's my buddy. His name is Brandon."

Her eyes lit up. He brought her over and made the introduction. This girl looked like a rock star's girlfriend, like she had just walked out of a Motley Crue video. Long, blonde hair, killer body, fake boobs - the perfect picture of a hot Hollywood porn star. It was definitely a go!

As it was getting close to the 2:00am closing time, I fed her multiple vodka cranberries and she waited at my end of the bar, hanging out through the insanity that strikes every night. When it hit 1:45am and the club lights went up and we yelled: "Last call," it was like the end of the world. Everyone rushed to the bar to get their last drinks like they were never going to drink again.

One cool thing about our unhinged club owners is they never sweated me or the other straight bartenders having girls wait around while we cleaned up after the crowd split. They knew that after closing these girls were coming home with us. And why not, after the amount of indecent behavior we witnessed from them?

After we wrapped up, the girl and I walked out together. I swear we may have said two sentences to each other and walked 10 paces before our tongues were down each other's throats. Making out hard-core, we shuffled ourselves to Koontz Hardware, a West Hollywood staple.

She pulled me into the garage underneath the store and I propped her up against one of their delivery vans. The mini-skirt went right up and I moved her panties to one side. She grabbed my fingers, put them in her mouth like she was going down on my fingers, then put them inside her.

I thought my heart was going to pop out of my fucking chest! My dick had never been so hard. Never had a girl done this to me or been so willing to do whatever in public. At the same time, I had never had a girl be so into me so fast.

She unzipped my pants and started stroking me while I fingered her, like the high school principal was about to bust us. Except we were adults and the only possibility of getting caught was by the West Hollywood Sheriff's Department. Honestly, they probably would have just told us to move on. I can only imagine what they see every night.

It was like 3am and we were in the garage of a hardware store ravaging each other with absolutely no control and no stopping in sight. She looked straight at me and said: "I want you to fuck me right here!"

Now I know what you're thinking: stupid Brandon, you did exactly as she said, right then and there, with no protection. Let's face it, most guys would have and they'd just deal with the paranoia the next day, hoping to God that she was clean. Or they'd live with the dread that three months later she'd walk into the bar with a baby bump.

Not me.

Thank God for 24-hour sex shops in West Hollywood. And thank God there was one right next to Koontz Hardware.

I told her: "I'm gonna grab some condoms really fast. Don't move."

Like mother-fucking Flash Gordon, I bolted into the sex shop, grabbed a three pack of condoms and some lube, paid the guy and had my tongue all over her body in less than two minutes. That's how badly I wanted this girl!

When I got back, she was still plowed against

the van, like she got hit by the Brandon sandwich truck.

I ripped apart the condom wrapper and put one on. As I slid myself inside her, I nearly fell over. She had a huge (I mean huge) tattoo on her va jay jay. I guess I was too preoccupied before to notice. As I was sliding in and out of her, I wanted to savor the moment. Holy hell, it was so hot. But all I could focus on was that fucking tattoo. It seemed to be a tarantula wrapped around her situation, but in the dark I really wasn't sure what it was - which really bugged me out.

If you don't have a tattoo then I'll tell you this: getting tattooed is a highly uncomfortable process. A needle drags across your skin over and over. Having a tattoo completely cover your pussy is a serious and painful commitment. It may have been the first but I'll admit it wasn't the last tattooed pussy I've seen.

She must have noticed how distracted I was because she grabbed my face and slammed her tongue inside my mouth. We fucked against that van for at least an hour, using all three condoms. While all that was going on, I still couldn't get the picture of that goddamn tattoo out of my mind. She was the wildest girl that I'd ever met. But still, to this day I'm so happy that I grabbed those condoms.

Even now I can see her face, with her eyes

closed, loving every minute of it. I'm one of those people who keeps his eyes open and watches. Looking at a woman's face while you're having sex and seeing her facial expressions - totally uncensored and uncontrollable - is so sensual, such a turn on and definitely a sight to see. Even when you're kissing, you can tell a lot about a person by the way their face twitches and moves when they are with you.

This whole experience didn't feel real. It felt like I was watching a movie, starring me. After I came for the third time and used the last condom, we finally detached from each other. We each caught our breath and wiped the sex and sweat from our bodies. She blurted out her name, which I hope to God I remember someday. I do remember that she was from Anaheim.

Anaheim and I exchanged numbers and gave each other one last licking of each other's mouths and a sweaty grope. I walked her to her car and saw her off on her journey back to Anaheim.

I don't remember my own walk home to my apartment on Larrabee Street, right below the Viper Room. I could have floated home for all I knew. I was on such a natural high that I didn't get to sleep until noon. I never saw Anaheim again. I'm sure she had a boyfriend; I definitely had a girlfriend at this time! Trying to have a serious relationship with any girl was virtually impossible. Plus, a girl with a tattoo on her pussy doesn't really seem like girlfriend material.

It was the same story with Mason, another bartender at The Firehouse. He and I became good friends. When two straight guys bartend together at a gay bar and they start meeting hot girls non-stop, they tend to get close.

Mason had started there before me, so he already had it going on for himself. He basically showed me the ropes, like my first teacher in Hollywood. He really knew how to work the celebrity crowd - and work himself into that crowd. At 6ft 3in, Mason was a force of masculinity in West Hollywood - a good-looking guy with a great personality and not homophobic in the least.

Mason was tight with Alexis Arquette (of the Hollywood Arquettes). You probably would recognize him from the movie *The Wedding Singer* with Adam Sandler and Drew Barrymore. He was the guy in the band who looked like Boy George. Alexis died in 2016. So fucking sad.

During this time, Alexis was dressing like a woman on occasion but hadn't fully transitioned. Back then, there was no Caitlyn Jenner on the cover of *People Magazine* making transgender mainstream news. Alexis would come to the club all the time, sometimes two or three times a week. He could bend over and put his junk in his own mouth. I'm fucking serious. I'd never leave the house! Mason would egg him on and Alexis would entertain us by doing it, like a party trick.

This was old school, hardcore West Hollywood. The crazy corner of Robertson and Santa Monica Boulevard alive with freedom, decadence and debauchery. Flames lit up the front of the club, warning that you were entering a den of sin. This was before the most profitable gay bar, called The Abbey, swallowed that corner and Bravo celeb Lisa Vanderpump popped up her trendy restaurants.

My mother lived in Northern California at the time but came to Los Angeles occasionally to visit me and other family. She wanted to see the madness of the neighborhood and The Firehouse for herself. So, I brought her to work on a night that I knew would blow her away. It was a Friday night, Victor's night for promoting. He loaded the place with good-looking, muscular guys. They called these kind of guys 'The Circuit'. The circuit queens were successful, hot as shit and always the biggest drinkers and the biggest tippers.

My mom got the royal treatment and was like the queen of the queens for a night (while I was busting a nut tending bar). We were at capacity, bodies pressed against each other, wall to wall, music pumping and skin everywhere.

It was a lot for her to take in. Her straight son surrounded by so much depravity. Hell, it took me a year to feel totally comfortable. I forgot to warn her about the restroom and I never did ask her what she may have seen. What I can imagine is that she saw what we all saw: guys fucking each other and people shoveling coke up their noses. There was no way to prepare yourself or someone else for what goes down - even my mom who is a former prison guard. You either roll with it or you roll out!

At the end of the night, she looked like she had been stuck for days in an elevator with the Village People. She was rattled. Naturally she asked if I was gay and said: "You know, if you're gay it's totally okay." I gave her a quick smile and said: "No, mom. I'm not gay." Just then we passed Koontz Hardware. Timing couldn't have been better or more awkward. Of course, I could never tell her about that night.

My life was going in a direction that no-one from my family had ever experienced. I was on my own, learning new things every day. The only reference I had was from Mason, who was getting with every girl in sight.

No-one forced me to stay in that crazy environment. I began to truly love it and honestly couldn't get enough. I figured for the gay men, if they couldn't have me, their girlfriends could. Then they'd dish about it afterward.

I am eternally grateful for the whole fucking experience at The Firehouse. Grateful because of the people, all the crazy fucking people, and it opened my eyes to whatever goes. And it was there that I met the person who absolutely changed the entire trajectory of my life.

His name was Ross. Ross wore a baseball cap and was one of the straightest gay guys I'd ever met. He was a regular at the bar and we got to know each other pretty well.

Being a hair stylist himself, one day Ross suggested that I think about being a stylist: "You're what we gay boys call the four quadrant straight guy."

I looked at him perplexed. "Four quadrant?" I asked.

He said: "Yeah, four quadrant. Gay boys want to fuck you, straight boys want to be you, women love you and, I'm sure if you were alone with a pretty lesbian, she would fuck you just because."

"Remember, Brandon," he said. "Women love straight hair stylists more than they love female and gay male hair stylists. I have no problem admitting that. You can make a fortune in this town. You could be famous!"

Being famous sounded really good. Being famous without putting myself through auditions sounded awesome.

"It's Hollywood," Ross said. "If you can make them blonde and do a good blowout, you're set!"

Walking home that night, I rattled the conversation around in my head. I hated acting by this point. Acting is a labor of love until you hit it big, if that ever happens. For every actor I met who just got to town, I knew one going back home because they ran out of money, ran out of their parents' money, or their ego was so hurt by being told "no" all the time that they just couldn't handle it anymore.

Ultimately, I didn't love the acting world the way you need to love it to make it a career. Trying to get acting work was like reaching for thin air. I was constantly living in the unknown and desperately wanted something solid to grab onto.

Other than Ross, I didn't know anyone who was a hair stylist. More and more I started to obsess about being a hair stylist. You know when you get a new car and then all you see is that same car everywhere? That's how it started to manifest itself. I started to throw out the idea to people around me. Hell, I did know hair stylists! At least ten guys at the bar. All of a sudden, I started to build a little fan club of hair stylists pushing me to go to beauty school. I had always been really good with my hands. My father was a pretty successful artist in his day and I inherited his artistic ability.

Even at 24 years-old, I was an all or nothing kind of guy. One day I woke up with a single thought in my mind: "Fuck it. I'm going for it!"

KING OF BEAUTY SCHOOL

The next week, I began my beauty school search. In Los Angeles, location is everything because it takes so fucking long to get anywhere on the freeway. Marinellos, a school in my neighborhood, was first on my list.

And Marinellos then immediately fell off the list.

You know when you are sincerely seeking information and the person on the other end of the phone couldn't sound more bothered and disinterested (and a bit ghetto)?

"Yes, can you please tell me how your beauty school program works?" I asked.

An audible, long sigh came through the phone.

Every question was answered with a rude, curt reply. Honestly, I don't know why Marinellos let that woman pick up the phone. "Probably for the best," I thought. The tone of the conversations in the background didn't sound any better. Hellsville.

I ticked down my beauty school list. Too far. Too ethnic. Too expensive. Even though I was investing in the rest of my life, I still didn't want to pay too much - or even pay full price for that matter! After all, I was used to opening doors with my good looks and bullshitting skills.

Ads for well known schools like Vidal Sassoon and Paul Mitchell looked so fancy and stylized that I could only imagine how the tuition would gut my bank account. Not that I was intimidated but it looked like fucking hair ninjas styled the hair in the ads. With the sharp lines and angles. It didn't look like anything I could ever do - or even want to do.

I called the Paul Mitchell School just for the hell of it. An over-caffeinated young woman cheerfully informed me, as she clacked her gum, that the tuition was $20,000. Suspicion confirmed. These big name schools were crazy expensive. Bartending was great money but saving $20,000 *and* living in West Hollywood was a bit of a stretch!

My standards were officially lowered.

At the bottom of the list was a school in Culver City, a neighborhood four miles south of West Hollywood. I know this sounds close. It wasn't. In traffic, I would looking at a solid hour commute. Still, there was some appeal. The neighborhood had a cool vibe with coffee shops and Sony Studios (formerly MGM), Culver Studios and other movie lots. Plus, my father lived in Culver City on what had been the Tarzan movie lot.

I grabbed the phone and called the Culver City Beauty College. Jim, the owner, couldn't have been more helpful or polite. I told him my situation and he explained what it would take to obtain a cosmetology license in the state of California - that it would take just 1600 hours working at the beauty school because they take actual clients, usually low-income types and some occasional weirdos (as I would learn later on).

Holy shit, I would be cutting people's hair right away? Where were the dummy heads of hair? This whole hair stylist thing began to sink in. As Jim continued to explain the process, he must have interpreted my silence as my head spinning (which it was!). "Why don't you just come down and we can talk in person," he said. "I think you will get a much clearer picture if you see it for yourself." I got on my motorcycle and was there in record time.

The fierce scent of hair color and perm solution greeted me when I walked through the doors of the Culver City Beauty College. To this day, whenever anyone is doing a perm I am transported to that first day of beauty school.

Jim was standing behind the counter ringing up customers (aka guinea pigs) as they paid the $5 fee for their 'cheaper than cheap' haircuts and color jobs. He spotted me right away. I stood out like a sore thumb - or a rock star. Ha! I was the tallest person in the entire building. That was a first. It was as if they had never seen anything like me before. And definitely not in their beauty school.

Stepping into this beauty college was like walking into a time warp from the 1960s or 1970s. There were more old ladies than I have ever seen under one roof, all sporting fuzzy, sheep-like perms. As if their heads didn't look big enough on top of those bony little bodies, the champagne pink or a silvery blue perms gave it that little extra size. You would think they were wives of astronauts.

Never in my life had I stood out like this. I had arrived. A flash went off in my head. Talk about a perfect set up for showing off, looking good and swallowing the room every time I walked in. From that first meeting at Culver City Beauty College, I was surrounded by women with not a masculine male in sight except the one that stared back at me in the mirror. It would be this way at every salon to this day.

Now I can hear how arrogant and cocky I sound. And I was. But it was more than that. I was about to get an education in more than styling hair. It was an immersion into the female mystique, deepening my respect and affection for women. I'm not saying I knew everything about women but I can say for sure that I've now done a lot of studying!

I'm not just talking about sex. As a hair stylist, you learn how to listen and respond in a way that feels good to women. This is a skill that many men don't have and I see them sabotage themselves over and over because of it. As a female insider, one of the most valuable lessons I can pass along to guys is to understand every women's most hated word. That word is **NO**. There is always a way to adjust to make women happy and give them what they want.

Most, if not all, of my friends today are women. If you're ever in the Los Angeles neighborhood of Brentwood, where I now live and work, look around and you're likely to see me alone or with a woman friend. I was never a bro-time kind of guy; maybe it's just that I hate football - or why I hate football. Like my ex-wife said. I was probably a woman in my past life and she was the man. Not that I'm effeminate at all, women just interest me more than guys do.

Jim introduced me to the three female instructors who were teaching on the first floor, which was strictly for the cosmetology students. I met Jim's Asian ex-wife and her twin sister. The ladies were still partners in the business with Jim and looked like porn stars. Jim was a decent looking Vietnamese guy and, as far as I could tell, totally straight and newly single in a sea of young women. He obviously got into the beauty school business to get laid. I liked him right away. Something felt shady about the whole situation but that didn't bother me one bit.

Jim continued to give me the rundown of the school and assured me that I would be able to make my own hours and pay monthly. For about five minutes I actually got dizzy from all the information Jim threw at me. In the big picture, becoming a hair stylist may not seem like such a huge deal but It was one of the biggest decisions of my life. Plus, making a career decision while seeming to have been transported to another dimension complete with fluffy pink perms and hot Asian twins and state board exams and payment plans and...I was just trying to get my fucking bearing straight.

I snapped out of it when Jim said: "You can come and go as you please. All you need to do is give me $500 up front for registration and your stylist kit."

Holy fuck, this was really happening.

"We will set up a $250 a month payment plan," Jim said, "Until the $4,000 tuition is paid off." Seemed like a fair and reasonable amount to pay for the keys to my new career. I stood there for a few minutes, contemplating the move towards total Brandon hair

Page 38

domination but I still wasn't quite sold.

Then Jim pulled a power move: he took me up a flight of stairs. My breath literally was taken away. The second floor was filled with really hot women, mostly Eastern European, who were working towards their esthetician licenses.

I turned to Jim: "Who do I make the check out to?"

Six months in and I was the king of beauty school!

Once my hands got a feel for the work and my head got a grasp on the job, it was full speed ahead. All of a sudden, I was rocking Culver City with the local betties lining up for their Saturday blowouts. (Shocking revelation: there are women who don't wash their hair for an entire week because they want their blowouts to last that long.)

As soon as I'd begin blow drying their hair, women would open their mouths and tell me everything that was going on in their lives. I mean everything. It was like tending bar without the booze. All I had to do was turn on the blow dryer.

It wasn't a surprise that the women opened up to me. Having someone touch your hair is intimate. It's relaxing and hypnotic. This is where I picked up the female language. Like I tell my clients today: "I speak female!" This ability has helped me in every single area of my life, not just at work. I swear, if men could blow dry their ladies' hair, there would be a lot less divorce.

Before I started doing hair and before I got married, the only experience I had with strong women was with my mother. That relationship hasn't been a bowl of cherries, so doing hair helped me be a better man, who understands women better.

But I didn't learn it all right away. The Warren Beatty in Shampoo lifestyle had already begun, even though that guy didn't hit the level of clientele that I would soon be attaining! Between the tattoos and the motorcycle, I was immediately accepted with open arms (and legs). It was as if the universe made it my destiny to be a hairstylist.

Being a 20-something, straight male certainly came with its privileges in that place, especially as I better acquainted myself with the second floor. I had my own Victoria's Secret catalogue and the stairs were the runway. Up and down all day long with those girls!

It brought me back to my high school days of little crushes and daily flirting. Only at the beauty school, we could both actually clock out, leave campus and get it on for a few hours, then come back, clock back in and continue our days.

No more having to compete with every other asshole guy on campus.

I quickly adapted to having multiple coffee breaks at the Argentinian coffee shop next door. The women's stories were all fairly similar. Either she hadn't scored the rich guy yet and in the meantime trained as an esthetician for the possibility of working somewhere like Beverly Hills where she could meet her future husband. Or she had the rich guy already, came to the States and, having gotten what she wanted, dumped the gullible rich prick who brought her from whatever country they came from. Marriage and kid equal citizenship! It was amazing.

That is when I met Dallas. With blonde hair down to the middle of her back and the body of a ballet dancer, she was about 35 and from South Africa. Our attraction was immediate and the chemistry was so hot I swear you could see it.

We were like Danny and Sandy from the movie Grease. Except I had a motorcycle instead of a T-Bird and Dallas was from South Africa not Australia. She would give me dreamy looks during school and at lunchtime we always managed to sit close to each other - or within each other's view - on the benches outside the coffee house next door with the rest of the beauty school crew.

Dallas was different. Not like any of the women I had met at the bar. She gave off a mature sexiness. A real woman with class and sophistication. Like me, she seemed to be a fish out of water at the beauty school.

Every time I would glance her way, I would see Dallas looking at me and the same when she would glance my way. After a few months, the flirting intensified. It was as if we were magnets being pulled together. Everyone in the school noticed. Then Dallas and I began hugging. Then the hugs became longer and we would hold each other tighter, talk to each other and lock eyes while in each other's arms.

Dallas was confident, smart and hard working. She spoke beautifully and talked about things that mothers would talk about. Becoming friends with her helped open up new levels of communication with females.

One afternoon we were eating lunch with a group of students at the cafe. Dallas and I sat across from each other. The flirting was so obvious that the other students, feeling uncomfortable, moved to another table.

Once they were gone, Dallas and I exchanged a

few words. Then, rather abruptly, I leaned in very close, looked her straight in the eyes and said: "I can't stop thinking about you, Dallas. I really, really want to fuck you." It just came out. Usually when a guy drops a comment like that he needs to brace himself for a slap across the face. Not this time.

Without hesitation she responded: "I really want to fuck you too."

The only problem was that Dallas was married - to an older, rich Russian man. And she had a son. But there was no going back for us. These things, these chemical forces of nature, happened like a freight train at full speed.

I know what you're thinking: "Brandon, you home wrecker, why do you want to mess with a rich Russian's wife?"

I've learned a lot over the years being a shoulder to hundreds if not thousands of wealthy women and living their experiences with them. When you're young, beautiful and married to an older, unattractive man for the money and a Green Card, you tend to become unhappy in your everyday life. It was shocking at first to see gorgeous, youthful women arm-in-arm with dinosaurs. I came to understand that for some women security feels much more important than attraction. In the beginning to talk yourself into being happy with someone who is 30, 40, 50...fucking 60...years older than you. You're living the good life. In the beginning. Then time passes and reality sets in. Now you're downing Vicodin and Percocet with vodka because you're stuck in an expensive jail. Relationships built on money are built on quicksand. It's just a matter of time before they collapse.

Dallas definitely had gotten herself into a quicksand marriage and was coming to the end of her prison sentence. She was in the process of filing for divorce and needed to release some frustration...on my tattooed body. I was not going to deprive her.

So Dallas and I had to get creative. We set up a rendezvous point, at a friend's apartment nearby, where there would be no interruptions. We arranged to meet during school hours, clock out and back in and finish the day without too many people noticing. That day, Dallas and I drove together in her car to the apartment, talking and giggling like it was Christmas morning and Santa had delivered all our presents.

Deep down inside, I was really nervous. I knew she was feeling the same. When we arrived, we started off slowly...actually it was a little awkward. Here we were, hot shots at school with mouths like porn stars, alone for the first time with nothing holding us back and we were at a loss for words.

I guess we both wanted to enjoy and savor the moment. I certainly didn't want to pounce on her like some rookie kid who walked around with his dick in his hand stumbling over it.

We began to kiss slowly and passionately. She was so sure of her every move, like a tiger who knows how to get around in the jungle and hunt for her food. Dallas knew exactly what to do and how to do it...with an alluring South African accent that drove me wild.

Ten minutes after we arrived, our clothes were off and tongues were everywhere. I can still see the goosebumps form on Dallas's flawless porcelain skin. Little points of energy raised up to the sky under my touch, because of my touch. We cradled each other and twisted our bodies together, intertwined in one synchronized series of sweaty movements. The flesh of my legs ran the length of hers, my feet found hers. Fingers grabbed other fingers and slipped away from the heat and sweat. She held me and kissed me with such confidence and affection, like a wife holding her newlywed husband for the first time after saying: "I do." Making love to Dallas was a turning point for me as a man.

Our eyes locked and never looked away.

Her smile told me everything. She had left her real life at the door and, if just for a moment, she had put down a heavy burden. She traced every inch of my body with her fingertips, studying me, the lines of my body, as if she didn't want to miss a thing.

Seeing her that happy was intoxicating. We were in a moment. A really special, simple and fun moment. We weren't drunk, stumbling over each other after a hazy night at the club. We didn't meet at the gym or the grocery store. And we weren't in a relationship and needing to deal with stress like who is going to leave work early to pick up the kids. We were just two friends. Two friends with a crazy, chemical connection who could have hot sex and be totally cool with it.

Dallas was a mom and had no intention of jumping from guy to guy. There was just this connection between us and a way that I made her feel free and safe. That's what made this experience really euphoric.

Sex fatigue eventually set in but we couldn't stop. We couldn't get enough of each other, we devoured every inch. Orgasm after leg shaking orgasm. We only stopped long enough for Dallas to light a quick cigarette and for us to laugh and chat while our bodies still clung to each other.

After reaching new heights of ecstasy five times, we came to the finish line of our sexual marathon. Never in the history of fornication have two bodies been so deprived, so neglected and then so goddamn satisfied.

Completely drenched, we talked for a while about life - and life after beauty school. Dallas asked so I told her how I had gotten into hair.

"You couldn't be more perfect for this career," she said. "You obviously have the looks and personality. Plus you just fucked the shit out of me, so your sex appeal is through the roof!"

Coming from Dallas, those words meant the world to me.

Then she added: "Just remember, Brandon, at the end of the day, it's all about the blow dry!"

Truer words have never been spoken.

ROCK AND ROLL HIGH SCHOOL

Sixteen hundred hours of beauty school. That was the finish line. Those hours made California licensure a reality.

When I was close to fifteen hundred hours, I started looking for a hair assistant job in Beverly Hills. The beauty - and vanity - capital of the world, the streets of Beverly Hills are packed with salons for every imaginable grooming need: hair salons, nail salons, eyebrow salons, waxing salons, make up salons...the list goes on.

Since beauty school, I had this idea that going to New York to do hair would be a possibility. My gut told me that the Luis Ferreti Salon - based in NYC with an LA presence - could be the right fit to launch my career. Shit. My gut was not wrong.

Luis lived and worked in New York the first three weeks of the month and then the last week at the Beverly Hills salon. He liked me right away. Technically, I wasn't supposed to work at a salon until I finished my beauty school hours, took my test and got my cosmetology license. But Luis bent the rules and hired me right away. I didn't mind one bit taking advantage of the good-looking, straight-boy privileges that would later make the other assistants' blood boil. I was too driven to give a shit.

The salon was very small, with only 10 chairs, so we would get busy really fast. I've never seen anyone serve more clients in one day than Luis. I'm talking an average of 25 to 40 clients with three assistants running around, mixing color like it was cake batter at a cake off!

I was thrown into the mix as the salon assistant, working for every hairstylist and colorist. The salon's bitch, really.

This salon was departmentalized; you could only be a haircutter or a hair colorist. You weren't allowed to do both. This real 'New York' way of doing hair grooms you to become a master of one or the other, instead of a jack-of-all-trades (master of shit).

Salon assistants learned both sides - cut and color - then decided which way to go. At that point, you would assist the person who does what you eventually wanted to do - unless Luis made a choice for you, claiming you as his assistant. Then you pretty much want to do color with him. Plus, there's a lot more money in doing color than strictly cutting. Women always get their color done more often than they get their hair cut.

After a month as the salon assistant, Luis handpicked me for himself above the other assistants who had been there longer. This was not a popular decision among the assistants. I had a few weeks of dealing with their nastiness but I didn't care. My main focus was getting from assistant to actual stylist or colorist as fast as possible.

Being an assistant didn't bring in great money but I kept my eye on the prize. When I became a real hair stylist, I would be making far more money than I would ever make at the bar.

Luis attracted a ton of famous clients. Everyone from Jennifer Grey (Baby from *Dirty Dancing*) to a former First Lady. It was the first time that I was up close and personal with real celebrities without thumping music and a bar between us. I maintained the attitude of treating everyone the same. My philosophy is that you get the most respect in return that way. Other assistants would get flustered and giddy when someone famous came in. All that did was make them look like idiots.

The former First Lady rolled in every three weeks with a posse of assistants and Secret Service guys, three or four of them at a time. I made sure I got her whatever she wanted...fast!

It was really funny to watch her interact with the Secret Service. Her fuse was short and she was very bossy. It seemed she had them on lock down; they would ask us assistants not to tell her where they went while they snuck off to the bathroom. These badass, ex-military, Secret Service guys were totally scared of a woman who stood at about 4ft 10in. That's power.

She almost didn't look real. When she sat in the salon chair, the gown swallowed her narrow shoulders and thin body so that only her gigantic head was visible.

It seemed like there were celebrities coming in every day. And for good reason - Luis was the best. Bobbi, the manager, called Luis 'The King of Color!' He would transform women in a matter of hours, taking their boring, soccer mom hair color and turning it into a work of art. Beautifully placed highlights set perfectly against their skin tone.

Five colorists and three haircutters worked at the salon. Glenda, one of the haircutters, had this certain way of giving me attention. She would look at me as if she knew me in another life, losing her train of thought while staring into my eyes.

Glenda was older, probably mid-40s at the time, and had the thickest New York accent I had ever heard. She looked like she was married to a rock star - or a rock star herself. A walking magazine shoot, she had killer taste in clothes and jewelry, always in short dresses and skirts that showed off her petite, fit body. Every day. With multiple wardrobe changes like she was coming out for another set. Never breaking character.

You could spot Glenda a couple blocks away. It didn't matter if she was surrounded by a sea of people. The way she walked, talked, moved and laughed was just hers alone. And when she laughed. Shit. It would start out like a whisper then, all of a sudden, it was as if a clown were blowing this horn on a unicycle.

After a few weeks of witnessing Glenda shower me with attention, an assistant said: "Haven't you noticed that Glenda gets away with murder? You don't know who she is married to, do you?"

"No, she hasn't told me who her husband is," I said. "It doesn't seem like she wants to bring it up."

Glenda looked like she was married to a rock star...because she *WAS* married to a rock star. Glenda's husband was Ronnie Capone. Lead guitarist of The Capones, the band who fucking defined punk rock.

Ok, I have to stop for a minute. I'm totally bullshitting you on the names as I'm sure you can tell. Seriously, from here on out the whole name thing gets complicated. When I walked in that door to the Luis

Ferreti Salon, little did I know that my circle of friends would soon change from normal everyday hair stylists and wannabe actors to the biggest names in the world. So, yeah, I'm using some fucking creative aliases to tell the story. What's not made up are the actual events and how meeting 'Glenda' changed my life forever.

Obviously, I knew who The Capones were as I love rock and roll. Glenda saw this in me; my tattooed body and wild hair. No-one else in the salon looked the way Glenda and I did.

Ronnie would never come into the salon. At the end of the workday, a brand-new Cadillac Eldorado would pull up front, with a mysterious figure in the driver's seat. Through the tinted windows, you could see the silhouette of Ronnie's iconic bowl-like, shag haircut. Being from New York, neither Glenda nor Ronnie had ever driven a car before they moved to California. Man, I wish I could have seen Ronnie get his driver's license. That must have been a scene. He drove his Caddie with two feet, making it a seriously dodgy experience to ride with him. I'm sure I would've taught him how to drive myself if I had met them earlier.

The Capones got famous at a shit-hole bar in the Bowery in Lower Manhattan in the mid-70s, as they were riding this loud and fast wave of music that was being created by a handful of bands. As it would turn out, pretty much every rock band after the late 70s would be influenced by The Capones, whether they knew it or not.

Ronnie, or Ron, as he preferred later in his life, was known for playing guitar fast, loud and aggressively. He would also beat you up if you crossed him or pissed him off. The Capones came from a rough neighborhood in New York, at a time when New York itself was rough.

When The Capones started to build steam in the beginning of their career, Ronnie stole the lead singer's girlfriend away from him. You could see how it happened with the lead singer being a passive kind of guy whereas Ronnie was a fucking bulldozer. Ronnie did it because he was relentless and knew he could do it.

The girl? Yep, it was Glenda. Classic rock and roll drama that played out behind the scenes for more than 25 years while the band stayed together.

"Yeah, Ronnie asked me again today who's that punk kid working for me," Glenda would say, laughing. Three months after working in the salon, Glenda had become my direct boss. I was now her bitch! After a month of working for Glenda exclusively, she had me come outside to meet Ronnie. It was a brisk night with heavy traffic on Canon Drive. Lots of people walking around, heading out to dinner. I was wearing a Van Halen t-shirt. Glenda knew this introduction either could go north or south...and fast. I walked up to the passenger side of the Eldorado, black exterior and interior. Ronnie may have been vintage punk rock but he had good taste.

He pressed the button to lower the passenger window as I approached the car. I can still remember the sound of the loud, automatic window coming down and this figure appearing on the other side. Ronnie fucking Capone smiling right at me.

"Hey, how are you?" he asked. "How do you like working for Luis?" His thick accent smacked me over the head like a jack hammer on 53rd and 3rd!

"Be cool," I said to myself as I told him: "I like working for Luis, he seems nice and it's a really busy place so that's what I'm looking for."

I could tell that Glenda had withheld from Ronnie some details about my muscular aesthetic. Working out was (and is) essential to my being, especially back then while I was still bartending at night. Keeping up with muscle queens took hard work and dedication!

Ronnie nodded his head as some sort of acceptance. Grinning, he said: "Well, we'll see you later. It was nice meeting you. Goodbye." Glenda blurted a short and quick nasally laugh and said: "Alright, mister. I'll see you in the morning." She called me mister from then on. Other names would come later on but mister was the first.

Then there was this moment. I opened the door for Glenda and, as she got into the car, I got a full view of her inner thighs, all the way up to her white panties. My eyes were held hostage for a full five seconds.

Shit! Ronnie is going to knock me all the way over to the Hollywood sign. He didn't. But he also didn't take his eyes off me. Trying to figure me out. Trying to figure out how I worked into the equation. Trying to figure out what the hell happened during the day while Glenda was at work and he was at home.

The next few weeks were business as usual. And business as usual for me, Glenda's assistant, was 1,000 times more enjoyable than the bullshit that the other assistants had to put up with. Glenda would do hair for photo shoots and commercial shoots all over the city and I'd tag along. Since she was the wife of a rock icon, we received the red carpet treatment everywhere we went. She may not have played an instrument in the band but she lived the same experience that Ronnie did. She was the instrument that drove Ronnie and the lead singer into making their songs so powerful. She created that tension, that competitive struggle.

At the shoots, people (and raving fans) would see me next to Glenda and automatically assume that I was just like her and her husband. That I was a rock star and part of the Capone 'family'. It wasn't long before I was sworn into Ronnie and Glenda's funny little family.

One night, my father and I were meeting for Italian food at La Scala in Beverly Hills. He had never been there and I finally had a career and was making some money. It was my turn to treat this man to a great meal. I walked in to secure a table and eating dinner at a corner table were Ronnie and Glenda.

"What are you doing here?" Ronnie asked. "You having dinner by yourself?"

Just then my father walked in. I hadn't really told my father about these two yet, since I was still pretty new at the salon. When I explained that I was taking my father to dinner, Ronnie gave me a look of total endearment. It was like he saw a piece of himself in me and that hit the hard-to-find soft spot in the tough-as-nails Ronnie Capone's chest.

Ronnie immediately asked if we wanted to join them. At first, I turned down the offer because I didn't want to impose or bail on the father-son solo dinner.

Very quickly I could tell that Ronnie wasn't going to take no for an answer. And that one decision, to sit down to dinner, started the bond between Glenda, Ronnie and me.

I talked of how my parents divorced when I was 10 and how I lived with my father. It was the reason my father and I were so close and being that close we never really moved that far away from each other. All of that fascinated Ronnie. Later I came to learn that he was very close to his father and was devastated when he passed away. I would also come to know that seeing the bond between my father and me showed Ronnie that I knew what loyalty really meant. Loyalty was big in the Ronnie and Glenda vocabulary.

I don't remember my father talking much at the dinner. He was really just listening and taking it all in. Even though he is a graphic designer and around artists all the time, my father is a bit conservative. I'm sure he didn't know what to make of these aliens from planet Rock 'n' Roll. Especially since he had heard the name The Capones but didn't really know who they were.

That didn't stop Ronnie. It seemed that he understood how to get through to fathers. Without being too obvious, he talked about how being a hair stylist is a great job when you work with people like Luis. How if you play your cards right, you can become as renowned as the celebrity clients. He said it in a way so that my father understood that I was in a great position, and that I had made the right decision on my new career.

A few days later, Glenda gave me a call to come up to their house. They lived in the Hollywood Hills, which meant that on my motorcycle, I would be risking my life winding through the canyons and across Mulholland Drive. Screw it! I was going to the house of my new friends who happened to be rock stars.

The air was warm and the sky, that Los Angeles-color blue that I swear doesn't exist anywhere else. I was living someone else's life. This was a fucking dream. But as we all know, nothing comes for free.

When I arrived, the driveway was so ridiculously steep for my motorcycle that I almost had to bail but ended up gunning it until I got to a level surface. The house was built into the side of a hill with a stunning view of the city from the front yard, which was complete with a badass pool. Glenda greeted me at the front door. Most women I know would be in sweats or maybe shorts and t-shirt when you come to their house in the middle of the day. Not Glenda! She was in a mini skirt, clanging jewelry and high heels that banged across the hardwood floors like someone was hammering nails.

The inside of the house was bright and busy. Not a thing was out of place. The furniture was 1950s, retro style and lining the living room walls must have been 10, no more like 15, classic horror film posters like Dracula and Frankenstein. It was fucking Happy Days Meets The Munsters!

Ronnie walked in and gave me the rundown on the posters, telling me that he's a big collector. He wasn't kidding. I got a tour of the house and every room had its own theme. There was The Elvis Room near the front door. Elvis lamp. Elvis pinball machine. It was like an Elvis gift shop.

Then we entered The Horror Room. A whole room dedicated to fucking real horror - not the manufactured movie poster kind. As we walked in, I immediately see Nazi / Hitler paraphernalia. Nazi flags and a Nazi sword. Glenda and Ronnie loved to shock people and seeing my face as I looked around at the collection lit them up. Beyond the Nazi stuff were a series of jars - with severed fucking heads in them. These heads in a jar definitely stopped me in my tracks! Glenda and Ronnie could barely contain themselves. No wonder they called this the horror room!

Before I could even speak, Ronnie asked: "Oh, you've never seen a shrunken head before?" He had such a nonchalant attitude, like everyone has a shrunken head in their house. "No!" I replied without hesitation. They both burst out laughing hysterically.

Next up was the Rock and Roll Room with rock band posters - T-Rex, David Bowie - kicking it like it was the lobby of the Hard Rock Hotel. Glenda had obviously taken over that room; her clothes and jewelry were everywhere. Not one pair of jeans in sight. She was very clear that she would never, ever wear jeans...*ever*.

Ronnie and Glenda believed that most successful rock stars, or rock bands, were successful not only for their talent but also because they made themselves look the part and fit the music they played. Jimmy Hendrix dressed like his songs. The Beatles dressed like their songs. We would talk about these things all day long. Being pretty much from the street, a lot of their style had that late 70s, New York vibe which carried over into Glenda's outfits. Ronnie, on the other hand, wore the same outfit every day: blue jeans and a black t-shirt. Just like Albert Einstein or Mark Zuckerberg. That way you don't spend wasted time deciding what you are going to wear that day. Ronnie definitely had that sign of genius. His was the first closet I had ever seen that had 10 to 15 pairs of the same jeans and black shirts.

As they continued the tour of the house, Glenda was becoming a bit more touchy-feely with me. At first, I figured it was just an innocent, affectionate thing because she liked me and I was working for her. There were a few times when she ran her fingers down my back or locked her arm through mine when we would walk through the house from one room to the next. She was doing it in front of Ronnie, so I figured that it was normal.

We ended the night back in The Horror Room, which doubled as a media room. We watched some obscure late 60s art film, which was just their time-warped style. During the movie, I sat in the middle. (Glenda would always make sure that I sat in the middle.) She kept moving closer to me, as if she was trying to burrow herself into me. Sweat was starting to form between our skin. I could tell that something was going on, that she wanted me on some level but with her husband on the other side of me I really had no idea what was happening.

About a quarter into the movie, Ronnie got up to use the restroom, leaving the light down as he walked off. Once he was out of sight, Glenda jumped on me. She started kissing me and putting her tongue in my mouth! I immediately pushed her off. "What are you doing?" I asked in a loud whisper. "Your husband is in the bathroom and he's going to be coming right back."

I'm thinking…this is the first time I'm in their house and Ronnie is definitely going to punch me.

It didn't matter what I said or did. Glenda was relentless! She ran her hands up my leg and started grabbing my cock while trying to make out with me. I didn't know what to do. As she put her tongue in my mouth again, I started to let her kiss me and I released my mouth and put my tongue in hers. As soon as we heard Ronnie walking back, she stopped and acted like nothing was happening. When he wasn't looking she stared into my eyes like she was in love with me.

To this day, I've never had a woman attack me like that. She fucking mauled me! Half of me felt violated, the other half of me liked the attention. Like an old lady, Ronnie got up to use the bathroom three or four times during the movie. Every time, she would go for me! How could Ronnie not know this was going down? How was she getting away with this?

Most of my friends and family admitted later that they thought Glenda, Ronnie and I were having a threesome. I could see how people would think that, but we weren't. I had never met people like this before and I had so many questions about what was going on. At the same time, I was kind of digging it, even though I knew what Glenda was doing was so wrong. Or was it?

I more or less became Ronnie and Glenda's adopted son, even though Glenda was molesting me every time she had the chance. All of a sudden, I was surrounded with the most famous people in the world and I was right there in the middle between Ronnie and Glenda as their new friend, or boy-toy, or whatever you want to call it. Hanging with other famous people went from 0 to 60 overnight.

Everyone wanted to be nice to Ronnie including the most well-known people in Hollywood. It wasn't unusual to be at a restaurant and, all of a sudden, an actor like Mick Rage would walk up and say hello. By his side was his girlfriend, LMP, the daughter of the King of Rock and Roll. She loved Ronnie because of his legendary status in the music business.

Mick and LMP were becoming close with Ronnie at about this time and I was right there to witness it. Mick had a huge personality that exploded like a bottle of champagne when he was around Ronnie. It was like being around two, wealthy children who found a friendship together through horror movie posters and other strange toys.

When he was young, Ronnie had set a goal that when he became famous he and Glenda would eat dinner at a really nice restaurant - every single night. He insisted that Glenda make him breakfast and lunch every day. But not dinner. It was a pretty awesome goal.

I basically had it made. Ronnie and Glenda took me to dinner every night! Imagine how many people I met just in the first week of hanging out with them. Glenda would go out of her way to make sure that the other assistants knew I was more special than they were, usually when they were eating their Subway sandwiches for lunch. Yours truly, on the other hand, was being wined and dined at top-tier restaurants like Mastro's, Madeo's and Il Pastaio. Glenda and Ronnie fucking loved exposing me to that shit. You have to remember that they both came from very humble beginnings. Ronnie knew I had a work hard, blue-collar attitude like he did. It was like they were getting to experience fame again for the first time through me.

It wasn't unusual to be sitting down to dinner with seven other people who were all some of the most famous people in the world: Teddy Sweater from Jam Pearl, Dirk Slammit from Alkoholika, Mick Rage and LMP, of course. When the holidays arrived, musicians like Mary Man and the rehabilitated heroin junky, guitar player from The Ice Cold Bell Peppers, Ron Curante, were weekly fixtures at Ronnie and Glenda's house.

Mary Man had caused a lot of controversy. People made him out to be this devil worshiper because of his stage theatrics, which were over the top and dark. American parents hated him for turning their kids into these goth, Mary Man disciples.

When I met Mary Man for the first time, I don't know what I was expecting but it wasn't the smart, perceptive individual standing before me. He actually was the most normal out of everyone. In fact, he seemed kind of nerdy deep down. You could tell that he created this Mary Man character to shock the general public, and our society completely bought it!

To get beneath the personas and see who these musicians were underneath was exciting and astonishing in the same breath. The art they created was from their souls, from the gut...then it was hypnotic in the way that it affects us and speaks to us at different moments in our lives. It's no surprise to me now, having met a lot of famous musicians, that a good amount of them fall off the deep end because of the impact they make on people. Moving mass amounts of people the way they do is probably really hard to prepare for.

What I saw was that so many of these extremely influential musicians and actors just wanted to be nice to Ronnie because he had influenced them so much. I'm sure, 20 years ago, Ronnie could never have imagined that super famous musicians and actors *IN LOS ANGELES* would be worshiping him the way they were. He never wanted to seem like he was affected by the music he put out. "It was job for me," he would say over and over. For him, it was a way out of Queens.

A year into our interesting relationship, people started wondering what Glenda and Ronnie were doing hanging out with me all the time. Some people thought we were all having a sexual relationship. (We weren't.) Some famous friends thought they were taking pity on me or I was using them. (Not true.) My parents, separately but equally, thought it was strange that this rich and famous couple was taking me in like I was their kid. (I agreed but didn't care.)

In the beginning, Glenda and Ronnie definitely seemed like they wanted to help me. Glenda was buying me clothes all the time and Ronnie picked me up CDs to broaden my knowledge of rock and roll, especially the early stuff like Elvis, The Beatles, etc.

"There is nothing worse than being boring," Ronnie would say. He told me he loved doing these things for me because these experiences would make me more interesting and give me something to talk about with my clients.

To this day, I tell all my assistants that you need to be a concierge to your clientele. You need to know what the good restaurants are, where the good clubs are and where the good parties are. You need to be a cultural encyclopedia. People come to us not only for their hair but also to know what's cool, what's in style and where to go.

One day Ronnie asked me: "So Brandon, what's been the highlight since you've known me and Glenda?"

There had been so many experiences and each one seemed to trump the next. A few months prior, Ronnie, Glenda and I had driven up to San Francisco to hang out with Dirk Slammit from Alcoholika for Dirk's birthday. All of the members of Alcoholika were there and, being that famous people attract other famous people like moths, the party was basically a mash up of The Academy Awards and The Grammys. Every face at that party had either been on the movie screen or on the cover of an album.

Glenda and I liked to drink red wine and got shit faced every night we were there, including the night of the birthday party. She had become more and more relentless about taking advantage of me. When we drank, it became worse. It was getting to the point to where I was getting upset and uncomfortable, not knowing when or how she was going to put her hands on me. With alcohol in her, she would get more aggressive and didn't know how to stop herself - nor did she want to. She also had started to make the moves on me in front of Ronnie. This, I didn't understand.

The night of the birthday party we had a huge fight that escalated to screaming and name calling. It didn't matter how loud I screamed at Glenda, she didn't seem fazed. In fact, when I screamed at her, she would burst out in a witch-like laugh, as if she enjoyed the fighting (which she did...it turned her on). This made me angrier and more confused, as it didn't matter what I said or did. Then after the laughing stopped, she just slipped back into her signature love struck stare.

I guess looking back, she probably didn't understand why I was getting upset. Maybe I should have been more accepting of the situation but I wasn't. It really made me uncomfortable. At the same time, I loved being part of The Capones, becoming friends with them and the experiences we were having. So, I let it continue.

After we got back from San Francisco, things were still a little strange. However, I didn't want things to stop. So, when Ronnie asked me what was the most exciting thing that we have done so far since we have been friends, I told him that going up to visit Dirk had been the highlight so far.

I could tell that was not pleasing to Ronnie.

Ronnie and Glenda always wanted themselves to be the highlight in our relationship. Jealousy was an everyday thing with both of them. Ronnie had a big smile on his face and I could tell that he had something very important to tell me.

"Well, I know you've never been to New York and I know you really want to go," Ronnie said. "Turns out that The Capones are getting inducted into the Rock & Roll Hall of Fame and I'm going to take you with us." Ronnie and Glenda really took joy in outdoing other people.

"Are you fucking serious?" I replied immediately. Ronnie and Glenda knew that going to New York was like a fantasy for me. "That's fucking amazing! Of course I want to go, are you kidding me?"

"Dirk and Teddy will be meeting us there," Ronnie said. "Teddy is actually going to be giving the induction speech for The Capones."

I looked right at Ronnie and Glenda and said: "Let me get this straight, you're taking me to New York with Dirk Slammit from Alcoholika and Teddy Sweater from Jam Pearl and we're all going to watch you get inducted into the Rock and Roll Hall of Fame?" Even though I tried to keep cool, I'm sure my voice went up about three octaves.

As I'm nearly jumping up and down with excitement, Ronnie said: "Well that's great because I already booked airline tickets. We are all leaving next week and we're all going to fly first class."

Seriously. I think I nearly shit my pants. I could see Glenda's wheels turning, though. Glenda was going to try to rape me in New York every chance she got.

Now I don't want to sound like it was all Glenda's fault; I did give in at certain moments. Especially when we were drunk. Then there were a handful of times when I initiated being physical with her. Glenda was doing to me what Ronnie had done to her when he stole her away from the lead singer 20 years earlier. Relentless sexual advances. I mean relentless.

Don't get me wrong, I was a grown man, even if I was young and stupid. No-one ever forced me to hang out with Ronnie and Glenda, or forced me to keep hanging out with them even with all the advances and the constant fighting about the advances with Glenda. I did it on my own. And there was no fucking way I was giving up going to New York.

The day finally came for us to fly to New York. It was fucking glorious. The Hall of Fame covered the travel and, hell yeah, they gave us the rock star treatment. Going through security with Ronnie and Glenda was surreal. We were the white exotic tigers at the zoo, free for all the public to see. Ronnie's haircut was so obvious, there was no hiding who he was. He must've signed 10 or 20 autographs while we were waiting in line and we couldn't go 10 feet without being stopped by an adoring fan. As we boarded the plane, the stares kept coming. At that point, I was totally used to people gawking at us everywhere we went. I had never flown first class in my life, or even thought that it would be possible. When we were shown to our seats, I felt like a real king.

From the moment we landed at JFK, the fans were relentless. A wall of screaming people immediately charged us as we walked out of baggage claim. It was that, 'I'm with the band' moment. People were staring at me, trying to find out who I was and why I was with them.

The limo picked us up and off we went to the Waldorf Astoria Hotel, where the induction was being held. I had arrived. Like an excited dog, I stuck my head out the window, letting the brisk, New York air hit my face. Ronnie could see the big smile that was permanently strapped on my face until the day we left. Never in a million years did I think that my life would be going this way.

A documentary of The Capones was being made during all this. The camera crew would be meeting us at the hotel and Ronnie wanted to make sure that I was in the documentary in some way. He knew that it would be something that I would have forever. (I'm in about three scenes.)

Since the Hall of Fame induction is a huge deal, the general public knows that New York City is going to be crawling with musicians and famous people of all sorts. Persistent fans have their ways of finding out when the artists are arriving and leaving the hotel. A crowd of fans were awaiting our arrival.

Once again, Ronnie took to signing autographs and allowed pictures to be taken of him. I started to become their security detail in a way because, when the fans would mob us, all 90 pounds of Glenda would be pushed aside like a rag doll.

Some fans have no idea about personal space. They just roll up on you very aggressively, wanting t-shirts signed, while holding handfuls of photos that they also wanted signed. (If you are this kind of fan, please reconsider your approach.) We literally had fans on top of us all the way to the elevators as we headed to our rooms.

As exciting as it was, it was very claustrophobic. I see now why The Beatles or The Rolling Stones would stay holed up inside their hotel rooms. The fans won't let you go anywhere. They would have loved to have ripped the clothes right off Ronnie's back.

That trip to New York was the first time that I saw Ronnie as the actual Ronnie Capone, not that more normal guy I knew back in Los Angeles. I was witnessing his full-blown celebrity status as one of his closest friends. The Capones set their goals and made them happen! This way of seeing the world rubbed off on me. And being in their inner circle affected me. It made me feel like there was nothing I couldn't accomplish, if I just set my mind to it.

Ronnie - as aggressive as he had been and sometimes still could be - was just not that dick that he could have been to the fans. He said hello and responded to every person that came his way as we walked to the elevators. He made sure that he signed an autograph for every fan that wanted one. He smiled at the fans. If you knew Ronnie, you knew that he didn't smile that often. But when he was getting mobbed, which seemed like a stressful situation, he was always nice. He told me that it's very important to be good to the fans, no matter how tired or irritable you might be. Being polite to the people who made you famous was a must. I had so much respect for that.

We finally made it up to the rooms. Wow, that was really fucking intense!

Glenda and Ronnie had gotten me my own room just down the hall from theirs and, to my surprise, Glenda had not tried to attack me yet. I think all the commotion actually startled her a bit. It had been awhile since they were both back in New York, and, from the time we landed, the mob scene didn't stop.

The next morning my head was screaming at me. We drank far too much the night before - at dinner with Dirk Slammit and Teddy Sweater and their girlfriends! We had already been in New York for 24 hours and it seemed like it was flying by. I didn't want to miss a thing. Before the ceremony later that evening, we all had to go downtown to meet Ronnie's manager to do some autograph signing, and to go over The Capones merchandise.

This skinny guy named Arturo handled the merchandise. When we met him at his loft, he was sporting a fresh, black eye that he gotten that morning from some random homeless person on the street. Arturo had been with The Capones since the band's inception. Like many other people I met, he obviously started from nothing and made it to where he was because of one rock and roll band. Since The Capones were being elevated to hall of fame status, so was everyone else that worked with him in the business. I loved that about Ronnie. He was always about the loyalty and he stayed true to the people who helped him and his band from the beginning.

As we headed back to the Waldorf for the ceremony, I started to get the looks from Glenda. I was wondering how long it was going to take for her touchy-feely hands to rub up on me. I knew that I was going to be in for it later on. Especially tonight, since we would all be celebrating at the Hall of Fame.

I justified letting her do what she wanted since she and Ronnie brought me all the way to New York. I didn't want any stress. If she wanted to fuck me somewhere where no one was watching, I would let her.

If she wanted to sneak off and give me a blowjob during the ceremony, I would let her. I knew we would get really liquored up, and I wasn't going to put up a fight this time. I surrendered.

As we got closer to show time, I could see outside my hotel window that the crowd was growing by the minute. I knew when we all got downstairs for the ceremony that there would be a crowd of people we would have to get through. Only, this time, it would be more stressful, because Dirk and Teddy were going to be entering the ceremony with us, along with the rest of The Capones.

The time had arrived for all of us to go downstairs to the ceremony. Glenda knocked on my door to let me know that they were ready. I opened the door to find her in a beautiful, orange dress that was really short. She never wore a bra, so her breasts would almost be revealed with every step. I could tell by the way she was looking at me that I was definitely in for it later on. I grabbed her tightly before we met up with Ronnie and kissed her hard and passionately.

Her eyes lit up as I stroked her back and grabbed her body as if I was going to take her right then and there. There she was, a 40-something year-old woman, looking like she was going on a first date with someone she really liked and she knew she was going to get lucky before the date even started. It was sweet, actually. Except for the fact that it was the biggest night of her husband's career. I started to not care anymore about that, as I knew he was fully aware of what was happening.

We all met up at the elevator and began our descent to the lobby floor, with the documentary film crew following and filming us. When we arrived in the ballroom, we were seated at the table of honor with the other members of the band. All except the lead singer who had died a few months prior. With his passing, Ronnie decided that The Capones would not perform at the ceremony, as most other honored performers do.

Ronnie wasn't just interested in The Capones and the honor that was being received. He was actually a fan himself of the other artists being inducted - like Brenda Lee and Gene Pitney. There was no way that Ronnie would ask them for an autograph, so he asked me to do it! I was already buzzed and my confidence was through the roof. I actually hadn't heard of these artists because they were popular before my time, but I loved the fact that Ronnie was so excited. I could tell that it meant a lot to him to be in the same room as these other artists who had influenced him in a big way.

Especially since he was being recognized as a rock and roll artist alongside them.

It seemed like we sat there for hours before it was The Capones turn to go up on stage. Every band that was getting inducted would play a three to four song set after they would give their acceptance speeches, which generally was way too long. Glenda, Teddy Sweater and I were getting pretty wasted on red wine while we were waiting. As The Capones moment got closer, we started drinking more. When the time came, Teddy just brought the whole bottle of wine up to the stage with him as he prepared to induct The Capones. Fuck it, right? It's Rock and Roll!

As Teddy stepped up to the mic, the crowd went wild as they knew what was coming next. After all, this was New York City: The Capones home turf. Teddy began his speech and paused to take a big swig of red wine out of the bottle. He gave this long drawn out speech that lasted at least fifteen to twenty minutes, filled with rants about things that are bullshit...that the business was crap and fake. It was a total, 'I'm a rock star and I don't give a fuck' speech, clearly taken over by the wine. It was long and embarrassing to witness. All of us at the table were pretty silent through all of this. I don't know if Ronnie and the rest of the band were prepared for this kind of induction. Teddy's speech finally came to an end and The Capones went up to the stage to accept their Rock and Roll Hall of Fame award, giving acceptance speeches that were about a third as long as Teddy's single speech.

Since The Capones weren't going to play for the audience, we all decided to split the ceremony early and go to Glenda's friend's downtown apartment. By this time, Glenda, Teddy and I were shit faced. As we all got up and walked out into the hotel lobby, we were swarmed. I remember specifically a woman coming up to Teddy and nearly crying from the moment she laid her eyes on him. She bee-lined it straight for him. Her hands were shaking with excitement just to be able to get next to him. She was the kind of fan that all rock stars and famous people are afraid of. It was the emotionally challenged fan that was scary to be around. She seemed unpredictable like she would kill herself over Teddy. I had never witnessed anything or anybody like this.

It sort of freaked me out and I remember at that instant, all of a sudden, I became sober. Teddy's mannerisms and attitude changed immediately when she got close. We were all extremely uncomfortable. We were also dealing with Dirk's fans and Ronnie's fans all at the same time. Once we were rushed, Glenda and Dirk's wife were blown to the side. Once again, I stepped in as a bodyguard to keep the aggressive fans back so we wouldn't be tackled. I was grabbing people by their collars and necks to keep them back. It was as if we had shaken a human beehive and were being swarmed with bodies, shoving pencils and papers in our faces. When it finally ended, the wives were about 20 feet away from us and we all took a deep breath, giving each other looks to make sure everyone was okay.

We got into the limo and headed to downtown Manhattan in a blur of street lights. We arrived at Glenda's friend's apartment. She was a female, fashion designer that Glenda grew up with - and was as cold to me as a polar bear in the North Pole.

By this time, Glenda, Teddy and I were back to being fucking wasted, laughing hysterically at absolutely nothing. To my surprise, Glenda and I were getting along really well. Since we were all together, she was holding back on the molestation. We stayed at her friend's apartment for about an hour as the group began to yawn and stretch. My head was beginning to spin. I don't remember getting back to the hotel as I had blacked out. I don't even remember saying goodbye to Glenda's friend... or maybe we never said goodbye. The next thing

I remember was waking up in our hotel room with one of the worst hangovers I have ever had. These two days had taken so much out of me. I can't believe that rock stars do this on a daily basis. No wonder so many of them die young.

Being famous seemed fucking weird to me after that experience. I liked it and I didn't like it. It was cool, but scary at the same time. These fucking fans would kill themselves over these guys and that's a lot of stress to carry. But, like Ronnie would always say to me: "What's life without a little stress?"

After we got back to LA, things started going south for all of us. Glenda and Ronnie were starting to become very possessive of me. They both acted like they owned me, which did not go over well with me. Glenda and I got into another screaming match because I was starting to see other girls, as any 25-year-old male should. We didn't speak for about three days. She kept calling me and I wouldn't answer. On the fourth day, I was at the salon working and all of a sudden Ronnie storms in, screaming bloody murder at me.

"Why haven't you called Glenda back!" He yells at me with spit flying out of his mouth. "Why are you ignoring us?" My whole body went numb. There he was, this retired rock star, who had just gotten inducted to the

Rock and Roll Hall of Fame and he was freaking out in the salon because I hadn't responded to his wife. It was very bizarre!

After he finished, he realized that the entire salon had stopped everything they were doing and were just staring at him - from the other stylists, to the clients, to the cleaning woman. He stormed out and the salon was silent for about five minutes. My boss looked at me and asked: "Why did Ronnie Capone come in here and scream at you for not calling his wife back?"

I didn't know how to respond. I just sort of shook my head and continued the blow dry. I'm sure that everyone in the salon at that point thought Glenda, Ronnie and I were engaged in some strange love triangle. My boss never looked at me the same after that.

We made up eventually and I continued to stay at their house three to four nights a week, sleeping in the pool house. At night, Glenda would try to put the moves on me. As much as I tried to make it normal, I just couldn't. If Ronnie would walk out of the room, she would immediately grab my cock and try to put her tongue in my mouth.

She told me more than once that I reminded her of her father. He was a handsome, Italian man with dark hair and green eyes. Glenda loved her daddy and saw a lot of him in me, but what she wanted to do with me was nowhere near appropriate father/daughter behavior.

It wasn't that I wasn't attracted to her, I was just uncomfortable with the fact that she was married and her husband was now my friend. I loved them both. I was so fucking torn.

More and more, the vicious fights continued between Glenda and me. Not talking for days at a time. From my side, it just looked like the whole relationship had become toxic. Like they were two lunatic, retired rock stars who were totally nuts. What I didn't know, because they didn't tell me, is that Ronnie was sick. He was dying. He had prostate cancer and they had found it too late to do anything about it.

The more sick Ronnie got, the weirder things got. It all started to become like a really bad acid trip. For my birthday, my mom was in town and Ronnie and Glenda wanted to take us out to dinner, and then go back to the house to give me my presents that they had so generously bought for me. We went to Madeo's on Beverly Boulevard, a very upscale, Italian restaurant that we went to quite often.

My mother had never been around famous people and was already skeptical of my two new, interesting friends. Glenda wanted to meet my mom right away. She was more excited to see my mom than I was. It was like Glenda was my new fiancée, and she was meeting her future mother-in-law.

Glenda and I picked up my mom from the airport and started heading back up into Beverly Hills. I was driving an El Camino at the time, so the three of us had to sit next to each other with Glenda in the middle. Glenda always insisted on sitting next to me like she was my wife.

My mother was turned off right away by Glenda. Growing up, my mother never really had girlfriends. Being a prison guard at Folsom Prison, this woman was not to be fucked with. Apparently, Glenda didn't listen to me when I explained my mother's personality. Since I was a little boy, my mother has suffered from migraines and she probably has never had as big of a migraine as Glenda gave her that day. The more Glenda talked, the bigger and more visibly painful my mother's headache was becoming. Within 30 minutes after we had picked her up, she winced with every word that came out of Glenda's mouth. Since I only had a little apartment in West Hollywood, Glenda insisted that my mom stay at their house.

We arrived at Glenda and Ronnie's house and my mother immediately needed to take a nap. A few hours went by, my mother woke up and Glenda gave my mother the tour. The same tour as the one I got, with the Nazi paraphernalia and the shrunken heads. I could tell that she was genuinely worried about me. At the same time, my mother loved nice things and when she was married to my father she spent all his money. After the divorce, she moved to Northern California and had to start all over again. This was very tough for her. Seeing me living it up with this rock star and his wife really hit a sensitive spot with her.

As Ronnie and Glenda got the car ready to go to dinner, my mother pulled me aside. "I know you're having a great time but none of this is going to last," she said. "They want something else from you. You have to know this!"

I knew she was probably right but I just wanted her to be happy for me and let me enjoy myself. We all got into the car and headed to Madeo's. We arrived at the restaurant and sat down at our table. I could tell right off the bat that Glenda was going to want to sit next to me. My mother tried to sit next to me, but Glenda pushed her out of the way. Disbelief was written all over my mother's face. So, what did my mom do? She shoved Glenda right back. My mom outweighed Glenda by about 20 pounds, so Glenda really went flying, and my mom won the battle.

We were seated for about five minutes when Glenda started in with my mother about how she always sits next to me, and my mother should just deal with it. Ronnie sat there loving every moment, with a devilish grin on his face. He loved uncomfortable situations.

Glenda's nasally, New York accent was exactly the pitch that drove my mother fucking nuts! It was like Chinese water torture. I could see my mom hating Glenda more and more with every passing second. We managed to get through dinner and dessert. My mom almost had a fucking heart attack when she saw the bill for upwards of $500. She wasn't used to eating at expensive places. My mother attempted to pay for her meal, when Ronnie grabbed the bill and insisted on paying.

We got back up to the house and the gifting began. Glenda and Ronnie gave me about $4,000-$5,000 worth of stuff. The first gift was a $1,000 skull belt buckle that I still wear to this day. They got me two vintage 50s movie posters, worth about $500 each. One bathrobe with my initials on it, a 25th anniversary

Capones Japan tour, tee shirt, and a handmade Mosrite, Ronnie Capone signature guitar!

Ronnie wanted me to feel like a celebrity. He wanted me to feel like one of them. He saw something in me early on, even before I could see it. There's no substitute for experience, and being on the road in a punk band for 30 years gave him plenty. My mom was blown away and very uncomfortable. My actual parents were never able to shower me with gifts like this. Somehow, The Capones had become my new rich parents.

We were all staying at the house that night. It was time to turn in, so I walked my mom into the Disney Room to say goodnight. She turned to me and said: "I know that they're famous. I know that you're infatuated and have stars in your eyes because of what they're doing for you. I know your father and I could never do for you what they're doing for you, but they're using you for some strange reason and you need to watch out."

I rolled my eyes and replied: "Yeah, yeah Mom, I get what you're saying." I knew she was right, even though I didn't want to hear it. What did they want from me? Where did I fit in? Why did they take such an interest in me?

Everyone has an expiration date and Ronnie knew his was up soon. Since they were first together in the 70s, Glenda and Ronnie had never been apart. As much as he loved her, he didn't want her to be alone when he died.

Of course, I knew none of this until it was too late. Glenda and I eventually got into a fight that kept me away for a long time through Ronnie's last days. I didn't get to see him at his worst. I didn't get to say goodbye. She cut off contact with me until he died.

Glenda invited me to the dedication of the statue of Ronnie that stands in The Hollywood Forever Cemetery where he was laid to rest, and Glenda and I started to see each other again.

After a few weeks of hanging out together, we started to fool around again. Ronnie was no longer around, so I wasn't worried about him catching us anymore. I guess I could have been Ronnie's replacement. The whole dynamic wasn't right, though. We both missed Ronnie. Without him, Glenda and I didn't make sense together anymore. There was a void that could only be filled by a rock legend. A guitar God named Ronnie Capone.

Eventually Glenda stopped all contact with me and I haven't spoken to her since. A few years later, I was driving and glanced over to my left. There was Glenda in the passenger seat of a car, being driven by some guy that I didn't recognize. She hadn't changed a bit, still larger-than-life. I didn't try to get her attention. I just drove for a while, watching her through the window. Funny thing about Hollywood, most friendships, like all the Ronnie Capones in the world, have an expiration date.

It's a shame, but that's just how life goes.

MURDER ON THIRD STREET

My relationship with Glenda was deteriorating – fast! After Ronnie passed, it just wasn't the same and working for her in the salon was becoming incredibly uncomfortable for both of us.

With Ronnie's cancer, we had all gone through such a dramatic transition. It's tough to see someone go through that. You take the journey with them and it really takes the spark out of you.

We had a really good run but towards the end, Glenda was off on another planet. She seemed completely lost without Ronnie and I didn't know how to fill that gap, nor did I think I could. Things had become really negative between us, which was sad.

But I still needed to think about my career and what would happen to me now that Ronnie was gone. So, secretly I started looking for another salon where I could work.

Luckily, I didn't have to look long for a new salon because out of the blue, just a few days later, I received a random phone call from a woman named Meagan, who managed a salon on Third Street in West Hollywood.

I had no idea how she got my contact information, but she said that is was a brand new salon and it was owned by a famous hair stylist named Rory Dowell. Well, of course, I had heard of Rory – everyone in hairdressing circles knew his name.

I was still puzzled as to how they knew about me, but I was intrigued enough to accept Meagan's invitation to come and meet Rory in person and check out the salon.

Since she was being so aggressive, I figured I would let Meagan pursue me and not reveal that I was ready for a move. Rory was actually a pretty known hair stylist around town who did color and cutting. It was very attractive to me that he did both services. But what was even more attractive was that Rory coiffed a lot of celebrities – a lot of hip young, relevant celebrities.

In addition, he was looking for new, hot talent and I was on the list. In my mind, it was a match made in hairdressing heaven!

We scheduled a meeting for the next day, as people in the hair business never waste time. When you leave a salon, there's no two-week notice and Meagan wanted me to come in right away as they were quickly filling up the chairs in Rory's salon.

I went down the next day to meet Meagan and scout out this new salon. It was all very cloak and dagger, James Bond kind of stuff. I just hoped no one I knew saw me sneaking into the Parlor!

I rode my motorcycle down to Third Street and saw the sign, The Parlor. I really liked the name! It had this upscale, beauty vibe ring to it. And Third Street in West Hollywood is a real hip, artistic street, with a lot of interesting, yet expensive restaurants, clothing boutiques and furniture shops. It's a very colorful and young-looking street that's booming with hip, wannabe actors.

And at the heart of this beating community was The Parlor. It was a new and exciting venture for Rory, who was known for making beautiful blondes even more blonde and even more beautiful!

Rory championed this amazing technique called Balayage, where instead of highlighting hair with foils, you would actually paint the color right onto the hair. I was mesmerized as I'd never seen this technique being done before. Coming from the Ferretti salon where Luis was crowned The King of Color, I was excited. I desperately wanted to learn everything I could and this was the perfect opportunity.

Meagan had made it very clear to me from the start that Rory was doing a lot of celebrities who were relevant at that time and that discretion would be needed. That was no problem for me. I was used to keeping quiet about the celebrities coming into the gay bar, so I knew how to keep my mouth shut. Of course, I didn't tell Meagan about those wild nights in the bar. I just told her that I knew the client came first every time.

I walked into The Parlor to find Meagan waiting for me in the seating area. But I hardly noticed her. I was too busy looking around the salon – it was amazing!

When you walked in, the whole salon was about three feet deeper than the front door. It was like a huge, sunken-in living room with salon stations perfectly placed throughout the space. It had beautiful, light brown, hard wood floors and gorgeous, parlor style mirrors. The salon definitely had swagger!

Meagan began our meeting and I was listening intently, trying to take it all in when, all of a sudden, I heard this huge cackle from up front. The laugh was so loud it stopped our conversation.

Meagan rolled her eyes. But I didn't mind. Finally, I'd found someone as loud as me. "Sorry about that Brandon, Rory is a bit loud when he does hair. Sometimes I think he's deaf!" Meagan apologized. But I didn't need the apology. I responded with: "No problem, I like that he has a boisterous personality! It means he's passionate about his job."

She quickly said: "Oh, he's passionate alright!" I couldn't tell if she was being complimentary or if she was being slightly sarcastic. I really hoped it was the first one! She then asked me about my hair stylist goals and about my training.

I had to be careful what I told her. I wanted to big up my talent, but at the same time, I didn't want to bad mouth the salon I was at right now or anyone with whom I worked. That would be one hell of a big no-no. Hairdressing is a small world and I didn't want anything I said getting back to any current co-workers.

I mentioned that I had worked for Luis Ferretti as an assistant and I told her that I wanted to be able to do both color and cuts. I explained that while I had learned a lot during my time there, Ferretti was a departmentalized salon and it didn't really fit what I wanted to do in the future.

Of course, I kept quiet about the fact that I was being molested by a dead rock star's wife all day, every day. It might be some guy's dream job, but it was causing me problems and I couldn't wait to get out of that situation!

And bringing up the whole Ronnie and Glenda situation wouldn't be appropriate for this meeting. After I got to know Rory, I knew he would have loved to hear all about it, but I still felt a loyalty to Ronnie and Glenda and didn't want to spread gossip about them all over town.

As it would turn out, we had a lot to talk about anyway as Rory knew about me through the gay bar. He was one of the customers that frequented The Firehouse. When I met him, I recognized him immediately.

Rory was an ultra-buffed, good-looking gay man with tattoos and a thick mustache. He was the gay version of Tom Selleck's Magnum P.I. He looked like a very handsome, manly man, right up until the moment he opened his mouth. Then it was like being repeatedly slapped over the head with a pink Chanel handbag!

He might look all man, but Rory was one of the gayest- sounding men I have ever met – and I've met a lot! He was a walking contradiction, strutting around with leather pants and a tank top, cackling at the top of his lungs at his own jokes! This big, beautiful, masculine male with facial hair, sounded like a prissy prom queen on her period!

Rory definitely had a mouth on him and he didn't give two shits as to who would hear him. One of his favorite phrases was: "Well, honey!" In fact, most of Rory's sentences began with: "Well, honey!" It was almost like a catchphrase. I wouldn't be surprised if he has it inscribed on his tombstone: "Well, honey, here lies Rory!"

One time he had a client in his chair, and this client was being kind of bitchy about God knows what, when all of a sudden, Rory yells out to her: "Well, honey, you must not be getting your pussy pounded enough!" The client's face turned white with horror while the whole salon grounded to a halt! You could hear a pin drop – until Rory just gave his usual loud cackle.

He was completely oblivious to the effect his comments had on people. Or maybe he just didn't care! He didn't say things in a malicious way; it was the raunchy, fun guy he was. He just didn't realize that he was one-of-a-kind and not everyone was like that.

Rory was completely wild but so, so talented! He's one of the most talented hair stylists I've ever worked for. He did the most beautiful hair color I have ever seen, and that's saying a lot having worked for Luis Ferretti. The thing about Luis Ferretti, the clients were famous, but they were old-school stars. It was different at Rory's salon - the celebrities were much more popular and current.

By the end of the first week of working there, I could see that Rory was 'Roaring' his way to highlighting fame! Just one famous blonde after another - from Kim Basinger to Tammie Mendez to Denise Withers.

It was a really busy place, but because of the layout, all the stylists were spread out instead of being on top of each other. We each had our own special, private nook, which gave celebrities a more intimate feeling and they loved that! Celebrities love nothing more than being made to feel special!

The salon mostly employed male stylists and I was the only straight guy there. The two girls that worked with us were lesbians and they acted like guys, so between the four guys and the two lesbians, we were a pretty masculine salon – despite Rory's super loud gay voice!

With Rory being right in front, it was definitely 'The Rory Show!' Since I had come from the West Hollywood bar scene, I knew how these personalities operated and I felt very much at home working with this crew.

There were two other women who worked with us that did the cleaning. Maria, who could also do shampoos, was the leader while Sabrina was the younger one. Sabrina didn't speak a word of English, so she would just nod her head and smile if you asked her something. Sabrina was from El Salvador and she was in her mid- 20s.

We also had a reputable and active publicity firm spending every day pushing the salon to all the magazine editors and television outlets. The salon was getting a lot of calls from women who had seen our salon in some magazine, or heard about a celebrity's new look and then wanted the same look. It's amazing how everyone thinks they can bring in a photo of a celebrity in a magazine and walk out looking exactly the same, so we were getting dozens of new referrals every day!

It was the perfect time for me to join The Parlor and take advantage of all these new clients. Getting on the Parlor ladder early, I was able to begin climbing and building up my clientele. And let's face it, women do not fuck around when it comes to their hair!

For me, this was a perfect learning opportunity. I was having fun at The Parlor, but I was also learning so much from Rory, a guy who had built it all on his own. That was a huge inspiration for me. Working at Luis Ferretti and working at The Parlor was like night and day. Luis would only be there one week a month because he was working in New York most of the time. But with Rory it was different. He was there, right beside you every day. He was the main artist in a group of other artists and the canvas was famous people's hair.

Once an actress is famous, they can get their hair styling paid for by the studios, who pony up an ungodly amount for hair and make-up. The actresses would come in, but they definitely would not want to pay for it themselves, especially when they're walking out having spent $800 on the cut, color and highlights. Sometimes bills would be over $1,000 depending on if you were going to bring your child with you.

Oh yeah! Some of these actresses, who earned millions of dollars, would try to get the kid's haircut paid for by the studio as well. We didn't care if you were 10 or 80 years-old. What we charged is what you paid. Kids under ten years old would walk out of the salon after getting a $150 hair cut, or $75 for bang trims that the studio paid for. "Fuck it," one actress told me. "I worked for this all my life so if they're paying, I'm doing it."

Actors are funny. Take your normal eccentricities and times them by a thousand and you've got your over-the-top celeb! When these actors came into the salon or sat in my chair, they always acted like they knew nothing about what was going on around them. They could all have auditioned for a role in the movie Clueless! That's how they behaved. They liked to pretend that being clueless was the hip thing to do.

For example, I would ask some famous person: "Hey, so and so, did you see that TV show on Channel Seven last night?" And they would always reply with: "I don't watch any television so I wouldn't know what that is." Or they would pick up the weekly gossipy tabloid magazines and pretend they didn't know who their peers were. They would show me paparazzi photos and ask: "Who are these people? I've never even heard of them!"

It was hysterical. It was so obvious they knew who everyone was and what was going on in the crazy world of celebrities. It wouldn't have surprised me if they'd picked up a magazine, flicked through it, spotted a photo of themselves and asked me who that was!

When we would order them lunch from the local diner or restaurant nearby, they would always want the restaurant to make them some dish that wasn't on the menu. Without fail, they would just make up some shit they felt like eating at that moment.

I found this quite amusing, although I'm sure the chef at the restaurant got pretty annoyed about it! It's appalling, yet accepted behavior in Hollywood. These are the ridiculous things you get to do when you're famous. When you're so famous that the paparazzi is outside the salon waiting for you for hours and the publicity girl is next to you the entire time, kissing your ass like it's her most favorite thing to do, that has to enlarge your head a bit.

But at the end of the day, the stylist's job to is to keep the celebrity's people happy. It doesn't really matter what the celebrity thinks. They have a team of people they have to report to – and they don't do anything without their say-so. That includes changing their look, or hair.

Week-in week-out the celebrities would all tell me the same thing: "Oh, I have to keep my hair the same so my people don't kill me! This color has to be perfect or my people will freak out! I'm doing re-shoots this week and it has to look exactly the same!"

This means that you, as the hair stylist, were always working under the gun. You'd have to perform at your best, or be crucified by the A team of people that could turn on you at any moment. Performers need attention – your undivided attention! It wouldn't be unusual to have three or four of their 'people' involved in what you are doing to the hair.

When this happens, it becomes a collaboration - almost like an art project with the talent being the art that's going on display. One would think that all of this was a bit much, but when you worked for a big, buffed, prissy queen in a muscular and tattooed body, the demanding celebrities were a breeze!

It wasn't that Rory was trying to be mean, he just didn't understand why people couldn't read his mind. Plus, when Rory got worked up, which was quite often, he would begin to stutter. It was like all of a sudden this big, muscle man with facial hair and tattoos would be reduced to a 10 year-old with a short fuse and a stutter!

I would have to learn to keep a straight face when he got worked up because the stutter would start and I couldn't help but get impatient while I was waiting for Rory to finish what he was saying.

With Rory in full stuttering mode, and celebrities snapping their fingers left, right and center, this made the salon a sight to see. Rory made it all the more interesting with his off-color jokes, loud cackles and ear piercing insults, which flew out of his mouth faster than a rich woman runs for a divorce.

You always had to have the right answer for Rory, or he would talk down to you. At first it seemed like he was making a huge insult, but every time there would be a laugh at the end of it, so it didn't seem like he was being mean.

He also had a way with his clients; he wouldn't take any of their celebrity shit. He had this slightly arrogant attitude with women, like his mother had done some damage that hadn't gone away. While the rest of us took our orders – hey the client is always right, correct? Rory wasn't going to let anyone tell him how to do hair. He would snap back at them, but then immediately laugh, and that would somehow keep people from getting directly offended.

He knew how to insult them and then smother it up with a loud cackle right afterwards, as if he was laughing at himself. It's a great technique, actually. The next time you want to insult someone, just say whatever insult comes to mind, then laugh out loud at yourself right after. I guarantee it will get you out of trouble every time!

Rory had perfected this technique and it worked really well for him! He could do no wrong, nothing was able to touch him, and why would it? He could do whatever and say whatever because he was the owner. And I think the celebrities loved that about him. They were surrounded by so many 'yes' people, it was a nice refreshing change for them to come into the salon and have someone like Rory insult them and tell them exactly what he thought of them for a change. That two hours in the chair was probably the only time during a week in their spoiled little lives that they weren't in charge. I imagine it was a relief for many of them to just kick back and let Rory be the boss.

And Rory didn't let up on anyone. Overweight people were particularly open targets at our salon. There was no mercy! For all of us there, nothing was worse than being fat! I think that's just Hollywood in general. No one wants to be out of shape in this city. All of us at the salon were really in shape and still are, for that matter.

Our publicity girl was a little chubby and I remember her wobbling into the salon and seeing Rory make faces behind her back, like silent, fat jokes. Rory had a six pack and worked out every day. He just didn't understand why someone would ever want to be fat, and I think that stems from the way he was brought up.

Rory was someone who didn't get along with his mother. He had major 'mommy issues' and this really shaped his attitude towards females. Like Rory, I also have had issues with my mother, although our mother issues were slightly different. Rory's 'mommy' problems were on a whole different level, and when you don't get what you need from the woman who is supposed to be there for you, it drives you in a certain way. Sometimes it creates major destruction, but other times it can create success if guided in the right direction.

Rory's mother was obsessed with him and wanted him sexually, along with other serious issues that I'm sure were beyond explanation. She definitely had a Jocasta Complex. Jocasta was the fictional Greek Queen who had a sexual relationship with her son Oedipus. When a child is sexually obsessed with a parent – usually sons with their mothers - it's called the Oedipus Complex. But when it's the other way around, it's known as the Jocasta Complex. Rory's mother would have definitely fallen into that category.

That said, she wasn't there for him in the way that a mother should have been. Not a shocker that they weren't best friends and certainly why she never came to the salon while I was there. A mother being obsessed over her son where it's almost a sexual thing had to wear Rory down as a child and really shaped the way he acted when he was around women. It definitely explained the stuttering.

This would come up in conversations with his clients and you would overhear him talking about it randomly as if it were a joke to him. It didn't sound like a joke to the rest of us, but this was Rory's way of dealing with it and working through his issues.

People don't realize that hairdressing is a form of therapy – on both sides. Not only do clients tell us everything, we end up divulging information about ourselves to our clients. It's a two-way street when it comes to doing hair.

Rory had grown up in the desert near Palm Springs, which is about two hours outside of Los Angeles. Living near there is a lot like the television show Breaking Bad. Bikers, crystal meth, and people who love Nascar! The intense heat does something to you out there!

It was no small task that Rory was able to overcome all of his childhood bullshit, be gay and overshadowed by his mother, then come to Los Angeles to strike highlighting gold! Being able to have your own salon, with a booming, celebrity clientele was a monster accomplishment!

The Parlor was our own little slice of Hollywood heaven - we had our own valet parking and a beautiful backyard area where celebrities could hide out. To me the salon was paradise. It was on fire with serious talent and seriously famous clients and I was surrounded by talented artists, who were all successful in their own right.

I felt like the amazing talent we had at this salon, drew in the customers. It was like our beacon of light shone across Hollywood, radiating our energy and trapping the celebrities inside. It was like the stars were aligning for all of us. But like any great rock band, egos and substance take over.

You suddenly find that the high you're chasing becomes more and more unattainable. When you're living the high life and pushing the limits, the limits sometimes push back. That's what happened to Rory. Throughout all the success and traveling, making all these famous women look gorgeous for all the major movies, Rory couldn't change who he was, nor could he break the cycle with which he grew up.

Being an excessive person in Hollywood can be a dangerous thing if you lose control. We see it so often - celebrities hitting the headlines when they go off the rails. They overdose or get arrested. Well, if it's happening to the celebrities, the people we admire and want to emulate, then it's happening to everyone else as well.

No one wanted to say anything but we could all tell that Rory was using drugs more often than not. Rory was beginning to act irrational and he was having extreme highs and lows. This comes when you take drugs that make you wired. Coming down off these drugs is always really hard on your mind and your body and can make you really irritable, especially if you're already in a stressful situation like he was, trying to make these women look and feel beautiful.

Drugs have the capacity to take the nicest person and turn them into a monster. You could tell when looking at Rory in the eyes that his pupils were dilated. And not just once or twice a week. It was starting to be all the time. The demons were beginning to unfold.

The other stylists in the salon were starting to take notice while I tried to ignore it. I just didn't want to admit that the drugs were getting to him. I was in complete denial. Things were going really well for me at this salon and I didn't want anything to jeopardize that. I was starting to style celebrities myself and I had just received a write up in a major fashion magazine. I was also on a high, but it wasn't from substances. I was on a work high and I was enjoying every minute of it.

After the death of Ronnie, I had felt lost, like I was floundering with no direction. As dysfunctional as they were, Ronnie and Glenda were still a big part of my life. When it ended, it was as if I had to start all over again. Being at The Parlor was a new beginning for me. I didn't want anything to stop the momentum that was happening with my career. So, I ignored Rory's drug habit. I was like an ostrich burying my head in the sand.

Even when the front desk told me: "Brandon, I smelled a really funny smell from Rory's office after he was locked in there for about an hour. I saw smoke, but it didn't smell like regular smoke. It smelled like chemicals burning," I tried to justify Rory's actions.

I answered with: "Maybe he was just burning a candle, maybe he had gas and was trying to keep the office from smelling." I didn't know what to tell her. When she told me about the chemical smell, I immediately knew it was drugs, but I didn't want to face the harsh truth.

Still, we all carried on like no one knew anything. We all pretended everything was OK. It was like an unspoken conspiracy. When Rory started to have random outbursts of laughter for no apparent reason we all would just go along with it as if this was how he always acted.

Rory always kept a bit of distance from me. Maybe because I was straight there was this barrier between us, even though he was nothing but supportive and nice to me. He even gave me these really cool pair of leather pants that were worth at least $1,200. His legs had gotten bigger due to his weightlifting and he couldn't fit in them anymore. He just gave them to me. That's the kind of generous guy he was. So, it was hard for me to see someone lose their shit, especially when it was happening right in front of me.

It didn't help that every conversation we would have was a positive one. This helped me rationalize it all. How could Rory be that bad when he's being so cool and collected? I could tell that he was really trying to battle his demons and by no means were the other stylists and myself angels!

Randi was a colorist who was gay and was closer to Rory than I was. They would go to the clubs together and party till the morning hours pretty much every week. One day I could see that Randi seemed really troubled by something. All day he had a look of fear on his face but he wouldn't tell me what was wrong.

I noticed that the clients could even tell that something was up with him. They would ask me before they would leave: "Hey Brandon, is Randi okay? He seems really troubled today." I could see that there was a look of terror on his face. It frightened me, but it was a really busy day with lots of clients coming in and out and there wasn't a moment to stop and take a breath.

When you're neck deep in clients, especially demanding ones like we used to deal with, there was no time to be down in the dumps. Clients want you to be happy and cheerful because part of the reason they're there is to not only be made to look beautiful, but they want you to make them feel beautiful as well.

But that day Randi was silent with his clients, which was so out of character for him. It was really troubling. Randi and I had become pretty close and had developed a bond as we were sharing customers together. He was doing color and I would cut his clients hair. That's how I knew something was really wrong.

We finally were able to slow down and he had a client under the dryer so he had about 15 minutes to spare and wanted to know if he could talk to me outside. I jumped at the chance to find out what was wrong. I told him: "Of course. I'm worried about you. You've been quiet all day and I can tell that something is up." He admitted: "I know, I know. I'm really scared right now." We walked outside and he immediately began to unload on me about what was wrong. He turned to me and said: "I had sex with a guy a couple of days ago when I was out at the club. We went home together and I let him fuck me."

Randi was a bottom. A bottom is a gay guy who takes instead of gives. Guys who give it are called 'tops' and guys who take it are called 'bottoms'. Randi was a bona fide bottom, which was a dangerous thing to be. Bottoms are more susceptible to catching AIDS.

Then he told me something that completely shocked me. And, believe me, after all I'd seen in Hollywood, it took a lot to shock me. It turned out that the guy he let fuck him was positive with the HIV virus. My mouth dropped wide open. A million thoughts were flying through my mind. But I had to ask the question. I didn't want to but I knew I had to: "You used a condom right?" The silence grew and Randi's eyes began to swell up. He shook his head. *NO!* And then he began to cry.

All I could do was hug him and tell him that everything was going to be all right. I didn't know if it was but what else can you tell someone when they've just told you some potentially devastating news? Randi said that he already went to the doctor and he was waiting for the results. I could only imagine how fucking scared he was. As his friend, I had to hold back from being mad at him for letting someone have sex with him without protection.

But take this as a warning. This is what happens when you use drugs. When you're fucked up on cocaine or crystal meth, you are obviously not thinking straight. When you add those type of drugs into the mix, it makes sex so much more intense and fun because you can fuck forever and not get tired.

Unfortunately, they don't pass out condoms at the clubs. They should do that with every drink. The West Hollywood gay scene is wild and decadent, and when you induce it with drugs, people make really bad decisions. Randi certainly made a huge mistake this time – and it could've cost him his life. He got fucked up at the club, went home with this guy and got fucked all over again when he let this guy screw him all night with no protection.

I guess a few days later when Randi tried to re-connect with the guy, the guy came out and told Randi that he was positive and that he should get checked out. Un-fucking believable! I wanted to find out who this guy was and kick the shit out him. Maybe beating him up would be a bad idea, but it would've made me feel a hell of a lot better. But Randi wouldn't tell me who it was and just wanted to get his test results. Basically, he had a 50-50 chance of catching it.

While he was talking I could see his lip quivering with fear. The conversation made me feel scared as well. One wrong move like that and you're gambling with your life. He cried for a little bit, then we went back in to the salon to finish the day.

I started to feel this huge grey cloud hovering over the salon. It was like things were starting to take a turn for the worse. Between Rory taking drugs in his office and Randi nearly catching HIV from a one-night stand, I felt this weird vibe overcome the salon for the next few days as if something else was brewing. I'm not at all superstitious, but weird things definitely happen in threes. And the third thing to happen was more horrific than I could ever have imagined.

By the next week things seemed to be cooling down. Rory wasn't hiding out in his office at all. Instead he seemed a lot more clear and focused, almost like he had turned a corner. Then Randi walked into the salon with the biggest smile on his face, as he'd received the results from his HIV test - negative on all levels. What a fucking scare! I was so happy, you would have thought that I was the one that had been given the all clear! That's how close we were to each other. Like brothers. Randi was my gay brother from another mother and I truly loved him like family.

I bought him a box of condoms and handed them to him while no one was watching. He just smiled and gave me a nod like he understood what I was doing.

The salon kept gaining new celebrities from all the write-ups we had received. Offers were coming in to do prestigious magazine shoots and fashion shows. The work was getting more and more heavy and it seemed like a perfect time for Rory to start thinking about expanding. But he didn't seem to have that vision.

I honestly felt that Rory didn't see past the existing salon. He wasn't thinking five steps ahead…and how could he? He wasn't given the tools from his upbringing to be able to think on an expansion level. He was only thinking about holding on to what he had right then and there.

Even though it seemed like he was keeping the drugs to a minimum and, on the surface, things appeared to be okay, I could see the stress on his face. Rory clearly wasn't CEO material. It would have been better to hire, or bring in a CEO to take over the business decisions so that Rory could focus on what he was good at, and that was the hair. But he just wasn't ready to hand the reins over to someone else. He couldn't relinquish control – but soon something would happen that took things out of Rory's control completely.

It was a Saturday morning that I will never forget. I didn't have a client until noon, so I had the morning to go out to breakfast, have a workout and enjoy the beginning of my day.

Sabrina, our maid who did the cleaning, would come in every morning around 6am to get the salon ready for everyone. Sabrina would always be listening to music on her headphones while she cleaned, so she usually couldn't hear when people would come into the salon.

I remember walking in to the salon some mornings and she would be cleaning my station and I could stand behind her for five minutes before she would notice me. I've often wished that this particular Saturday morning she had forgotten her headphones so she could hear what was about to happen.

Sabrina lived in east Los Angeles, in an area that was predominantly Latino. LA has a lot of street gangs that sell drugs and raise hell in these parts. Sabrina's boyfriend was a gang member who hung around and sold drugs in these areas. He was part of a gang called MS13. MS13 is an extremely violent gang that is known for some incredibly brutal murders.

MS13 would constantly fight with other Mexican American gangs that far outnumbered MS13, so they tried to be more dangerous and scarier than their rivals. Sabrina had a couple kids but that didn't stop her from being affected by the gang life. In the Latino community, it's an everyday thing that they have to deal with. Often in the poorer LA communities, if you're illegal and can't get work, you get pulled into selling drugs to make a living and that's what Sabrina's boyfriend did.

It turns out that Sabrina was cheating on her boyfriend with a rival gang member. I never really found out why she was doing something as dangerous as this, but she found out exactly what the repercussions were for cheating on her man when he walked into the salon at about 7:30 am that morning and stabbed her to death in our break room.

He obviously knew that she wore headphones when she worked that early and he knew she wouldn't hear it coming. He stabbed her all over her tiny little body including her face. None of the stylists were there yet, thank God! Who knows if he would've stopped at just Sabrina if anyone else had been there? But he stabbed her over and over again until he thought she was dead. Then like a coward, he fled the scene.

A week before, we had just hired a new salon manager named Michael. He got to the salon that Saturday morning early because he was meeting our new assistant, who was going to start working that day. Both arrived and they began a walk-through of the salon. They opened the door to the break room and found Sabrina on the floor, lying in a pool of her own blood.

Miraculously, she was still breathing then. She was holding on, gasping, trying to stay alive, although sadly she died a short time later. I couldn't have imagined what was going on in Michael's and the new assistant's head after seeing this. The fear, the confusion, the hysteria that they must have both felt probably changed their lives forever.

After they called the cops, they then had to call Rory to break the horrible news to him. I don't know what Rory's state of mind was at that time, but from what I was told, when he arrived at the salon, he looked like he'd fought his way through Dante's Nine Circles of Hell and somehow survived.

Besides Sabrina being dead, the police were not helpful at all – or even remotely sympathetic. They didn't seem to give a shit about Sabrina or Rory for that matter. When someone is killed, or dies in your place, the police are not responsible for cleaning up the bloody mess for you. That's down to a third-party company who specializes in cleaning up murder scenes.

I think because of the shock that Rory was going through, he couldn't wait for this cleaning crew to come the next day. He ended up getting down on his hands and knees and cleaned it up himself. I think cleaning up

Sabrina's blood off his break room floor was Rory's breaking point. That has to fuck your head up royally.

All the appointments were obviously cancelled for that day. The completely stunned manager had to pull it together to answer the phones all day and make up some excuse as to why we were suddenly closed on a Saturday – our busiest day of the week.

We all had to make sure not to let the murder slip out as we didn't want the clients scared away. Something as awful as this could shut down a business instantly.

When they told me what happened I was in total shock! I remember pacing my apartment for hours not knowing what to do or how to handle it. I'd never known anyone who died or was murdered. Even though Sabrina and I weren't really close, I still saw her every day at work. She was part of our family and to go back to work and not see her again was incredibly strange. It was one of the most surreal things I had ever experienced.

When we finally went back to work, the mood was quite different from the week before. I could see that the spark had been taken out of all of us, especially Rory. He looked completely lost. How do you deal with someone getting murdered in your salon? How do you move on?

Michael, our new manager who had found Sabrina, quit. He left Los Angeles and moved back with his parents in San Francisco, even though he was in his 40s. To move back with your parents at that age was a sure sign that he was forever changed by this experience. The other hair stylists then started quitting one after another.

Rory was no longer available as he tried to hold on to his sanity and keep his clientele going. None of the clients knew what had happened. We'd managed to keep the murder quiet and, bizarrely, it didn't seem to make it into the papers or gossip columns. But they could tell that something strange had happened.

Within three weeks of the murder, every stylist had quit.

Even Randi quit and he and Rory were very close. I begged Randi to stay and told him that we would build it back up and that everything would be okay but he knew that Rory was done, and so was he.

It ended up just being Rory and myself for the last month we were open. I still was optimistic for our future. I felt that we would get through this and I was prepared to be there for Rory as much as possible. I figured we would get new stylists and everything would go back to normal.

Oh, how naïve I was!

Sadly, Rory couldn't even be there for himself. He was holding on by a thread and I'm sure the drug use increased to an all- time high. Rory and I ended up getting into a huge argument over something insignificant and I ended up quitting as well. I knew deep down that it was over so I packed up my gear, left the salon, and fled into the unknown.

I will always miss The Parlor. To this day, I still talk about how it was the place where I got my first magazine write-up, my first celebrity client and first murder experience. Rory closed The Parlor just one month after I left. He stayed there by himself until the very end. I wonder how sad and lonely it was for him those last weeks at the salon. None of us were the same ever again, although it affected us all in different ways.

I would run into the stylists over the years either at parties or just bump into them in and around West Hollywood. Weirdly, we would never bring up what had happened. None of us ever spoke of it again to each other.

The really sad thing in all of this - apart from Sabrina's death - is that while I still see Rory around town, these days we don't even acknowledge each other. That might seem strange, but honestly, that's how it goes in Hollywood sometimes. People who were your friends, best friends, can easily become strangers. It's sad but just a fact of life.

      * Note to self: don't let anybody get killed in your salon.

MENTORS & MEGALOMANIACS

After slaving away for four years as an assistant, I finally was given my own chair in Beverly Hills. For the next six months, I turned myself into a hair concierge, kicking around Beverly Hills and networking in clubs, restaurants, grocery stores, bank lines and fucking malls!

Then I met Jordy, a girlfriend of my pot dealer. Call it the Universe. Call it fate. Either way I was in the right place at the right time. Reality television hit the airwaves like a fucking snowstorm. Out of nowhere, soap operas were being replaced by TV shows supposedly documenting unscripted, real-life situations (which were completely produced and induced with big personalities, alcohol and high-definition cameras).

Jordy was starting a beauty agency, handling hairstylists and makeup artists for celebrity photo shoots, productions and at-home services. She had big plans for me. I was so new and really wasn't that good as a hair stylist yet, but with my sheer drive, I was game for whatever.

After three or four smaller jobs through Jordy, a TV show opportunity knocked on my door. The producers already had a successful reality cooking show and were looking to do the same, except with hair stylists in Hollywood - similar to a UK show called *The Salon*. I had the look they wanted. Jordy just about peed herself. And then she set a meeting with the producers.

So, I had given up acting to be a hair stylist and now I was meeting a producer for a TV series at Universal Studios. Life is funny. For some reason, I wasn't nervous at all, as I had been as an actor. I guess because they were looking for a character just like me. I'd always been brilliant at being myself. "When I die, I want to come back as me," I'd always said. If that's not confidence I don't know what is.

The day of the meeting finally arrived and I was ready as ever. The wardrobe was simple: jeans, snakeskin boots, leather jacket, big hair and, the icing on the cake, my vintage 1973 Motoguzzi motorcycle.

The main gate at Universal Studios was pretty well guarded and rightfully so. The lot was huge and busy as hell. There must have been 20 to 30 productions happening at the same time. Actors in costumes, assistants driving in golf carts and messengers on beach cruisers delivering mail, scripts and lunches.

I rode up to the production office and parked my bike. When I strolled through the door of their bungalow-style office, the receptionist's eyes opened wide. In my mind, I must have looked like The Fonz. Ha!

Soon I was greeted by two young television producers - Ben, the lead producer, and an English dude named Mark, his partner producer. "You are perfect!" Ben said as soon as he met me. He looked like a taller version of Ben Stiller, but really energetic. Mark had a thick English accent and was a quieter individual. He and I are still friends and, even after all this time, I still have a tough time understanding him now and then. (Sorry, Mark!)

I sat down and Ben and Mark started to give me their show pitch. Ultimately, I was down for whatever was going to make me more famous as a hair stylist. Being on television just seemed like a great fit for me. Ben's voice was so filled with excitement, as if he had just hit the jackpot.

The next step was to meet with the president of Bravo to pitch this new salon show idea and, like with all pitches, see if it had legs. Even if the network said yes and we got the show, it didn't mean that it would air. There are so many steps to getting something on television that it almost seemed impossible. Fortunately, I didn't know all of this yet. I was so gangbusters on this idea - and so was Ben - that we went in like it was going to happen and that was it.

Bravo was going through a major facelift. It was a pretty sleepy network with arts and culture shows like *Inside The Actor's Studio*, with the host James Lipton interviewing actors about the craft of acting. I'd watched this show a few times and, even though I sort of enjoyed the conversation, it was kind of a snooze fest. I could see why this Bravo network was going in a new direction and, boy, did they!

We got into the meeting and there were a few other people in the room besides Jeff Gaspin, the president. I could tell from the way he was looking at me that Jeff knew we had the goods. One thing I have always been a winner at was having the look. Not necessarily good looks, although I fancy myself as a good-looking guy, but more about having swagger and confidence. Ben had his swagger on, too. The level of excitement and flare that came out of Ben's whole being...good God! He was pitching me like I was the best hairdresser in the cosmos.

The whole room was nodding their heads up and down at each other. In one surreal moment, Ben was pitching, then my mouth opened and I was pitching too. Ben was talking and then I was talking. We were in unison back and forth like two beautiful boxers in the biggest fight of our lives! Jeff and his people were no match for us. I was throwing ideas at them like I was the one who created this pitch. Hell, it was my life so I might as well have!

I even started to step on Ben's words, which I apologized for later. It was a beautiful scene. A straight, woman-loving male hair stylist in the middle of Beverly Hills...where *Shampoo* and *The Restaurant Show* collide. Our badass hero risks it all to open a salon for the first time. The stress, the drama, the crazy hairdressers and, of course, the women!

These network executives knew from the shit coming out of my mouth that I would have the sound bites to deliver drama like their audiences had never seen. Being a hairdresser is a profession of juicy secrets and confessions. As I started telling them my stories of the gay bar and beauty school and my rock and roll celebrity friends, I saw dollar signs in their eyes and they were laughing hysterically.

Every fucking person who cares about their precious strands knows that once you find the person that can do your hair well, you will do anything not to leave them. And those network executives were no different. They totally got it.

Even in really famous salons, there are always

hacks. It's the same in every profession. Some lawyers are monster attorneys who never lose and some are just OK. You still pay the high rates when dealing with the firm, but you don't always get the best attorney unless you have a solid referral.

The execs asked me a question that I hear every day: "How can you tell if someone is going to be good?"

Here's what I told them and what I'll tell you: Judge a book by its cover. If the person looks like a mess, they will most likely make you look like a mess. The person who jumps right in and handles your hair quickly is usually the one that's good. A real pro, with real taste, knows what to do right away without overthinking it. Beware of stylists who are slow, timid and do things over and over like brushing your hair for 10 minutes while asking you a million questions about what style you want.

Ben and I wrapped up the meeting and walked out knowing that we nailed it. The network bought our pitch and I landed a major role on the show, launching me into the reality TV revolution that - little did we know - would change our culture irreversibly.

Blow Out was born. The first season was to revolve around the construction and launch of a new, upscale salon in Beverly Hills. I was really green - still only a hair stylist with my own chair for a year - so it would be nearly impossible for me to open my own salon.

Not a problem.

They created a new spin. They would find a seasoned salon owner to open the new salon. I would start as his or her protégé and eventually graduate from young, wild apprentice into a professional, more sophisticated Hollywood hair stylist. Having me as the protégé would give the viewers someone to root for and would create instant drama with conflicts and disagreements played out on camera. My imagination was going crazy with ideas to create tension and excitement: making out with girls in the salon, ruffling the feathers of the salon staff, clashing with the more refined salon owner. I was born for reality TV!

The show would help bring the salon owner to the forefront of the hair world in Hollywood. It was an easy sell, I thought.

Well, not exactly. The first established salon owner the producers found was a guy from England named Charles. Mark, one of the producers who was also from England, and I met with Charles at the Chateau Marmont. This hotel is a famous Hollywood landmark known as a home-away-from-home for actors and musicians since the Golden Age of cinema. Comedian John Belushi died of an overdose there. Greta Garbo slept there. Sting has been seen hanging out in the lobby. Films and songs have been written there. It's definitely a movie star and rock star hang out.

Charles also was a straight male hair stylist. In cool boots, new-to-market $250 True Religion jeans, a sick blazer and clean-cut hair, Charles just oozed success. I looked like a real Hollywood adolescent compared to him. I'm not saying that I looked un-cool, but he sure gave me ideas of how I could progress with my wardrobe. Perfect set up for mentor and protégé.

Charles listened to our pitch with complete concentration; he did fly from London for this meeting after all. Mark and I said that we would help him find a space in Beverly Hills since we knew the lay of the land. Charles said that it's one thing to be famous in England, but who gives a fuck about that? It's only worth being famous if you're famous in America. So, it was appealing to extend his brand to Beverly Hills.

A few days later we learned that Charles passed on the idea.

I was shocked. Charles didn't want any drama when it came to his brand. Reality TV was just getting started and it wasn't for everyone. In fact, most other hair stylists I knew didn't want to be on TV either. (They all were kicking themselves in the ass later when they saw the recognition the salon owner and I received.) Either way, it wasn't a fit for Charles. Which was just the way it was meant to be. When the Charles door closed, one opened with the perfect guy walking through it.

Benjamin Stantin.

I had interviewed with him three years back before I worked with Luis Ferreti. He seemed cool at the time. Both of us were from Los Angeles. I went to Santa Monica High School; he went to Beverly Hills High School. We were both talented, straight male hair stylists, although people would question Benjamin's sexual orientation. He probably has about ten years on me, but other than that you would think that we would get along. Well, not by a long shot!

Benjamin was a chain-smoking, tattooed, megalomaniac prone to temper tantrums, crying fits and lots of self-loathing. As soon as the cameras starting rolling, this Mommy Dearest drama queen would have the tears pouring and cell phones launching across the salon like fastballs at a Dodgers' game.

Reality television really means 'reality-based'. There is still a script and storyline, and changes can be made either by the producers or the network executives themselves after they watched the 'dailies' (rough cuts of scenes, literally shown daily). It's like acting, only you are cast as yourself. Well, a more hyped-up version of yourself. If you weren't a big personality, you pretty much got no camera time on *Blow Out*. At times, the producers even used ear buds to feed us lines to get the most drama as possible. Of course, filling us up with liquor didn't hurt either.

Benjamin would yell, scold and lecture me about pretty much everything. From the first day of shooting there was this jealousy that exploded during filming. Technically, I didn't work for him. I was hired through production before he was on board and was the only hair stylist who was outsourced. Maybe that drove him nuts. But what seemed to really sting Benjamin in the ass was that for whatever reason, I started to have more clients coming in and out of the salon than he did.

On the show, clients had to sign release forms so they could be filmed. About fifty percent of my clients were OK with it. The others were uncomfortable. I have to admit that I was so pumped up about being on TV that I didn't really care what my existing clients thought about it. I just wanted my chair to be full at all times. The more action I provided, the more camera time I would get.

To keep the action moving, the producers staged dramatic scenarios among the staff and the stylists. They didn't have to ask me twice. I took off my shirt to show off my ripped body. I washed my hair in the shampoo bowl (a huge no-no!) to cause an uproar - and ended up shooting water all over the floor. My bartender experience at one of the craziest gay bars in West Hollywood really paid off. Those antics were magnified in the confines of a salon. Benjamin knew I was going for broke to get attention and he hated me more and more because of it.

Fuck this Benjamin guy!

All he did was bitch and moan about everything. He wasn't busy at all. He only knew how to do one haircut. His whole fucking act was throwing his phone when he was upset and smoking like a chimney. Then, at the end of his little bitch fits, he would always start to cry.

I became the Omarosa of the show. She was the character you 'love to hate' on the first season of *The Apprentice*. All the other *Blow Out* 'cast' members aligned against me. I was busier and more electric than everyone else and had the best-looking clients. When my clients walked in, the camera people would immediately head down my way because they didn't want to miss one single shot of gorgeous women or one sound bite that exploded from my mouth!

I was known as the 'Salon Villain' who didn't give two shits. I knew that the audience would be rooting for me. Plus, I wasn't putting my real job in jeopardy. Benjamin wasn't my boss; I had a salon job to go back to that was getting a great deal of press on its own.

After a few months, three or four episodes were under our belts but the environment had become totally toxic for me. I felt like a whole fucking year had passed. Dealing with Benjamin and his drama was getting to me; he was anything but a mentor. At night I would have violent, thrashing dreams about him. I could see that the stress of filming, opening a salon for television, dealing with me and the rest of his staff was starting to eat away at Benjamin, too.

He played himself right into the hands of the producers. They took advantage of Benjamin's every flaw and made sure that everyone saw just what a real jackass looks like in the form of a salon owner.

Like most days on set at the salon, I was really busy actually doing hair, unlike Benjamin who routinely paced up and down the alley behind the salon smoking like he just got off a 12-hour flight from Beijing. One day, at the end of the fourth episode, Benjamin told me he needed to speak with me before I went home.

Even though we were on the outs with each other constantly, I still wasn't quite prepared for what happened. The end of the day came. I was beat and not in the mood to deal with his bullshit. He pulled me outside and gave me a talking to all right.

He fired me.

Firing me wasn't in the script.

A producer behind the camera went ape shit. It was a surprise to them as well. And, of course because no-one was aware of his plan to fire me, we had to shoot it over like it was fresh.

It was one of the few times that I didn't deliver a huge, dramatic performance. I was both in shock and relieved. As much as I loved the idea of being on TV, I was ready to get the hell out of there. It took a lot of fucking energy to be on camera, day in and day out. I see now why so many reality television stars crash and burn in real life; it takes everything out of you. You give it your all to be on television and you let everything in your real life go to shit.

That's exactly what happened to Benjamin. Once I was fired, the show became a full-on Benjamin bitch-fest. I stayed friendly with the producers after I left and continued to get the scoop. Benjamin could have been the next Vidal Sassoon, yet he couldn't hold it together. He was a nightmare for the producers. He would say no to everything, to all the ideas they threw at him.

Since my exit from the show was so dramatic, the network wanted me to be interviewed by all the big weekly magazines like STAR, US Weekly and People. I knew that my 15 little minutes of fame was about to expire so, damn straight, I was going to milk it for everything it was worth.

Now the adult thing to do would have been to take the high road on this one. I could have told the magazines that it was a great and positive experience. That Benjamin was just under a lot of pressure opening a new salon in Beverly Hills and that's why he acted the way he did. It's not like the entire world didn't see how he treated me on television.

Unfortunately for Benjamin, that's not how I played it.

STAR magazine was up first. A PR woman from Bravo would be patching me into the interview call with STAR and she'd stay on the line. She called me first to go over a few things: I couldn't say I was fired because the episode hadn't aired yet. I could dish on Benjamin Stantin and his salon. Don't forget, this is bloodthirsty

STAR magazine, so the more candid and catty the better.

The call came through for the interview - my first interview with a real magazine. The STAR Magazine editor led with the question: "How do you feel about being the Bad Boy on Bravo?"

"Bad Boy on Bravo," I thought. That has a nice ring to it. There's nothing better than being given a network television title. I was proud of myself. Then she moved on to asking about Benjamin. That was the moment. A real crossroads. Like an angel on one shoulder and devil on the other.

The Devil won.

I started with insults and didn't seem to stop until we hung up: "Benjamin isn't busy at all in the salon. He spends his days in the alley smoking." Then I added: "His voice sounds like Jeff Spicoli from *Fast Times at Ridgemont High*." The devil nudged me again: "He only knows how to do one haircut. It's called the Dumb and Dumber. By the end of your haircut, you realize that the hair stylists at Super Cuts have more intelligence and better skills." The STAR magazine editor laughed uncontrollably while the network PR woman was dead silent.

"I feel like I died and went to chump heaven," I

think the editor snorted while laughing at that one.

I was on a roll now: "Benjamin is jealous of me because I've been doing hair for barely two years compared to his fifteen. I think he dislikes me so much because he is secretly gay and really wants me. That's why he gets upset when my hot female clients arrive and flirt with me. Believe me, I worked in gay bars before I got into hair so I know a closeted gay man when I see one!"

It was like I had a disease and burying Benjamin's name was the cure. The STAR magazine editor was typing away, furiously catching every vicious nugget. Looking back, it was like I was having a cathartic, out-of-body experience, releasing all the pent-up stress from those months on set. Once that ball was rolling, I couldn't stop. Even though I was the wild child on the show, it wasn't normal for me to go off at someone like that.

The editor closed the interview: "Well, thank you so much for this candid interview, Brandon. What's next for you?"

"I am now working at a real, professional salon with real, celebrity clientele," I said. "I know that I will become more successful than Benjamin could ever dream of becoming."

The editor thanked me and we ended the call. The publicist for the network was still on the other line. There was total silence.

"Well, Brandon that was quite entertaining!" She said. "I wasn't really thinking you were going to take it that far but this is television and drama sells. If I need anything else, I will contact you. Thank you so much."

We ended the call and I walked away with a huge smile on my face. Since I was the first stylist to get fired from Benjamin's salon, I knew that the more I dished on what happened and the more elaborate I made it sound, the better it would be for me in the long run. Even though I knew Benjamin would freak out and possibly try to retaliate, ultimately there is no such thing as bad publicity. Whether he liked it or not, me giving that interview the way I did, was the best thing for both of us. Like Ronnie Capone used to say to me: "What's life without a little stress?"

My STAR magazine interview was released the next week. Benjamin flipped his lid. After he called me for the fifth or sixth time in a row, I hesitantly picked up. "Hello," I said into the phone. He let it rip: "You motherfucker. How dare you say those things about me! Who do you think you are calling me gay and all that other shit? I'm going to fucking kill you when I see you!"

"Fuck you, bitch!" I said right back to him. "You ain't gonna do fucking shit, you high hair-lined, bitch ass mother fucker! You're nothing but a chump! Come and get it! You and your shitty salon that's in between Subway and Quizno's! What the fuck are you going to do about it? Now that I'm gone, your show is gonna fucking tank!"

His head must have nearly exploded. I'm sure he was foaming at the mouth at this point. I just let him continue with the insults and eventually hung up the phone and went back to my day of cutting hair. I moved on but he kept calling over and over, maybe 20 times. After it came to a stop, I was prepared for him to show up at the salon where I worked. I knew he was all talk so I wasn't too worried about it.

I guess word got out that he threatened me and was stalking me by phone. Television networks get really nervous about situations like this. The next day, one of the producers called me to find out what had happened. I explained my side of the story and told him what I had said about Benjamin to STAR magazine. He laughed and said: "Don't worry, we'll handle this!" There was nothing they could do to me as I was already off the show. Fuck it! People love drama and the producers knew that to be true. The more drama, the more ratings.

Now the readers were definitely going to tune in after I was gone.

Unfortunately, Benjamin was too stupid to think that far ahead. Or he just really wasn't cut out for reality television.

A few days later, Benjamin was pulled into the producer's office with the network on speakerphone. They read him the riot act for calling me over and over again and threatening me. Since he was under contract, the network could be held liable for his actions. Once they pulled him into that meeting, he changed his tune really quickly. Because he reacted the way I knew he would and freaked out at me, he had to return to the show with his tail between his legs. As *Blow Out* went on, Benjamin became a bigger and bigger cry baby. The message boards and fan sites lit up with comments about all of us on the show. Some good comments. And lots of mean ones: "Brandon's hair is so big. It must be a wig." I didn't care what people said. The more they commented, the more publicity it was bringing for the show. Some people were glad that I was gone and others said that I was the best thing about the show.

Being on television catapulted me ten years ahead of the game. I was getting noticed all over town. People were stopping me on the street for my autograph and they all wanted to take pictures with me. I remembered how Ronnie would stop what he was doing to say hello to fans and answer questions. That's what I did. It was like the Universe had prepared me for my television debut by giving me a legendary rock star to model. Ronnie would've been proud.

About a month after I was off *Blow Out,* the producers came to me with an offer. They wanted to create a one-hour spin-off special about me called *Salon Diaries.* Turns out that those message boards were getting enough hits about me to spark their interest. It was all about the potential of ratings.

I about hit the floor.

They wanted to give a big fuck you to Benjamin for firing me by giving me my own special. Only this time, instead of working for some hack like Benjamin, they would have me work for two of the biggest hair stylists in the world.

The premise of the show would be that after I got fired from Benjamin's salon, I would start hustling to find hair jobs. I would do photo shoots, fashion shows, whatever came my way. Then I would find out that a big salon outfit from New York would be opening a salon in Los Angeles. I would go and work for them and be mentored by the two owners, 'Edward and Joel'.

They would take me into their salon family and teach me how to do hair in a high-end, fast-paced, midtown Manhattan salon. The cameras would follow me into the lion's den of New York, running from one fashion show to another as our filming would coincide with Fashion Week.

The producers had already negotiated how the show would go down with the real salon outfit that would be called 'Warren Tricomi' on the show. Edward Tricomi and Joel Warren, the two owners of Warren | Tricomi salons, would be cast as themselves and were coming to Los Angeles to oversee the construction of their new salon. This would be the perfect time to have our initial meeting to make sure everyone was on board.

The producers set up the first meeting at the historic Roosevelt Hotel in Hollywood, where Edward and Joel would be staying. They are both straight-male hair stylists. Edward, the hair cutter. Joel, the colorist. Turns out that Glenda, Ronnie's wife, had worked for Edward back in New York.

I entered the Roosevelt and walked out to the hotel's pool area to meet Edward and Joel. I was alone on this meeting as the producers were going to sit this one out. In between Edward and Joel sat a pretty, blonde woman. At first I thought that she was one of their wives. Her name was Roxanna and she was there for one reason: to talk business. Roxanna was their business partner. Starting out as a nail technician, she was now running their Warren | Tricomi salons. Talk about sheer drive.

Edward and Joel were the real deal. Edward looked like a rock star with long hair and immaculate clothes. He resembled Mick Jagger or Iggy Pop, with a thick, Brooklyn accent and a very confident, yet peaceful look to him. I immediately felt like everything was going to be all right when I met him. Like this guy knew what he was doing and there wasn't anything he hadn't seen. His energy was unlike anyone I had ever met before. Joel also exuded confidence in a way like nothing bothered him. Like there wasn't anything he couldn't handle. His laugh was infectious.

Even though they were the power trio of one of the most successful salons in the world, with locations in New York, Los Angeles, Tokyo and India, they knew how to behave like civilized and respectful human beings. I'm used to other hair stylists, AKA Benjamin Stantin, talking at me. These three looked me in the eye and made me feel so comfortable, probably because they were so comfortable with themselves.

Regardless of how the TV show turned out, I

knew that working with them was going to be a great move for me personally and for my career. Getting fired from Benjamin's show started to seem like the best thing that ever happened to me.

Edward, Joel and Roxanna were new to reality television and genuinely curious. They had done a lot of on-camera makeovers for shows like *The Today Show* and *Access Hollywood,* but not a reality-type television show. I don't think they quite knew what they were in for!

Edward asked me about my experience on the show. This wasn't a STAR magazine interview. I didn't want to just blurt out any stupid comment or a stream of insults. "It was interesting," I answered in a confident tone. "I learned a lot about what to do and what not to do! I'm not going to lie, I hammed it up for cameras but that's what was expected from production."

They all smiled as if I wasn't telling them something they didn't already know, vibing on my LA vibe. Besides the one-hour special, they really were opening a salon in Los Angeles, and were looking for strong, male hairstylists to carry the Warren | Tricomi method in LA.

Then we came around to talking about New York, about me learning a level of hairstyling to which I hadn't been exposed. We would film in LA for half of the show and New York for the other half. My heart started racing. It seems like I was being pulled to New York again, as if there were something - or someone - waiting for me. I had always heard about hair stylists being bi-coastal, traveling from LA to New York and vice versa just to do hair. I wanted *THAT*.

We wrapped up the meeting and they offered to pay for lunch. I let them. This time, going into the show, I had come with my own swagger. Having just been fired from the first 'hair reality television show' gave me some serious street credit, since the viewers were pulling for me instead of Benjamin, the so-called star of the show.

Not to be cocky, but as lucky as I was to meet Edward, Joel and Roxanna, they were equally as lucky to meet me. My stock was up and they were snagging me to be the face of the Warren | Tricomi LA salon. We were coming together to create more success for all of us.

"Come work with us now in the LA salon," Edward said as we were leaving. "Bring your clients there, so we can get a sense of how you work." They had taken over an existing salon, so I'd be able to start right away. Since the murder of our cleaning woman at the salon on Third Street (where I worked before and after *Blow Out*), business was slipping anyway. This was my opportunity to make a move.

A few days later, I heard from production that our one hour-special was approved by the network and we would start filming in about two weeks. I took all my gear to the new Warren | Tricomi Salon in West Hollywood. When I walked in, Edward introduced me to the other stylists and immediately gave me the station in the front of the salon. Prime real estate. Since I was going to be getting filmed a lot, it made sense to show off the salon's number one stylist.

Edward and I talked while I moved into my station. About Glenda. About Ronnie. About Ronnie's passing and my falling out with Glenda. I held back on telling him about the molestation. Even though Glenda wasn't in my life anymore, I still thought of her and Ronnie as family.

Edward was a fucking hair encyclopedia and really into sharing ideas to further the craft of hairstyling. He talked a lot about fashion magazines, which ones I should be reading. He talked about music and art, and watching vintage films for inspiration.

"I'm already successful," Edward said to me. "Now I want you to be successful. Not only will it feed you, it will feed the salon and me." I loved this way of thinking. Help the people around you, and you too will prosper!

Finally, I had found a fucking mentor.

The next day, the producers told me they wanted to shoot some B-roll with me doing hair in the new salon with Edward and Joel. (B-roll is extra footage usually without dialogue.)

On that day, we were to get B-roll of me pulling up on the motorcycle, walking into the salon and making the introduction between me and my new salon owners. Even though this was a reality show, it still was shot like a real television show or a movie. Pulling up on the motorcycle and walking into the salon could take about two hours, just to get those shots right. We might have to do two or three takes depending on the skill of the camera crew.

I looked like a huge star since the shots were really focused on me. The front desk girls lit up when I walked into the salon that day. Having your own camera crew is like having your own Ferrari. All the girls want a piece of you.

As I was pulling up on my motorcycle outside, a celebrity tour van drove by. The driver slowed down to see what we were filming and who the guy was on the motorcycle. "Hey, that's the guy from that hair show!" A tourist on the van yelled out. That recognition was definitely amazing for my ego - and it confirmed to Joel and Edward that their new hairstylist was bringing the goods.

As we broke for lunch, I wanted to better acquaint myself with the hot front desk girls, Lisa and Casey. They started asking me about the show and how I was chosen to be the guy for the series. I turned the Brandon charm up to level 10 as these girls, who happen to be roommates, seemed like they were into having fun.

Edward and Joel were walking around the salon, making sure everyone had what they needed. They came over to me and could see that I was doing just fine! Being surrounded by women wasn't new to me - or them.

Lisa invited me to join her and Casey for a dinner at Beso, which, at the time, was the new business venture of the actress Eva Longoria. I thought it would be a group of people but it actually ended up just being us three. Right away, Lisa and I started flirting in a big way. The attraction was chemical, very similar to the relationship with Dallas in beauty school. Lisa was Mexican-American. Really beautiful with an edge. She looked like an Aztec princess. A wild creature with a powerful sexuality.

Casey was beautiful in an innocent way. She had gorgeous long, black hair and really cute freckles that would light up her face with a playful vibe. Casey was in her early 20s, whereas Lisa and I were already 30-something. Casey had just finished college at San Diego State and moved back home to LA.

Lisa and Casey had only been roommates for a short time. The two of them together were a really hot combination: sexy, mixed with sweet and innocent.

We didn't have a reservation but the hostess recognized me from TV, and gave us a corner table that was tucked away. Definitely one of the best tables in the house. I sat in the middle and we ordered drinks. The laughs quickly followed. I had them nearly peeing themselves with my stories. They both had watched *Blow Out*, so they were hammering me with questions. As I was holding court and giving them the behind the scenes on what went down with Benjamin, Lisa and Casey were moving in closer to me.

Lisa was in a short, flowing dress that showed the silhouette of her body. She touched my hand when she talked to me as if I needed any help paying attention to her. Then her hands moved to my lower back. Our eyes met a few times and locked. The heat was rising.

Casey was laughing and really enjoying herself.

She also was very handsy. Hell, we all were. Knees rubbing knees, hands suddenly moving in all different directions like we were all part of a human octopus. As I stroked the soft skin of their bare backs, chills ran down my spine.

Is this really happening? I asked myself. I won't be able to choose. I want both of them. What's going to happen if one wants me to come back to their place, since the other lives there as well? All this is running through my mind as things were becoming quite interesting there at Beso (which means 'kiss' in Spanish).

Maybe this isn't the first time Lisa and Casey have done this. Now is not the time to be judgmental!

Before they finished their first drinks, I was ordering the second round. I'd never had a threesome before and wasn't really sure that it was going to happen that night. But it would be pretty fucking amazing if it did!

Sitting there, flanked by those young beauties, I was fully conscious of how fleeting fame could be, and that I should enjoy the hell out of this crazy, hair adventure. I thought to myself: "Man, all those young guys trying to be actors, auditioning and waiting tables and bartending to survive. All I had to do was go to beauty school and voila! I'm on TV."

We slammed round two down our throats. As we laughed about salon nonsense and the joys of shooting a reality show inside a salon, Casey abruptly blurted out: "I want to have a threesome!" She'd read my mind. The table went silent as we gazed at each other like all our birthdays were happening on the same day -TO-fucking-DAY - and we were all going to exchange the best gifts to each other.

"Check!" I screamed out, before the waiter could even ask if we'd like to order appetizers.

We were really buzzed and got ourselves to their apartment, probably by cab, although I cannot be totally sure. Suddenly I wasn't with Lisa and Casey from the salon anymore. It was like their faces had taken on a whole different look. This, I remember specifically. I was turned on, but there definitely was a change in both of these mysterious creatures. It was like split personality.

By no means was I in the driver's seat. Lisa was in charge and directed all three of us in the best game of Twister. "Don't do anything stupid to mess this up, Brandon," I thought to myself. God forbid, I made the wrong move or moaned in the wrong way. I did not want to give anyone a reason to opt out.

After a short while, they had me naked and were having their way with my battle snake. My hands were all over both of them. We did this for a while. I stared at their eyes to try to figure out what they were thinking. They exchanged looks with each other and then gazed back over to make sure I was watching them. They remained on their hands and knees making out with each other and at the same time swallowing my cock. The two of them snapped me out of any buzz that lingered.

How glorious was that night, you ask? Right up there with going to The Rock and Roll Hall of Fame, but better!

Casey laid on her back and opened her legs for Lisa. Then Lisa spun around so I was behind her. She grabbed me from between her legs and slid me inside her without warning. To my surprise, Lisa stopped, got up and grabbed a box of condoms from one of the kitchen drawers. Who keeps condoms in the kitchen drawer? If that kitchen could talk, right? I mean, holy shit, these girls seemed like professionals.

Next thing I knew Lisa was going down on Casey as if she was showing me how it gets done. Everybody was having an equal amount of pure fun, because that's what it comes down to. It was a much different scenario to be with two girls who you don't have deep feelings for, but you are all friends now and have this deeply intimate relationship going on.

Transition number three. Lisa sat on Casey's face while I was sliding in and out of Casey. Like a perfect triangle, Lisa and I leaned in towards each other to kiss with incredible sensuality.

After an hour or so of various positions and experimentations, Casey - the most buzzed of us three - started to fade from the madness. Her sleepy clock was ticking. I, on the other hand, was running on adrenaline and definitely didn't want to stop. We all stopped to catch our breath. They both smoked. Lisa lit up a joint and passed it to me for a hit.

Casey headed to her bedroom without a sound and Lisa and I started up again. Since we had both just come out of this intense session, all inhibitions were completely shattered. We put out the joint and she lay back down on the soaked bed. I moved down to begin her salad tossing and what did I see? A fucking tattoo on her situation! I couldn't believe it.

I obviously didn't catch that when we were having the threesome. This tattoo was considerably larger than Anaheim's tattoo that revealed itself to me underneath Koontz Hardware store. It said a lot to me about Lisa. Or maybe it made me assume a lot about Lisa. Maybe it was about sexual addiction. Maybe I had a slight sexual addiction. Or maybe I was just doing what heterosexual, sexually liberated males would do in this situation. Or maybe saying yes was - and is - just a part of my way of life and dealing with females.

We both couldn't stop having sex with each other and we both weren't on anything except alcohol and a little pot. Chemistry, adrenaline or whatever...we were high on each other and we didn't stop until we saw the almighty sun crack through the window shades.

Stopping seemed insane. She could have kept on going but I eventually gave out. "You win," I whispered in her ear as I pulled the covers over us. She lit up the same joint we were smoking earlier. The room had a thick, heavy smell of sex and green bud.

Lisa was like girls I knew in high school. Her parents were both Mexican, so she spoke fluent Spanish. But she didn't look Mexican at all. You could tell that she grew up in LA like I did. Maybe she hung with gang members when she was young. That could explain the tattoo on her Yoo Hoo, as if it's a sign of toughness. She was beautiful, but she was jaded like I was.

The beauty business is a safe harbor for troubled, damaged individuals - artists like myself who have dodgy backgrounds. That makes us wild. What had just happened between Lisa, Casey and me was wild at the highest level.

"Brandon, can I ask you something? Something important?" Lisa said as we were lying in bed, eyes practically closed from the fatigue.

I thought: "Girl, after the gift you and your roommate just gave me, you can have anything that you want."

"Of course," I said. "But I don't think I can have sex for at least a couple hours."

She laughed out loud like the reality of what we had done for the last few hours just caught up with her. "Don't worry about that. As it is, I think I'll need a wheelchair to get to work tomorrow," she said. "No, I really need to know...will you do my hair? I'm really picky about who does my hair, but I want you to do it."

"You better not fuck it up, Brandon," I thought. "Bad hair will kill any relationship!"

A couple weeks went by and I was settling into my new salon position of TV, rock star, hair stylist. The shooting in LA was going really well. As we got closer to the New York shoot dates, a certain anxiety started to arise.

In itself, the New York hair market was a whole different scene that came with a different level of expectation. Now take the intensity up 10,000 notches and you have New York Fashion Week. I was willingly being catapulted into the fray, with only two years of hairstyling holding me together. I wasn't that great at up-dos or any type of styling. To be honest, I wasn't that good at doing hair period. I didn't know my way around Manhattan, having been shuttled around with Ronnie and Glenda in a limo during my whole trip. It would be freezing and snowing in New York while we were there, and I get cold when it dips down to 60 degrees in LA!

All this added up to great reality television. It would be sink or swim for hot shot Brandon and the cameras would be following me every step of the way. There was no way out of it. I had to be good. Actually, I had to be great. There was no way of faking it. I prepared myself like I was going into battle. I knew that all my cylinders would need to be firing to watch, learn and perform like my life depended on it. I wasn't a quitter and I wasn't a loser. So, the only option was to be a rock star.

But I wasn't alone. I had Edward. With 30 years of experience, he was my Yoda. The opportunity to learn from him would be tremendous. He approached hairstyling like a surgeon.

After all, I once saw him use scotch tape and an overhead dryer to achieve a certain look on a model.

FASHION WEEK

I was heading to New York. The Big Apple. The city that never sleeps. Everything in New York moves about five steps ahead of the laid back, sunny Los Angeles pace.

Los Angeles is fast paced, but you can still wear flip flops while conducting business. Wearing flip flops in New York is like wearing shorts to a wedding. A big no-no! The busy New York streets would eat up those flip flops like a cop at a Dunkin Donuts!

Having been to New York so many times since, I can see now how different New York is from LA. LA is the laid back younger brother to NY's uptight, neurotic older sibling. NY is a sea of lights, buildings, jackhammers, people having arguments in the street, strange smells in the subway stations and hair flying everywhere!

And Manhattan is the crème de la crème for runway hair in the US, so I knew this week was going to be intense – especially with my big personality. This fancy NY salon with its conservative staff and clientele was in for a shock.

The running around I would do between the salon and the shows, while having a reality show camera crew following me around, already had me in dire need of alcoholic beverages! One thing New Yorkers can do extremely well, at least my friends in New York is, drink…a lot!

I had quickly made friends with the stylists that worked at Edward and Joel's 57th Street salon. The hair stylists in New York have a completely different attitude and temperament. New Yorkers tell it as it is. They can be brutal, but they are also some of the friendliest people in the business. Looking back, I'm so grateful that these New York hair stylists took me in, or I wouldn't have made it. They accepted the reality television 'bullshit' and baggage I brought with me and rolled with it because they liked me.

And I made sure that I wasn't going to be a party pooper while being in the city. Regardless of the work, I was determined to see the wilder things that New York had to offer and the stylists at Edward and Joel's salon did not disappoint!

Once I arrived, I had plans for every night of the week. Right off the bat I was in alignment with the city. I was able to meet so many people, in such a small amount of time, exchanging numbers, telling them about the salon and the shows we had lined up.

It was constant! I could see how New Yorkers get burnt out unless they have the ability to ground themselves deep, or just become really fucking rich!

And I had made sure I had a partner in crime with me for the ride. I didn't want to be in the city alone – although once I'd actually arrived in NY I'd realized being alone was impossible - so I'd brought one of the stylists from the LA salon with me. Ramses.

Yes, his name is Ramses. Ramses Martinez, a half-Mexican, just like me. He had been working in the salon and the producers liked his look, so they gave him a minor role, if you can even call it that. We basically got to be on television for just being ourselves!

Ramses was also a straight-male hair stylist and was someone that looked like he hung out with Glenda and Ronnie. You would describe Ramses' look as Heroin Chic. He was an even scrawnier version of Steve Perry from Journey, looking like he weighed in at just 110 pounds while sopping wet. He was a sight to see with his stringy, long, brown hair that had an early Rod Stewart thing happening, like when he was the lead singer of The Faces.

But he was cool and fun to hang with! I was letting him stay in the apartment with me in Chelsea. Since I had a big enough space, it made sense for him to stay with me. We both figured, fuck it, we probably won't be coming back to the apartment much. And we both agreed to the 'guys going out code,' which is as follows:

1. If we both go to a club, and one of you doesn't get it, you're on your own.

2. If one of us gets drugs, we have to share with the other depending on the drug!

3. If you bring a girl home, the other guy has to sleep in the tub. 'Deal? Deal!'

I definitely wanted to sleep with the girls that worked at Edward and Joel's salon. It was so refreshing to walk in every day to their salons and see hot, female hair stylists in every corner! I was like a kid in a candy store. And the cherry on top was there was another salon in Connecticut, with another slew of East Coast hotties! I had died at Benjamin's shit show, only to be reborn in hair heaven on the other side of the country.

But right now my main focus had to be on Fashion Week. Things move fast in NY – and the fashion shows are no different. Your adrenaline gets kicked into overdrive as you get caught up in the whirlwind of shows and catwalks.

Ramses and I were on our way to Bryant Park for the first of four fashion shows that were on Edward's list for that day. Of course, it was cold as shit in Manhattan and Ramses and I were not quite prepared for the brisk weather, being used to the constant LA sunshine!

We hit the first show, full of excitement and enthusiasm as we unloaded our hair bags in a slot designated for two working stylists. A long mirror ran parallel along the tables where we were going to work. Make-up had their own section that was filled with busy little make-up bees, running around like little bursting volcanoes of make-up pleasure!

The elite of make-up artists that saturate New York during this time is astonishing. To see a 6ft tall Swedish model transformed into a Japanese Geisha Girl in a matter of ten minutes is a sight to see! Think of the Indy 500. Instead of a pit crew consisting of highly trained mechanics that work at the speed of light, it's blow dryers, curling irons and make-up brushes being wielded by a team of highly trained beauty magicians.

Hair and make-up is an art. We are artists who create art. And like all art, when you put it down, it's there forever, for all to see. That's what it was like for each show at Fashion Week. I would be helping to create something stunning, something beautiful, something that would set the trends for the rest of the world.

Each show would have a key hair stylist and a key make-up artist. These two would have the highly intense and thankless task of making sure everyone underneath them kept to the look that had been rehearsed prior to the actual show. The key hair and make-up person would answer to the designer, or the designer's second hand, if they had one. And like all empires, the King is the boss and at Fashion Week, the designer is the King!

Hair and make-up are only two little pieces of what goes on at these shows and we have to work in unison with everyone in a calm, yet expedited fashion to create the bigger picture, to make sure our piece of the puzzle fits in perfectly with the designer's vision.

But at the same time, it was like being at the zoo!

Everything was over the top! Edward was already playing with a model's hair when we arrived at our tent. I loved watching Edward do hair. He is like a fucking Jedi Knight when it comes to transforming hair. I would watch him create hairstyles that seemed completely intricate and confusing, but he had a way of touching hair like he was Keanu Reeves from *The Matrix*.

Like Neo, he would anticipate his next move when he would do hair. He would be thinking a step ahead, flowing through the hair like dodging bullets in slow motion. It was as if he could suspend the hair and complete it in the blink of an eye. After all, for thirty some years, Edward has been right smack dab in the middle of all the changing styles, trends and clothes. He started as an apprentice, then moved up to one of the most successful hair stylists in the world with multiple salons pumping out clients like Apple pumps out iPhones!

The look we were doing for this show was really intricate, or at least it looked like it. My palms always get sweaty when I get nervous and it seemed like I just spilled personal lubricant all over my hands. I have to admit that my couture, hair designing skills weren't quite up to par at this point yet. Edward could totally tell that I was nervous and as I glanced at one of the mirrors, I could see that I had that 'deer caught in headlights' look all over my face.

I was so nervous, that I didn't even notice the models until I started working on one. They were already walking around naked by this point. I always compare models to tall, graceful giraffes. I stand at a very average

5ft 9in for a guy. These towering infernos of international beauty were averaging on a low end at 6ft tall. Some looked like they could even have been 6ft 5in! When they sat in the chairs, I still felt short!

I wish that young girls in America could all witness what real runway models look like behind the scenes, because it would open their eyes about what models really look like. It seems like every young girl in America who is remotely pretty, wants to be a model, or thinks that she should at some point in her youth. But if you're not at least 5ft 11inches, then don't even bother. Also, models don't have boobs, so if you are well endowed in the chest area, it will most likely work against you. Models are usually completely flat chested freaks of nature that could probably slam dunk like a college basketball superstar.

If you have boobs and are pretty, you'd be better off at acting. It seems like only in New York are there super tall woman - and men for that matter. But it seems like everyone in Los Angeles is short! I've never met a really tall, female movie star. They're all pretty short for the most part.

Fashion Week is like being in the jungle and the models, like giraffes, are the most visible animal. Another observation was that not all of the models were that beautiful in person. Don't get me wrong; more than half of them were jaw-dropping gorgeous. However, a fair amount of them were not that pretty in person. A decent amount of them had something very interesting about them that when in front of a camera, with the right lighting, wardrobe and make-up, they would transform into something else, like it was a magic trick! Even the models that were obviously more beautiful still had an interesting and different beauty about them. You would see a 6ft 2in Brazilian girl who had skin like a black girl, but would have piercing green eyes like a white Swedish girl.

And the fashion shows had the most beautiful red-headed girls I had ever seen in my life. Usually when you see red-headed people, they're not that cute but, when you're at the top of the ladder as a red-headed person it's a whole other story. These red-headed models I saw at Fashion Week were the obvious reason why God created freckles! Perfectly placed freckles over perfect pale skin! And usually all over the body, which actually enhanced their model hotness!

Regardless of how hot these girls were, there is absolutely no time for idle chit chat, or to exchange contacts. All of that is done later on at the parties, if you're lucky enough to get invited. The shows are all about fast and efficient work! It's controlled behind the scenes.

Before I could even blink, I had finished one girl's hair. And Edward was almost pleased with my work! He only had to fidget with a couple strands to fine tune the look. I wasn't looking for acknowledgement on my work at this moment. I was just happy to keep my mouth shut and learn whatever I could. The one thing that was different about Edward, was that even when he corrected you or your work, he never did it in a condescending way. His approach was much more educational and interactive. He would turn whatever was wrong into a lesson.

He loved to teach what he knew and this was so valuable to me! He had me come over to watch the model he was doing and he showed me how he was taking the hair to get it to what that look required. You would think they would design road maps for some of these hairstyles! The way that Edward demonstrated this particular look helped to make more sense of what I was going to do for the next one.

As I continued to move through the constant assembly line of the hottest girls in the world, my hairstyles were getting better and better. Even the models were complimenting me for taking Edward's suggestions and putting them to work.

Ramses on the other hand was struggling terribly. To his credit, he had no idea what he was in for. I had some inclination as to what I would be walking into as I'd done my homework on Edward and Joel, so I knew just what to expect from taking the time to gather that background information.

The great thing was that Edward spotted how green Ramses was and basically made him an assistant without any lectures or short-fused attitudes. Ramses was absorbed into the show without any bad feelings or stress. This attitude that Edward worked and lived by was something that I wanted to attain. Coming from a train of train-wrecked hair stylists - apart from Luis Ferretti - it was so inspiring to see someone like Edward be so cool and humble in his position..

Since I started to do hair, every step of the way had its level of stress and excitement. Finally, I could at least be relaxed in who I was personally. Edward didn't care so much about my personal life. He cared more about my work and what I wanted to become as far as a hair stylist.

Being under the microscope of a reality television crew really meant nothing to him because he figured he already had the goods before I showed up with them in tow. He cared more about me as an individual, especially after the television show.

Let's face it, reality television is quick. It's powerful, but it's quick and Edward was going to make sure that there weren't any train wrecks on our show. It wasn't in him to be crazy and I respected that tremendously!

As we narrowed the number of models left to finish, Edward was going over every girl. Fine tuning each piece that he saw out of place. When it gets close to the start of the show, the designers' heads are usually about to explode in these last moments, as they are incredibly stressed and the shows are all usually running behind schedule. Let's face it, the whole fucking world is watching!

The only time the models really wear clothes during the shows is when they're on the runway. When they circle back around behind the stage, the clothes are stripped away in seconds by the designers' assistants, who are handling the wardrobe changes. It's like being in a pack of naked, confused flamingos flopping their arms and legs around getting out of one outfit and getting into another. They go through the models' outfit changes before show time, but that requires the models to think. In a time-crunch, that all goes to hell!

The wardrobe people are screaming out the models' names to get in the next look. The models are stripping off the current outfit and trying to get into the next. It sounds like the fucking Nasdaq stock exchange! The hair and make-up people are in the middle of all of this since the wardrobe changes aren't really respectful of the hair and make-up that's been done, so the hair stylists are buzzing around in all of this madness.

And in the middle of all this chaos is Edward, and he's as cool as a cucumber! He could stand back and look at all of it from another angle. The angle of experience! Like Yoda, my mentor of mentors, become he would.

Being able to rally people's brains together to work on a project of this magnitude was no small task, yet Edward seemed to do it so simply and effortlessly. Especially since we had three more shows to do for that day.

The madness lasted for just 15 minutes and then it was all over. Just like that my first fashion show in New York was over faster than a New York minute. The models were already changed back into their clothes and heading off to do more shows as we were too. The smell of hairspray and airbrushed make-up filled the room and all that was left were forgotten bobby pins scattered on the styling tables.

We packed up and headed outside the tent into the park. It was time for lunch, so I grabbed a burger and joined Edward and Ramses. It had warmed up a bit and we sat outside and all took a breath from what had just happened. Edward started to talk about the craft of doing hair. He said in his very thick NY accent: "Treat the hair like it's art."

I loved the way Edward would explain things when it came to hair. He knew how to explain things in very simple terms. He knew how to compare things in a practical, yet educated way. Of course, his extremely thick, New York accent would hit you like bag of Brooklyn bricks! You could tell that he came from humble beginnings as every New Yorker whose accent is that thick usually does. But being the rock star, badass that Edward was, he could get away with anything!

To me, one of the coolest things about my business is that you can make a shit load of money and still remain the individual you always were. You are encouraged to look like an individual, act as one and create individuality for others. You're given the green light to get tattooed, have wild hair, dress extremely cool and it's to be expected!

There's this huge contrast between you and your clients when you do high end hair. When you're charging over $200 for haircuts, the clientele tend to be rich, conservative, and most likely un-cool. They come to you so they can be cool, so they can show off and tell their friends that they go to Edward and Joel on 57th St.

Doing hair is like selling drugs, not everyone has the best shit! A crack dealer on the corner in Brooklyn is not going to have the same A-grade coke as a dealer on Park Avenue. It's just a fact. Hairdressing is the same. A stylist working at Fantastic Sams is not going to give you the same quality cut for $30 as someone like Edward - charging $400 - will.

When you work at a place like Edward and Joel's, the money is insane because the clientele have insane amounts of money. Billionaires need haircuts too and they definitely are not going to Fantastic Sams, unless they're Warren Buffett – and he's a rarity! The billionaires I know want someone like me to cut their hair – and they expect the best. That's the benefit to being a straight, male hair stylist. You attract every type of client that exists. Your appeal reaches every type of person, especially if you're good looking, too.

When it comes to the hair business, everyday political correctness is non-existent. Most of the time, in busier, hotter salons, the staff are always aesthetically more pleasing than in a normal establishment. People don't just want to be beautiful, they want to be surrounded by beauty as well.

And I was in the mecca of the beauty business at Fashion Week. All forms of beauty, intersecting for one week of ridiculous excess and indulgence. The most beautiful women wearing the most expensive clothes, being styled by the most expensive hairdressers and make-up artists in the world. Believe me, I was thanking my lucky fucking stars!

Due to my nervousness and anxiety for the first show, I had forgotten that one of the shows was going to be an all bikini line, being modeled by mostly Brazilian girls! It was just my luck that our second show just so happened to be the bikini line! We walked into the tent where the show was going to be held and I thought I'd walked into heaven!

There they were - real life Brazilian models and I mean all the famous ones! You know, the girls that you dream of when you see certain lingerie ads where the girls are so beautiful, they're wearing wings! I did everything I could so that my jaw wouldn't hang open! It was unreal! Not one of them was shorter than 6ft tall. Brazilian girls seemed a lot more relaxed being naked and because they were wearing bikinis, there wasn't much for them to change in to. It was like I was on another planet being next to these Brazilian beauties, seeing their perfect caramel skin with green eyes and perfect asses like you've never seen before.

These were the kind of girls that I can only imagine must make men completely fucking crazy! The kind of girls that could hand pick anyone they wanted. The kind of girls that marry rock stars and professional athletes.

Amongst all the perfection that surrounded us it was time to get to work! We were again swept into the tornado of the next show that was now under a time clock. I'm so glad I got to gawk for the first five minutes when we walked in. One thing about Brazilian girls, they have a shit-load of hair! They definitely kept us busy! Remember, we still had a camera crew following us around and we're working on the hottest women in the world for everyone to see. Every model was flawless from head to toe. They're picked specifically for their beach bodies, so out of all the models that do Fashion Week, these are the girls that are not only super beautiful, their bodies are dangerously perfect.

There is such a thing as an out of shape model, or as we like to call it in my business, *'SKINNY FAT BODIES'*. During Fashion Week you would see these models. They were no doubt beautiful, but their bodies were a bit lazy and not as tight as they could be. Due to the fact that their faces are really beautiful and they would be 6ft plus, they could get away with it.

But this bikini show didn't have one single Skinny Fat Body. These models were all the Perfect 10. The look that we were doing was a softer, more simple, wavy look and our hair team was whipping through one beautiful Brazilian after another. While I started to style my third or fourth girl, a model named Alexandra began to ask me why the camera crew was there.

"It's a reality show I'm doing for the Bravo network about me, the hairstylist coming to work for Edward and Joel's salon. Do you know Edward?" As I pointed to Edward, Alexandra's eyes lit up. She told me: "Yes I've been out with them at clubs, their salon is the best in the city. I go there myself. You must be really good then." She then winked at me. At me! I smiled back at her and said: "God, I hope so! I'm really worried about looking like an ass in front of Edward and his stylists. This is only my second fashion show, ever!" She gives me an obvious 'once over' from head to toe and then says: "I'm sure you'll do just fine!"

By now my mind is in overdrive! I'm questioning everything that's happening, everything that I'm thinking! Is it me, or am I really getting action from one of these super hot Brazilian girls? It was an obvious flirt and I definitely fancy myself as a good-looking guy, but I have to admit, when I walked into this Brazilian bikini fashion show and got one look at these girls, my ego was reduced to a pre-pubescent 11-year-old Brandon!

Alexandra was by the far the hottest girl that I had ever exchanged words with let alone flirted with. I already knew this week was going to be a special week as far as experiences go, but this was something else! After all, it was only 2pm right then in Manhattan - people don't even start going out at night here until at least 11pm - and here I am, flirting with a supermodel in the middle of the afternoon!

Alexandra and I exchanged a few more flirty looks until we were both swallowed by the business of the fashion show. These girls do about four rounds of catwalk, so basically they're changing four times during the show. Once the catwalk begins, that's when all hell breaks loose! The designer's assistants go ape shit, making sure the right girls get into the right outfit, or in this case, wearable dental floss! These $1,000 bikinis were so small I couldn't tell the difference between them and an eye patch!

The girls are literally surrounded by hair and make-up people in between each change like an Indy pit crew. Outfit switches, hair and make-up are touched up and off they go again down the catwalk in front of the who's who of fashion and pop culture.

Famous people are all over the place. You would see rappers next to socialites, athletes next to actors. I loved being able to see them really up close and personal. You really get to see what famous people look like in person, which more than half of the time, it's a different story in person than it is on the screen or on television. Most of the shows we did, famous people would come back stage and say: "Hi," to the designers.

Of course, the celebrities only want to meet the designers. The hair and make-up people are invisible backstage. And even if any A-list star had approached me, I wouldn't have been able to shake hands - my hands and fingers were all shiny and sticky from the hairspray and other various hair products that I'd been using on the models.

And if my hands were covered in product, you can only imagine what the models were going through –

they weren't able to wash their hair in between any shows. They have to run from show to show pulling bobby pins out of their hair en route before sitting down and having more and more product slapped on them to pull off each different look. Their hair gets really trashed during Fashion Week as it's blown, teased, sprayed, pulled and twisted for more than a week with no stopping! Due to the constant time crunches in between shows, the stylists do whatever we can to get the hair to look the way it should for the look that's set. If we have to slam 100 bobby pins into the hair to get it right, the models have to suck it up and deal with it.

At the end of Fashion Week, I actually saw models breaking down and cry because of all the hair and make-up they had to endure for that period of time. They really are treated like pieces of meat. The models are told what to wear, how to look, what to eat. Pretty much like beautiful cattle! As the show winds down and the designer steps out on the catwalk to take a bow, the models come back in and prepare to leave the show.

As the bikini show came to a close, Alexandra came up to me to say goodbye. "Maybe I'll see you out this week?" She asked me. I could feel my eyes popping out of my head. "Control yourself, Brandon," I said to myself in my head. I wasn't feeling calm inside, but I managed to get out: "Yes I hope so! I'm supposed to go to some club tonight called The Box." Her eyes lit up as she sneaked a slightly dirty look: "Oh, The Box isn't really a nightclub, it's so much more than that!"

The way she said it was as if she saw something there that she had never seen before. The fact that she had this thick, Brazilian accent made it all the more intense. She could've honestly told me anything and I would have melted in her hands. She grabbed my phone and put her number in my contacts. She looked at me and asked: "You remember what my name is?" I quickly responded with: "Alexandra, of course I remember. I doubt anyone forgets your name." She then gives me a wink before taking off to her next show. I took a deep breath and started packing up my gear. Two shows down, two more to go!

One of the field producers for our show was a really sweet blonde who was giving me the eye and I could tell that she saw the exchange I had with the Brazilian. It's true what they say – you wait ages for a bus, then two (or more!) come along at once! When it's dry it's dry, but it finally looked like I was entering the wet season!

The field producer's name was Mindy. Mindy had a tomboy attitude about her but that was no surprise as she was surrounded by men on location every day. Being around big, sweaty camera and lighting guys has to rub off on you. Mindy wore a baseball cap, set really low to cover her pretty face. You could tell that she was a little shy and I'm sure it didn't help that she was thrown into this situation where she was surrounded by the most beautiful women in the world. That has to be shocking and humbling at the same time. I know it was for me!

Still I could feel Mindy's attraction - and she wasn't being soft or sweet to me. Her approach was more of a ball-busting, wise-ass attitude. It was like being on the playground and having your crush punch you or push you over instead of kissing you! Soon everything I said to her became a joke or a dig. At first it was cute, but then it became a bit excessive to where she was teetering on being rude.

We all started heading out towards the next show and the camera crew went into another gear as far as being aggressive and in your face. Now that Mindy and I had broken the ice, sort of, the crew started to feel more comfortable with annoying us.

In turn, I think we were just as annoying to everyone else at the Fashion Shows. We had 20 hair stylists racing to the next show with a crew of about eight. So basically 28 people are bombarding the backstage of the next show. We had more people in our entourage than there were models for the show!

Mindy wanted interviews from myself and Edward before the next show, but the designer for this show was extra stressed because half of her models were going to run late because of their prior shows running late. There's nothing more amusing than watching models racing into the shows late. All you see is extremely long arms and legs flapping everywhere as their clothes just drop! I saw more naked female bodies in one day than I think I have seen in my entire life!

As soon as the designer saw Edward, she immediately ran over to him in a panic. Edward had obviously known this designer for some time given the way he was able to cool her down. Edward had that way with his clients. He's like the fucking Woman Whisperer! The designer was almost instantly relieved when she saw Edward. Even Mindy was visibly calmer around Edward. With me she seemed like her pussy was on fire, but with Edward, he kept everything and everyone cool around him. I guess that comes with experience.

When I first met Edward in LA, I noticed this power he had over women, especially ones that can be a little highly strung, like Janice Dickinson! Janice was a model back in the days when Studio 54 was the hottest place to be seen and Edward's been doing her hair since then. She visited the LA salon when it first opened and I witnessed Edward do his magic as she came flying in, all hysterics, crying, complaining, hanging off the salon chair like a four-year-old. After all these years as a retired model turned reality TV star, she was a real sight to see. That being said, Edward was able to neutralize her personality, just like walking a big mean dog on a leash. Every compliment he gave her and every piece of advice he threw out to her soothed her and transformed her.

Some of these young girls could take a leaf out of Janice's book and learn how to survive the business. When you rely completely on your beauty, there can be a price to pay later. Models always have it easy when it comes to scoring rich men, but if they don't get married or if they don't accidentally get pregnant, then they're usually fucked later on. Rich men want young girls! I don't know too many rich guys who are into older women.

This designer didn't seem anywhere as hysterical as Janice had been that day but, regardless, Edward was able to comfort her in a way that only a pro knows how to do. As Edward was taming the designer's near meltdown, I was asked to give a quick on-camera interview about how the experience was going so far.

In my best television voice I said: "I'm having the most amazing time here at *NEW YORK FASHION WEEK* with Edward and Joel! The hair that we're doing is really hard and I'm being tested beyond my skills. I'm hanging in there and I hope to make it out of this show in one piece!"

Then within a blink of an eye, we were swept into the next show! With each show the styles were getting more and more intricate. Some of the styles needed a fucking road map to follow them! Surprisingly enough, my hands were really starting to work for me. The last two shows were so intense that my skills improved immensely in just that short amount of time.

This designer's overall look called for braids and there would be more than one. Braids, at this time, were definitely not my strong point. All I wanted to do was survive the next thirty minutes as we were all suddenly buried with thirty models! Even the more seasoned hairstylists were looking nervous, which in turn made me nervous.

Mistakes weren't an option! As we're neck deep in French braiding, Edward turned to me and said: "I've never lost a show Brandon, never!" With those words all my fear disappeared, I kicked it up a notch and our team together kicked things into a new gear. Like a well-oiled machine, we got through each girl's hair faster and more effectively because we would all pitch in to help one another.

There wasn't even that much speaking going on. Everything was working in unison and it was incredible to see in the flesh! By the time the girls started walking down the catwalk, you know it's almost over. We wrapped this show and then breezed through our final show with flying colors.

On the way back to the apartment I was still in a bit of a daze, like I just ran a marathon holding my blow dryer in one hand and my curling iron in the other! Stopping was not an option, unfortunately, as I had to continue shooting the reality show for a dinner scene with Edward, Joel and their third partner Roxanna.

We were going to have an on-camera dinner meeting with some induced drama no doubt. I had a little time to get back to the apartment to change and freshen up, especially since I smelled like I had bathed in a pool of hair gel!

The production crew usually stay at a different location than the stylists, so Mindy kept calling and texting me about where we would be meeting and at exactly what time. I technically had two jobs going on at the same time. One was being thrown into this new salon environment that went a hundred miles an hour faster than the LA salon. And then on top of that I was more or less being an actor without having to rely on a script. Almost everything is ad-libbed when you're doing reality television.

And I wasn't really being completely myself for the cameras. I would amp it up about ten notches so it was me, magnified, which took a lot of energy! Soak that up with alcohol, late nights and whatever else and you have a recipe for messy television gold. I promised myself that I would hold it together while I enjoyed the partying lifestyle and not get too crazy. At least I would try.

I arrived at dinner at this restaurant in the meat packing district called Spice Market. "Chef Jean-Georges Vongerichten's elevated take on SE Asian street food served in an exotic setting." I'd read the review as I looked up the address for this restaurant. This was supposed to be an on-camera meeting with my new bosses who were taking over the hair salon business throughout the country. This was my opportunity to shine as an appreciative apprentice, candidly expressing feelings about this new world to which I've been introduced.

I knew for TV purposes they would put me on the hot spot as far as my inexperience, which was fine. I knew it made good television to show that I was being forced to get better and to show the progression during each episode. I had no problem hamming it up for the camera and the audience.

Roxanna, the third owner, was known for being tough. Word on the street was that she was not to be fucked with and I'd been in the business long enough to take notice of those kind of words. But I was running behind as I took a quick detour to get some pot on the way, and it was a whole different experience than buying in LA.

After the fourth phone call from Mindy the producer, I finally picked up and started in with her before she could say anything. I didn't even need the cameras there as I turned into the spoiled talent that throws hissy fits when they don't get their way. I don't even really remember what I actually said, but when I arrived to the restaurant, I could see that Mindy had been crying.

My heart just dropped I didn't know what to say at that moment but I know I had a sorry look on my face.

She had to buck up quick and give me the run down on how they wanted this conversation to go because, of course, it was reality TV and it was going to be artificially induced.

Mindy and I didn't have to time to get into the prior phone conversation we'd just had. But there was definitely some sexual tension there, although neither of us acknowledged it. Everything was happening really fast. She was looking at me, explaining what I was supposed to talk about, the sound guy was wiring my microphone and my three new bosses were already there and waiting.

I entered the private room that was booked for our dinner meeting. Roxanna was sitting in the middle of Edward and Joel, sizing me up a with camera crew catching every moment.

I should've been paying attention, but all I could think about is the night ahead at the club and freak show at The Box. And on top of that, I had Mindy giving me awkward and uncomfortable looks in between the starting and stopping of filming.

Since this conversation was going to be contrived, we would have to get the correct reactions from one another that would satisfy the producers. I'm sure for Roxanna, being on camera for the first time, it had to be pretty uncomfortable in the beginning. Having cameras in your face isn't for everyone. You either light up, or you fade out. And out of the three, Edward was by far the one with the most personality.

I remembered a good amount of starting and stopping due to the noise level and being that it was Roxanna's on-camera debut, it took a minute for her to warm up. It worked in my favor that she was a bit flustered and I wasn't in the least. I was able to control the meeting and actually ask for more money. I felt that because I was bringing the television show, that I should be able to get a bigger commission cut in the salon, than the other hair stylists. Their commission structure was really low compared to everywhere else.

The fact that they were providing a big, beautiful salon where I could grow and learn from the best didn't matter to me. I figured, fuck it, 35% was not going to cut it, no pun intended. In my mind, I was bringing a TV show as well as some new Park Avenue clients I'd recently acquired through an LA connection. There was no point in even thinking about coming back and forth to New York if I was only making 35% of my money and they would be getting 65%.

Everyone knows that once you step foot in Manhattan, money just flies out of your wallet faster than a pick pocket can steal it! So many stylists are infatuated with wanting to go and travel to either New York or LA to do hair and make it a constant thing every six to eight weeks. Having been there, done that as a hair stylist, it's more work than it's worth, in my opinion. In addition, what it does to your body, money can't fix!

I knew I had to show these people that I meant business right up front so they knew I was serious. What did I have to lose? Nothing! As I continued with the subject of wanting more money, I started to take over the conversation by not letting them get any words in. I even had to pull back so there was some back and forth dialog. I could see the frustration on their faces and I don't know if it was real, or if I was really pissing them off.

And I still wasn't giving them 100 per cent. In the back of my mind, all I could think about was the possible Brazilian dream girl situation that still seemed completely surreal. I was still trying to wrap my head around getting her number, but I'd checked my phone twice and her number was still in there, so I knew deep down that is was real.

I'm also thinking that now I kind of want to fuck the producer Mindy, too. Hey, it's always good to have a back-up plan! Probably not the smartest plan I realize now, but it was a plan.

Due to the constant starting and stopping in between our heated business arguments, we actually talked it out between takes and Edward and Roxanna basically told me that we would work something out that would be better than their first offer. I said: "Great but I'm still going to be upset while were on camera, cool?" They both just laughed as we started to get to the end of this shoot. The tension was broken and I got what I wanted.

Still, I didn't want them to know that I was going out after this since we had more shows to do the next day, plus they were going to pile me up with clients in the salon so I could get my first taste of New York salon clientele.

We wrapped up the last shots that we needed and the production crew would now disappear for the rest of the evening and I would be free to meet up with some of the other stylists to check out The Box.

One of the benefits to being a loud person like myself in New York, was that I never had a problem getting a cab! For some reason, they would always hear me, no matter where I hailed one! So I grabbed a cab and headed downtown to meet up with another stylist and their friend who was going to try to get us into The Box.

Since it was new and everyone would be trying to get in, it might not happen but I was committed to seeing this freak show, so fuck it! As I pulled up in the cab, I could see the line for the club was already building and it was only 11pm. New York nightlife starts really late and clubs are open till 4am, so showing up somewhere at 11pm was a bit early, but it also showed how popular this place was.

The stylist's friend had the hook up at the door. We walked up and he started negotiating with the bouncer. The bouncer looked over at us and like magic, we were in! We walked with some swagger into this old-looking theatre playhouse. It looked really old inside and it kind of smelled too!

There were different levels from where we could watch the stage. They don't have theatre playhouses that look like this in LA. The crowd was growing by the minute, so we were directed closer to the stage so we could get the full effect of what was about to happen. At first I thought it was going to be some burlesque show with a bunch of hot girls dancing around naked, but that would've been like watching a child's tea party compared to what was about to happen!

It was so loud and crowded inside that is was difficult to talk to each other. The house lights went down and the stage lights came up to introduce the MC who looked liked he worked for the Devil. He was tattooed and horned, with a ripped body. He looked like a Minotaur, just without the bull body.

It suddenly went silent as he introduced himself and the show that awaited. He told us what was to come in the next 45 minutes would for sure blow all our minds. The crowd quietly awaited the line-up of performance art that was about to be thrust into our memories like strange dreams that we experience and never forget.

The music kicked in. The lights went black, then quickly the stage lit up to this buffed transvestite riding out on the stage astride a Harley Davidson. It was wearing a construction helmet and carrying a piece of two by four. It - I say 'It' simply because I didn't know what to call It. I tried to really look close to see if It was male or female but It strangely looked like it was both!

It burst out into the song 'I Am Woman, Here Me Roar!' First of all, the voice was incredible. I mean seriously like *The Voice* status! The performance level was at 10 and all three of us were looking at each other like: "Man, I'm getting into this!" The singing just took over and you couldn't help but like it. As the song reached the ending, the performer started to do a little dance and then began to unbutton It's pants.

Then It whips out a COCK!

Well, I guess that answered the question that had been on everyone's mind, including mine! The performance was coming to a close and this guy is whaling away like Jennifer Hudson. It then reached under his cock - and pulled a bloody tampon out of It's own PUSSY!

"Holy fucking shit Batman!" I yelled out as the other two guys started laughing their asses off! I was stunned! I'd never seen anything like it and I'm pretty sure everyone else in The Box felt the same way. Well at least I can now mark that one off my list of weird shit to see.

The performer gave the crowd another good look at it's snatch just to confirm to everyone that it was real before it ended the performance. My first night of going out in New York had been beyond interesting.

A fight with my new bosses, seeing a pussy and a cock on the same body, what the hell was next? Surely it couldn't be girls going down on each other right on stage? I guess I spoke too soon!

The weird hybrid performer finished the number and threw the bloody tampon at someone in the

Page 194

audience and rode off stage on the Harley! The lights went out and the stage hands cleaned the stage for the next number. And then my intuition was proved correct!

Two girls holding hands came up from the audience. They looked like they could be twins, but because it was so dark it was hard to tell. As they walked up to the stage you could see that they were stroking each other and playing with each other. It was like watching a porno in real time. They got up on the stage and stripped down to what looked like nothing. I tried to look close and they both had tiny dental floss underwear on and that was about it! They immediately started getting into a 69 position on a table that was placed on the stage. It was as real as you can get and it was definitely hot! Everyone in the audience was loving it, both male or female. No one was turned off or grossed out by it because we all knew going to this place that it was going to be sick and twisted!

As raunchy as it sounded, it was still done in an up-scale, old-world circus freak kind of way, so it was really artsy at the same time, especially with the DJ and the theatre space. It wasn't distasteful even though it was extreme. The girls were doing pretty much everything they can do to each other. They both were obvious acrobats, possibly even contortionists, so they could get themselves into all sorts of positions with each other. They were doing things I had never seen before!

And the whole time I was thinking: "Who are these girls? What's their daily life like?" I'm always fascinated with people who have these extremely perverted occupations like porn stars or strippers. What's their deal? Is it just a fucked-up background? What happened to you that makes you think that a profession like going down on a girl in public is okay? Maybe it was drugs.

Oh yeah, the drugs were starting to go around as the two stylists I was with were already sniffing a great deal like they had bad allergies. I felt like I was in the movie *A Clockwork Orange*. Just weird shit going on all around us in this place. I actually did see a few girls making out in the audience. One of the guys I was with asked me if I wanted some coke. "Why not?" I thought to myself. "A little can't hurt." The guy gave me a little bump on a key and I snorted it really quick so no-one saw, although it's not like anyone's hiding anything here.

As soon as the coke hit my throat, my face went completely numb! What a fucking rush to head this stuff gave me! No wonder New Yorkers can stay out till 4am! After that first bump I was ready to fucking do anything and go anywhere! All the fear I had from earlier in the day with the fashion shows and dealing with the production and the new salon in Manhattan suddenly disappeared in a cocaine-infused nightclub that was throwing down everything it had to give.

From twin lesbian lovers, to the hermaphrodite who could sing like Beyonce, the night was unfolding the way I thought it would. I would hang on for the ride and live in between the blurry lines for the week. I looked down at my phone and there was a text from Mindy. It read: "Hey, you want to come over to the hotel tonight?" I gave it a few minutes to respond so I didn't seem eager.

One thing about cocaine, it makes you really horny! It also makes you do stupid shit! Fucking the producer while filming is a recipe for disaster. But when you're on coke, you feel like you can conquer the world, disasters are non-existent, nothing is a bad idea!

Watching these twins up on stage go at each other like they're on a porn shoot is starting to look like something I want to do. In my twisted mind, Mindy was skinny and flexible so I'm pretty sure we can downward dog in her hotel room until the morning.

But the freak show wasn't quite over in the club. I was ready to start my own freak show with Mindy, but there was still some action to be seen!

The twin lesbians completed their session for the evening and the next performer came out looking like he was one of those balloon magicians. He walked out blowing up balloons and turning them into little characters really fast for the crowd as he threw them out one by one. As he threw his last balloon shape out to the crowd, the balloons started disappearing in other places. I learned quickly that balloons weren't going to be the only appetizers for this object hungry performer. Off to the side was a chest full of different objects that he was going to ingest.

The first thing he put down his extra long throat was a sword that was half the length of his body. Somehow he was able to get it all down his mouth and inside his belly. He held it in for a while too. The crowd was utterly fucking shocked! You could hear people gasping out loud at this guy. I had suddenly forgotten about snorting that bump of cocaine and was suddenly sober again watching this. He kept it up with other objects each one more dangerous than the next.

But the final thing he did had me at my limit with freaky shit for one evening. He went back to his balloons and began to blow one up that was really long and fat. Not too fat because he had to be able to get it down his throat, but it was really long like the sword. So he finished blowing up the balloon and put it down his throat. He kept going and going till it was all the way down his throat and into his belly. I thought: "How is this guy breathing? How is he not suffocating right on the spot? If it blows up in his body, what happens?" All these things were running through my mind, but then he did the unthinkable.

He reached behind and stuck his hand up his own ass with his pants hanging off. He pulled the balloon that was inside of his body, out of his *ASS!* He was pulling the balloon out of his ass that he just swallowed a minute ago. It's coming *OUT. OF. HIS. ASS.* I could see the shit on the balloon as it slid out of his shitty asshole. I thought I was going to faint. It's definitely the freakiest shit I've ever seen!

It was now 2.30am in the morning and nothing good can happen at a time like this. Against my better judgment, I was on my way to where Mindy was staying. I was lucky enough to find a cab at this time. I got to her hotel and it was a weird sort of stare down with each other, as I never really apologized for screaming at her earlier and like any tomboy, she wanted to show her annoyance for my behavior.

Now that she was out of her work clothes I could see more of what had been attracting me to her. She looked softer and less rigid in the mood controlled lighting of the Tribeca Grand. We started making out and she pulled me to the bed. I still had a little bit of the cocaine feeling going on, but thankfully it was wearing off. She put her tongue in my mouth like it was that performer's balloon! Her hands were all over me as she was tearing my clothes off and unbuckling my belt.

I pulled her shirt off and she had these beautiful, little breasts that were poking straight out with the hardest nipples. She covered herself like she was embarrassed. She told me: "Don't look at me, I have no tits!" But I grabbed her arms away from her and started rubbing her body as I moved myself closer to her. She started to complain about something else and I immediately went in and kissed her. I threw her down on the bed and we started fucking.

She was beginning to loosen up and move her body against mine. She went from arms crossed, to legs straight in the air. She grabbed my hair and pushed my face down in between her legs. Before I started, I looked at her and said: "I'm going to pull the cum out of your little body with my mouth!" Her head just fell back and she let out this huge moan! We continued to fuck until the morning. Call it adrenaline, call it sexual frustration, call it the leftover buzz from the coke. It was probably all three, but it kept us going like a freight train until the sun came up!

In my profession, sex comes at all angles. It comes when you least expect it. Was it right to fuck Mindy, who was the producer on my show? Probably not. Was it right for her to fuck me? Definitely not. Usually when these kind of things happen to me, the girls usually go home to their boyfriends. For some reason I attract woman who are unavailable. Maybe I'm the bad boy they always wanted to fuck but never had the opportunity until now.

We both were aware of the next few days ahead. We still had three days to work together and we would be in each other's face, literally. When we finally finished, it was already 6:30am! I started to yawn but she looked at me and said: "Hey, you can't stay! My other producer is meeting me here in an hour to prep for today's shoot. I also have to call my boyfriend in 15 minutes."

Of course she had a boyfriend! The guilt was already kicking in with Mindy and every moment I was in her room, the more the guilt was building! Without an answer, I grabbed my stuff and split! For once I kind of felt used! Did I just get taken advantage of by the producer? I did come on my own, but could she have been any more rude asking me to leave? I tried not to make too much of it. It was just a weird feeling that I was the one being kicked out for a change.

I headed out of the hotel and into the early morning streets of Manhattan. Wow, for once, I was the one doing the Walk of Shame out of someone's place! Served me right I guess. The way I looked at it, the Walk of Shame doesn't count if you're not in your own town!

As the next few days flew by, the mood between Mindy and myself took a sour direction. Talk about not shitting where you eat! The one night of dirty, sweaty sex with someone who's not available never works out! You'd think I'd know this by now! Things always get weird because now I'd changed the trajectory of someone else's relationship.

I've learned this the hard way in life as this wasn't my last unavailable woman I would fuck, or try to fuck. But it was damn fun for those few hours and it was the perfect ending to a weird and wonderful night.

Fashion Week started to slow down and I had fulfilled my expectations, between getting fucked up on coke, fucking a producer and seeing balloons coming out of people's assholes. More importantly I was able to survive Fashion Week and hang with the 'Big Boys' in the hair world. I would say it was definitely a week to remember!

The New York salon had given me so many priceless experiences in such a small amount of time. They had so graciously taken me in without any judgment and Edward had taught me so many tricks that I still use to this day! I don't remember if he knew that during the shows I was still high from the nights before. Did he care? Probably not!

I was living it up and he was observing my behavior and keeping me in line when I needed to be kept in line. We got to the end of the week of shooting and I was scheduled to go back to LA and work at their new salon there.

We didn't know if the TV show would happen or not. This was still technically a pilot episode, so there was no guarantee that it would go on air or not. The networks often wait till the bitter end to green light a show and they don't want to pay shit for them, so you are always left hanging by a limb, waiting to see if it's going to air so you can prepare your life for more shooting.

You also don't get much money in the beginning of reality shows. Maybe later on when you're three or four seasons in, you can negotiate more money depending on your TV street credit and ratings. In the beginning, it's not much at all and they don't consider your life or your regular schedule. At the end of the day, it's all a gamble, but a gamble that can pay off big time if you've got the right combination of talent and screen presence!

I had a late afternoon flight to catch out of JFK airport back to LA. I woke up early so I could leave the apartment in good condition and get to the salon to say goodbye to everyone before my departure. Edward and his partners had agreed to my commission terms regardless of the TV show happening or not.

Since I'd arrived in New York, I'd experienced all of my emotions from one spectrum to another. I went from scared, to happy, to coked out, to sexed out! I did the trip the way it needed to be done. I always promise myself that when I come back, I'll be more tame, I'll see more of the city and sleep more. I know that never ends up happening. The more I came back to New York for work, the deeper I went into the finer things the city had to offer. When there's more money, there's more indulgence, more backstabbing, more adultery.

Even though it went fast, it seemed like I was there forever. I wanted a quick bite before taking a cab to the airport. I went to Rue 57 on 57th Street, right up the street from the salon. Rue 57 is a French Bistro that's on a corner and is busy all day long.

I went in for a fast lunch and as I walk in, I hear: "Brandon!" I turn to my left to be completely surprised by Alexandra, the Brazilian model! There she is at a table with another gorgeous model girlfriend and this interesting looking guy who's sitting in the middle of them.

She waves me to come over and sit with them. I didn't need to be asked twice! The way Alexandra was smiling at me was pulling me closer and I was powerless against her. I quickly sat down and introduced myself to the other two. "This is Peter. Peter lives across the street. We always come here." Alexandra said while devouring her Cobb salad. One thing I learned about Brazilian girls, they can eat! They're definitely not shy about getting their grub on!

So Alexandra was eating and talking about Peter and explaining that he was a photographer who had these amazing photos of animals in the wild. Peter appeared to be mellow. He only spoke when it mattered and had this tan, leathered skin like he was a surfer or a mountain climber. He was good looking and as it turned out, he'd been a model back in the day as well. He became this famous, professional photographer after shooting animals in the wild in the African jungle. He looked like he had been in a war. He was like Tom Berenger in *Platoon*.

The three of them seemed like a fun bunch. Alexandra seemed full of life and she wasn't afraid to let you know it. I had only been sitting with them for 20 minutes and we had already had two rounds of drinks. Alexandra had said: "Cheers," like four or five times already!

Laughing and drinking with two hot models and some random, famous photographer in the middle of Manhattan, thousands of miles away from home. It was just another chapter in my crazy New York story.

I was looking at my watch to make sure I left in time to get to the airport, but Alexandra gave me this look and she started to touch me when she talked to me. Nothing overly aggressive, mind you. It was a social type of touching, but she was still putting her hands on me and I was totally fine with that!

They were talking about the wardrobe malfunctions during Fashion Week and how some model totally ate shit on the catwalk. The girl just tripped on her own lanky legs and did a face plant right in front of the front row and Alexandra laughed at the other model's mishap. The girls were getting liquored up and louder by the second.

Alexandra looked at me and asked in her thick Brazilian accent: "Brandon, why didn't you call me this week?" She was totally putting me on the spot and I didn't really have an answer other than I didn't think it was real. Of course, I couldn't say that to her so I just responded with: "The shows just wore me out. The week went by so fast, time just got away from me." She gave me a long smirk like she didn't believe a word I was saying, then she grabbed my hand and held it like she was my girlfriend.

I was aware of the time and knew if I had any chance of making it to the airport on time that I had to leave now. "We're going back to Peter's apartment after this. You're going to come, yes?" Asks Alexandra. I was torn! Of course, I wanted to go back to the apartment, but also I didn't want to miss my flight!

"Well I have to fly out of here in two hours. I want to but,…" She cut me off and ordered me: "You're coming for a little bit, I'm making you!" Before I knew what had happened, Peter had paid the bill and we were outside, walking to his apartment that was just a couple of blocks away.

I looked at my watch and it was definitely time to get a cab to leave so I could get to the airport with enough time to not worry. But we entered the apartment to find Peter's wife there. I wasn't expecting that one. Usually when a guy hangs with two hot models, he doesn't bring them home to his wife! Or maybe they do and I'm the one that's naïve!

The wife wasn't really social and she ended up just being in the background while Peter rolled up a joint for us to smoke. Alexandra planted a big kiss right on me as we sat down on the couch. I guess she was making her point known.

But I was getting nervous about the time and I was starting to think with the wrong brain. I was already contemplating staying while trying to figure out how much it would cost to rebook my flight. One part of my brain was saying: "A girl like this doesn't come around too often," while the other part was screaming: "Flight! Flight!" But the other part took over again and I asked myself: "When are you going to get this caliber of hotness again?" She didn't even seem real and all of this seemed like a dream and I was on the outside looking in.

Even after the surreal week I'd had in NY, this was the hardest thing to process. Here I was, sitting on a couch making out with a Brazilian supermodel. By this time, I was running on empty and I didn't have the gas to fight off Alexandra, not that I even wanted to. And her wanting me so aggressively was also turning me on. It always works out better when you're not putting out too much effort and the girl is doing all the work. That's exactly what was happening here - even though she was the hot model - and I knew right at that point that fighting it was useless.

We were all getting high and looking at Peter's work. What a career this guy had had. The whole time, Peter's wife didn't partake at all. She just kind of stood in the background and observed the whole scene.

I summoned up the courage to look at Alexandra while she was clinging to my body and said, rather weakly: "I have to get to the airport before I miss my flight." I don't know why I was nervous to tell her this since I was the guy, but when they're tall and Brazilian, they can be intimidating! She looked at me with no hesitation and declared: "You're not going anywhere!"

She grabbed me and kissed me again. I looked to Peter for support, but he just passed me a joint. He looked at me, then at Alexandra, then back at me and basically gave me a look like: "Don't be stupid, buddy. You see what you have in front of you?" Or maybe that's just what I rationalized in my mind that he was thinking!

I'd never missed a flight before. Looking back, it doesn't seem like a big deal, but at the time it definitely was! As I took another hit of Peter's joint, I fell back into the sofa and into Alexandra's arms.

It's no surprise that I ended up missing my flight that day.

THE BITCH OF BEL-AIR

During my long and strange relationship with the Capones, Glenda had this client and friend named Jane. Jane's husband was in his early 70s - he was so old, he had something to do with creating 'test screenings' for movies. He's no longer alive, but at this time he was hanging in there!

They lived in Bel Air, up the canyon through the beautiful and elite West Gates. Right before my friendship ended with Glenda after Ronnie's death, she was gracious enough to let Jane know that I was a really good hair stylist and that she should have me do her hair. Jane loved getting her hair done and would get her hair colored by Luis!

However, Jane is what we would call in the business a 'sniper'. A sniper is a woman who looks for really rich, old men for financial security. She was hot tempered and loved money like a crack head loves an eight ball! Ronnie used to make fun of her for obvious reasons, especially when you would see her and her husband together in public. The contrast was so extreme that you couldn't help but laugh inside because he was so much older than her! Every time we ran into them, I would be with Ronnie and Glenda and Ronnie would always make a joke either before or after we would say hello to them. Ronnie loved to make fun of Hollywood and the people in it. But at the end of the day the one having the biggest laugh was Jane. Laughing her way to the bank!

The 'sniper method' is a great formula - snipe the old man, get knocked up, divorce him, or wait till he dies and then you're set! The house is yours! Or sometimes it's the houses that are yours! Just looking at women like Jane sometimes made me want to be a woman! To me, the best job, or the best life is being a rich mom. Work out all day, hang with your girlfriends and compare Hermes Birkin bags. Drive around in the fucking Range Rover all day having overpriced acai bowls and protein shakes! What the fuck is acai anyway? Sounds like a plan to me!

And Jane wasn't fucking around when it came to her lifestyle! She wanted to wear the best, look the best and surround herself with the best! There are people like actors and rock stars who are really rich, but then you have another layer of rich that's on top of that and Jane and her husband belonged to the higher layer of wealth. When you're rolling in that kind of money everything comes to you, you don't have to go anywhere if you don't want. No more going to the nail salon, the nail girls come to you. Forget the days of trying to park at the hair salon. Your hair color, cut, blow-dries, anything you want comes to you.

I went to Jane's house so many times to do her hair that you would have thought that she invented the words 'house call'! I remember one week I counted six times I went through those Bel Air gates to do her hair for God knows what. I was practically there every single day, whether she had an event or was just hanging at her house. All of a sudden, this woman's blow-dries are paying the rent to my apartment and the lease to my car! I would charge $150 per visit, so you do the math. And it didn't seem like this was out of the ordinary. A highly strung European woman getting her hair done six times a week. But I knew it was this type of compulsive behavior in someone else that could really take my career to the next level.

I could see that Jane was kind of crazy as far as day-to-day behavior went. I really loved to observe people's habits and eccentricities. With Jane, her eccentricities stood out like a homeless person standing on the street in Bel Air. In the few short weeks that I had been doing her hair, I noticed that there were a couple different maids. At first I thought that she had multiple maids. Turns out, they were either walking out or getting fired by the end of each week. That was a huge red flag, but I was the hair stylist, not the maid, so I ranked much higher in the domestic food chain when it came to being part of the help.

Also, lucky for me, she hadn't thrown me any attitude since I had been coming to do her hair so I wasn't going to sweat the constant firing of the maids. Thankfully Jane's husband was really laid-back. They were like Yin and Yang – at different ends of the laid-back scale! He seemed like he was her son's grandfather more than the dad.

At this time their little boy was two or three years-old. Sometimes when I would be over there, the kid would be running around the house while her husband was chasing him. I'd be thinking: "This guy is going to drop dead of a heart attack at any moment trying to chase this kid around." It was a sight to see. The old man would be chasing this toddler around the house while Jane was getting hair and make-up done six times a week! If that's not LA living, I don't know what is.

This being said, I have to give credit where credit is due. Jane was responsible for getting me some of the richest women in the world as clients and I'm not kidding when I say that. Jane was a great cheerleader –

temporarily - for me because she loved to turn her girlfriends on to new things like up-and-coming hair stylists and make-up artists.

It was completely for selfish reasons of course as these hook ups were thrown back in your face if you crossed her later. I hadn't done any crossing yet so I had been spared from that experience thus far.

The struggles of being a frustrated actress who was now married to a studio executive who's twice her age, playing make believe was a full-time job. Being a mother just solidified the money. Another great thing about Jane, besides the daily blow-dries, was that she went to every event that you could possibly imagine.

From the Oscars, to the Golden Globes to The Emmys. If there was an event in Hollywood that required hair and make-up, Jane was all over it. They would get invited to all the big events that had to do with the movie business and she took full advantage of that. I made sure I made myself available for each event. I would even move other people in my schedule out of the way for her, which would get me in trouble later on with my salon clients. I knew Jane had to be the top priority.

However, Jane hated coming into the salon and when she did, she would totally throw my day off as she would just roll in whenever she felt like it with no prior warning. It would be a sight to see! She would text me last minute to get her hair done – literally my phone would buzz with the text and she'd walk in the door moments later - and because she was using me so much, I just couldn't say no! She would barge in and grab my assistant, whoever they were at the time, and have them wash her right away regardless of how many clients I would be doing at that moment.

She would look at my clients and apologize to them for barging in on my schedule and taking over the chairs. She would say: "Sorry!" but it would never occur to her to wait her turn or call ahead for a proper appointment. The $10,000 purse would get plopped on one chair - yes, the expensive bag would get its own chair! - and she would throw her coffee and phone right on my station without worrying about what I had up there.

Jane was like a force of nature! She was a European heat wave that would move at a typhoon's pace! Fortunately, she didn't come to the salon very often. As work was increasing with the wealthy crowd, I started to weed out the old customers that were paying less, even though they had been with me since I had started. I wouldn't stop seeing these people completely, but I would just become less and less available for them.

I was hungry for the big money that was being presented to me. I was becoming the real-life Warren Beatty in *Shampoo,* but better! These people had way more money than the women in the movie *Shampoo*! There was no way I could pass up these opportunities. I would basically have the blow dryer in my pants when I would arrive at Jane's house while riding up the canyon on my motorcycle, that's how much I was becoming like the movie!

It wasn't irregular for me to show up and she would be running late, nanny-less, feeding her kid then handing her two-year-old off to me while she jumped in the shower so she could get her hair blown out! I didn't mind holding her son and feeding him. It's really funny to see a rich woman trying to deal with her kid when the nanny has just walked out. Jane wasn't used to not having help around. She just had a problem keeping them around! I stopped trying to learn the names of the maids as I knew they wouldn't stick around long.

Soon I was becoming like a girlfriend to Jane and seeing her in these vulnerable situations was only just the beginning. There's no way to not get close to your clients when you make them look beautiful for a living. At $150 just for a blow dry, I was OK dealing with her everyday madness. I thought: "No problem, I'll feed your kid while you run into the shower to wash your hair." Also, I knew that any friend coming from Ronnie and Glenda was going to have a big personality, and that there would be times where things might get weird and uncomfortable.

Every event that would happen in Hollywood, Jane would rustle up a top beauty team to prep her for the red carpet. It wasn't that she was famous or anything like that. She just knew that because of who her husband was, she would get some attention when they would show up to these events. She would walk the red carpet, so it would be guaranteed that she would be photographed. She was also friendly with a lot of celebrities, so she could ride their coattails during the red carpet arrivals.

After events, I would check out the big photo agencies like Wire Image or Getty Images to see the work I had done as I knew there would always be at least two or three shots of her. There were never dozens of photos of Jane, but what did I care? It was a great experience for me and she always paid in full. Unlike celebrities who always try to get things for free, Jane came through with the cash!

In the beginning Jane and I had a good relationship. It would stay this way for a while, but I could see her craziness through the money. I had a hunch in the beginning that she and I would end on a sour note because she didn't seem like the kind of person that would allow you to ever leave her or tell her no. This was evident from the number of staff she blew through – I'm surprised there wasn't a revolving door installed at the house. The maids appeared to do most of the work in the house but, unfortunately, she was so demanding that most of the nannies would walk out on her, too.

What I've learned about these women who want to live the good life is, they are willing to sacrifice themselves for an old rich guy, or a dorky, unattractive rich guy simply for the money, but they end up living in an expensive jail. The next thing they know, they're trapped with kids and married to a guy old enough to be their grandfather, or some ugly dork who is more interested in his money than them. They eventually become more and more unhappy because the sexual frustrations grow more and more intense as the years go on. Even with all the money, they might not even be allowed to buy certain things without the old man's approval. That's why you see these women running to the hot, straight yoga instructor or personal trainer, or the hot, straight hair stylist.

These things don't happen by accident. That's why straight hairdressers become successful way faster than women or gay hairdressers. Gay men and women do hair to make you look pretty, but a straight guy will do your hair to make you look hot – believe me there's a difference! Most women out there will sabotage their own girlfriends, while us straight guys will do whatever it takes to get our clients looking hot. It's just how it is. That's why I have a waiting list.

So back to Jane. She had started to become a little too demanding for her own good. It didn't start with me. The first time I saw her freak out on someone, she freaked out at this little clothing stylist named Nuncio. Nuncio was from Italy. As you could imagine with a fucking name like Nuncio either you're a gay stylist, or you're a waiter at an Italian restaurant.

Nuncio, was a stylist for Bvlgari. He would bring her the dresses and the $50,000 tiaras and necklaces she wanted to rent for an event. Yes, even rich people and celebrities rent diamonds! Most of the bling you see walking down the red carpet, especially at the Oscars, is loaned out to the star. They don't own it!

Remember, just the hair and make-up alone was an easy $1,000 for every event and there would be two to three events a month, not including the two to three visits a week at the house for blow outs. When it was award season, Jane would be at everything from the Globes to the Oscars and every party in between. Nuncio had other clients who were more famous than Jane and it would really bother her when he would have his assistant come and drop off the dress rather than himself.

I could understand his dilemma. Celebrities help stylists because of their name and the publicity they bring by just wearing a dress or carrying a bag, but women like Jane would pay the bills. Most celebrities would try to keep the shit after an event knowing damn well they would have to give it back whereas Jane would just buy the fucking dress.

Nuncio told me once when I gave him a ride back to the Beverly Hills Hotel after an afternoon with Jane, in his very thick Italian accent: "Brandon, it's great to do people who are famous but it's better to do the women who could really afford it." I liked his attitude. Use the celebs to get the really rich girls. Besides, the really rich women would love it when you did celebs, whether they want to admit it or not.

But Jane would pitch a fucking fit when Nuncio wasn't available. Yet if he didn't have the clients he had, Jane wouldn't give a shit about using him. It was a big

Catch-22 situation. It was all very fucked up. I remember one Oscar day, she was screaming at him on the phone in Italian about who she hooked him up with and the things she had done for him. Jane would scream bloody murder at Nuncio, but to them this was all very normal. At the end of the day, it's abuse, but it's all very accepted in our world.

During the time I first met Nuncio was about the time Jane started asking me to get her drugs. At first, she would ask me for a little bit of cocaine. "I don't do coke." I would always say. "I don't really know people who sell coke, I'm more of a pot guy." Then she started asking me for pills - Vicodin, Percocet, things like that. I have never been a pill person either, so again I was in the dark as to where to find these kinds of drugs.

Because she continued to ask me, I would get anxiety about going to her house because she was so fucking relentless and it was starting to make me feel very uncomfortable. I finally asked my pot guy if he could get me some harder stuff! This was before the pot stores became legal in California, so I still had to have a pot dealer. (In LA, pot dealers are now extinct.) So, my pot dealer was able to get Vicodin because of an accident he had so he had an endless prescription, plus he had a famous friend who could also get more pills for my relentless client.

So, on my next visit to see the pot dealer I asked: "Hey, this fucking broad that I do keeps asking me for dope. Can you get pills?" He said: "All I can get is Vicodin." I replied: "I think that's what she wants. Let me text her to see how many she wants." I was thinking she might want like two or three. She texted me back saying she wants a hundred fucking pills! I looked at him and said: "She said she wants a hundred." He just started laughing. He knew the game. He said: "Let me guess, younger woman, older husband?"

By this time, I was laughing too: "Yeah, really old husband, like wearing Depends old." He asked: "How rich?" " West Gate of Bel Air rich," I told him. He shook his head. "What do you mean?" I asked. He said: "If I had to fuck someone that old I'd probably have to be pretty wasted and need that many pills. I don't care how much money is involved, I'd rather be poor."

On that note, I grabbed the hundred Vicodin and headed back to Jane's. My dealer was in Brentwood so it wasn't far from Bel Air. Just 20 minutes along Sunset Boulevard and I started going up the hill to Jane's house.

I love Bel Air. It just screams success. People who live there are fucking winners! A lot of old-school celebrity legends have lived in Bel Air including Elizabeth Taylor, Judy Garland, Alfred Hitchcock, Zsa Zsa Gabor, Clark Gable, Tom Jones and Nicholas Cage. All those stars had money – and class! What a contrast to the West Hollywood neighborhood I was living in.

I guess I wanted to keep Jane happy not only so I could do her hair but also because I didn't want to stop coming into Bel Air. It was so beautiful to drive up the hill surrounded by 20,000 sq. ft monstrosities overlooking all that Los Angeles has to offer. I have been in homes where they might have a view of the city, but to have the ocean and the city at your feet all in one panoramic view was the best! I knew the more I worked in these kinds of environments, it would shape my own life and I would end up in a neighborhood like Bel Air or Brentwood, where I currently live now.

That's what my father used to say to me. He wanted me to live around people that were successful, so that I would be exposed to successful energy. That's why I couldn't say no to Jane. For some crazy reason, I felt that she held the key to all the rich people. She was my way in and I had to suck it up. I never thought that bringing drugs to clients would be part of the job description, but I am in the business of saying: "Yes!", so fuck it! Back to the house, deliver the goods, blow out her hair and I'd be on my way back down the hill to West Hollywood to my reality.

But then things started going south with Jane.

The problems began when I received this huge write up in Allure Magazine. Allure magazine does this piece once or twice a year called *The Directory*. It's a write up that every beauty person who matters gets. If you get the write up and your picture is in the magazine, it's fucking priceless! I got the write up with picture and all. It was the only magazine write up I really ever wanted. If it was the last magazine write up I would get, I would have been happy. OK, maybe that's not entirely totally true but either way I got the write up. It's the kind of write up that makes the other hair people around you very jealous.

When I got the Allure Directory, things started to change. I knew that when the Allure article published, I would probably lose some hair stylist friends. Hair stylists are not good at hiding their feelings. If they were jealous, I'd know it! All of a sudden, I had people calling in to the salon to book with me because they saw the Allure write up. I was really starting to get busy. I think in one month my clientele almost doubled.

Everybody I knew had seen the article, including Jane. And when she saw it, she knew that our end was near because she knew that I was going to be less and less available as time went on. She knew she would lose control of our situation and Jane did not like to lose control!

After she saw the article, she started to become more difficult with me. This is how it went down. She tried to book me on a Saturday in the middle of the day, which is always my busiest day. Then she wanted me to come up to the house at 5:30pm to style her for some red carpet event she had to attend.

Saturdays are always the busiest days at the salon for any stylist. By this point I was booking up fast, so it wasn't easy for me to just cancel on people any more, even for Jane. The night before all of this, which was Friday night, she wanted me to come to the house for a quick blow dry, even though I was coming back the next night to do it all over again.

So, it was Friday night, the night before her event and as I was blow drying her hair, her elderly husband wobbled out from their bedroom to confirm that I was coming tomorrow at 4:30pm. "4:30?" I asked. "Jane, you told me 5:30! I've already booked my entire day. I can't move ten people back an hour just so I can be on time for your event." She responded with: "I knew once you got that write up that you were going to become difficult." "So now I'm being difficult?" I thought to myself.

Before I mouthed off something that could end this relationship, I bit my tongue and said: "No problem, I'll take care of it." She just smiled and nodded her head like she had won! How the fuck was I going to move ten people on a Saturday? What could I do?

Cut to Saturday. It was really hectic. I had been slammed all day and I'd had a minimum of three women going at once, pretty much the entire day. As 2:30pm rolled around, things were still looking pretty good but I didn't want to speak too soon, especially on a day like this. Any problem, like someone coming in late or my assistant fucking something up, could happen at any time and all hell could break loose.

Everything was going okay until my second to last client text messaged me and says that there is traffic and she's going to be late. "Fuck!" I said out loud as the text came through. My schedule wouldn't allow any mistakes! As soon as I put the phone down, I told my assistant that we had to work double time to finish and get to Jane without any problems. My clients who were currently in the chair could see the stress on my face. They knew I was in a predicament.

Another thing about Jane was, when she would get mad, it took her some time to calm back down. She wasn't really one to hold back on giving you a verbal ass kicking. To this point, her and I had not had a real 'blow out' with each other. Mostly I think because I always made her hair look great and I always was on time. Plus, being friends with Ronnie and Glenda gave me a 'get out of jail free card'. I was friends with a legitimate, legendary rock guitar player and this bought me the ultimate respect from everyone.

Jane knew that if she did explode on me, I would most likely walk, given the fact at how Ronnie and Glenda were. They would ghost anyone's ass in a heartbeat if they thought they were being disrespected in any way.

I was also 100 percent sure that Jane did not want to have to find another hair stylist at that very moment. Or did she? Then again, when it came to Jane's personality, think of a freight train ramming in to your day with no apologies and not taking no for an answer. It was her way or the highway and right up to that day, my schedule had always seemed to permit her eccentricities and craziness.

On that day, which was for the *Pirates of The Caribbean 2: Dead Man's Chest* premiere, I was doing my very best to keep our relationship from being 'shipwrecked'! Her self-entitlement was astounding.

I was compulsively looking at my watch to make sure that I was staying on time. My second to last client had not shown up yet and I was getting into the red zone as far as time was concerned. I looked down at my phone to see if anyone had cancelled and my worst nightmare appeared.

Jane had sent me a text demanding: "I really need you here earlier than 4:30. Can you make that happen?" I was afraid to respond. I figured I would just tell her that I was slammed and I didn't see my phone, even though it was a flat out lie! My second to last client finally showed up after being 30 minutes late…and 30 minutes late in a salon is an eternity!

As I began to start on my last client the intensity was growing by the second. I was doing her hair so fast that I didn't even remember what I did! I didn't even say anything about her being late, I just wanted to get her in and out as fast as possible. My assistant washed her and sat her down. Just as we sat down my second to last client, my last client comes in early! Yes, there was a God!

As my last client, Jaime, walked in, before she could say anything, I say: "Hey girl, so glad you're here. I can start you right now!" My assistant threw my last client in a robe faster than she could grab that US Weekly and we got her color going!

My assistant and I were working like fine-tuned machines ready to go into hair battle! So, to clarify - Jaime was my last client on the list that day, Valerie was my second to last client of the day and they were both currently in my possession. I had to be at Jane's in Bel Air in an hour and a half from that moment. The salon is in West Hollywood, so I really need to leave at least 20 minutes before to make it on time.

I had to finish cutting Valerie's hair, which usually takes me longer than normal because she has enough hair for three people! Jaime was early, but I still needed to do her base color, which was currently being put on by my assistant, then I had to throw a few highlights in and then blow her out. So, a haircut, base color, half a head of highlights and another blow dry, all in one hour and ten minutes! I could feel the sweat on my forehead and it wasn't even hot.

I was working furiously trying to make sure that I didn't have to do anything twice and I was also praying that my current clients weren't going through anything stressful like a break up or a new boyfriend or whatever. I couldn't afford to take any extra time out to be the fucking therapist right then. If I didn't finish in time, I would be the one that was going to need a fucking therapist! Drowning them out as much as possible was my only option for maintaining the least amount of conversation without being obvious.

My clients know me as a positive, high energy person ready to take on the world! Right then, I was stressed, focused and quiet, which is not my usual temperament. As I was blowing out Valerie's hair she asked me about Jane and why I was so stressed. She said: "Why do you even deal with that Brandon? That woman is so demanding! I've heard you talk about her before. Is she paying you extra for all this stress?"

In a way, Valerie was right. I was working on overdrive for this woman and I was becoming her drug dealer. I was making so much money from her that it blinded me from the possible dangers of this situation. Getting her a few pills here and there wasn't that big a deal, but when it's a hundred pills at a time or cocaine or whatever for her and her friends, all of a sudden I was the 'go to guy'. What if I got caught? What if she got caught? Would she give me up? Probably. What if she started hitting on me? How could I turn that one down without losing her as a client? All these questions started piling up in my head.

Valerie was becoming louder as she was voicing her opinion on the subject of Jane. I realized I needed to wrap her up and get her out of here. That's why I like loud blow dryers. I not only like the power, but it's a great voice reducer. This was one of my many talents in the salon. If a client was annoying me and I was trying to rush them out, I would just drown them out with the blow dryer.

Of course, I would maintain an interested look on my face. However, I wouldn't have the foggiest idea as to what they would be saying! It was like reading lips, but better because I can tell by the way they would be moving their head around and how they would move their eyes that would just give me enough to give them a half- ass response to whatever I thought they were saying. I got really good at it, and most of the time when I would do this, my assistants would ask me: "Brandon, how did you hear what she said?" I would just say: "I heard what I needed to hear!"

So, I was trying to get through Valerie as fast as possible. She was yapping away about this and that and I was bobbing my head up and down pretending to be listening. But what I was really doing was trying to time when the other three clients were going to be ready as I know Jane and she doesn't give a shit about the other women. It's a funny thing about women. They're fucking brutal. They will cut you if they think you're going to take their appointment away from them, or make them late. As the clock was ticking, I could feel my phone blowing up in my pocket and I could only imagine who it was. I still hadn't responded about being able to come early because, let's be honest, I was really fucking scared! Minutes seemed like seconds and we were getting close to the finish line.

My assistant had a look of terror on her face because she knew that after we were done here, we would be off to Jane's house and there would most likely be more stress there. I finally answered Jane's text and said that I wouldn't be able to get there earlier. Not one second goes by and she immediately responded as if she was yelling right in my face! Once I saw the exclamation point in her text I started to become upset. I hated the feeling she was giving me in the pit of my stomach. After all, it was just fucking hair!

Sometimes when you have so much money, but no hobbies and you're married to someone 30 years your senior, that plays a big role in your personality. Other than the money, I couldn't see that there was any happiness in her life. There was something strange about a woman getting her hair styled four times a week. I wasn't complaining about the money, but deep down I knew that this woman was probably certifiably nuts!

We finally wrapped up my current clients and started to pack up to leave. I basically ran out of time as I was too jammed all day to get to Jane's early. At this point I was running 15 minutes late. The text messages kept rolling in, the next one meaner than the last. I started to think that Jane was getting immune to all the Vicodin I was getting for her.

My assistant and I jumped in the car and off we went. I immediately started speeding west on Melrose Avenue towards Bel Air. My assistant had a look of horror as I sped through a couple red lights and stop signs. I could see my assistant was gripping the passenger seat tightly as I headed up the canyon. The text messages kept coming and the last one demanded: "Why aren't you fucking here yet! I told you to be here 15 minutes early."

At that very moment, I lost all desire to continue doing Jane's hair. I released my foot off the gas and began to slow down. My assistant looked at me like: "What the hell are you doing?" Because we were close to getting there. I handed my assistant my phone so she could read the text. My assistant looked at me and asked: "Is this what I have to look forward to when I start doing hair?" I responded with: "Because you're a girl, it will be worse!" After I said that to her, I pulled in the left turning lane and turned around back to the salon.

"Fuck that bitch," I said as I made the U-turn on Sunset Boulevard. My assistant said: "What are you doing?" Her voice trembled but I knew exactly what I was doing. I told her: "I'm turning around. I can't take this abuse from this woman any more. Let her do her own fucking hair!"

It just wasn't worth it at this point. To have to take this abuse from this crazy woman wasn't in the cards any more. Once you curse at me in a negative way you automatically become my enemy, regardless of the money. That is how I have maintained my soul throughout my career. Be kind to others, but know your worth and don't take shit from anyone regardless of what they pay you or how famous they might be.

At that moment, I was still nervous about what I was doing because she did help to get me some extremely wealthy clients. But in the end, I didn't care. I knew I'd get new clients without her. We got back to the salon to return my gear. My assistant was being really quiet at this point. I was quiet too even though I felt like jumping up and down and screaming from the roof top that I was free from the craziness.

The only sad thing from the whole situation with Jane was that I think it completely freaked out my assistant because she quit working for me and the entire hair business a week later.

ASIAN PERSUASION

I was living the high life. In fact, I was living beyond the high life thanks to my seriously rich clients. I was being flown around the world just to style someone's hair. It didn't matter to them what the cost was – or how ridiculous it was to fly someone 6,000 miles to another country – just to get a haircut. It was crazy and I was lapping it up. I was like the cat who got the cream – and then some!

The only negative at this time in my life was that the relationship with Jane had not only ended, but ended badly. But in a strange way, she was the one responsible for my new crazy lifestyle.

Before the relationship with Jane was over, she had brought some seriously rich women into my life and I had to admit that's when things started getting really good! Now, for safety sake – mainly my own safety – I have to change the names of these people because the clients I was getting from this point on are so powerful, it's best to disguise their true identities. (But I'm sure you, the reader, will be able to figure out who is who.)

The money was seriously increasing and I would be flown all around the world, just to do hair, which at the time sounded crazy to me!

For some reason Jane's husband was doing business with this man who pretty much runs the media. I'm going to call him Mortimer and, at this time, he was married to this really pretty Chinese woman named Sandy.

What happens to these women who are married to powerful men is that you're almost forced into fake friendships with other women because of the husbands doing business together. I knew that Sandy and Mortimer were way above Jane's league. Sandy and Mortimer had an air about them that I had never really witnessed. These people were among the top one percent of the wealthy people in the world. It's a whole different kind of rich! While some people in the smaller cities in America think they're big shots with homes that are a mere $1 million, these people's homes are upwards of $20 million to $50 million!

I love meeting people outside of LA or New York who think they're hot shit because they have a little money and a nice house that might have cost them $1 million, which in some cities, will get you an entire block. In LA, you're lucky to get a two-bedroom condo for $1 million! Homes in Compton these days are almost $1 million!

People like Mortimer and Sandy make regular rich people look poor! The seriously wealthy love showing off what they have. Inviting people on their yachts, or lending an associate and his wife their house in Malibu for the summer, where they hang works of art like Picasso or Pollack. When you have a home on Pacific Coast Highway in Malibu and the art alone is worth a couple hundred million, your mind begins to expand about how much money there really is in the world. That's why I can't stand when normal people say that there isn't enough money out there, or that rich people are greedy and keep it all.

Since I've been a fly on the wall for a lot of these uber wealthy people, what stood out the most to me was that they all have one thing in common - they all work their asses off! They work at home, they work while they're on vacation. They work hours that most people don't.

When readers see the title of this book 'Sex, Hair and Billionaires', their first reaction might be that I am going to fill this book with stories that trash people unnecessarily.

Well, I hate to disappoint because that's not how it went down. I don't feel bad about revealing Jane's crazy, gold-digging personality, or Rory's crazy lifestyle, or Glenda molesting me half the time because, at the end of the day, I didn't force them to act the way they did. I'm just here to report it. As we move forward with this book, you will discover that the people that I would meet through Sandy and Mortimer helped me tremendously through my career.

When hard working, successful people spot talent in someone and they can see the drive in you and they know that you're not there to take advantage of the situation, they actually embrace you. Like Sandy. Sandy was and is still one of my biggest fans to this day. She brought me more attention and more clients than any other woman to this day. She basically became my agent without taking any commission.

After I had the blowout with Jane, she actually went to Sandy and told her to stop using me for hair. What Jane didn't realize was that once someone finds a good hair stylist, they pretty much stick to that person and friendships become secondary. It was Jane's own fault for referring me to Sandy and now that I was no longer doing Jane, this sort of backfired on her. After she demanded Sandy to stop using me, Jane and Sandy's friendship soon deteriorated. I'm sure I can't take full-credit for that since Sandy, being a really smart person, probably saw Jane's crazy side from a mile away.

Sandy loved setting me up with her friends because it made her look good! I was making Sandy look hot, I'm sure it was giving Mortimer's old penis some adrenaline! Scoring Sandy as a client was like scoring ten movie stars because her husband, Mortimer, owned the fucking movie studio and that was just one aspect of what he did.

When you're the one paying the actors and directors millions of dollars, just imagine how much wealthier they are than the normal movie star. I say normal because Sandy and Mortimer made famous people look like small, insignificant babies! Being able to service clients like Sandy and her friends gave me a whole new outlook on my profession. While all the other hair stylists were scrambling to nail celebrity clients, bending over backwards and kissing their asses like their lips were a toilet seat, celebrities just became regular, normal clients for me.

I wanted the big ballers and people like Sandy and Mortimer were the biggest! From my understanding, Sandy and Mortimer had homes all over the world. New York, Los Angeles, London, Sydney, Beijing. That's a lot of cities! Plus, they're so fucking far away from each other, but when you have your own jet, or should I say, *jets*, that will make any long-distance travel much more enjoyable!

Once Sandy's friends caught wind as to who her new hairstylist was, they wanted me to do their hair as well. The first time I did Sandy's hair, I knew she was hooked! It was all down to me being able to tame her cowlick. No one could control the cowlick right on the top of her forehead. Before I came along, she tried so many other hair stylists and the blowouts would fall apart after a few hours especially around her face where the cowlick was. Well, call me the cowlick tamer because I busted out that blow dry like she had never seen before.

The first time I met Sandy and Mortimer was back at Jane's house. Jane had invited Sandy to her house to get their hair and make-up done together before an event. Sandy and Mortimer were also having dinner at Jane's house, then they would all go to the event after hair and make-up.

While this was all going on, Jane's little boy Sean, who was maybe three at the time and a little wild, was always getting into everything. When I arrived, we had to kid-proof the living room with a gate that would keep him out so we could work. Plus, I had hot curling irons on, so the gate was a must to prevent him from walking up and doing something stupid like grabbing it while it's hot. So, the gate was up and locked.

In the room was Jane, Sandy, the make-up artist and me. The make-up artist's name was Gabriel. He was a young, good looking gay guy with tattoos and a great head of hair. He was Hispanic like myself and we hit it off right away. The husbands were in another room talking business and catching up.

Also, each party had their own nanny team with them. Jane had one at the house who was supposed to be watching Sean and Sandy and Mortimer had brought their own nanny as well. You know you're fucking loaded when you bring the nanny with you to someone's house for dinner! So, you would think with all the help that was there, that nothing could go wrong.

Everything was going great. I just finished Jane's hair, she went to make-up and I start on Sandy's hair for the first time. I'm halfway finished when, all of a sudden, Jane's little boy gets through the makeshift gate that we assembled. He gets in without us really paying attention and what the fuck does this kid do? He runs right over to the most dangerous thing and sticks his entire hand on my big curling iron! He didn't just put a finger on it, he fucking grabbed it for like three full seconds. Of course, it took about five seconds before the pain kicked in and he began to scream at the top of his lungs beyond anything I have ever heard. Fucking bloody murder is the sound that was coming out of that child's mouth.

Both husbands rush in. I've never seen two old men like that run so fast. I was afraid they would both shit themselves and have a heart attack. They asked what happened, and Jane tells them that Sean grabbed the curling iron and of course who do they look at? Me. Of course, it's totally my fault. Jane's husband starts in on me with this condescending attitude as if I was the gardener and had chopped off his little boy's finger. "How did he get in?" he asked. "Someone opened the gate," I replied. "I have to have the irons on to work. They don't work when they're not on." He didn't understand. Basically, to him, it was my fault that his kid got burned. I started to respond to him with a little more attitude: "It's not my fault, buddy. Don't you have a nanny who is supposed to be watching him? Obviously if we're doing hair, there's going to be curling irons on. We set up the gate for a reason. Who let him through?"

I was starting to get pissed with his tone that he's giving me because in my mind I'm thinking: "I'll throw you in the middle of the street, you old fuck, if you

Page 244

keep talking to me that way." I had to just hold my tongue and finish up with Sandy while they tended to the kid's hand. Regardless of her son getting burned, they still wanted us to finish the hair and make-up. At the same time, Mortimer is also asking how he got in and basically is looking at me to blame as well, like I was the disobedient butler or something.

I was fucking sweating serious bullets at this point! I finished up Sandy while they were wrapping up Jane's little boy's burnt fingers and preparing to take him to the hospital. It's funny how through all this, Sandy didn't even have me stop doing her hair. It was her daughter who opened the gate and let the poor little boy in. Of course, they didn't get blamed. Easier to blame me, I guess. I actually never thought they would call me again to do their hair. I went home and wanted to throw up.

Much to my surprise, Sandy loved what I did and wanted me to do her hair again in the future. Perfect! I was back in the saddle and it was perfect timing to score Sandy as a client right before Jane and I had our falling out. Some days later, Sandy called me to come up to her house to do her hair.

Mortimer and Sandy's LA house was sick! It's literally at the top of the hill way up in Beverly Hills. All the way up the hill where the street dead ends. When you get to the gate that leads to their house, they have a guard who sits in a car at the entrance of the gate, ready to alert the house that you are there. I pulled up to the gate and pressed the call button to be let in. On the other end of the line was a really pleasant male voice who I figured must be the butler. I heard the buzz of the gates and they began to open. I drove up the really steep driveway that was about a 60 percent incline.

When you get up to the house you realize that Mortimer is no joke. Jane's house was in Bel Air and really nice, but this place was a fucking compound! Complete with a full staff of gardeners, a butler, nannies - yes that's plural on the nannies - and also a full kitchen staff, with a chef. They had their own personal teachers for the girls, which totally blew my mind. One teacher was Chinese and the other was Australian.

I parked my car in their enormous circular driveway and walked to the door. As I approached the front door, there was a really nice-looking man standing in the doorway wearing a white dress shirt, slacks, and I also noticed that he had a really clean-cut hairstyle. He greeted me at the door and said: "Welcome, I'm Bill. The Mrs. is awaiting your arrival." Bill was Mortimer's butler. An extremely important figure in the Mortimer and Sandy household. "Would you like a water or coffee?" He offered but I politely declined as I gazed through this palace fit for a king.

He showed me upstairs and there Sandy was waiting patiently. She had just had a massage because that's what you do when you're filthy rich. You get a massage in the middle of the day! You schedule all the beauty people one after another. Sandy, at this time, was in her late 30s. Mortimer must've been in his 70s or something like that. Just a wee bit of an age gap! Her bathroom and closet was the size of my entire apartment. The closet was a separate, yet connected room that had all the shoes, bags, anything you could imagine. Basically, everything she had was right out of the fashion magazines. In fact, she probably got things faster than the magazines would get them.

She also was sporting the biggest pink diamond ring that I had ever seen in my life. That pink rock on her finger was bigger than an actual quarter. I had never seen a diamond that big before in person. The only time I had seen a diamond like this was on television, or in the movies, with many people in the movie being murdered over them. You've seen the movie Blood Diamond? She could have made her own movie about her ring and could've called it 'Pink Diamond', a movie about a ridiculously gigantic rock. Of course, I acted like I didn't notice anything, unpacked my gear and started.

Sandy is a tall woman. Probably 6ft. She towered over her much shorter, much older husband. I think that in the beginning, Sandy was probably telling Mortimer that I was gay. I'm sure a guy like him who is quite a bit older and comes from the old school probably thinks all male hairstylists are gay. What did I care? I was getting $150 a pop for just a blow dry and $300 for every haircut. You can go ahead and think I'm gay all you want. It's not like I didn't have enough practice as a bartender.

Sandy has a really thick Chinese accent, so she has always been a bit difficult to understand. You would think that someone who has been in the country for a long time would work on their accent, but it's funny with Asian people. They still sound like they just got off the Dim Sum boat. Even if they've been in the country for 20 years, you still have to listen closely so you don't miss anything. Sandy also talks really fast as well, which made it even more difficult. Thank God my blow dryer was loud so I could act as if I didn't hear anything. I've always found that when dealing with this type of client, saying less is always more. I try not to be super chatty with people when I'm working on them. I like to work fast and talking always slows you down. I also feel that they respect you more when you say less.

Every job I've done, whether it's a photo-shoot or any kind of freelance job, the make-up and clothing people are always so fucking chatty. I swear most of them don't know when to shut the fuck up and get it done. No one wants to hear your life story especially when it's the first time you're meeting them.

In fact, the reason I'm not chatty is because of talky fucking make-up artists. I'm very good at reading someone when they're becoming annoyed and it's usually when you're doing an important person and the make-up artist doesn't know when to stop talking. It actually worked perfectly that Sandy's English wasn't great. The less I had to say, the better. It is only after the fifth or sixth time of doing someone's hair that I might begin to talk about myself, if asked. I don't like to give up too much information.

Here's some advice to young, up-and-coming hair and make-up people, act like a model, be seen and not heard. Wealthy people hate overly-chatty people and they especially hate when you try to give them advice. They have plenty of dough, they don't need your advice! If they want it, they'll ask for it – but probably not from you. That's why they have therapists! But when it comes to clients, my philosophy is that they mostly want to talk about themselves. You're there for them, not the other way around. Being a bit mysterious is a better position to be in.

I could tell that Sandy liked me right away. Let's not confuse that with anything sexual, at least, I never picked up that vibe from her. Besides, Sandy would later on be responsible for getting me laid twice by other woman. It was the biggest compliment to me as a young stylist. I feel she genuinely liked me as a person and loved the way I did her hair. She immediately started referring her friends to me. Her friends were also really loaded and powerful. She actually was kind of like my agent in the beginning. She was telling her friends that they had to have me do their hair. She would almost force them. It was a huge compliment. I thought to myself: "Wow, Chinese women are pushy!" It felt great!

Basically, styling the richest people in the world does not suck! This whole time I had been trying to focus on getting celebrity clients to make a name for myself. Little did I know that the very rich and powerful, would be the ones to make it happen for me. Celebrity types are much more of a pain in the ass. Always running late, really full of themselves and acting like they're doing you a favor! Pretty much how Jane would act all the time except she wasn't famous in the least.

People like Sandy didn't seem to have that sort of attitude. I guess because women like Sandy don't have the time. They're too busy meeting with important people. The parties they were going to were more about business than about mingling. Sandy didn't need to go to a party to get noticed. Her husband pays everyone. In fact, he pays the studios, who end up paying the actors. See what I mean?

As time went on and the more I did Sandy's hair, the more I would get exposed to her friends and her lifestyle and was able to be around Mortimer. At first, I didn't think he really liked me or at least didn't even notice I was there. Then one day I went to do her hair while they were staying at this sick house in Malibu. It was on Carbon Beach. Carbon Beach is known locally as Billionaire Beach. It's one of the most expensive strips of real estate in America. These houses cost anywhere from $10 million to a $100 million. Maybe even more!

As I was driving up Pacific Coast Highway, I could smell the ocean filling my senses. I always like to roll the windows down when I'm driving and I noticed as I was getting closer to the address, it seemed like the houses were just getting bigger and bigger. As I pulled up to the address, it seemed like this one was the biggest one out of them all. I parked, grabbed my gear and headed to the door. I rang the bell and a young, blonde-haired butler answered the door with what sounded like an Australian accent. He knew who I was and I told him that I was there to do Mrs. Mortimer's hair. He politely let me in and announced my arrival to Sandy.

As I walked in, I noticed a lot of paintings and sculptures. You could also see the ocean from the front door. The butler offered me something to drink and I waited for him to take me to Sandy. I was looking around and from what I saw there was another family there as well. I could see the children playing in the backyard that looked out to the ocean with teams of nannies following them around waiting on them hand and foot. It was funny. The kids were chasing each other around with the nannies chasing them so as to make sure they never fall down or get hurt.

As a kid, I always played with my friends alone. I guess this is what it's like when the silver spoon in your mouth will also wipe your ass for you. It was odd to me to see kids play with so much supervision, but when your parents are worth so much money, I guess everyone and everything could potentially be a risk. Why risk it if you have the bucks?

The butler came back to get me and he escorted me to where Sandy and Mortimer were waiting. On the way there he started pointing out the paintings and the sculptures that were scattered around the mansion. He was telling me who they were created by and what they were worth. At first, I couldn't believe the names he was rattling off and the amount for which they were purchased. I'm thinking to myself: "Did he really just say Picasso and $15 million? Did he really just say Warhol and $5 million?" This house was better than a museum because it had all the really rare pieces and you could walk right up to them. The museums probably borrow these pieces from these people.

"Wait a second," I thought to myself. "These people probably own the fucking museums!" It was me who had to adjust to the type of money that was surrounding me. Most people who don't grow up rich, can't even fathom this kind of money. They limit themselves when they say things like: "Oh, that's too expensive," or: "I can never afford that." That's why they stay poor. Whatever you put out to the universe, the universe puts right back out to you. These new clients I was getting did not think poor. Their thoughts were focused on the most abundance possible - and they got it! Wow, I liked this house, and I liked these people! As I walked upstairs where Sandy was hanging out, she popped her head out and invited me in.

Mortimer and Sandy appeared to be chilling out in what seemed like the house gymnasium. Everything in the room was top of the line, as well as an indoor-pool that faced outside into the ocean. This gym was nicer than any Equinox I've ever been too – and for those of you that don't know, Equinox is one of the most expensive gyms in LA!

Mortimer said: "Hello," and called me by my name. He actually remembered my name! Sandy asked me to start Mortimer's hair first. I was actually going to cut and color his hair. What little he had anyway. I have to admit I was a little nervous. Not nervous about doing his hair because he didn't have any. I was more nervous about being able to have a conversation with someone this rich and powerful. Let's face it - this guy was Daddy Fucking Warbucks!

What do you talk about with a man who runs the media and everything else? What could I possibly say that would be interesting to him? I was so afraid to sound like a dumb ass, that I just kept quiet. He was wearing swim trunks and nothing else. His accent was a lot thicker than I had originally thought. Sandy said she would be back and to go ahead and start Mortimer. Her accent was so thick, I'm thinking: "How the hell do they understand each other?" Obviously, she's a trophy wife, so maybe he doesn't want to know what's she saying. I guess it's more exciting that way?

Then, he proceeded to strip down to his bare ass which, I have to admit, I wasn't quite prepared to see. Here was possibly the richest man in the world completely bare ass naked! I guess there's a first time for everything! I sat him down and quickly wrapped the cape around him to save myself from looking too long at his naked, old man body.

Just as I was about to start, the butler pops in and tells him there was a call that he had to take. He excused himself and said: "Brandon I have to take this. I'll be right back." He gets on the phone and says to whoever he was talking to: "Hello? This is Mortimer." I've never felt such power from someone by just saying their own name. Whoever was on the other line must have been just as important as he was because he was talking to this person like it was his equal. He stayed on the phone for about 10 minutes, talking about business affairs.

As he was taking his phone call, I took the opportunity to look around a bit. Everything about this house was incredible, from the floors to the ceilings. This home just screamed billionaire! He hung up the phone and sat back down. He sincerely apologized for taking so long, as if your grandfather had kept you waiting. I say grandfather because he had that old-fashioned, polite way about him that wasn't like any of the younger successful guys I had as clients. You could tell that he learned manners in a different time. Nothing like what my generation taught for manners. Usually I'm annoyed when someone makes me wait but in this case, I was obviously patient and attentive to whatever move he made, or whatever came out of his mouth.

I put the cape back around him and began to cut his hair. For an older guy, he was kind of tall. He was definitely taller than I expected. He had old person spots all over his body. Like moles and freckles that I don't have yet. He would breathe deep when he sat, to relax himself, I guess. I had heard that he had never taken a vacation from work and that he is basically always working, even when he is relaxing. I guess that's what you do when you're that powerful and that busy. Just create a luxurious environment around you so that you can constantly work, but have some peace at the same time.

I would see this later on when I would fly on their jet or be in their house in Beverly Hills, or at their New York apartment. When you're that rich you can make it so that your surroundings are beautiful, including your wife. I could see why he was attracted to Sandy, besides her just being a lot younger. After all, she was very beautiful and exotic. It's like you work so hard at your job that everything in your home should just be beautiful and relaxing. Even though they seemed so different from each other you could see the calm and peace between them.

During his haircut, I thought that I would be a nervous wreck but instead I started to feel my normal self again, even throwing out a compliment about how beautiful I thought his wife was and telling him what a lucky guy he was. I guess because of the Australian accent, he seemed more like a normal guy. We just happened to be standing in one of the most expensive homes I have ever set foot in. Mortimer had the power to make you forget all that and just get on with whatever you were doing.

After 20 minutes I finished, dried his hair and started on Sandy's blow dry. She told me I did a great job with Mortimer and that he really liked what I had done. As I began to blow dry her hair, she started to talk about her friend Anne, who was going to marry one of the founders of Google. She was telling me about their wedding plans and that they were both very nerdy. Sandy was laughing to herself about the wedding dress and their ideas about the ceremony. I guess one of the ideas was to swim out to a sand bar and deliver their vows, while the whole wedding party would be there watching.

I asked Sandy: "How will the guests get out to the sand bar?" She said as though it was the most natural thing in the world: "By boat of course! Anne and her husband will swim from the boat to the sandbar to recite their vows." Only rich people think like this. I asked Sandy: "What is she going to wear for a wedding dress, a bathing suit?" She laughed and said: "I have no clue what she is thinking. I'm trying to help her with her wardrobe because the wedding will take place for an entire week on a private island in the Bahamas."

The more I got to know Sandy, the more I realized that she would always play style council for her girlfriends, whether they asked for it or not. If you lacked fashion sense and you were friends with Sandy, she was setting you up with jewelry, hair and make-up. She would suggest ideas that only someone with a shit ton of money could afford. She would suggest a certain type of diamond necklace or a famous designer's dress, or use a certain hairdresser.

Then, just like that she would say: "You have to do her hair Brandon, it's so terrible! You need to tell Anne how to wear her hair for her wedding! She is going to be here in LA next week because I'm helping her pick a dress so you need to do her hair because I know it's a disaster!" I asked if the dress she was going pick for her would be the swimming one and she just started laughing. She said in her thick Chinese accent: "Oh Brandon, they so nerdy. Very, very, nerdy!" We were dying laughing as I finished the blowout.

A few days later I get another call from Sandy. I answered the phone and she asked me if I could come to the house again for a blow dry. Of course, my answer is: "Yes, when do you need me?" She told me she wanted me there in two hours and that she wanted to run something by me. Two hours roll by and I found myself in front of their gate again. As I pulled up to the house I see Bill's welcoming smile as I walked towards the front door. Their butler Bill is the definition of class! Talk about service and manners. He spoke so well it made me check myself as far as my speech and diction.

The last thing I wanted this family to think was that I was low class.

I really began to step up my game as far as the way I presented myself. I wanted to maximize this situation and elevate my personality from regular hairstylist to famous hairstylist. No more curse words, no more slang words. I wanted to speak properly around these people because I really wanted to be a part of this uber wealthy lifestyle.

I started to watch how I was carrying myself. When I would do Sandy's hair and there would be a new make-up artist who didn't carry herself well, whether it was that they talked too much or that they would be chewing gum with their mouth open, the contrast between them and me grew tremendously with each visit.

The only way to break into that lifestyle is to live that lifestyle. I got working on her hair and Sandy started talking about this conference that they're going to in Sun Valley, Idaho called *The Allen & Company Conference*. This conference is where all the heads of the media meet to discuss what goes on in the world of media. As she was talking, I was just trying to listen to her as hard as I could because she was a bit hard to understand. It took me a year or so before I really was able to decipher what she was saying.

After a couple years I was able to basically read her mind, but this was still early on. Then Sandy chimed in with: "You should come with us to the conference. All my friends are there and I will line them up for you." I responded with: "Do I need to book a flight?" She laughs out loud: "No, you will fly with me and Mortimer on our jet." When she said jet, my dick got hard! She added: "All my girlfriends are going to be staying on or near the resort, so it will be great for you to be there!"

My stomach hit the floor, then went up through the roof, then back down again. It was like I was on a rollercoaster as I told her: "Of course, I would love to come. Do you think it's going to be okay with Mortimer?" She responded with: "Oh, it's not going to be a problem, I'll tell Mortimer that you're gay!"

Did she just say what I think she said? I wasn't offended because she obviously wanted me to go. She could have been joking or maybe she wasn't. Either way what the fuck did I care? Being flown on a private jet to a ski resort where the most powerful people in the world were going to be, I'm fucking there! The one thing about Sandy, she made everything sound like it was no big deal. It was only going to be people like Barry Diller,

Diane Von Furstenberg, CNN's Anderson Cooper. You know, the usuals! The list went on and on! I really had no clue how heavy this conference would be, but ignorance is bliss and I was for sure game for the ride!

Sandy then told me: "We are going to be leaving in three days. I'll text you the address to the airport where our jet is. You can meet us there. Just make sure you're on time!" To say I was excited would be an understatement. Wow, what a difference in attitude from Jane to Sandy. Sandy was so elegant, sophisticated and sexy! Let's not forget this woman is six foot tall and gorgeous. Talk about making me look good. I couldn't wait to tell the other stylists about this trip!

The day arrived to go to *The Allen & Company Conference,* and I took a taxi to the private airport. As I boarded the plane, there was Mortimer sitting there with his son Blain. Mortimer had a really surprised look on his face to see me. Mortimer said: "Brandon, what are you doing here?" The shot of fear hit my stomach like a left hand to the liver from Julio Cesar Chavez!

I had to brazen it out. I smiled and told him: "Sandy told me to come so she could have her hair done!" Mortimer's son Blain gets this look on his face like he's disgusted and amused at the same time. Then Mortimer asked: "Brandon, who are you going to be staying with?" I cheekily said: "You, Uncle Mortimer!" The look on his face was so priceless I wish I could have taken a selfie with him at that moment!

Fucking Sandy didn't tell her own husband that I was coming on their plane to one of the most important conferences in the world! How did she leave that one out? "Oh, sorry honey, I'm bringing my hair stylist with us. I guess I forgot to tell you." What women will do for their hair! They'll do whatever it takes, even if it means telling your media mogul husband that you're bringing your hair stylist and, don't worry, he's gay! First of all, I'm the farthest thing from being gay. Plus, I act really straight and that's from my gay friends telling me that. I'm sure, looking back, Mortimer obviously knew I was straight. Mortimer was running the world's media - for sure, he was no dummy!

After the few seconds of being uncomfortable, Mortimer immediately said: "Well, we're glad to have you." Such a politician. He probably wanted to kill Sandy! His son Blaine was a good-looking guy in his early 40s. He lived in London and was helping his dad run the empire. Mortimer also has another son named Brock who would be there as well. Blaine and Brock. Brock was known as the more wild and edgy son. Brock was married to a retired, Australian supermodel turned television producer in Australia. They would be there at the conference as well. I must have looked like a deer in the headlights as I was taking my seat on the plane.

There is nothing in the whole world like being on a private jet. Everything inside was so luxurious and perfect. The leather seats, the wood trim, the chrome finishing that seemed to be shinier than any chrome I had ever seen. When you opened a drawer to get some potato chips, they were the best potato chips that you could buy, like full on artisan potato chips. The candy they had served was the best candy and, oh yes, the stewardess. Fucking hot stewardess. She comes over to me and asks me: "Can I get you anything, Brandon?"

The dirty thoughts started running through my head faster than a crack head can smoke up an eight-ball! In my mind I'm like: "Yes, can you take me in the lavatory and fuck my brains out while we're thirty thousand feet high? Oh, and a chicken sandwich while you're at it!" Of course, I responded with just: "I'll take a chicken sandwich, if that's okay?" She sweetly replied with: "Of course, Brandon, I'll get right on it." She gave me a wink and turned to get my sandwich, wiggling her ass in front of me like that's going to be the dessert. "Manners Brandon, manners," I thought to myself as I watched her tight skirt walk to the other side of the plane. This was going to be a fun trip!

I looked down at the table where Mortimer and Blaine were sitting and in front of them was a private plane brochure, like from a private plane dealer. I'd never seen a private plane brochure before. It made the Ferrari brochure look like a flyer with a car for sale on it. This brochure looked like it cost $500 just to look at the damn thing. The paper was so thick and glossy and I could hear that Mortimer was shopping for a new jet because the one we were currently in was getting old.

This jet that we were flying in cost a meager $40 million. That's all! But what's $40 million when you're running the world? I was able to relax and kick my feet all the way up, which I had never been able to do on a plane before. Private jets are like high performance sports cars. I felt everything which can be a bit unsettling, especially when taking off. I really felt the plane take off like a rocket ship!

A few hours went by and we landed in Sun Valley. As we began our approach, you could see all the other private planes parked around the private airport. It was private for sure because there wasn't a commercial airliner in sight! We landed and de-boarded the plane. As we exited the aircraft, there were black SUV's already there, awaiting our arrival.

On our way to the actual resort where the conference was being held, I was overwhelmed by the beauty of this place. Driving in a black SUV with one of the most powerful families in the world, all just to do hair. I also thought that if I was already starting to travel with Sandy, imagine how much more I was going to be traveling after I met her friends.

We arrived at the resort and as we approached the hotel, or I should say the main building of the resort, there were hundreds of paparazzi standing outside waiting for people like Mortimer to arrive. We got out of the car and the flashes from the cameras lit up the front area like a UFO landing. It was everything like you would imagine. It was fucking *ROCK STAR* shit! Here I was with Sandy and Mortimer, getting hounded by paparazzi. We all had sunglasses on, we all looked really important and there I was right in the middle of it, milking it for everything it's worth.

I even pointed my face towards the cameras in hopes of being put in the newspapers and magazines that were covering the conference. I'd never made an entrance like that in my life! I was on this major incline that was unfolding right before my eyes. It seemed like every day I was experiencing something that I had never experienced before. Every day was becoming better than the next and I hadn't even met Sandy's friends yet.

We settled into the condo where we were staying and I was given the entire top floor! I was already getting hit up by Mortimer's son to have his hair cut by me. I also forgot to mention that our pilot and the hot stewardess wanted their hair done as well, so my schedule was already building. I unloaded my gear in my new quarters and began to unwind. My stomach was still in knots and I wanted to finally settle into the situation. I decided to go for a jog to release some nervous energy. Since I wasn't going to have to work until the next day, I wanted to take advantage of the time I had. I changed into my sweats and headed downstairs to exit the front door.

I walked out the door and looked to my right and there was the designer Diane Von Furstenberg and her husband Barry Diller. I don't know what possessed me to do this, maybe because I was feeling like hot shit, but I walked right up to her and introduced myself. I told her I was Sandy and Mortimer's hairdresser and I would love to do her hair if she wanted since they were staying in the condo next to us. She and Barry both had this look on their face like: "Why the fuck is the hair guy talking to us?" They both kind of nodded their heads and kept going. "Oops," I thought to myself. Oh well, you can't fault me for trying.

I headed out on my jog as this was always a good way to explore new surroundings while getting in a workout. I hadn't run more than 50ft when I see this young guy run by me with really noticeable white hair. Holy shit, that was CNN's Anderson Cooper! Brandon Martinez and Anderson Cooper jogging in the same resort, I think I'd made it! I continued my run through the resort and then I headed out on the main road towards the actual town of Sun Valley.

I remember it being hot and kind of humid. Everything was in bloom so my allergies started to kick in. What it must be like to live like this all the time! What an exciting situation to be a part of! So many thoughts were running through my mind while jogging. What were Sandy's girlfriends going to be like? What other adventures was I going to get into? I promised myself that I wouldn't try to fuck anyone on this trip, as I was sure bringing a girl back to the condo where Mortimer and Sandy were staying probably wouldn't be Kosher! I was already so high on the experience, it was enough just coming down from that.

The next morning, I had Sandy as my first client. I got up, ate some breakfast and got ready to blow out some hair! As I was doing Sandy, she said: "Brandon, my friend Hayden is here with her husband. They are staying close. I told her you were here to do hair. She would love a blow dry." I quickly responded with: "Yes of course just let me know where and when." She gave me the time and address of where they were staying, which was really close to us as well. Sandy said: "My friend Hayden is really beautiful. You will love her and she's really sweet. I told her that you have to do her hair. I know she needs something new." I was excited as this would be the first person that Sandy was going to refer to me. I wrapped up Sandy's hair and finalized the time to do Hayden's hair.

On the way to blow dry Hayden, I was thinking to myself: "How much better can this get?" The money I was making on this trip was like an entire month in the salon. What these women would pay for their hair was insane! I approached the condo where Hayden and her husband were staying. I got to the door and what happened next, I wasn't quite ready for. I knocked on the door and I heard this voice that sounded like an angel was on the other side. The door opened and I saw Hayden for the first time.

I know this sounds kind of corny now as I'm writing about it but nevertheless, she answered the door, and I swear I was looking at the woman of my dreams! All my life, all my thoughts about what kind of woman I would want to be with, how she would look, sound and smell, Hayden had it all. She hit me like a beautiful blonde Mack truck! I actually had to keep myself from staring at her uncontrollably as she introduced herself to me. It was like the Charlie Brown cartoons when they're listening to the teachers and all you hear is sound but no words. She took my breath away! One look at Hayden and I completely forgot about every girl I had ever been with.

Looking back now I have to give Hayden so much credit for me wanting to be the most successful person I could be because if I could have a woman like this, I wouldn't even think about looking at another woman for the rest of my life! Beautiful tan skin that showcased her blonde peach fuzz that that hovered lightly over her body and you could see it when the light hit her body. Crystal blue eyes that stopped me dead in my tracks. Gorgeous blonde hair and I guess the one thing that made me so attracted to her was her smell. The best way I can describe her scent would be an addictive, chemical reaction that truly changed my life and changed my look on what type of woman I want to be with. Her scent was like walking into the Jo Malone counter at Neiman Marcus, finding your favorite scent and attaching it to the most beautiful woman in the world!

For me it was love at first sight! I had to give myself a stern talking to: "Control yourself, Brandon, this woman is married and she is friends with your biggest client, stop staring at her like she just descended from heaven." But I could barely talk, let alone stop staring. I had to tell myself: "She's going to think you're weird if you don't pick up your jaw off the ground." I did everything I could to keep cool and seem like I wasn't being affected as much as I really was!

Hayden invited me inside and began to tell me how she wanted to wear her hair and I began the blow dry. I start to section her hair and my fingers accidentally grazed her neck to move the hair out of the way and I could see little goose bumps rising on her neck. I was so turned on, I thought I was going to faint! I acted like nothing happened and continued the blow dry.

All of a sudden it was like I was back in junior high and I was in front of the prettiest girl in school and I just didn't know how to handle it! Most men never even get to meet the woman of their dreams, let alone do their hair! Here I was standing behind this woman who I just met and I already felt this connection to her.

I don't know what it was, other than the universe putting something in front of me, but I knew from the moment I looked into her eyes that I wanted this woman, and I would be willing to do whatever it took to have her! How did I get so lucky? Why was she put in front of me? But then I had to remind myself – she's married! Women like this aren't waiting around single. Women like this are well tended. So, I kept quiet and continued the blow out. Then I hear: "How did you meet Sandy?" Oh, shit I have to talk to her. I was so fucking nervous. You know that kind of nervous when you try to speak and nothing but garble comes out? That's exactly what happened to me!

I started to mumble a bit and I had to catch myself by slowing down my words to get them out clearly. What was going on with me right now? But I finally answered with: "I met Sandy through this woman named Jane in LA." Hayden didn't know Jane because Hayden was one of Sandy's New York friends. She replied: "Well you must be good if Sandy and Mortimer flew you here!" I just smiled and played up the humble bit: "Oh thank you, that's sweet! Yes, Sandy loves the way I do her hair. I'm so lucky to have her as a client!" I left the part out about Jane and I having the falling out.

At that moment I realized that if I had never met Jane, I would have never met Hayden. In a way, I kind of owed Jane and after meeting Hayden, Jane didn't seem so bad anymore! Boy, did I owe Sandy for this one! I finished her hair and I have to admit, I was on such a cloud while doing Hayden's hair. All of a sudden, I was done and I wasn't going to be able to look at Hayden again for another 24 hours. "So, Hayden, you live in New York?" I asked her. She gave me an angelic smile and said: "Yes, we live on Park Avenue near Sandy and Mortimer's apartment."

I was already trying to figure out how could I get this woman as a regular client, even though she lived on the other side of the country. "Do you come to New York to do hair?" Hayden asked. This was my opening: "I haven't yet but I would love to come and try it out! Hopefully Sandy will have me come." Hayden said: "Well, if you do come to New York, you can sign me up too. I can refer a lot of my friends as well. I think they would love you. Park Avenue needs some LA hair!"

Wow, she wanted me to do her hair in New York! I could hardly contain myself. I was bursting, but forced myself to say politely: "Thank you so much, if I come there I definitely will let you know ahead of time." At the same time, I was thinking to myself: "Can I make your husband disappear and move in?"

I left Hayden's room floating on a cloud of love at first sight! The moment I walked out of her room I told myself that: "I want that woman, and I am going to do whatever it takes to become successful enough to have someone like her." It wasn't like I was thinking I was going to try to hit on her in any way because she was married and that would be stupid, but I had this feeling deep down like I was connected to her. She was so nice and sweet to me right off the bat. It was almost like I was meeting a long-lost family member or some old friend that I hadn't seen in a long time and we were being reunited by chance.

I don't know why I felt this way, I just did. I know it's probably silly to think that one woman could change a man and make him want to be the best that he could be, but that's exactly what Hayden did and does for me to this day. She makes me want to be the better me. I left her place feeling like I had grown up so much more during that blow dry.

All of a sudden, girls that I had been into were no longer good enough for me. Things that I was looking for in a woman had suddenly changed. I wanted Hayden, or at least someone like her, but that's the tragedy, isn't it? I knew that deep down, there wasn't going to be anyone else like her and even though I knew it was wrong, my uncontrollable longing for her was born.

I couldn't stop thinking about her! It hurt inside my gut. It was like the best and worst aching I had ever experienced. The best because I was so happy she entered my life, but the worst because she seemed so unattainable.

I tried telling myself that I could be happy with someone who was like her but the truth is, I just met the woman of my dreams and she was real. And married to someone else. No one else would ever be good enough and I would compare every girl I would date in the future to Hayden. It's like one of my favorite songs from The Capones. In fact, Ronnie wrote a song for Glenda. It's a really simple title and it says everything, The song is called 'She's The One'.

The rest of the trip was amazing, but as far as I was concerned, the trip's highlight was meeting Hayden. I left a day earlier than Sandy and Mortimer since they were going straight to New York from Sun Valley. They booked me a flight home on a commercial airliner. All of a sudden, I became too good to be on a normal flight. To have to be slammed in with the rest of society on a coach flight brought me back to earth. All I could think about was Hayden.

I went home a different person after this trip. It was at this time that I was contemplating putting together a product line. I had thought about it before, or better yet, I would think to myself: "How does a hair stylist make money while he sleeps? He creates a product line!" Now that I had met the woman I really wanted, it gave me the drive to better myself and expand my talents into more of an entrepreneurial space. I guess it's safe to say that meeting Hayden made me want to grow up and be more successful than I ever thought I wanted to be.

I was back in the real world, if you could call my world the real world because it was becoming more and more like a fantasy or a dream. I felt like I had gone through a whirlwind and came out the other end, smarter, more driven and more focused! Sandy had returned from New York and wanted me to go to the house again for her regular, weekly blow dry.

Sandy sent me a text asking me to come at around noon, and if possible, can I cut her friend's hair as well? I responded with: "Yes, of course, no problem, is this a man or a woman?" Deep down I'm hoping it's Hayden and she's decided to leave her husband and be with me. Well, no such luck! She responds with: "It's a man. He's my friend. He will be here at one. You can do his hair after mine." Here we go, another one of her 'friends' – but at least I wouldn't fall in love with this friend!

I arrived at Sandy's house right on time. As usual the extremely polite and welcoming butler, Bill, greeted me at the door. I walked in and notice that there is a staff of people that I've never seen before inside the kitchen area. It was like this group of people sort of took over the kitchen and dining room space. They looked like a staff for someone important but given the fact that this is Mortimer's house, it didn't seem that out of the ordinary.

I headed upstairs and started on Sandy's hair. As I was blowing out her hair she was telling me about her friend that was coming by in an hour. She kept saying: "My friend, he coming soon," in her thick Chinese accent. So halfway through the blow dry I ask: "Who's this friend that you're having me cut?" She responds nonchalantly with: "His name is Tony, Tony Blair." "Oh, cool," I said not thinking too much of it, but then I thought to myself: "Wait a minute, I know that name. Wasn't he the President or Prime Minister of England?"

So, I asked her: "Is this the same Tony Blair that was the former Prime Minister of England?" She quickly replied with: "Yes, my friend Tony, he coming soon. You can wait for him, yes?" I looked at her like she was nuts. She basically just asked me if I could make the time to stay so I could possibly cut the former Prime Minister's hair! If that wasn't a silly question, I don't know what is.

I finished her hair and headed downstairs to wait for Tony, since he was running late. I walked down to where Tony's team was sitting. There was a woman who appeared to be Tony's secretary and this guy who appeared to be one of his security detail. Call me naive or just really American but I had no idea what Tony Blair actually looked like!

I walked up to his secretary and politely introduced myself. She was a small, kind of chubby little English woman who was typing away furiously on her little laptop. I told her: "Hello, my name is Brandon. Looks like I'll be cutting Tony's hair soon. I'm kind of embarrassed but can you pull up a picture of Tony? I have to admit I don't know what he looks like." She looked at me with this big smile because I'm sure I'm one of the first people who has ever said that to her. I'm sure the whole fucking world knows what Tony Blair looks like, except me. Well I'm not big on watching the news so deal with it!

His secretary bursts into laughter and his security guard overheard and started laughing as well. I mean to them, it was like someone not knowing what the President of The United States looked like. After his secretary stopped laughing, she said: "Here's what Mr. Blair looks like and I can't wait to tell him that you didn't know what he looked like!" Man, I was so embarrassed.

She pulled up a photo and to my surprise he was a very good-looking guy. About a half an hour goes by and the butler, Bill, said: "Brandon, come to the front door and check this out." I walked up to the front door and a motorcade of police and Secret Service vehicles begin to arrive in Mortimer's driveway. I couldn't believe that I was about to cut the hair of someone who was brought to me by a motorcade, let alone the former Prime Minister of England!

To my surprise, as soon as Tony got out of the car, he looked right at me and said: "I'm so sorry for keeping you waiting." As he said this, I could see a smirk come over one of the cops faces as the cops realized that they just rushed Tony back, just so he could get his haircut by me. I quickly responded with: "Well, what took you so long?" I quickly added I was kidding and that it absolutely no problem. I couldn't help the wise ass remark, I am who I am!

With Tony was the famous and powerful David Geffen. I had heard of Mr. Geffen, just from being in Hollywood as he's known for being a huge producer and Hollywood mogul. I didn't know what he looked like until that moment. David was bald, so he wasn't going to need a haircut.

We all walked back into the house as the motorcade exited the property. We all walked upstairs and up to Sandy's bathroom where the haircut would take place. I was so nervous doing this haircut because here is the former Prime Minister, David Geffen - who's a billionaire - and Sandy, all watching me while Mortimer and the rest of the staff were downstairs.

David had the shiniest skin I had ever seen. I was so tempted to ask him what moisturizer he was using because it was working for him! I've been around some of the most beautiful women in the world, with amazing skin, but David Geffen had the nicest skin I have ever seen on a man!

I sat Tony down and started the haircut. As I was cutting his hair, they were all talking about random things. I was so focused on the haircut, I tried to stay out of their conversation as much as possible just so I could listen and soak all of this up. I mean, this was a huge moment in my career and I didn't want to forget anything.

Sandy was talking away and laughing about God knows what because again, she was a bit hard to understand and then all of a sudden, David Geffen hit Sandy on the shoulder and said: "Girl, when are you going to learn some English?" Oh my God, I almost fell over laughing at that one. Great skin and a sense of humor. I really liked this David Geffen guy! He was fucking hilarious.

That's what's cool about this job. I got to see the wealthiest, most powerful people in normal, everyday situations and believe me, they say and do funny shit! We all laughed at David's comment. By this time, I was almost done as they had a busy schedule ahead of them for the evening. Dinners, meetings, drinks and more meetings. Life for powerful people is very busy! As I got close to the end of the haircut, he looked in the mirror and gave me a thumbs up. "Phew," I thought to myself. Thank God he loved the haircut. Before I knew it, it was over. We all walked back downstairs and there was Bill, waiting for me with the crispiest, $100 bills I had ever felt!

Between Sandy and Tony, it had been a nice little score! I always loved Bill the Butler because he always made sure I got paid in cash. Every time I was paid by them, it was always in $100 bills and they were always really crispy - as if there was a money printing machine somewhere in the house and they would have them ready for me after every visit. I thanked Sandy over and over for this one and made myself disappear back down the hill, back to West Hollywood. What a fucking day!

Sandy sure had a way of getting people to do what she wanted. I've always told everyone the same thing when they ask me about Sandy. People always ask me: "What's Sandy like in person?" I always respond with the same answer: "Mark my words people, one day, Sandy will be running the world. She's no fucking dummy, that's for sure."

Just as I thought things couldn't get any better, she hit me up a few days later and said she had two jobs for me. The first job was going to China with her to do Cosmopolitan magazine in Beijing. The next job was a referral for her friend Anne. She texted me and told me that she gave my contact to Anne, who was about to marry one of the owners of Google and said that Anne would contact me shortly.

Sure enough, I got the call from Anne, who was in LA. She wanted to know what would be the best time to come to the salon to talk and possibly do her hair? I booked her on the schedule for a few days away and told her I would see her then. Sandy was also going to be in town and she had me come back to the house again for a quick blowout before I would finally meet Anne.

As I was blowing out Sandy, she gave me the full run down on Anne and her soon-to-be husband, Sergey Brin. He's one of the two owners who founded Google. Sandy insisted: "I'm going to tell Anne that she should hire you for her wedding!" I couldn't believe this was all happening! I never thought in a million years that I would ever go to a private island just to do hair. Anne would end up flying me on a private jet for a whole week, to do hair for this wedding! Just when I thought it couldn't get better, Sandy hits me with China and a wedding on a private island for the fucking owner of Google!

Talk about Asian Persuasion!!

GOOGLED

Usually when I get referrals from clients, I Google their name. Most of the time I know who they are if they're a big celebrity, but occasionally I get the rich clients that are not in the spotlight, but behind the scenes. That's when I pull out the phone and do a quick search for them.

So, when Sandy referred me to her friends Anne and Sergey Brin, I typed their names into Google – and was left grinning at the search results. Ironically, Sergey was a huge name in the tech world – he actually owned Google!

Of course, I jumped at the chance. Not only was I getting some prestigious clients, but I was also going to be flown out to a private island to do their hair. This was a dream job. Sandy revealed that Anne and Sergey were about to get married and she thought that Anne might need some help with her hair. Sandy was going to help her with a dress and she was going to have Anne come see me when they visited Los Angeles.

Anne and Sergey were not the usual Hollywood type clients. In fact, they weren't Hollywood at all. They were from Silicon Valley, which is right near San

Francisco and the center of the tech world. All the world's largest high-tech corporations, including the headquarters of 39 businesses in the Fortune 1,000 and thousands of start-up companies, are based there, including Google, Apple, eBay, Facebook, Intel, Netflix and Tesla.

In fact, Anne and Sergey were as far removed from the Hollywood 'type' as you could be. They would've been much more at home in *Revenge of the Nerds* than *The Aviator!* They looked – and behaved – like any normal couple. They didn't flash their wealth about or throw it in your face. It was a refreshing change after being in Hollywood.

Anne was beautiful in an understated way. I was used to all these glamorous Hollywood stars who had been nipped and tucked and everything's tight and in the right place, looking half their age. But Anne was a natural beauty. There was nothing fake about her at all and I loved having that canvas to work with. Honestly, it was refreshing to see.

At first, I was surprised that a guy liked Sergey, with all his billions, didn't have a 20-something trophy wife on his arm, but I soon realized that Silicon Valley is like the rest of the world - they care much more about how big your brains are instead of the size of your boobs.

Anne did all communications through email. The one thing about all these tech billionaire types – or at least all the ones I met – is that they all communicate completely through email. I guess they want to have a track record of everything they do. They never call on the telephone and hardly ever do they text message. I found that strange but then again, who am I? Maybe I'm on the late train.

Anne came to LA and emailed me to book an appointment at the salon to do her color and possibly hire me for their wedding. In the background, Sandy was pushing my name to her, telling her that she should hire me for the wedding. The way Sandy explained how and where the wedding was going to be, it seemed like a pretty awesome wedding.

So, Anne came into the salon and I had booked out extra time especially for her so we could have time to discuss what she wanted to do with her hair. All in all, she was pretty nerdy, but a hippie at the same time. I immediately knew what to do with her hair, but I waited to see what she had in mind. That's the one thing about me as a stylist, I try to always listen to the client first before I chime in on what I think.

The way I figured it, they're the ones paying me, so the least I could do is listen. Also, it's better to let the client work out what she wants in her head, so that whatever we do seems like her idea. That way, in the end, they feel like they're part of the process. Only then will I add some critiques to their suggestions. I never let them think that it was all me.

A good lesson for any hair stylist is to let the client seem like they're the ones coming up with the ideas. People love to listen to themselves talk. When they think that they're coming up with something genius and you add to it by saying: "Oh yeah, that sounds amazing," they love you that much more, even though I usually end up doing what I want!

So, Anne started to tell me what she thought and I nodded and said: "Yes, that sounds amazing," even though I hated what she was suggesting. She actually wanted me to put bright red streaks in her hair, like she was going to a rave or something. I tactfully said: "Anne, are you sure that's the look that you want for your wedding?" Again, I made her answer the question. She thought about it for a second. "Maybe not so bright," she answered. I'm thinking to myself: "Of course I'm right." But out loud I told her: "What I'll do then to give you that warm feel is, I'll add some warmer pieces through, along with the highlights. This way you can still have the red, just not 'punk rock' red. We don't want to give Sergey a heart attack at the rehearsal dinner."

She thought that was a great idea and said: "I would love that." So, I mixed the color and we began. The whole time I was thinking: 'When is she going to ask about the wedding?' I've never been on a private island and I'm dying to go!" But, of course, I had to keep my cool. Better she comes out and asks me, but my stomach was in knots waiting for her to say something. As I'm doing the color she is mostly doing emails, of course.

Then she started to open up the conversation. She asked me how I met Sandy, how long had I been doing her hair? She told me: "Sandy says you're the best! I totally wasn't going to come in today but Sandy pretty much forced me to get my hair done today, and is even helping me with my dresses." "Dresses?" I asked: "As in plural?" She smiled and told me: "Yes. We're going away for a week for the wedding. I'm having a different themed party every night of the week on the Island. Sandy is pretty much my style council."

"Island?" I thought to myself. Now, Sandy has an aggressive way about her. Plus, with the thick Chinese accent you're kind of helpless in doing what she wants.

You usually end up saying: "OK Sandy, OK." I've seen this happen in person. It's best to just agree with whatever she says.

As we were talking, I could see how smart Anne was. She said she was starting a company that offered a way to swab inside your cheek and analyze your DNA. From this they can see what kind of diseases you might be prone to. It's like being able to map out your family genes. She said it was called genome-mapping. It sounded really hard and really fucking confusing to me, but ultimately brilliant. Being married to someone who can tell you what you're going to die from is a good thing. I guess there are people out there who marry for brains instead of looks. Just goes to show how shallow I am!

As she was telling me about her company, I think she started to realize that she was losing me. I was about to finish up with the color and put her under the dryer. I asked her if she wanted something to drink and did she want any magazines? She answered yes to both questions and I said: "I'll be right back," as I brought her the water, then I went over to the magazine basket.

Now most of the time with magazines I would bring an assortment from the good stuff like US Weekly, In Touch, you know...the gossip garbage, then throw in a fashion magazine to mix it up. But I had a hunch that she wouldn't care about either of those subjects. I needed to get this job and I needed to do a little nudging to close this wedding deal. So instead, I take her a Women's Health magazine and two wedding magazines.

The vibe I got from Anne was that she was not too concerned with the celebrities like Sandy, so I figured giving her the US Weekly would only insult her intelligence. I also figured that with her fit figure she is into being healthy, so the Women's Health magazine would fit. Then, hit her with the wedding magazine at the end to try to push an offer out on the table.

I handed her the magazines, gave her a wink and said: "I'll be back to check on you in 10 minutes." I was fucking dying inside at this point. Every minute she was under the dryer was like an hour. I found myself pacing up and down the salon like a mad man with nowhere to go. Finally, her bell went off! I lifted the dryer and made sure the color was perfect before I started the cut. I send her to the shampoo bowl to be washed and I just know, at this point, that she's going to ask me to do the wedding.

I mean, who else is she going to get? I can't imagine that there is anyone good in Palo Alto, wherever the fuck that is? My assistant brings her back after her hair is washed. Right as I'm about to start cutting, Anne quickly asked me. "So, how do you think my hair should be for the wedding?" My heart starts pumping! Inside my head I'm like: "Yes, here it comes!" I'm a wreck on the inside, but I'm so fucking calm and collected on the outside.

So completely nonchalantly I asked: "Well, what are you planning on wearing? Or better yet, what are the dresses going to be like, since we have more than one?" She threw out some options to me that Sandy had picked out for her. Then I remembered Sandy telling me that she was finding her a dress because Anne was going to buy a wedding dress at Target!

And then she actually told me about Target! I started to laugh and scolded her: "Oh no, Anne. You can't wear a wedding dress from Target. Do they even have wedding dresses? I don't remember a wedding section."

She immediately responded with: "I love Target! It's my favorite!" How do you respond to that? But I still didn't want her to think that I was pushing to do the wedding. In situations like this, it's always better to play dumb.

Anne then launched into an explanation of the entire wedding week. It's really crazy to me what rich people will spend their money on. She said: "I want there to be a different theme every night because we're going to be on the island for a week. The day we get married Sergey wants to take one of the yachts out to a sandbar about a mile off shore and have the ceremony there, on the sand bar." I asked her how she planned to do all this without getting wet? She laughed really hard.

She then said the actual day she was getting married, was the only day she wouldn't need her hair done since they'll be swimming into the ocean once they're married. That's how the ceremony would end. She's swimming for her wedding ceremony! That was definitely a first - and a last - as far as weddings I have done. Not one of my brides I have done had ever wanted to swim for the ceremony!

I was totally engaged in what she was saying, laughing with her about the swimming part. I even said: "Oh, I've never heard of a wedding like that before. You'll be the only couple I ever heard of doing that." Whether the compliments worked, or whether it was the fact that she liked the color, I don't know but then she just blurted out: "So can I get you to come down for the week to do my hair?" I didn't even flinch. Without skipping a beat I said, "Absolutely!"

Right at that moment I was the King of Fucking Cool. "Of course, I would love to go. When and where?" I asked. She responded with: "In a few weeks. I'll have our life manager email you everything." Life manager? What the hell is a life manager? But I didn't care as long as I got the email!

So, there I was sitting with the future Mrs. Google, and she just asked me to do her wedding. Movie stars don't even come close to the amount of money these people have. Maybe a Saudi Prince. As I'm about to start the haircut I asked her: "What island are you getting married on?" Now I'm thinking it's going to be something like Hawaiian or somewhere like that. Somewhere nice and tropical. She told me: "Oh, the island is private. David Copperfield, the magician owns it. It's called Musha Cay. You'll most likely fly in on the jet with our DJ and security. Tony, who does our air-traffic control will coordinate the transportation." A million things were going through my mind. I thought I was going to faint. I didn't know that you could hire your own air-traffic control person!

To this day, I don't even remember cutting her hair. It all seemed like a dream. Someone's else's dream! Everything she said about the wedding came true. It was one of the most amazing places I had ever seen.

A few days later I received an email from Anne and Sergey's life manager. I finally found out what a 'life manager' was. It was a really politically correct - and fancy - way to say assistant! The 'life manager/assistant' emailed me the details of the trip. I was going to be gone for six days. The assistant asked me how much I was going to charge for the six-day trip. I asked for $10,000 for the entire trip. They came back at me with $8,500. What was I going to do? I didn't want to lose the gig. I was a little shocked that these billionaires were working me down $1,500 but fuck it. $8,500 for six days of work doesn't suck either! That was the most money I had ever made in six days of work.

I was going to be flown commercially from Los Angeles to San Jose, then hop on their private jet, a G5 to be exact. I would be on the G5 with the DJ, their head security and Tony, the personal air traffic control person. I really wanted to meet this guy Tony! His job seemed so interesting to me!

Not two weeks later, I was on the way to LAX to fly to San Jose where Anne and Sergey house their jets. I say jets as in plural because the Google crew had about three jets at that time. They had two G5's and, according to Tony, they had an actual commercial jet that they turned into a party jet. Sergey, Anne and the other owner of Google, Larry and his fiancé, would fly down to the private island with the rest of the wedding party on the big jet. I even think that Sergey was flying the jet himself, from what I remember. I had the absolute luxury of flying on their G5 with just three other people. So amazing!

After I landed in San Jose, there was someone there to pick me up and take me to the private airport that wasn't far from the San Jose Airport. I arrived at the private airport and I see the G5. I know it was dorky, but I had to take a photo of myself getting on this jet. I have to admit that this jet was much nicer than Mortimer's jet. Sorry, Uncle Mortimer!

I walked onto the jet and it was like a fucking dream! It looked like a flying Bentley! The inside was so beautiful. The wood trimming was shiny and perfect. Even the carpet was amazing! I sat down in my seat and I could have just melted in the chair. The leather smelled like it was brand new. The seats were a beautiful, off-white, creamy color that felt so good against my skin. It made me never want to fly commercially again!

Just a few minutes after I boarded the plane, DJ Spider walked in. DJ Spider was a pretty well-known DJ in Hollywood. I had never met him before, but I had sure heard about him. He was tall and skinny and had this longish, curly hair that hung down past his shoulders. We immediately hit it off! I'm glad that I would have someone close to my age and from my hood to hang out with.

Next in walked Tony! Here he was, the famous Tony! Tony - the air traffic control guy. Tony was a tall, thin guy who looked like he could be either Hispanic or Middle Eastern. Tony asked me if I had a good flight coming here on Southwest. I responded: "It's no G5, but I was able to manage." He just laughed. He confided: "Believe me I know. After working for Sergey and Larry, you get spoiled really quick." He went on to tell me how he had gotten the job and said that he basically handled all transportation, whether it's on land, sea or air.

The plane began to take off and we accelerated like we were in a sports car. The take-off was so fast, I felt like I was on Space Mountain! We hit the cruising altitude in the blink of an eye. The other guy that was on board was their private security guy, Eric, who was coming with us because we would actually get to the island before the rest of the wedding party. The wedding party would arrive a day after us depending on weather conditions.

For a private security person, Eric was very low key. He had a really mellow personality and a real sweetness to him. We all talked about our lives, where we all came from etc. We had five hours to get to know each other and the private jet was so nice, I would've been fine if the flight was 10 hours!

We landed in Nassau where the private jet airport was located. What I didn't know was that we were all going to have to take a smaller 'Island Hopper' plane to the actual private island! The island hopper plane didn't sound that safe, but Tony assured me that these small planes were fine. I assumed Tony knew what he was talking about, I mean, he did this for a living!

I'm admitting now that I'm totally afraid of heights. When I'm on a commercial airliner, I always feel a bit safer because it's big, so I feel a lot more protected on a bigger aircraft. The smaller the aircraft, the more vulnerable I become. The first five hours being on the private plane was a dream come true, but that dream come true was about to turn into a small nightmare. As soon as I got a look at this island hopper plane, the movie *Six Days, Seven Nights* entered my mind. That plane crashed down on an island even with Harrison Ford flying it - and this plane kind of looked the same as that plane.

Tony went up to speak to the pilot who looked like the only thing he could fly was a paper airplane. He was a bit slovenly and chubby. His shirt was half way tucked in and it appeared that he hadn't shaved in a few days. What a contrast from the pilot that flew us over on the private jet.

But I didn't have any choice. If I wanted to attend this wedding, I would have to get on the island hopper. So, we all boarded the little plane and another movie entered my mind – *La Bamba!*" I started to whistle the Buddy Holly song *Peggy Sue*, as we began to board. The DJ gave me a look of terror as he knew what I was whistling. The seat belts on the plane looked like they had been through the ringer and the inside was pretty bare.

Now I'm not a religious person, but I felt this was the perfect time to say a prayer as we started to take off. It was like we flew from San Jose in a Ferrari, but were finishing the trip in a Pinto! I admit that my eyes were closed on take-off! We hit cruising altitude and fortunately this was going to be a short, one-hour flight.

The DJ and I were talking, trying to keep our minds off the fact that we're in this jinky little plane. He was also a bit nervous. Just as we started to relax, we noticed that the pilot was flying the plane with no hands!

He literally had his hands, relaxed on the back of his neck as if he was taking a siesta! I took a photo of it, but for the life of me I couldn't find it for this book. It kind of took our fear to another level! We all just had to laugh at this point.

We got closer to the island and off to the left I could see a tiny, little landing strip that was detached from the main island. It was like we were landing on an aircraft carrier, but with no crew or help standing by. If this landing strip was compared to a bikini, it would be the skinniest, G-string you could imagine. The butterflies in my stomach started to increase and I thought to myself: "Maybe I should have negotiated more money!"

We begin our approach to the small, minuscule, landing strip. I felt like there was no point in keeping my eyes open for the landing. I just shut them tight and hoped for the best. Luckily, before I could throw-up, we were on the ground. There was a boat waiting for us that would take us from the landing strip to the island, which was only half a mile away.

The island was already being set up for the wedding. On the island were about five mansion-style houses where guests would be staying. There were also luxury tents that were spread out on the beach just a few feet from the water. I was given one of the tents to stay in while I was there for the week. Since the entire wedding party was going to come the next day, we were pretty much alone on the island, which was kind of eerie but, then again, there's no other land in sight so you're completely safe. I've never felt so alone and safe at the same time.

I unpacked my gear and threw on some swim trunks and went for a swim, right in front of my tent. It was just steps from the tent to the ocean. Such a paradise! The ocean water was 80 degrees plus and it was marvelous!

As I was floating on my back looking at the early night sky, I thought to myself: "If this doesn't show you how good you are Brandon, then nothing will!" Being flown to a private island on a private jet is about the ultimate you can achieve as a hairstylist as far as freelance jobs go. I finished my swim and retired to my luxurious, Four Seasons-style tent. Look at me now, Mom, I've hit the big time!

The next morning was going to be another day of just hanging out. The wedding party wasn't arriving until later in the day, so I wouldn't have to do hair until then, if Anne even wanted her hair done that night. I walked around and introduced myself to the staff. Most of the workers were Bahamians that lived on neighboring islands. I figured that the Bahamian workers might be able to score me some pot. I started a conversation with one of the workers and hinted that I was bummed that I couldn't bring any weed on the trip. I told the worker that I was the hair stylist, so he knew that I was cool and wouldn't rat on him.

He then told me, in his thick Bahamian accent: "I can get you weed, man!" I mean, not to stereotype anyone, but most of the Bahamian workers looked like they played in a reggae band, so I figured there would be weed everywhere. I literally was on an island in the middle of nowhere, so I would've paid whatever for a gram of pot! He informed me that I would have to wait a few hours, but the pot was on the way. I continued my introductions with the rest of the island crew and made myself available if anyone needed any help setting up.

What's a lonely hair stylist to do on a private island with no hair to do yet? Swim naked in the ocean, of course. I headed back down to my tent, stripped off my clothes and swam in the ocean as naked as a newborn baby. "This is the fucking life!" I said to myself.

Speaking of the life, let's talk about the food that's served on a private island.

My first meal was on a yacht. Oh, I forgot to mention the yachts! Besides the mansions on the island and the tents on the beach, Sergey had chartered six yachts to sit right off the beach. They were there for people to stay in and they could travel back and forth to have lunch or dinner. Each tent on the beach came with its own Sea-Doo, which is a brand of jet-ski. I hopped on my Sea-Doo and headed over to one of the yachts for my first meal. This was the first time that I would set foot on a real yacht! I drove my Sea-Doo up to the yacht and anchored it where the rest of the Sea-Doos were parked. I climbed up on the yacht and was greeted by the boat's captain.

The captain looked like a fucking pirate in shorts and sandals. He sported a big, Santa Claus belly and was smoking a cigar on the deck. He asked me how I was doing and what would I like to eat. He grinned and asked: "We have fresh lobsters and the chef is preparing lobster tail salads. Would you like one?" Like he even had to ask me that? "Yes, please, thank you so much!" I started to tell the captain who I was and what I was doing there. He asked: "So let me get this straight, they're paying you to be here just to do hair? Like that's it? Wow, Brandon, what a life you have! You must be really good!" I responded with: "Well, I was referred by a really powerful woman named Sandy, who's really close with Anne the bride. I feel really lucky to be here. You're right, I do have the life. It's going to be hard to top this job!"

I go to the dining room of the luxurious yacht and sit while I await the lobster tail salad. Before the food comes, one of the boat's waiters or service person came over and asked me: "Good afternoon Brandon, the chef wants to know if you would like romaine lettuce or spinach lettuce? Would you like one lobster tail, or two lobster tails in your salad?" So many options for one salad! What service, what attention! Man, I am going to be rich too because if this is what it's like, I'm fucking in!

The waiter came back with my salad and it's all lobster tail. Usually when you go to a restaurant, they give you only so much of the good stuff, but this yacht was giving you the goods! Chunks and chunks of the most delicious lobster I'd ever tasted! I swallowed my first bite and got chills down my spine because the lobster was so good. Who needed lettuce at this point? I had two lobster tails staring right at me saying, "Eat me Brandon, eat me!!!" To this day, I still remember that lobster salad as one of the highlights of that trip.

So, there I was, sitting on one of the most beautiful yachts I had ever seen, eating the biggest lobster salad I could imagine, on a private island! I must have died and gone to heaven. Maybe we did go down on that shitty little plane and now I'm in heaven! I wrapped up lunch and headed back to the island on my new Sea-Doo. As I walked back to the tent, I saw my new pot dealer flagging me down so we could do the weed exchange. He unloaded like an eighth of pot, which street value was $60. I throw him a nice crispy Benjamin for his troubles. His eyes lit up when I said keep the change! I promised him that I wouldn't tell anyone and that I would just say that I brought it myself.

I walked over to the bar where they were still setting up and asked them for a can of soda. I had to get junior high-style by making a pipe from the soda can. I headed back to my tent and proceeded to light up! Ahhh, I could definitely get used to this for sure. My first day on the island was really just a mini little vacation for me. I smoked a few bowls of the weed and retired in my tent. I knew this was going to be a great trip, but nothing like this! The only thing I was missing was a naked girl in my bed.

Well, Brandon, ask and you will receive.

The next day, the wedding party arrived. I met Sergey and his partner Larry for the first time and Anne got an excited look when she saw me. She asked if everything was good and if my trip was okay. I responded with: "Yeah, the G5 didn't suck and the lobster salad I had yesterday on the yacht wasn't so terrible either!" She introduced me to Linda, who was her business partner in her new company, 23andMe. 23andMe is huge now, but back then it hadn't been born yet.

I met all the nerds that were going to party like it's 1999 for the next week. Big brains pay the bills and then some with this crowd! Not only did they fly in their close work friends, but they also flew in their massage therapist and their yoga instructor. The island now had the total beauty squad! Hair, massage and yoga, all on one island. I could see the yoga instructor checking me out. It turned out that the yoga instructor was staying in the tent next to mine.

As everyone started to settle in, I headed back to my tent to see the sunset. I walked down to the beach and got nice and comfy on the sand. I started to light up and smoke more pot. Some of Anne's friends saw me smoking and their eyes lit up when they saw that I had pot. "Where did you find pot?" asked one of her girlfriends. I lied: "Oh, I brought it with me. I figured I'd be good flying on the jet. "Can we smoke some too?" Asked the friend with an eager look on her face. "Yes, of course, I won't be able to smoke all of this while I'm here." I packed up my soda can pipe and passed it to Anne's friends. All three of us were getting lit as the yoga instructor walked up.

Monica, the yoga instructor was really excited that I had weed as well. Now remember, this was only the second day that I'm here and already I'm making friends through marijuana! Monica was checking me out hard. We had only met a few hours ago and she's licking her chops checking me out. I was trying to be conservative as far as sleeping with anyone on the island because of just that. We were on a small island, and if I fuck someone, everyone is going to know. I played it cool as we all smoked into the late night. We were all getting to know each other, while getting high. It was amazing.

Meeting new friends, exchanging Anne and Sergey stories, which was great for me because I really didn't know them well. They all asked me how I got this job and I told them that I did Sandy and Mortimer's hair. They all knew who I was talking about since Mortimer was so damn famous! "Wow," they all said. "What's it like doing people like that?" At first, I was sort of taken back by the questions because here were the friends of some of the most powerful people in the tech world and they were interested in knowing about my famous clients.

Tech people are really low-key, at least this crowd was. The Google crowd didn't act like celebrities. They acted exactly the way they were, like nerds! I was the first, 'celebrity hair stylist' that these people had really met and they were so interested in Hollywood. I started telling all my crazy, rich women stories, the murder on Third Street, what celebrities are like, which ones were assholes and which ones weren't.

The yoga instructor Monica blurted out: "You should write a book. I would read that book immediately!" I responded with: "Oh I could write an amazing book. Who doesn't want to read about Sex, Hair and Billionaires?" I went on about what my salon was like and the other crazy hair stylists that I worked with.

I guess living in Silicon Valley is very much like a bubble and it couldn't be more different than Hollywood. I held court all night as the sun went down. I was catching the yoga instructor checking me out relentlessly. It was humid, so I took my shirt off to get her all hot and bothered. It definitely worked!

The next morning came like a flash. I was a little groggy from the cheap, brown weed I had scored from the island worker, but beggars can't be choosers! I walked over to one of the main areas to get some coffee and maybe enjoy a ridiculously luxurious omelet. Most of the guests were already up and moving around. Even though this was a nerdy crowd, it was a fitness crowd as well. Most of these people weren't into partying so it was also an early crowd. I met up with Anne and we discussed the evening ahead.

That night the party was going to be on one of the yachts. I would need to be on that designated yacht by five o'clock. I had the day to fuck off and do some more relaxing. She told me how she wanted her hair, which was going to be kind of intricate. She wanted her hair curled with the curling irons for a beachy, bohemian look. Anne's hair is as straight and fine as it gets. Holding curl, at night, on a yacht no less, was going to be challenging!

I headed back to my tent to get some more rest before the evening. Monica, the yoga instructor saw me and said: "Hey Brandon, I'm teaching a yoga class in an hour on the beach and I want you to come!" I could see where this was going. I was definitely game for whatever this girl wanted to throw my way. She was really pretty, but a little thicker than what I was used to. I'm really into skinny girls and Monica had a little bit of meat on her bones, but when on a private island, beggars can't be choosers.

Plus, she had a very sexy way about her. Long brown hair, beautiful skin that she probably doused with coconut butter or some natural hippy dippy body cream that all yoga people use. She smelled like patchouli oil, which I didn't love but again, I was game. I agreed to do the yoga class and told her that that I would show up before it started.

I headed into my tent and searched through my luggage to find something that would be appropriate to wear while I'm downward facing dog! I found a pair of shorts and figured I wouldn't need a shirt since were on the beach. I showed up to the class, shirtless and ready to get my stretch on! Monica was giving me fuck eyes while she started her instructions.

Anne was also taking the class as well as some of the other wives that came out for the wedding. We are all doing the poses that Monica is calling out. My body was tan and sweaty at this point and I was really in shape, so I kind of stood out from the crowd. I was in a class with Silicon Valley moms who were definitely not into their looks like women in Hollywood. I was getting extra attention from Monica. Helping me with my poses. I could feel her hands press down on me when she would adjust me. I could feel her fingers stroking the side of my body. I knew that she wanted to touch my body and I could see the other women staring at me while I went into the different poses. She knew what she was doing.

I always find that female yoga instructors would push their boundaries with me…and Monica was pushing for sure. I had absolutely no problem with her pushing anything of mine! I was game for anything on this trip. Traveling and doing hair abroad wouldn't be complete without someone fucking me good and Monica was already giving me the signs that sex was going to be a possibility.

Monica was wearing a tiny, skimpy outfit with basically nothing underneath. I have yet to meet a yoga instructor who wears a bra because I could see Monica's tits from the other side of the beach! Every time she bent over, I got a full view of what was to come! As the class went on, we were giving each other looks out of the corner of our eyes. When attraction starts, it becomes chemical! It's like trying to slow down a train at full speed. No point in slowing down. It's full steam ahead. I've always loved aggressive girls and I've never shied away from what obviously is going to happen.

I actually like when girls get super aggressive with me. When I was a child, my female babysitters were always trying to molest me. Even at an early age. I guess nothing has changed! We finished the class and I headed back to my tent. It was getting to be mid-afternoon at this point and I was supposed to be on the party yacht by 4:30pm.

I had a quick shower, gathered my gear and headed towards the beach and onto my Sea-Doo with my hair bag attached to my back and off I went! I never imagined that I would in a million years be en route to do hair on a yacht via a Sea-Doo. I arrived at the yacht and grabbed a quick lunch before Anne arrived.

I was given a designated spot to do hair on the yacht where there were electric outlets for me to plug in my curling irons. An hour went by and Anne and company showed up for the night's themed yacht party. We were docked about a quarter mile off shore, so I could see people coming to the boat from the sand.

Anne sat down in the chair that I had prepared for her and I started to blow out her hair to get it ready for the curling iron. Her soon-to-be husband, Sergey, boarded with his partner Larry and his Russian cousin who was also a scientist or computer engineer. As I was blowing out her hair, I realized that my blow dryer was running extra hot! Like it had been super-charged or something. Then, I plugged in my curling iron and it started popping, like it was getting too much voltage! Turns out, the voltage on the yacht was European voltage! It was too powerful for my tools and I didn't know what to do!

This was a huge problem as here I was, stranded on a yacht and I couldn't finish her hair. I started to stress as I wanted to do a good job, but I didn't want to burn her hair! Sergey and his Russian, scientist cousin overheard what was happening and came over to see what was going on. Anne said: "Sergey, Brandon's blow dryer and curling irons are running too hot because the voltage is higher than what they can handle."

Before I could blink, Sergey and his Russian cousin jumped in and one grabbed my blow dryer while the other one grabbed my curling iron. They started examining my hot tools, no pun intended, and proceeded to adjust the blow dryer and curling irons accordingly to be able to handle the voltage.

First of all, I dropped out of high school so math class was a wash for me. These two brilliant brains mathematically calculated the voltage with what my tools could handle and with a few adjustments to the settings, I was able to use the tools without them burning out. So here I was on a yacht, with the creators of fucking Google and the owner himself was adjusting my hot tools with his Russian scientist cousin, while I'm standing there in awe. It almost seemed like it was a dream and sometimes I felt like it was.

I couldn't imagine any other hair stylists having these experiences. With a few turns of the knobs and a couple minor tweaks, my curling iron and blow dryer were back in business. I think I was safe to say that I am probably the only hair stylist in the world that has had his hot tools worked on by the fucking owners of Google!

I curled her hair like a champ and made her look like the princess she wanted to be. They asked me to stay for the party because they were casual like that. I could tell that they didn't want to act like they were above anyone. They wanted everyone to feel like an equal and it showed! I loved being on this job!

Not only were the aesthetics incredible, but everything about these people was so different than people in Hollywood. Usually when I'm doing an actress or someone in the entertainment business, they want all the attention on them. In this case, Anne and Sergey were concerned with everyone else and their well-being, including mine. To jump in like that and help me fix my curling iron and my blow dryer without throwing me attitude and to have just genuinely helped me because it was their instinct, that said a lot about who they are as people.

Anne's hair turned out really beautiful and everyone was happy. All the while, Monica was on the boat looking really hot! She was wearing another outfit that barely covered her body. Her skin was shiny and tan from being in the sun all day. Granted we were still on the boat, so she was staying somewhat away from me, but that's when you know they want you. When a girl has to force herself to stay away from you, it's an inner struggle that they have.

Little did I know that she was actually engaged to be married! I didn't find this out until later. As the night carried on I was getting tired and it was time to head back to my tent on the beach. The rest of the party was winding down and everyone was headed back to the island. In my tent, I rolled up a nice fat joint and sat my tired ass on the sand and stared into the beautiful starry sky.

The lingering scent of my pot carried its way to the other tents and before I knew it, I had a crowd around me sharing my Bahamian weed, including Monica. We laughed, we smoked, told stories and laughed some more. I was holding court for about 10 people, so my fat joint had quickly been reduced to a fat roach! The crowd didn't want to stop smoking and asked if I had more. Fortunately for them, I had a huge, Jamaican-style bag ready to be smoked because I wasn't flying home with it.

As I waltzed back into my tent, Monica followed. We left the others outside, chatting and laughing. I sat down next to my bed and began to roll up another spliff. Monica sat down next to me as I'm rolling up this joint like a professional pot smoker and she takes one look at me and asks: "Do you want to fuck around?"

Even though I was high, there was no hesitation on my end. I immediately kissed her deeply. We put our tongues into each other's mouths. Her hands were traveling up and down my body and she began to unzip my pants, or shorts, I should say. She grabbed my cock and went right down and started blowing me.

I was taking her clothes off while she was blowing me and after about five minutes of that, I grabbed her body and I had her sitting on my face while she's sucking me off. What we both didn't realize was that with the lights that surrounded the tents, and the fact that the tents were somewhat sheer, everyone saw our silhouettes doing each other!

After I made her cum the first time, I pulled her up to the bed and starting fucking her from behind. She had a fuller, thicker body but because she was a full-on Yogi, her body was still tight and sexy. We fucked for about 15 or 20 minutes not knowing that we were giving a show to the people outside! When you're in mid-fuck, you're not really concerned with being quiet and she wasn't really holding back. Our bodies were so tan and sweaty from the sex and her pussy was so wet, it was like we were bathing in lubricant. We kept going for a bit longer until we both came.

The moment she finished we started to put our clothes back on. I immediately noticed a look of guilt on her face. She kept quiet as she finished putting her clothes back on. I looked at her and asked: "You okay?" I'm thinking to myself: "I didn't do anything wrong. She came on to me, so I know I wasn't being aggressive or out of line." But it was like she had split personalities and all of a sudden, she turned into her quiet self.

She went from wild animal to quiet animal. Then she really surprised me and came over to me and put her tongue in my mouth one more time. She looked into my eyes while we were making out like it was going to be the last time she would see me. The way she kissed me was like I was going off to war and she knew I wasn't coming back.

After she detached her mouth from mine, she quickly said: "I'm engaged to be married next month!" "Holy matrimony Batman," is what blurted out of my big mouth. She started to laugh, but I could tell that the wave of guilt was growing. Was she guilty for fucking me? Did she maybe realize that she didn't want to give up sex with other people? She fucked me like we were boyfriend and girlfriend. She loved it and it showed.

Maybe I came into her life for a reason. Maybe getting married was going to be a mistake for her. Either way, it was really hot for me and, ultimately, I knew that, especially after telling me she was engaged, that I would probably never see her again.

Well, that's exactly what happened. I never did see her again. I don't know if she ever got married. Whether she did or not, by the end of the week, everyone on the island knew that the hairdresser and yoga instructor fucked each other under the moonlight in an over-priced, luxury tent! What can I say? Someone has to be me!

PARK AVENUE

Traveling to New York to do hair had started to become more of a reality instead of the grandiose dream for which every hairstylist yearns. And it was all thanks to Sandy for introducing me to some of the most powerful, socialite females on the planet!

Sandy had pretty much guilted these women into having me do their hair! She had that Asian Persuasion I mentioned earlier. Ultimately, I would forever be indebted to Sandy, and not just because she championed my work and sent some amazing clients my way.

No, I will be forever indebted to Sandy because one of those socialites she practically forced into hiring me would be the woman with whom I would fall completely head over heels in love with!

Now when I say 'in love' you're probably thinking: 'OK Brandon, how do you know that it's real love? Is it love, or are you just in lust with this woman?" This is a completely valid question, as you've read through this book, you obviously know by now that I've had a lot sexual experiences through my years as a hair stylist – and I've not once mentioned the word 'love' before!

So how did I know? Now that I'm older and have had all of these experiences, I can tell you that no woman in my life, to this day, has haunted my thoughts and my gut like Hayden. I had that longing pain you get for someone, especially when you know that they are off limits.

When I first met Hayden, it seemed almost easier to travel to the moon than to get this woman. Although it would take me over eight long years to finally tell her how I felt about her, I wasn't going to say anything immediately!

After I met Hayden, my life was no longer the same. I had briefly met her when I was traveling with Sandy and Mortimer to the Rich Guy conference. From the first time I met her, it was clear as day that this stunning, amazing woman was my dream girl. I know that might sound silly, but it was true.

Most guys dream of scoring a model or a famous actress. I fell for a Park Avenue socialite and I promise you, I wasn't trying. It was kind of sad for all the girls that I would date moving forward as I would always be comparing them to Hayden, knowing damn well that no girl would ever match up to her.

By the way, did I mention that Hayden was married? Not the best person to fall in love with, especially when they both become your clients. Hayden and her husband lived on Park Avenue way up in the 70s. This was an area of New York City that I wasn't too familiar with. I had traveled to New York in the past, but most of my time spent there was spent in mid-town and downtown. It was only after I met Sandy, that I started traveling above 60th street. Hayden was the first woman in New York that Sandy referred to me.

With Hayden came another four classy women who seemed to have more money than anybody I'd met in Los Angeles. The universe has a way of putting the right people in your path when things are meant to be, they just happen regardless of you being aware of it. Hayden came from New York, but came from humble beginnings.

Hayden was and still is the most beautiful woman I know. Her eyes are crystal blue like priceless gems that belong on an expensive necklace. The kind of eyes that you could stare at until tears roll down your face. Her skin was my most favorite thing about her as it was always perfectly tan, and I don't mean a spray tan. For a white woman, she had the perfect color skin, and it never seemed to get pale. It would always stay a beautiful warm tone. So smooth and delicious that when I would blow dry her hair and my fingers would brush against her neck, she would get little goose bumps that would instantly make my heart jump.

My heart still jumps every time her name comes up on my phone when she needs her hair done. Hayden has a smile that would make you do anything and everything for her. It was no wonder to me that she lived in a palace of an apartment on one of the most expensive streets in the world. She was a beautiful princess who deserved to live in a palace on Park Avenue.

Seeing her for the first time was like in the movie *Scarface,* when Al Pacino sees Michelle Pfeiffer for the first time when she comes down the elevator in that famous white dress! Just like Pacino's and Pfeiffer's characters in *Scarface* - Tony Montana and Elvira Hancock - Hayden and I couldn't have come from more different backgrounds!

Hayden took to me right away as far as being a generous and caring client. She immediately introduced me to a few of her ridiculously wealthy friends who all were the elite of the elite in New York. Coming from Los Angeles I didn't quite understand the New York social scene. In Hollywood, it was all about celebrities and movie business folks, but New York was a whole different ball game. The money that these investment, or real estate, or just straight up trust fund guys, would have far surpassed Hollywood money!

I was able to hook a really amazing apartment to stay in. Turns out that Jane was good for something other than hooking me up with Sandy. Jane also hooked me up with this woman named Frannie, who was a stylist on major movies. Frannie was also the mistress to a very, very famous actor. He was also a very, very married actor!

This actor had put Frannie up in this amazing apartment near the Dakota building in New York, where John Lennon lived and was killed. This apartment was across the street from the Dakota. I had briefly met Frannie through Jane, and when Jane and I split ways, because Frannie lived in New York most of the time, she wasn't aware of my falling out with Jane.

Frannie had offered her apartment to me if I ever needed it because she was away on movie sets most of the time and she felt it was a shame to have this amazing place with no-one occupying it. Now, being from Los Angeles and not understanding the space factor in New York, I didn't quite understand how amazing this apartment was. It was a huge two-bedroom on Central Park West, one of the most prestigious addresses in NY. And it had a yard. A big yard! Again, to me, having a yard was very normal in LA, but I guess having a yard in NY is incredibly rare!

Frannie was leaving town again and had left me the keys to this super-sized apartment on the Upper West Side. Sandy had lined up Hayden and a few other friends for me to do their hair, LA style! I arrived at the apartment after a long flight from LA. The cab dropped me off and I walked up to the ground floor apartment. As I walked in I could see how nice this place was. I was really surprised at how much room there was. What was interesting was that Frannie's lover, the actor, had his scripts just lying about all over the apartment.

This was the kind of life you read about or you watched in the movies. Being a famous actor, you could put up your girlfriend in an amazing apartment and fill it with your scripts so you could escape from your wife, fuck your girlfriend and get some reading done at the same time. There were also pictures of the two of them scattered around the apartment. I'm sure this made Frannie feel like she was important to him - and I'm sure she was important to him.

I know from experience from listening to clients when they confide in me that any marriage can get stale quick. When you're famous and rich, and your marriage goes south, why not have a girlfriend? Better not to divorce so you don't lose everything. Plus, there are a lot of women in Hollywood who will tolerate other women in the picture, as long as they're being taken care of, and Frannie was definitely being taken care of!

After I had unpacked my stuff and taken a shower, I have to admit I was being nosy and was checking out everything in the place. The actor was someone I really loved to watch and I even found the script from one of my favorite movies. The character he played was one that I was really good at imitating!

It was getting late and I knew it was time to hit the sack! Sandy and Hayden were on my schedule for tomorrow and since I was new at hailing cabs and taking the subway, I didn't want to be late for their appointments. Frannie had told me I could stay in her bedroom, which was the master bedroom.

Wow, I would get to sleep in the same bed that one of my favorite actors slept in. This trip was already getting good and I only just got here! Park Avenue had always seemed like a fantasy to me. Like a different planet. Well, I was Neil fucking Armstrong and I was about to take one giant leap for mankind and conquer Park Avenue - armed with a blow dryer of course!

The next morning I was awoken by the sounds of the busy city. Even though I was in a nicer part of town, I wasn't excluded from the noise of jackhammers, buses and loud people on the street. Talk about getting the Manhattan experience, no-one could escape the craziness here, rich or poor! Once you hit the streets, you're an equal with every other New Yorker! The city stops for no one.

Sandy was my first stop on the list which was a good thing because she would be able to give me the run down on the other two women I would be doing after her. I had already done Hayden's hair once, but the other two ladies I had never met before. Fortunately for me they all lived very close to each other on Park Avenue.

I arrived at Sandy's apartment, which from my understanding, used to be owned by a member of the super-rich Rockefeller family. I got to the front of the building and I was greeted by the doorman. Doormen in New York play an important role for the families that live in these prestigious buildings. One thing that was different about New York from LA, was that the service people in New York make a career out of it. Doormen in New York become almost like family to the people who live in the buildings because they see each other every day. Most of the powerful people who live in these buildings want to feel comfortable and at-ease when they come home and these doormen are masters of that!

The doorman called up to Sandy's apartment to let them know that I had arrived. He directed me to the elevator, which took me up to Sandy's place. I got to her floor. Yes, the apartment was the entire floor! In fact, it was two floors from what I remember. As the elevator door opened to her apartment, I was greeted by two beautiful Rhodesian Ridgebacks! I was a bit shocked when the first thing I saw were two big ass dogs, but they could sense that I was friendly and I love dogs so I immediately crouched down to pet them. I had never seen a Rhodesian Ridgeback in person, let alone two of them. But they weren't the most magnificent things to look at.

The apartment was nothing like I had ever seen before. It was more like a mansion, inside a building. Saying the word 'apartment' didn't really do it justice. The butler greeted me after I'd been licked to death by these two gigantic canine babies!

The butler's name was George and he was in charge of the New York apartment. George was a lot like Bill the Butler back in Beverly Hills. George had an elegance to him and seemed incredibly at ease in the apartment. He looked like he belonged there even though he was the staff.

Everything in the apartment was perfect. There was nothing out of place! I could've run a white glove over any surface and I'm sure there would not have been a lick of dust! Most people have one maid to clean the house, but Sandy had two! Plus, she and Mortimer had a chef, tutors for the children and I even think they had someone specifically to look after the dogs!

I was directed upstairs to where Sandy was waiting. George walked me up a huge, curved staircase that looked like it was one, solid piece of dark wood. Obviously, this staircase had to be installed somehow. I was thinking to myself: "How did they get something like this in here? Maybe it was built inside of the apartment before they moved in? When it comes to having shit loads of money, anything is possible!"

I walked into Sandy's bathroom and it looked like it was built for a queen! She greeted me with a big smile and a look of hair happiness on her face! Sandy loved the way I did her hair. She would always compliment me on the way I styled her hair and she would always say: "No-one does it like you do!" That was an enormous compliment, coming from a woman like her, who could just snap her fingers and have any hair stylist in the world do her hair. She asked me if her friends had booked their appointments with me. I responded with: "Yes, thank you Sandy, I have three of your friends on my schedule including Hayden."

"Ahhhh Hayden," I said under my breath. A big smile was plastered across my face at just the thought of her. I did everything I could to suppress my emotions when the name Hayden was spoken. I had a poker face as I added: "Yes Sandy, I'm going to Hayden's place after you, then I have Cassandra and Caroline after. I also think I'm doing your friend Emily tomorrow. I'm still waiting for her to confirm."

Sandy started telling me about these girls and what they're like. It seemed that a lot of these woman meet each other because their husbands do business with each other and they are not best friends, at least not the kind of best friends you've known your whole life and who you could tell anything to. Instead they are socialite friends. Real Housewives anyone? You know the sort. They appear to be besties in front of everyone but, being a socialite, they are forced into events and situations where they meet other ridiculously rich people. Some of them become close and then some of them are enemies who become friends. These women might be blonde and coiffed, with many of them looking like trophy wives but believe me, they are anything but trophies. These women are incredibly smart and clever – and they know that if you keep your friends close, you keep your enemies even closer!

So many of these relationships have been built on artificial situations. I was cutting Sandy's hair and she was openly chatting about these women that are on my list. I didn't really know how close she was to these girls, but she only said very sweet things about them. Her true feelings about these women weren't important to me.

Sandy was like a politician. She was genuinely an incredibly nice person, but she also knew the people in these circles never exposed their true feelings and always stayed diplomatic when dealing with these types of circles.

One thing that she did say was that Hayden was a solid person. Hayden was the one she spoke the most about because it was impossible to not like her. She was - and is - so real, that you could strip the money and the possessions away from her and there would be nothing different about her. I think that's why Sandy really liked Hayden. Hayden was real and that's a quality that people are born with! It's undeniable! I could tell that Sandy could let her guard down around Hayden because it was impossible not to.

Hayden only lived a few blocks away and since I was almost done with Sandy, I would have about an hour to kill before Hayden would be ready. I wrapped up Sandy's hair and before I left, she wanted me to come back again in another two days to blow her hair out for an event. Perfect, I was already stacking up more appointments while I was there! I left Sandy's apartment and headed out onto Park Avenue. The streets were busy with businessmen, construction workers, street people and the ground level stores and restaurants were booming with customers. The energy in New York is like no other city that I had ever visited!

I found a nice little cafe to sit down and relax for a little while before I headed to Hayden's place. I was greeted by a really beautiful Russian waitress who took my vanilla latte order. Why do all the girls in New York look like models? For some reason, people in New York appear to be taller than normal. All the business guys looked like they were all above 6ft and the women were a close second! Another waitress came out to take the neighboring table's order and she was taller and more beautiful than the waitress who was helping me! "Wow," I said to myself. "I am a short person compared to these people."

I had an hour to chill but in the blink of an eye, half of that time was already gone! Was my watch working faster than normal, or was it the city that was making things move faster? I thought I would be able to relax, but that thought was a thing of the past. The closer the time got to see Hayden the more nervous I was becoming, which was unusual for me. I downed my latte and headed over to Hayden's place to cut and color her hair.

Since I was going to be at Hayden's for a few hours, I had to prepare myself and bury my emotions so that I didn't give her any inclination that I was attracted to her. Try being around the girl of your dreams for four hours and let's see how you perform! Well I would say that I should've got a medal for suppressing my feelings. If digging a hole to bury my feelings was an Olympic sport, I would definitely have scored gold right then!

I strutted up to Hayden's place with an all business attitude, but the minute she opened the door, the business attitude went out the fucking window. All of a sudden I was reduced to an excited, 13 year-old boy who just got his first boner in math class! Hayden was like every beautiful, popular girl that I had ever went to school with. She was that girl that seemed so unattainable. I would've been putty in her hands, or better yet, putty in her hair!

I started to unload my gear and I was dropping shit! I couldn't seem to keep the comb in my hands to save my life. I was afraid to talk too much because I was fumbling on my words. I was a fucking mess. Nevertheless, I pulled it together as I began to highlight her hair.

Thankfully these women have busy lives even though they don't technically work. Being the wife of someone as rich as Hayden's husband was a job in itself. Parties, school meetings, lunches with the other socialites and of course, shopping! Hayden and her friends were professional shoppers! These girls knew how to get it done! The average woman would have to save up for years to be able to afford a Chanel bag, or if they get lucky enough, the almighty Hermes Birkin, named after actress and singer Jane Birkin. Most normal women never even get to see an Hermes Birkin in the flesh. The cost of a new Birkin bag can range anywhere from $12,000 to more than $200,000. There is no designer handbag in the world as elusive as the Hermes Birkin – celebrities love them and David Beckham, who is worth $350 million, bought his former Spice Girl and clothing designer wife Victoria, an albino Nilo crocodile

Himalayan Birkin, back in 2008 for a reported $100,000. Victoria reportedly has 100 Birkins in a collection that's estimated to be worth a whopping $2 million. So, it's no surprise that Park Avenue women like Hayden have four or five Birkins.

Between the phone calls, nannies, and events in the evening, these women are always busy with something. Compared to the other women I would meet on Park Avenue, Hayden was noticeably different. She had a very down to earth, easy going attitude. Almost like an LA girl. She really seemed like she was out of place there in Manhattan. At least that's what I thought.

The first thing I noticed about her was her beautiful blonde hair, which was about to get even better because I was going to make her even more blonde! Her crystal blue eyes and perfectly tan skin made her seem like a California girl. Here she had this perfect tan and it was fall in New York! While I was doing her hair and painting on her highlights, the business going on in her apartment was apparent. Hayden had a nanny called Carrie, who was an African-American woman with a big personality!

Carrie was from Queens and had been with Hayden's family for a long time. She had a real boisterous attitude. Carrie was high energy and I could tell that she knew how to run their household with authority! Carrie liked me right away. Carrie was all 'Sista,' if you know what I mean! She moved her head around when she spoke like a girl from the 'hood'. She didn't take any shit from anyone and it was clear that anything Hayden needed, Carrie would be there to handle it.

As I was brightening up Hayden's hair, trying to make her look more like a California girl, she was asking me how I met Sandy and when I started doing her hair. I told her: "I met Sandy through a woman named Jane in Bel Air. Do you know Jane?" You never know who knows who in these types of circles. She responded with: "No, I don't who Jane is but Sandy has a lot of friends that I probably don't know." Phew, that was a relief!

It wasn't even really clear to me how Hayden knew Sandy but in New York, there are some key socialite events that happen every year and both Sandy and Hayden would have attended these events. The more we talked, the more comfortable I was becoming. After all, this was a completely new environment for me and it wasn't like I didn't stand out like a sore thumb in New York. I guess that's what the draw was for these women. I was unlike any other hairstylist here in

Manhattan. The way I do hair was completely different from the stylists there.

First off, hair stylists in New York only do one service. Either you're a cutter or a colorist. I have never believed in that method. I was doing both color and cutting and for most women, doing both is much easier for them. It's a huge inconvenience to have to go to two people when you're getting your hair done. Here I came, flying in from LA with my magic bag of tricks like I'm Willy fucking Loman and I was turning these girls' hair out in record time and they didn't even have to leave their apartments. Plus, now they had the prestige of their own stylist flying in from the West Coast specifically for them! What woman doesn't want that?

Now, I'm sure being easy on the eyes was also helping my situation. But while it's a bonus to be good looking, if you suck at doing hair, I don't care if you're a male supermodel, women of this caliber will drop you quicker than a fucking hot potato! All women – whether they are rich or poor - never ever want to risk their hair! Never! Fortunately, my skills were paying the bills so between my level of expertise and the way I looked, I had an edge over other stylists.

Then Hayden asked me a question that totally took me by surprise: "What are you doing about promoting yourself here in New York. Do you have a publicist?" Hayden casually threw this out there into the universe, as if everyone should have a publicist and it was the most natural thing in the world. A blank stare came over my face because I didn't have an answer for that. I figured Sandy was the one who was acting as my agent/publicist. I had never even thought about hiring a real publicist.

I then blurted out: "I'm working out of the Warren | Tricomi Salon down on 57th Street and I know they have a publicist, but since I finished working on the reality show, I've kind of slowed my roll on PR. You can always come to the salon on 57th Street, if getting your hair done in your apartment is annoying."

Hayden looked at me like I was crazy. I thought to myself: "Why would she ever want to go to a salon if she doesn't have to?" Of course, I was right. She told me: "I don't go below 60th Street!" Of course, she doesn't! What was I thinking? Clearly I wasn't thinking. And even if I was, I didn't move in that world. Who knew if you lived on Park Avenue that traveling below 60th Street was a big no-no?

Hayden then added: "You should do a PR party here in New York so that more women know about you. Since you were on TV, it's good to get yourself in the magazines here like the New York Post, Page Six and so on." Hayden was already thinking ahead for me. She had such confidence and sounded like she did this kind of thing all the time, like it was second nature. I had no clue about any of it and I didn't know how I would even get that started.

In a desperate tone, I said: "I don't really have a place to have a party and I only have about four or five women here that I'm doing. I'm afraid that I don't have that many people to invite."

Then Hayden did something that completely floored me. She offered: "I used to do this kind of work. I can throw you a party here in my apartment! Have the publicity girl at your salon contact me and we can throw you an amazing party in my apartment!" I was in shock. Hayden barely knew me, I'd been with her for less than an hour and already she was offering to throw me a party! In her sick apartment, in this amazing building? I couldn't believe what I was hearing.

In my most humble voice – well, I tried to sound humble though I was secretly on fire inside - I said: "You don't have to do that. I feel like I would be talking advantage and I definitely don't want to impose on you in any way!" For a woman like this to open her apartment to me and offer to work with the salon publicist was such a gift! She was like my angel from above, who could reach down from high up on Park Avenue to help a stranger, as that's really kind of what I was to her.

I had only just met Hayden and already she was offering to help me out on a level like Sandy! Now, I know this might look like Hayden was hot for me and that this gesture could've been because she was attracted to me and was trying to get closer to me, but now after knowing Hayden for some years, I can say that this was just the way she was. She was just very generous to me and to the people that she worked with.

Honestly, I wish it had been because she was attracted to me, but I can say that there weren't any sexual vibes coming from her end. It was me who was totally attracted to her and I knew deep down that she was unattainable, and married. I knew it was stupid to think I would ever have a chance with this woman! Why fuck something like this up? Here she was, really becoming my friend and that alone was worth more than anything!

Having someone like her on my side was so valuable because now I had both Hayden and Sandy pushing me to all their friends. When I started to going to New York every six weeks, I didn't think that it would catch fire as quickly as it did. Hayden really lit the fire for me and she wasn't using matches. She had a fucking designer blowtorch that she could access at any time she wanted!

She was just being nice to me and was doing this for me because she knew that it would be hard for me to have a party like this, in an apartment of this caliber, with the friends that she had, on my own. She knew that having a party for me at her spot, on her level, would blow away any media that would be invited. Well, she was right!

As I wrapped up her hair she said: "Have your publicist girl call me and we'll co-ordinate a party for you here. We'll invite the magazine editors and I'll bring all the girls. I can even handle the catering for you!" My head was spinning at this point. I don't remember if I even charged her for her hair. I honestly don't even remember leaving her apartment because I was floating with excitement – I was on cloud nine! I couldn't thank her enough: "OK Hayden, if you really want to then I will definitely take you up on that. I'll do all your hair for free for the party. Thank you so much!"

This is why I get annoyed when poor people, or working- class people, talk shit about the rich. Most normal people on a whole think that the rich are greedy, or that they did things that were shady to get to where they are. This infuriates me because here I am in a strange city, meeting these women for the first time and they're the richest of the rich and they did nothing but try to help me! These women didn't know me from Adam! I've always said that I have angels looking over me and Hayden just moved to the number one 'angel position'!

Hayden has never asked me for anything. She didn't want anything in return and she turned down the free hair services that I offered because she was throwing me the party. She didn't need it. What made her happy was helping a guy out who was hard working, personable and talented. Like Ronnie did back when I started. Although now instead of the help coming through a retired rock star, I was getting it from one of the most influential socialites in Manhattan!

I hugged Hayden and thanked her so much for the opportunity. She gave me a smile and said: "You're welcome." I left her apartment more excited than I have ever been. I walked into her apartment nervous, like a boy with his first major crush, fumbling my words trying to keep it together while I was in her presence.

Now I was leaving with a new, life-long friend who was about to give me the biggest favor yet. Hayden was going to make me the hot new thing in her hometown and wanted nothing in return. Call it an accident? I think not! This is my advice to all of you who are poor or middle class, but who want more out of life than what you have: work hard, be appreciative and the right people will take notice. I promise!

I left Hayden's place in a state of shock. The woman of my dreams was about to throw me a party, in her amazing apartment for free and all I had to do was connect her with the salon's publicity girl to coordinate it. Other than that, all I had to do was show up and mingle. I was off to the next client that Sandy had hooked me up with – but my mind was still with Hayden! I had to force myself to concentrate as I made my way across town to Trump Towers. This woman lived at the top of Trump Towers and her name was Emily. I had to travel south about twenty blocks to get to the Towers.

Once I arrived I gave my name to the front door person so they could tell Emily that I was here and before I could sit down, I was being escorted to the elevator. The Trump Tower residences looked a lot like a hotel. It was right next door to the Trump Hotel, but the Towers is where people actually lived full-time.

I boarded the elevator and braced myself for the ride all the way up to the top. As I mentioned before, I am afraid of heights. I don't know where this came from, but when I am exposed to great heights, my body freezes. As I rode up in the elevator, I prayed that Emily's apartment in the sky wasn't full of windows! I arrived and Emily was there at the door waiting for me.

Emily was a really pretty, 40-something year-old woman who was a bit shorter than me and had a couple of kids that were home with her. Her apartment was the most badass, baller style apartment that I had seen since I arrived. It wasn't that I disliked Sandy or Hayden's apartments. Theirs were just more traditional and conservative, whereas Emily's apartment looked like an art gallery! The colors were bright and powerful.

I remember her son's room had a really deep blue carpeting and it looked like a room that every boy dreams of having. The ceilings were so high you could've had a trapeze act swinging from left to right and they wouldn't be in anyone's way! Seriously, Cirque du Soleil could've put on one of their spectacular shows in there!

We entered the kitchen and I could see the floor to ceiling windows. I gulped as I dared to approach them. Fuck it. How many times in your life do you get to be in an apartment of this magnitude? I looked out the window and I could see all of Central Park! Emily was more than gracious to me as I unpacked my gear. I could tell that she had a sweet soul and I don't quite remember what her husband did but whatever it was, it was obvious he was pretty damn successful!

As I put the cutting cape around Emily's shoulders, she asked: "What do you think of my current haircut?" Now, this could easily be a loaded question, so in my experience, it's always best to turn it back on the client, to say, or ask: "What do you think of it?" When in doubt, answer a question with a question! She answered with: "I think it's good but I'm not blown away by it! I paid $1,000 for this haircut and it doesn't seem that much different from other good haircuts I've had."

My eyes lit up without my control. In my mind, I was thinking: "$1,000? For a haircut? What the fuck am I doing?" I had only been charging $200 for a haircut. I needed to get with the program and raise my prices! It hadn't dawned on me that these women were paying that much to get their hair done! It quickly put things in perspective for me as far as who these women were and how much money they were used to spending.

Hayden was so humble and kind, that she made herself seem very normal. She had captivated me so much that I thought of her as an equal. At least that's how she made me feel. Now being in Emily's apartment, reality suddenly kicked it and I became very aware of the situation these women were actually in. I was cutting

Emily's hair and she was definitely digging the work I was doing. After her comment about her $1,000 haircut, I told her that I was actually going to charge her $2,000 because I flew in from LA just for her! I laughed right after I said it as I was obviously joking!

I did everything I could to keep things light in a society where everything is anything but light! It wasn't that Emily was or acted more like a socialite or acted like she was really rich, but she was definitely more businesslike than Sandy and Hayden. She kept firing question after question: "So how did you meet Sandy? Last time I talked to Sandy, she insisted that I should have you do my hair. Are you going to be coming to New York often? I would like to make this a regular thing if that's the case?"

This woman was definitely Type A; she was already wanting to have her appointment on lock-down for six weeks ahead. I didn't know that these women would be pre-booking, but I guessed with the party that Hayden was going to potentially throw for me, I had better start thinking about booking my next flight!

I tested the waters: "Yes, I will be back for sure in about six weeks if that works for you? Your friend Hayden mentioned that she might throw a PR party for me at her apartment, so if that happens than I will for sure be back!" Her eyes lit up: "Oh, a party? That sounds like a fabulous idea! That was nice of her. When did she say this?" I admitted: "I just came from her place before you and she told me this while I was there doing her hair. She thought it might help me to get more clients and also would be a great way to meet the magazine editors while I'm here. She actually offered!"

I could see Emily's mind working overtime as I snipped away at her beautiful locks. As I was cutting, she was giving me the thumbs up on the work I was doing! My trip so far had been seamless, almost like it was too easy! Could these New York girls be that easy to please? I couldn't believe it. Why hadn't I come here before? Emily seemed just as excited about the party as I was: "I will call Hayden and talk to her about this party. It sounds like a lot of fun and I will try to bring some people. Is Sandy going to come?" She asked as if that's the ultimate guest that I needed. I told her: "I sure hope so. Hayden just brought this up today, so I don't know if Sandy knows yet, but I'm hoping she will."

I wrapped up Emily's hair as she handed me a nice wad of crisp $100 bills for the haircut. Yes, that's plural with the hundreds! Three down, one more to go. "Who are you seeing next?" Emily asked. I replied: "I'm seeing another one of Sandy's friends, Caroline. Emily exclaimed: "Oh I love Caroline, she doesn't live that far from here. Caroline has a lot of hair so watch out!" I gave Emily a grin and boasted: "There's no head of hair I can't handle, Emily!"

Back on the street level, traffic had already kicked in and even though I was only ten blocks away, it's ten fucking blocks away and getting a cab during New York rush hour can be tricky. I attempted to walk it. I figured I'd just walk fast and hope for the best. I was 30 minutes away from Caroline's appointment and I definitely did not want to be late! A few twists and turns around Central Park and I arrived at Caroline's place.

I got to her address and at first, I couldn't figure out if her apartment was a hotel or a house. It seemed to be one gigantic house with five floors. I was looking for an apartment number, but there was only one address for this entire place. Now, you're going to laugh at me because what I didn't realize was that Caroline lived in a brownstone. Now coming from Los Angeles, I had no idea what a brownstone was. This place was fucking huge! I rang the doorbell and Caroline answered the intercom.

"Hello, who is this?" Came the voice through the intercom. I must have looked strange to her with the hair bag and my LA attire. Plus, my hair was really big back then so I probably looked like a ruffian on camera. I looked into the camera and said: "Hello, this is Brandon, Sandy's hairstylist. We have an appointment?" I could hear children in the background and she was ordering them around while she's buzzed me in. Caroline had an authoritative tone in her voice when she spoke to her kids. I was already nervous about her. She buzzed me in and I stepped in a few feet only to be greeted by their nanny. The nanny was an older, Jamaican woman who pointed me in the direction of Caroline.

I walked into the kitchen where Caroline was talking to her kids like they were little soldiers and she's the Drill Sergeant. I didn't speak until she finished talking to her kids because I didn't want to interrupt the lecture she was giving to them for fear that I would be the next one getting lectured! She wrapped up their talk and looked over at me.

I smiled and said: "Hi, I'm Brandon, Sandy's hair guy. How are you?" She looked me up and down like she was the Terminator, giving me a full body scan. She then walked right towards me in a direct sort of way and extended her hand to me to shake it. I firmly shook her hand as I could tell that this woman was nowhere near as laid-back as my other three clients that I did earlier. I had a feeling that this woman was going to be tough!

"Hi, I'm Caroline, so nice to meet you!" She was very aggressive and direct! She looked me right in the eyes when she spoke to me. She kind of made me feel uncomfortable. I thought I was the aggressive one, but this woman had me beat. On the flip side, she was really pretty. She was a bit older than Sandy and Hayden but nevertheless, she was really pretty and her hair was so long and thick! She had enough hair for three women!

I knew this was going to be a big job and that was just dealing with her. As a seasoned hair stylist, when you meet someone for the first time you kind of know what you're going to be dealing within the first few moments. I knew what this woman was going to be like when I heard her talking to her kids. She was type A to the max and I knew that nothing was going to get by this woman. She would look at every detail, every move I made.

I was afraid to talk too much for fear that she would talk down to me. Don't get me wrong, she was nice, but I knew that if I pissed this woman off, she would switch on me like a bi-polar patient! She said: "Come with me, we're going to do my hair upstairs." We walked out of the kitchen and down the hall. I saw the staircase so I started to walk towards it when she said: "Oh no, we're going to take the elevator."

Now I feel like I'm little Orphan Annie, walking through 'Daddy Warbucks' house for the first time. She led me to the elevator which was a bit narrow and old world-looking. This brownstone was a least over a hundred years old. She pushed the fifth floor button and up we went. I couldn't believe how big this place was! I couldn't make out how many floors there were. I guess in total there were six floors including the basement. She could've moved out and turned this place into a hotel if she felt like it.

She started asking me about myself, where I'm from and how I met Sandy. It seemed like these women had no clue who crazy Jane was, so I was safe on that front. These women were Sandy's New York crew and these women had enough to deal with in their own city. Their bubbles didn't carry over into Los Angeles which was great for me because it was like having a whole new world of women to do that didn't have anything to do with home.

I was a free agent here! No salon owner looking over my shoulder, no crazy regulars who knew my business. New York City was a blank canvas that was being filled with some of the richest women in the world.

Caroline was aggressively asking me questions like: "Who do you do In LA?" Meaning what celebrities did I do. Then the questions got more personal: "Where do you live? Do you have a girlfriend?" She couldn't help but ask all these questions. She was someone who had to know everything around her. A true type A personality.

I had never really met a woman like Caroline. It was like she was a man in another life and was reborn as this pretty blonde woman, but she demanded everyone's full attention and was going to get her way, whether you liked it or not.

We walked out of the elevator and I could see the amount of hair that was in front of me. Swaying back and forth with every step she took, it was almost hypnotizing! I knew I was in it for the long haul on this one! I was doing her color and I was going to cut it as well.

She then told me very matter-of-factly: "Sandy told me you're the best so I cancelled my regular person for this! I love the fact that you'll come to my house. I hate having to go the salon!" I knew that she was telling me this to try to compliment me, but at the same time underneath was a warning. Basically, the warning was: "I cancelled my normal hairdresser for you. You better not fuck it up!"

I can read people's tone very well and Caroline's tone spoke loud and clear! I started to do her color and it was actually going quickly. Her son was doing his homework on the same floor as we were and she was directing him on how to work out the problems himself to get the better grade. I would be scared shitless to come home with a B on my report card in this household. These people were winners! There was no second place. There was no such thing as being lazy. It was all about winning!

While she was multi-tasking as I'm doing her hair, she was also watching intently through the mirror to make sure I was doing a good job. She was also giving me a running commentary on what I was doing! She told me: "I've never had my color done this way, where you paint the highlights right on to the hair. I'm excited! I wonder why my guy doesn't do my color like this?"

When a client brings up their other hairdresser, or current hairdresser, you have to be careful on how you respond. You want this person to start coming to you instead of their normal person but at the same time, you don't want to say anything negative about the other hair stylist's work because that makes you look like an insecure dick!

Again, answer the question with a question. "How do you feel about your hair?" I asked. She responded: "I like it. I think it's fine. I'm excited to see what you can do. I like that this process is fast because as you can tell, I have a ton of hair and not a lot of time in the day, so the faster the better."

Hint, hint Brandon, less talking more working. Well. I took the hint and I finished her color in record time! Once the color is processed, she ran to her bathroom to wash it out. As she walked to the bathroom, she turned around and said: "Aren't you coming?" I looked like a deer in the headlights for a second. There was a strange pause, then she said: "I need you to help me wash it out in the sink. I can throw my head in the sink while you shampoo it out."

For a second there I thought this woman was going to have her way with me in her shower, which because of her personality being so strong, I would have let her for fear she would scream at me if I'd said no!

I laughed under my breath and said: "Of course, coming now!" We walked into the bathroom and she threw her hair into her big sink and I started washing it. Now washing your client's hair in the bathroom sink is always a bit awkward because you have to get behind them to do it. She was bent over, ready to go and I was standing behind her, but I was trying as hard as I could to not rub my dick against her behind. All I was thinking was: "Please Brandon, don't get a hard-on while you're shampooing this woman's hair."

It's literally impossible, not to rub against each other when you're trying to shampoo someone's hair in their sink! It wasn't like I was instantly attracted to her or anything like that but at the same time, she was a pretty woman and I'm sure every man can relate to this because sometimes our dicks get hard when the wind blows and it's hard to control.

So, she was bending over and I could see her G-string poking through from the side of her jeans and I was literally breathing deep to not get a boner! Plus, she had more fucking hair than I bargained for, so it was a lengthy process. It took me over five minutes just to do the shampoo and I still had to run conditioner through it as well! "Are you getting the shampoo completely out?" She yelled at me while the water was getting all over the place including in her mouth. "Yes, I'm rinsing it all out," I said in a super loud voice as my dick was centimeters away from grazing the top of her ass!

My forehead was soaked with sweat even though she had the air conditioner turned on full blast! We headed back to the chair and I started to blow out her hair. Before I was even completely done with one section she asked: "How is it looking?" She was fumbling through her hair as I'm blow drying. Her OCD was kicking in for sure. She was quite the contrast from the woman I did earlier!

I said to her with excitement: "It looks great! I think you will love it!" The blow dry took me twice the amount of time that the color took because of how much hair she had. My arms were getting more muscular by the second and I'd only done a quarter of it. She lifted her hair up and I could see a smile on her face. "Thank God!" I said to myself as I ripped through this blow dry faster than I'd ever done before!

I was almost at the end when I heard: "Uh-oh! I see a spot on the side. Shouldn't there be one more highlight right there?" I started to play stupid and asked: "Where do you see a spot? It looks really blonde to me!" She actually got up while I was still blowing out her hair and walked toward the mirror. She started examining the hair like it's under a microscope and she found one spot where she said the blonde should be. It already took me an hour to blow out this woman's hair and I will potentially have to redo the entire blow out, just to add one more highlight. I knew it was too good to be true.

I could see her face turn from nice to not so nice! Before she even had a chance to breathe another word, I jumped in and said: "Don't worry I can add another highlight if you want. No problem." I could tell that she was restraining herself from being snappy with me. I mean after all, I'd been here for four hours by now and it looked like it was going to be another two hours by the time it was all said and done. That also meant that I was going to have to shampoo her again, which was a job in itself! This was the kind of woman that if she hears the word: "No," her fucking head would explode! Back to square one.

Two hours later after adding the one single highlight to Caroline's hair to make her happy, she thanked me over and over for being so patient with her. She asked me how much and then she disappeared to her bedroom and returned with a wad of crisp $100 bills. I thought to myself: "What is it with these girls and all this new, crisp cash? Do they all have money printing machines in their houses? How do I get one?"

I thanked her over and over for her generosity and I bolted out of there faster than an Olympic sprinter. Once I hit the street, I hit a wall. My body all of a sudden just gave out on me. I managed to grab a cab and I headed back to my fancy apartment. I had been at

Caroline's house for a total of *SIX* hours. That's a full day for some people. The money was definitely worth it but now I know, when it comes to doing blondes that have OCD, or as I like to say, '*blondearexia*', I make sure that I blonde the fuck out of their hair! Leave no dark spot untouched was my new mantra!

The next day I contacted the publicity girl from the salon, whose name was Rachel. I told her about Hayden's offer to throw me a party and asked if she would be interested in helping me. The publicity girl sounded like she was having an orgasm on the other end of the phone after I told her that Hayden was going to throw me a party with Sandy. She practically panted down the phone: "Are you serious, Brandon? Do you know how powerful these women are in New York? Of course, I want to be involved! Every magazine editor I contact will want to come for sure! So, let me get this straight, you're here from LA and you got Hayden to throw you a party at her apartment? How did you manage this?" She was blown away!

I calmly told her: "I didn't manage anything. Hayden is my new client that I got through Sandy. You know who Sandy and her husband are, obviously? Sandy referred Hayden to me and when I was at her apartment, she offered to throw me a party for the

Page 356

magazine editors. Cool, right?" Total silence on the other end of the phone. Then Rachel said: "I don't believe you. She's really going to throw you a party with Sandy and their friends? All the biggest New York socialites in New York are all of a sudden your clients?" How is this possible?"

So, at this point I know Rachel wasn't really getting it yet. I said in a cocky tone: "You can actually talk to Hayden personally because she wants you to call her and deal with her directly. You can handle that, yes? Here's her number." As I was rattling off Hayden's phone number to Rachel, I heard the other PR girls high fiving each other in the background because I was on speaker phone and this conversation was getting blurted out to the entire PR firm.

This PR firm that technically worked for Edward and Joel was made up of all young, aggressive fashionistas that would work 12- to 14-hour days. To land the type of clients like Hayden, Sandy, Emily and Caroline takes years for these girls. I was able to make things happen within 24 hours!

I remembered back to when I first got into hair, people would tell me the power I would have because I was straight and good-looking. The straight male really does stand out in this business and I was so fortunate that my career was headed in that direction so rapidly. I was on a roller coaster, but there was no sign of it slowing down.

So far, I had managed to get on television, land the most powerful women in the world, travel to far and distant lands like I was fucking Anthony Bourdain, and now several of the biggest New York socialites were going to attend the PR party that was being thrown by my fucking dream girl! How was this possible? What did I do to deserve this? Did I die on that little island hopper plane back in the Bahamas and this was God's way of rewarding me? It was all so surreal!

Since Rachel appeared to be in a state of shock, I re-asked her if she thought she could handle dealing with Hayden. She testily replied: "Yes, of course. Oh my God, you don't really understand who these people are, do you Brandon?" Well, I had to admit: "To be honest, Rachel, no, I don't. I'm from LA and we don't really have socialites in LA, it's mostly just celebrities. These women are just being really nice to me so I'm taking it day by day. I was shocked about the party offer as well but she insisted so I didn't want to tell her the word that every woman hates the most!" Rachel paused and then asked: "What word do women hate the most?" I replied quickly with: "Rachel, the word women hate the most is *NO!*"

The PR girls in the background burst out laughing as they agreed with me wholeheartedly!

Rachel connected with Hayden and the party was set. Every magazine editor that was invited confirmed their spot. Hayden's apartment building was a very famous building on Park Avenue. Everyone that lived in this building were really powerful in their profession.

I spent the day doing all the girls' hair. Hayden, Sandy, Emily and Caroline, plus a few more. I had to make sure that I looked really hot for this party. Hayden had handled the catering and decorations with Rachel the PR girl. I arrived at the party right on time so I could meet everyone as they entered.

Hayden looked incredible and not just because I did her hair! She was such a beautiful woman and she had basically taken charge of helping me in New York. Throwing parties like this was Hayden's specialty and she really made me look like the biggest hair stylist in the world! Sandy and the other girls started to arrive along with the magazine editors.

At first I found myself following Hayden around like a lost puppy. I couldn't take my eyes off her. My heart would pound when I was next to her. If I ever had to shampoo her hair in her sink the way Caroline made me, I didn't know if I would be able to keep it together! She was wearing a really elegant dress that exposed her shoulders and back. As I have said previously, Hayden's skin was like nothing I had ever seen on another human being. She smelled like Jo Malone and her skin was softer than butter. How did I get so lucky to have a woman like this in my life?

Sandy was really generous and had definitely helped me so much, but Hayden was on a whole other level. Allowing me to have this party at her apartment, to actually bring me into her home and allow me to entertain some of New York's top magazine editors just really took it over the edge for me. Plus, being so attracted to her at the same time was the icing on the cake!

At this point, I would've done anything for Hayden. If she'd said: "Brandon, light yourself on fire," I would have asked her where the matches were. What I would've given to just be able to kiss her once! I would've given up this whole party, I would've given up Sandy and the rest of the girls to have one night with her! I would've given up being on TV, the Google job, really anything to touch Hayden's lips! That's how I knew that I was in love with this woman.

My family life as a child was a tough one and my mother was a piece of work. To be honest, my own mother could be a royal pain in the ass and after meeting Hayden, it really showed me how horrible my mother had been because Hayden gave me so much in such a short time, and wanted nothing in return.

If my mother had been at this party, she would've wanted to be the center of attention, she would've been talking about herself the entire time. But Hayden was completely the opposite, she only cared about me and how the party was working for me. Hayden earned a huge spot in my heart that evening and I never, ever wanted to lose her!

At this point, I was even thinking about moving to New York, just to be near her. Why not? Things were working so well for me. Maybe it was a sign to live there. Of course, I kept this idea to myself, I certainly didn't want to freak anyone out, not while everything was going so well.

Hayden insisted that I go and mingle, which I did. What was funny about the party was that the magazine editors, who are usually kind of bitchy and full of themselves, were scared shitless to meet Hayden and Sandy. It was like the socialites were on one side of the room and the magazine editors were on the other.

I walked up to the woman from the New York Post and started talking to her about my career and how I met these women and in her trembling voice she asked me: "Do you think I can go and say hello to Hayden and Sandy?" A big grin covered my face because for once, these fucking magazine editors, who usually take advantage of their power and act like their God's gift to the beauty business, were scared shitless of my clients, and me for that matter! It was unreal! They were walking on eggshells in Hayden's apartment, tiptoeing around, barely eating any of the food, acting like scared little bunnies in a room full of beautiful tigresses.

Women like Hayden and Sandy could chew these women up and spit them out, because women like Hayden's and Sandy's husbands own the fucking magazines that these editors work for. That's the power that these socialites have over normal celebrities. Celebrities are famous and they make a lot of money, but Hayden and Sandy's husbands can buy the fucking actresses! They owned the movie studios, they owned the companies that owned the magazines.

It was a whole different deal here than in LA and I was now being loved and protected by these women! I always felt that God rewarded me because my mother was so terrible to me growing up. God was showing me what real, loving women are like. Hayden and Sandy were mothers who really cared for their children and the people around them and after growing up in a selfish environment where I had to fend for myself, they were a breath of fresh air!

After all, Hayden and Sandy owed me nothing. In fact, I owed them pretty much everything I had! My entire New York existence was created by Sandy and Hayden. It was clear that my life was becoming like a fantasy.

My mother later told me that my life was like Cinderella. She would know because to me she is like the evil stepmother in my life! I not only surrendered to the Cinderella way of life, I did a fucking back dive into it and never looked back.

The party was a huge success and I got a huge article in The New York Post showing all of New York City that I had arrived. New York City now knew who I was and who my clients were! As I said before, I owed my entire career to Sandy and Hayden. The hard part for me now was keeping my true feelings away from Hayden.

I'd never been one to keep quiet but in this situation, silence was the best - and only - move!

BRANDON TAKES BEIJING

I'd always dreamed of traveling abroad. Here I was at the age of 34, and besides going to the Bahamas for the Google wedding, I'd never set foot outside of America. Well, all that was about to change!

Luckily for me I did have a passport – unlike most of my fellow countrymen. For some reason 36 percent of Americans don't own a passport, according to the State Department, which means they can't travel internationally. But here I was - ready, willing and more than able to get that second stamp in my passport. And thanks to Sandy, my traveling dreams were about to come true.

When I began to do hair, I would have never thought that someone would fly me to the other side of the world to blow dry their hair! Being flown to a different country to do hair is by far the biggest compliment in my business. It was something that was on my professional bucket list, but never in a million years did I think that I would ever be going to a place like China!

I could barely contain my excitement when Sandy called and told me that Cosmopolitan magazine in China was going to do a spread on her – and that she really wanted me to style her hair for it. Of course, the answer was yes!

"China," I thought to myself. "It seems so far away. I might as well have been asked to go to Mars!" And I probably knew more about Mars than I knew about China – a quick Google search (thanks Sergey!) of the country revealed that it's the world's most populous country with 1.381 billion people and is the world's second largest economy.

Sandy told me that she was going to coordinate with Cosmopolitan Magazine to fly me out there. She said that she was going to go first because she was flying from New York and that she would have the magazine fly me directly from LA to Beijing. Smart girl having the magazine pay for me so she didn't have to fork out the cash for the last-minute coach ticket on Air China.

Besides the Bahamas, New York was the farthest I had ever flown, which is just six hours from LA. This would be the longest flight I'd ever taken. It's 13 hours from Los Angeles to Beijing, which is where the magazine was based and where we would do the photo shoot.

When you're married to a guy who runs the media you don't necessarily have to be famous in

Hollywood, to be profiled in a top fashion magazine. I'm pretty sure that in China, her native country, Sandy would be more or less a legend given the way she scored Mortimer as a husband. What a life! For a woman to fly out her hair stylist from Los Angeles to Beijing just for a one-day shoot is fucking awesome!

Oh, did I mention that the shoot was in just 10 days? Sandy then told me that I had to go down to the Chinese consulate and get a visa to enter the country. Growing up in America, I always kind of made fun of Chinese people. I'm not a racist, believe me, being Latino I got my fair share of cultural teasing as a kid, so I didn't think anything of teasing other kids who didn't look like me. I just remember making fun of the way they talked while I was growing up.

Even as a kid I remember my father yelling at them in traffic because he said they sucked as drivers. My dad would shout obscenities at them out the window of his red Corvette while he would be the one speeding through traffic, getting more and more annoyed with their slow and terrible driving. Now I was going to the place where I'd be completely surrounded by horrible drivers! The joke was on me I guess!

What's traffic like there? Are there accidents all day long because they all drive so terribly, or do they all just ride bicycles? So many questions were popping in up in my head. I called the Chinese consulate in LA and they said that I had to come down in person and they were only open till 3pm every day. 3pm? Fuck! Since I was on a time crunch, I knew I had to get on it fast.

The next day I went ahead and cancelled some hair appointments so that I could get down to the Chinese consulate on time. I'm glad that I had to go down there in person because it sort of prepared me for what was ahead. When I got there, I realized why my father used to scream at them in traffic all the time. What a cluster fuck!

I knew I was at the right place when the cars parked near the building were parked all fucked up! It was like the people from the Braille Institute took a field trip for the day to the Chinese consulate and were allowed to park the cars themselves! As I walked up to the entrance I could see tons of Chinese people smoking cigarettes as if it was their last act on earth.

But the best chaos was yet to come! When I walked in the building there was no real order to the way people lined up. It was crazy in there – a kind of organized crazy but still! And boy did the men like to pick their noses! Good lord! You would think it was gold country and they were never going to stop digging. I made sure I didn't touch anything.

I finally got to the window and filled out what I needed to fill out and the woman behind the glass tells me in a thick Chinese accent: "You need to come back three days to pick up passport. "Excuse me?" I asked. She repeated: "You come back, three days, pick up passport. It take three days for approval." Having been doing Sandy's hair for a while, and given that her accent was so thick, I actually was able to make out what the women was saying fairly well. I was just bummed that I had to come back to this place.

Still, I knew it was a small price to pay for a trip to China, fuck it! When you do hair in Hollywood, being flown to another country to do someone gives you ultimate bragging rights – so spending a couple of hours in this crazy place was worth every minute. I was really going to enjoy this! I couldn't wait to tell people that I was being flown to Beijing for Sandy.

I could see the jealousy from the other stylists. When I told the owner of the salon I was leaving for China for a job, we went out for drinks to celebrate! He never once told me I couldn't go or I would have to get permission. It was more like: "Have a great time, I'll block you out while you're gone. Happy hour?"

Three days pass and It was time for me to pick up the passport. I drive back to that God-awful Chinese consulate place to pick it up. During the three days, I took it upon myself to try to learn a few words in Chinese. I wanted to try it out at the consulate to see if it would work. I learned a few basic phrases like thank you (謝謝您), please (請), you're hot (您是熱) and more milk (更多乳汁). The essentials, right? So, I get to the Chinese consulate and wait my turn. I wasn't as annoyed this time as I was the first time. Maybe because I knew that I was going to these people's motherland and I better get used to the disorder. Finally it's my turn at the window and the woman behind the glass stamps my passport with the People's Republic of China in print. I figure now is a good time to try my hand at speaking their language.

So, I say thank you in Chinese, or at least I think that's what I meant. I'm sure I completely butchered it. I must've messed it up because the woman didn't even crack a smile. She just shook her head at me and gave me a look like: "You stupid American. "

Now I was ready to go. I had all my gear, my passport. It's on! Just a few days away from take-off. The flight to Beijing from LAX is 13 hours. I'd never been on a flight that long before. I was thinking I'd definitely have to do some serious drinking to knock myself out. Sandy had told me that they were finalizing my flight just a week before the shoot in Beijing.

I don't know if you know, but the closer you book your flight to the date, the more expensive it becomes. So, I was thinking to myself: "Damn, that must be a very expensive flight for the magazine to pay for."

But Sandy was smart, she wasn't paying for a single thing. She had the magazine pay for my flight, hotel, plus a daily per diem and they were obviously paying for her, too. When I received the itinerary through e-mail I saw the amount of the airline ticket with Air-China. $5,600!! "Holy fuck!" I said to myself. "That's insane!" I really felt like I was the fucking bee's knees at this point! I couldn't believe it.

Then the doubt began to creep in. I wanted this so badly, but did I deserve it? I thought: 'Wait a minute, am I worth it?" I had to mentally slap myself and give myself a stern talking to! I told myself: "I *DO* deserve this." But of course, once I'd accepted that, the ego crept in a little too! I then thought: "Why am I not flying first-class? I worked very hard to get here and I'm going to enjoy every minute of it. Sandy could have had any hair stylist come with her but, she chose me." But, hey, a little ego is not a bad thing and I was going to enjoy this. It was the ultimate compliment. Of all the stylists in the world, Sandy had picked me!

I wondered if Mortimer would be joining us for this trip? If he did, great but if he didn't, the thought flashed through my mind that - hopefully - Sandy wouldn't expect me to put out for this trip. If she did, I would definitely give it to her, if that's what she wanted! But then I had to shake that thought out of my head - the truth was, the relationship was nothing like that. There was nothing sexual about it. She loved the way I did her hair and she loved offering new experiences to those around her. She was an incredibly generous woman. It was like Ronnie came back to life in the body of a Chinese woman. She did as much for me as Ronnie did and I appreciated every second of it.

The day arrived for my departure. I made sure that all my gear was ready. Bobby Pins, curling irons, two blow dryers. Everything I would need while there. Next to doing the Google wedding, this was the most exciting job I'd done so far. The Air China terminal seemed a lot like the Chinese consulate in downtown LA, where I got my visa stamped.

Is it just me, or do the Chinese seem like they had no clue what the fuck they're doing? They sort of wander around aimlessly, like they're blind or something. It blew my mind! I was curious to see how they behaved in their own country. I could imagine that there's near accidents almost every minute of every day because they don't seem to really pay attention. Or maybe they are and that's just how they roll. Maybe I was just being impatient!

I checked in, got on the plane and away we went. As I sat down I noticed that all the flight attendants were pretty cute. This was going to be a long 13-hour flight, so I started to plan my entertainment for the evening.

In my travel naiveté, I sat there in my seat hoping they spoke English. Of course, they did! It was an international flight, there were people of all nationalities on the plane, we were flying out of the US, so naturally they would speak English. But then I thought: "Maybe I can practice my Chinese on them!" These poor stewardesses had no idea what they were in for!

But first things first, I needed a drink. I always find that drinking on planes makes me a much friendlier person. So, I'm sitting there on the plane and I'm getting wasted. I see the flight attendants checking me out so I started asking them all kinds of questions. At first it was about their homeland: "What's it like in China?" But it soon progressed to more personal questions like: "Have you ever been with an American guy?" I blame it on the alcohol! I'm sure they get this all the time from male passengers, so they just played along and good-naturedly laughed at me.

While talking to them, I discovered that two of the flight attendants just so happened to be from Beijing. They asked me why I was going there. I totally played it up and told them I was going for a photo shoot for a very famous Chinese woman.

Right away they asked who it was. I told them and they genuinely seemed really impressed, even though they had trouble believing I was just a hairdresser! "Wow, you're the hairdresser?" They seemed so surprised, like it was the last thing I was going to say. I replied: "Yes, do I not look like I would be a hair stylist?" They giggled and said: "No, not at all. You look like you're in a rock and roll band."

Now it was my turn to laugh. I decided to play it coy at this point: "Well, so sorry to disappoint you both. I'm just a humble hair stylist." Then they started to ask me what my client was like. You could see in their eyes that the interest was growing. They knew how my client met her husband, Mortimer, those flight attendants knew all about her and knew how she got to into the position she was in. I guess her story was pretty famous, but I was oblivious to how it all went down. I was actually getting a history lesson about Sandy from two strangers! They were telling me all these things that I didn't know about her.

I picked up that there was a bit of jealousy in their tone, but I totally understood that. Sandy had hit the jackpot and regular, working-class women are always going to be jealous of someone like her. Sandy just made things happen for herself. She did what the others wouldn't do, but deep down know they wanted to. The stewardesses were talking to me every time they passed by. They kept asking me about Hollywood and what celebrities were like.

One stewardess asked: "Do you know what you are shooting in China?" I told her that we were going to shoot a spread on Sandy for Cosmopolitan Magazine. Their eyes lit right up! One of them exclaimed: "You know that's the biggest and most famous magazine in China?" "It is?" I replied. At this point I'm wondering if any of the other customers are getting attention because both of these girls have been talking to me for at least 30 minutes. I was fortunate that I didn't have to pay for any of my alcohol on the flight. They kept me boozed up which makes me even more talky.

Since both of these flight attendants were from Beijing, they told me about certain areas I should visit. Wangfujing was one of them – it's one of the most famous shopping streets of Beijing. Wangfujing is a big market place and promenade that is in the center of the city. They asked me where I was staying and I told them the Grand Hyatt. Their eyes got big again as they instructed me: "That's a very nice hotel. You should definitely go to Suzie Wong." The World of Suzie Wong was one of the most popular nightclubs in Beijing. It was part 1930s Shanghai opium den and part postmodern lounge – totally flamboyant! Founded in 2002, it was named after the protagonist from British novelist Richard Mason's book and was the place to hang out with the rich and beautiful in the capital.

The stewardesses told me about another area that was up and coming called Gongti Dong Lu, but they could tell that they were losing me on the names of these places. One of the girls looked at me and said: "I'll write these places down for you." I was thinking to myself: "Thank God because in the condition I'm in now, I'll never remember." These girls were getting me wasted! They wrote these places down for me and fed me yet another red wine.

I could see that other customers were flagging them down and giving me dirty looks. All of the places and things they told me to check out were racing in my head. It seemed so amazing to be going to a different place than where I'm from. Just 13 hours away, I'd be in a completely different country. I was very excited! But then the liquor started to kick in and I crashed out for a few hours.

As we began our descent into Beijing I felt myself sobering up. The plane got lower and lower and I was getting more excited by the minute. As the flight attendants did their last walk through, I got some flirty looks from the two attendants that helped me earlier. They wished me good travels and said they hoped I would have a good time. They then told me that Chinese girls love American guys and giggled as they said I wouldn't be alone for too long.

I looked out the window and could see that it was really cloudy where we were landing. At least it seemed cloudy, or maybe it was just dirty. As we descended, the flight attendants began to push a cart through the aisles to do their last rounds. Then I noticed the cigarette cartons. They were actually selling cigarette cartons on the descent! I'd never seen that before. Just goes to show how much the Chinese loved their cigarettes.

Between what looks like brown air outside, the window of the plane and the cartons of cigarettes, I was just hoping I wouldn't get lung cancer while I'm there! On the way to baggage claim I was blown away by the airport. It was an architectural masterpiece! One of the most beautiful airports I'd ever seen in my life!

To get to the baggage claim you have to take a tram. I stepped into the tram and who was standing right in front of me? John Paul DeJoria. Yes, the guy with the ponytail who owns Paul Mitchell Hair Care! What a coincidence that the owner of Paul Mitchell Hair Care was on my flight!

It was a sign! I have no fear, so immediately I go up to him. You only live once right? I said: "I hope I'm not bothering you, I just wanted to tell you that I'm a big fan." John Paul had flown his entire hair team there for a huge international hair show. He was so friendly. I said: "I've always dreamed of starting my own hair care company. Any advice for a young hair stylist like myself who's on his way up?" He actually gave me some pointers and told me that the name of the brand should have a 'personal flow to it'.

Here is this billionaire, who just got off a 13-hour flight, doesn't know who I am, and is totally taking his time to engage in conversation. I thanked him for his time. I didn't want to seem like a pest. And the best part of it? He asked me: "What's your name?" "Brandon," I answered. "What a pro!" I thought to myself. "That's what I want to be when I grow up. I want to be like that guy. Hopefully one day, I have young, aspiring hairstylists approaching me, telling me that I was their inspiration when they were getting started."

This was going to be a great trip, I thought to myself! Already off to a great start, I couldn't wait to see what would happen next. We got to baggage claim and I waited for the luggage to appear. I could see my bags right away, so I grabbed them and headed for the entrance. The magazine was sending a driver to pick me up. I kept my eyes open for the guy holding up the Martinez sign. I didn't think there would be a lot of people called Martinez flying into to Beijing, but you never know!

There he was. I walked up to him and pointed to the sign that he was holding to let him know that I'm the Martinez he was looking for. I asked him if he's Hugo. Hugo was the guy who was coordinating the photo shoot. I think he actually owned the magazine, but I wasn't quite sure. The guy holding the sign shook his head no. "I'm driver", he quickly said. He motioned me to go with him and away we went. I asked him what his name was, but he looked at me like I was a Martian. I guess he didn't speak any English.

I was a little concerned that I was getting into a car with someone who didn't understand a word I was saying, in a foreign country and I didn't even know if my phone was going to work. Plus I'm a bit hungover, so the nice hotel room sounded like a great idea at this point. He grabbed my luggage and proceeded to walk to the parking garage. We walked up to this black Mercedes G-Wagon and he loaded my luggage into the back. Now this is what I'm talking about! This is the way to get picked up from the airport.

I offered to help him load the luggage, but again he looked at me like I was speaking gibberish. I could have been talking baby talk for all he cared and he still wouldn't understand shit. I wondered if they didn't bother to learn English here or at least didn't care to. It was pointless talking to him, so I just said to myself: "Fine, load my luggage and treat me like the rock star that I am. Now drive me into the city!"

As we were driving, I realized that the cloudy air was, in fact, really severe pollution. The sky looked way more brown when I was looking up at it. We began our road trip into the city, which took about 45 minutes. As we started to get closer to the hotel, I could see these really amazing buildings. I'd never seen skyscrapers shaped like this before. They were built with weird angles and different colors of glass like blues and reds instead of the traditional clear windows.

I was waiting to see if this guy's driving was good or not. Since the Chinese have this stereotype to really suck at driving, I wondered if I would see any accidents on the way. No such luck. But I kept my seat belt on pretty tight just in case.

As we exited off the freeway I really got to take in the city. Beijing was nothing like I had ever seen before. So many people! So many people on bicycles, and mopeds riding through the city! What was interesting was that most of the people on the streets wore hospital masks over their mouths and noses to prevent the toxic air from entering their lungs. I wondered what the lung cancer rate was there? Or did the Chinese people adjust to it between smoking and the shit-stained skyline. The sky was seriously brown like a toilet!

As I expected, the driving got worse as we entered into the heart of the city. Between the cars, buses, bicycles and mopeds all over the place, I must have seen 20 near-collisions before we reached the hotel. I guess this is how they drive and live. I could see buses and bicycles driving mere inches away from each other in traffic. So many people were running red lights as if it was the popular thing to do. For a Communist country, they obviously didn't care about breaking the laws, even if they were just traffic laws. With this many people in a city, there is bound to be a fatal traffic accident every 10 minutes.

We approached the Grand Hyatt Beijing hotel and pulled into the parking area. The driver unloaded my luggage and walked me to the front desk. I thanked him, or at least nodded at him with the words thank you in my mind as he turned and left, completely emotionless. The front desk person greeted me - in English! Thank God! I gave him my name and he said: "Mr. Martinez, welcome to the Grand Hyatt Beijing. Would you like some help with your luggage to your room?" I told him: "Yes, that would be great."

He gave me my room key and up I went to the 15th floor. It was a very nice room. Within five minutes the bellhop was there with the rest of my stuff. I dropped him $5 for his troubles. He sort of bowed his head and said something that sounded like 'shit-shit'. I'm sure shit-shit wasn't really what he said, it just sounded like it.

Maybe it meant thank you, what did I know. I was more occupied with the comfy looking bed. I knew my body was tired, but how was I going to sleep while I'm here and this excited? My body wanted me to sleep, but my mind wanted to explore.

I didn't have to work till the next day so I thought: "Why not just go and check out the city?" I went downstairs and walked up to the concierge and asked him where I could go that was close by. The concierge was this German guy named Heiko. He said: "You're in luck, right outside is Wangfujing." I was thinking: "Great! I know I've heard of this place before. The flight attendants told me about this place." Heiko told me: "There's lots of shopping and restaurants to choose from. You will love it!" Then he asked me with a grin: "You're American, yes? Where are you from?" I told him: "I just flew in from Los Angeles." He looked me up and down: "You must be in a famous rock band!"

Now I was grinning: "No, I'm actually a hair stylist. I'm here with Sandy for a magazine shoot." He knew who I was talking about straight away: "Oh yes, of course. She stays here a lot when she's in town. Well, just go out front and make a right and you will be at the beginning of Wangfujing. You will have very good time while you are here." He said this in a way like he knew something that I didn't. I thanked him and off I went.

I started to walk down the lobby and outside of the hotel. I made a right like Heiko said to do and there I was. Wangfujing. It was a lot like the Santa Monica Promenade, which is an outside mall in Santa Monica that runs alongside the coast, although it was a lot bigger and obviously the Chinese version. But it still had the same set up as the Third Street promenade, just everything written in Chinese. Most of the spaces were filled with junky little tourist shops. Little statuettes of dragons and Chinese temples in every window.

To the average American tourist, this might seem interesting, but to me it was the same as the junk they sell on Hollywood Boulevard. Also, the people who ran these little stores were very pushy. They would yell out things like: "Hey, you. You American? You come with me. You come with me, I show you many fun things."

I just kept walking, sort of ignoring them as I would pass by. Not 15 minutes of walking and a young girl with a little dress approached me: "Hello. You American? Yes? I saw you from over there where I was standing and I knew I wanted to talk to you. You want to walk with me. I think you're very handsome."

Already I felt like Matthew Modine in *Full Metal Jacket* with the hooker soliciting him in the town the Marines were occupying. I was just waiting for her to say the cheesy line: "Anything you want, I love you long time." I figured she was a hooker and she was trying really hard to get me as a client. Her English was not good at all so when she spoke, she didn't really make any sense. I thought it was cute. Poor girl.

Having to sell your pussy for money is a tough gig in any country, I'm sure. She asked me where I was going and what I was doing here in Beijing. I made up some bullshit lie and told her I was meeting a friend down the way, but thanks anyway for the offer. She gave up just as fast as she approached like I was just a number in her long day of trying to find a John.

A soon as I got to the next block, another girl approached me with the same rap. Really broken English. She had a similar outfit on, trying to ask me pretty much the same questions. This could have been the other girl's sister for all I knew. I told this one the same thing, that I was meeting a friend down the street, but thanks anyway. Then the girl asked me: "You buy me something? You want to buy me something and take me home?" I couldn't help but laugh. I had to tell her: "No, no I'm good but thank you," and basically kept going. Boy, were they aggressive!

I kept walking, taking all of it in. I had this cool video camera that Sandy had given me before the trip. It was one of those Flip Video cameras that took videos and you could instantly hook them up to your computer with the USB. It was a really great little camera. I took some cool video of the buildings and of the people on the streets. I didn't want to shoot too much for fear of looking like a tourist and attracting another hooker.

Uh oh. I spoke to soon! I figured this time I would have a little fun with it. So, the hooker rolled up to me and spewed out the same questions - asking me if I'm American and if I'm in a band. So funny how tattoos make you look to rest of the world. Every place in the world that I've been, all the hookers and the drug dealers always approached me and asked if I'm in a band. Then they try to sell me sex or drugs. So, this one started in on where I'm staying and do I want to hang out with her? So I just went for it. "How much?" I ask. She said $100 for 30 minutes. Of course, she wanted to be paid in US dollars, not the local currency!

Then I asked her: "Do I get to fuck your mouth?" She looked perplexed. Then I tell her: "I'd really like for you to put on a strap on, fuck me in my ass, then jerk me off at the same time. In America we call that a 'reach around.' How much for all that?" At this point she's looking totally confused. I don't think she's ever been asked that before. Once I said, 'reach around,' she was totally lost. She kind of shook her head at me and said: "OK, OK, $50 for 30 minutes." So I then asked: "Is the reach around included?" Again, just a blank stare.

So, she answered really slowly: "Whatever you want." I was now thinking, "Wow, what a dirty little birdy." If I didn't care about getting AIDS from some random hooker in some foreign country, I would've totally violated every hole that was attached to this poor little Chinese girl. Either that, or there's the possibility she would've lured me into some dangerous situation where I would've been robbed and killed. God knows if I had screamed, no one would understand a word. Mainly because the language sounded like screaming half the time anyway, no one would know the difference.

I opted for the safer approach and said: "Thanks anyway, I'm meeting a friend down the way. Maybe next time." She had no clue what that meant. I kept walking. Sometimes people just make it too easy for me to fuck with them.

As I was walking down a new street, I could smell the food coming out of the restaurants. Even though I've had plenty of Chinese food at home, the smells here were much more intense. I could tell that the flavor here was like nothing I'd tasted before in the States. The people passing by, the language, the entire vibe – it was all so different from what I was used to.

I'd been in the country less than 24 hours, but I could feel myself really falling in love with it. I didn't think I would love it as much as I did. I almost envisioned myself living here. Could I do it? What would it be like? I was pretty sure coming from Hollywood I would be a star in the hair world here. What would my parents think? It would be like: "Hey mom, I'm moving to China!" She'd think I was fucking nuts! They would never have believed me. I love adventure. Think about it. An American, tattooed, straight hair stylist living in Beijing? I knew I'd fucking crush it here!

As all these thoughts were going through my head as I continued my stroll through Wangfujing. I noticed a salon in my sights. I walked over to this, funny little hair salon. These hairdressers were really busy. The place was jamming actually! I opened the door and walked in and the whole fucking place stopped and checked me out. You would think I'd walked in naked or something.

So me, the wise ass, started waving at everyone like I was the mayor or something. They all waved back at me and smiled at me in that real Asian way. You know, when you drop off your dry cleaning and you know they don't speak English and you don't speak Chinese, but there's this mutual nodding that goes on between the both of you? That's what was happening to me with every fucking client and stylist in this salon. I felt really famous!

So, I just started walking around the salon like I owned the place. I went up to each stylist and started validating their work with a thumbs-up or a nod of acceptance like they were doing a good job and I was approving. It was awesome. As I made the rounds in this place I noticed these contraptions that hung from the ceiling. They looked like electrical jelly fish with tentacles that obviously attached to peoples hair in some way. They looked like the machines that movie stars from the old days used to hook themselves up to get body in their hair before curling irons and blow dryers were invented.

In China, these contraptions are still in full effect, which was shocking to me. In a country that's so far advanced in the tech world, I couldn't believe what I was seeing! These contraptions were so outdated, I had only seen these types of hair curling machines before in books and old movies. And they were using them like it was the newest, hottest thing! It was surreal!

I walked out and only a few feet away was another salon. I realized I had hit 'Salon Row' in Beijing. Each salon greeted me the same and each time I went into a new one they all had these contraptions hung from the ceiling to make these women's hair curly.

So, after all my rambling around, I realized that I'm a bit lost. That's one thing that I'm not good at is remembering where I was or where I parked. In fact, I'm really bad at it. I get lost at The Grove in West Hollywood. It's a mall in Los Angeles. I go there all the time and I never remember where I park. So here I was walking through downtown Beijing thinking about what it would be like to live here, thinking about everything in my life, and all of a sudden, I'm fucking lost. Oh shit! For the first couple of blocks, because I'm a pretty typical stubborn man, I refused to ask for directions.

Of course, I think I'm smart and I can get myself out of this. I took a few rights, a few lefts, then realized that I was more confused than ever! How did I even think I'd be able to find my way back to the hotel when I get lost in The Grove's car park? At least when I'm in the States, even if I get lost I can read the fucking signs to sort of navigate my way back to wherever I came from.

Well, not the case here. Oh, and by the way, no one, I mean no one speaks a word of English. Not a fucking lick! Believe me I tried. I must've gone up to at least 10 people and all of them gave me the same look - sorry motherfucker! That's the look I was getting from everyone I approached. At least that's how it looked to me. They were no help at all. It was like being in New York City, but instead of rude New Yorkers, there was only rude Chinese people.

Some of the people I asked even threw up their arms after I tried a few sentences to see if they could help me. I'd never been in a situation like this before. I'm afraid I turned into a typical tourist abroad at this point as I caught myself speaking louder and louder to them, trying to explain where I needed to go. Just like a stupid American speaking louder to people in hopes of being understood better, like they were all fucking deaf or something. It was like a bad comedy sketch – and the joke was on me!

Where were those hookers now when I needed them? Of course, the hookers were the only ones who could speak any English. I guess they didn't hang out this far off the beaten track. I must have walked pretty far. It was starting to get dark and I was really sweating it.

What the fuck was I going to do? I even looked for a cop or someone, anyone, in a uniform, in the hope of finding anyone who could speak English. I was really starting to freak out at this point. I just stopped, gathered myself, took a deep breath and tried to back track as well as I could.

I remembered that the hotel was not far from the Wangfujing. "Okay, I can do this," I said to myself. I turned a few corners, went down a few blocks and started to remember these buildings I had walked past. Then miraculously, I saw the salons that I had walked into. So I walked back into one and walked up to the front desk person and kind of threw my arms up in the air and asked: " Wangfujing? Wangfujing?" She smiled and walked me outside and pointed me in the right direction. She didn't speak a word of English, all of this was done with pointing.

But I wasn't out of this just yet. She pointed me to the Wangfujing mall, but I still had to get back to the hotel. I started walking in the direction that she pointed me to. I walked down a couple of blocks. "Phew" I said to myself. Everything was looking more and more familiar.

I started to feel like I was going to make it out of this. In my twisted mind, I even began hoping to run into one of those hookers who spoke English! Maybe they would help me out. I'd even drop them a $20 to point me in the right direction. But it was dark by now and not a hooker in site.

"What kind of city is this?" I said to myself. It seemed like the hookers might have some sort of curfew because there wasn't one single one of them around. But then, standing there on a street corner, was every horny man's dream. A hooker! She saw me, recognized me from earlier and made a beeline straight for me.

I was so glad to see her and she seemed just as happy to see me as her face had lit up. But as she got closer, she hesitated. I think she saw the panic and stress in my face and held back. I took a step forward and said: "Can you please tell me where the Grand Hyatt Beijing is? I'm so lost." She smiled and pointed me in the right direction. She said, "It's just down the block, make a right then a left and you will be there." I was so grateful that she had decided to be nice to me, especially after the way I treated her earlier. I gave her a $20 bill and thanked her very much. She was so thankful. Not as thankful as I was.

I finally got myself back to the hotel. As I walked back in, the concierge asked me if I enjoyed my first walk in China. I said: "You have no idea, brother!" He then asked me if I wanted a massage from one of the massage therapists. I was stressed and achy. Not thinking too much about it I said: "Sure." I got to the room, took off my shoes and started to relax. I had actually totally forgotten all about the massage until I heard a knock at the door.

I let the girl in, undressed down to my underwear and got comfortable under the sheets. She started doing her thing. Massaging my neck, then my shoulders. It felt great. She was a real pro. She would give anyone at Burke Williams Spa a run for their money. And the best part? She didn't speak at all.

There is nothing worse than going to get a massage and the fucking massage therapist starts talking to you as you're trying to relax. Don't ask me what I do motherfucker, just massage my body! I don't care if you're trying to be an actor. Fucking good for you! That's one thing that I love about Asian women, the silence! It's extraordinary. She didn't say a fucking word. She just kept doing her thing.

I'd booked an hour massage, so thirty minutes into it and I was half asleep, drooling on my pillow. She had to wake me up when she was done. Maybe it was because of the 13-hour flight. Maybe it was because I was so jet-lagged and stressed from my little adventure of getting lost. Whatever it was, I was beat. As she began to finish I was waiting for her to pack up so I could give her a tip when she asked me the inevitable question. She asked: "Want me to finish you up?" I jerk you off for extra $100."

It actually took me by surprise. Believe it or not, I have never had a person offer me a happy ending after a massage. I guess most guys would probably take her up on her offer but not me. After the day I had, I actually started busting up laughing. I don't think that was the reaction she as expecting. But I couldn't help it. I was so delirious from the trip and the lack of sleep. Plus, I was really hungover from the flight.

My laughter made her very uncomfortable because I'm sure men usually said yes. She definitely wasn't happy with me laughing at her when she asked me about the happy ending, so she packed up as fast as she could and split. She didn't even wait for her tip. I crashed out, had a great sleep and woke up to a beautiful morning in Beijing.

The next morning I awoke to breakfast in bed. Since I wasn't paying for anything, I decided to order whatever I wanted. Full breakfast, coffee, orange juice, even a Mimosa to get the day started. I didn't have to start until the next day, so I had another full day to chill out before the shoot. Sandy had arrived and sent me a text message to see if I made it in OK. I texted back saying: "Yes," and that I was actually going to the gym for a workout. She told me that she was going there as well and that I might see her.

I went down to the gym for my workout. Sandy was already there pounding away on the treadmill. We talked a bit. She asked me how the flight was and if I had a chance to walk around a bit. I decided not to tell her about my drama the day before. She said that she had a friend here that worked for a music website called MyPlace, that was just acquired by Sandy's husband, Mortimer. She was going to hook me up with this, Chinese-American guy named Peikwen, who lived here with his wife.

Peikwen was working for MyPlace in China and since Sandy was the wife of the new owner of MyPlace, she pretty much could have anybody there do whatever she wanted. She told me that she already called Peikwen and had asked him to take me out. Peikwen was really cool. First of all, he was an American-born Chinese guy. He had been living in Beijing with his wife for the last year, working for MyPlace. Peikwen and his Mrs. were both my age and knew everywhere to go in Beijing. It was awesome! They showed me everything that a young guy would want to see in Beijing.

Peikwen and his girl came to pick me up at the hotel. We hit it off right away. He was originally from Los Angeles, believe it or not. Peikwen and his wife were tripping out on the fact that Sandy had actually flown her hairstylist out just for this photo shoot. Right after we met he asked: "So let me get this straight, Sandy actually flew you in just to do her hair? She couldn't find someone here?"

I responded by saying: "Of course she did, I'm kind of a big deal." They both looked at each other and just laughed. It had been a while since they had seen someone from Los Angeles and my slightly arrogant attitude made them feel like they were back home.

I guess, cocky, straight, tattooed hair stylists in Beijing are a rarity. I stuck out like a sore thumb. You could tell that they loved it. They asked me: "What do you want to do first?" I said: "I don't want to put you guys out. I feel bad that Sandy has kind of stuck you with me. I'm down to do whatever. Whatever you guys had planned, I'm more than happy to just tag along." They responded with: "Perfect! We have an art gallery opening to go to, then, we had tickets to a soccer game later. We can grab another ticket for you if you want?"

I agreed with whatever they wanted to do because regardless of where we went, it was going to be an adventure! They added: "We have a friend who you might like as well. She has been here working for about a year teaching English. She's going to love you!"

I was ready for whatever they were going to throw at me. Their friend was going to meet us at the art opening. So off we went. We took cabs everywhere because they didn't have a car and since Peikwen spoke fluent Chinese it was easy for us to get around. Being driven around in a cab in Beijing was like being in a cab in New York but on steroids! In China, the driving etiquette is a bit different than it is in the States.

In the States, when a pedestrian is crossing the street and the driver and the pedestrian's eyes meet, that automatically means that the driver will yield for the pedestrian and will stop. Not the case in China. In China, if you want to cross the street and you look at the driver who is going to make a turn, you looking at him means that you are letting him go before you. Completely backwards from what we are used to doing.

Basically, if you want to jay walk in China, you have to cross the street without looking at a single car, trusting the drivers not to hit you, because if you look at them, that signals them to go ahead and keep going. It was fucking bizarre. The whole time we were driving in the cab, I would see near accidents all day long. People would walk in front of buses without looking at the bus drivers and automatically the bus drivers would stop on a dime, nearly hitting the pedestrians. I thought to myself: "People are human. Mistakes have to happen all the time. People have to get hit and killed daily." You've never really had an adventure in a cab, till you've been to China. Trust me!

We finally got to the art opening and Peikwen's eyes lit up because he was also a budding artist. This opening was also featuring his work, which I didn't know till we got there. This wasn't like any art opening I had ever been to before. You couldn't even call this place a gallery. It was like an art compound. It was huge! It was like a modern apartment complex, turned art gallery. There were a lot of Americans there as well. All guys with Chinese girlfriends.

I've always said that a lot of white nerdy guys love Asian chicks. Well, here was the Mecca for that. Most of these guys left home in the States to find love in China. And it appeared these Chinese girls went nuts for these guys. Not one American guy at this art opening was single. They all had their little Chinese girlfriends following them around giving dirty looks to the other Chinese girls. It was like they were each guarding their own priceless Terra-Cotta Warrior and they couldn't let them out of their sight!

I met this guy named Chuck from Omaha, of all places. He had been there for about three years and had no intention of going back. Chuck probably had no game with the girls back in the States, but here, Chuck was a fucking pimp! He was Beijing's Dennis Hof, you know the guy that owns Nevada's notorious Bunny Ranch? He had these little girls following him around everywhere like he was an A-list movie star. He certainly didn't look it, but he had the pulling power of fucking Brad Pitt.

None of these girls were that cute either, but what did he care? Getting a lot of attention from girls does something to a man's ego. I could see where he was coming from. Back in Hollywood, a guy like Chuck would never get into the club, never get any ass unless he was filthy rich.

Here, he had the world at his feet. Besides, Asian girls love to please. I could totally see why he didn't ever want to leave. As an American, you only get 90 days there, then you have to go home and apply for another visa to get back in. Chuck had already been back like eight times! Good for him. He asked me I what I was doing there. I told him I was there doing hair for a rich Chinese women. He had never met anybody like me before. "Getting flown overseas to just do one person's hair for a photo shoot is not common here," he informed me. "Wow, what's that feel like?"

I didn't really know how to respond to that. "It's very normal to me," I replied, trying to be cool. "In Hollywood, women will spend whatever it takes to look their best for an event. This is technically my second trip overseas for a job." He was in disbelief. I'm sure the hairstylists in Omaha weren't getting flown anywhere!

We talked some more, but his Chinese girlfriend was a bit pushy and was starting to feel neglected, so I backed off from our conversation and quickly ended it with a: "Hey, so nice to meet you, bro. Take care."

I walked on down the corridor to another section where all the pieces were done with projectors that were being blasted on huge concrete walls. They all had a futuristic theme, mixed with machines in the middle of these beautiful natural landscapes like an ultra- modern forklift in the middle of a beautiful forest. They seemed to represent technology interrupting nature's beauty. I was intrigued by these pieces of artwork.

As I was staring at these pieces, Peikwen walked up to me and asked if I liked them. "I love them," I said. "These are mine", he responded. I was stunned: "Wow, these are awesome. You're so talented! You both seem so happy together!" I barely knew these two, but already I liked them both very much.

They both were immediately warm to me and I felt honored that they had shared their experiences with a total stranger as they had only known me for a few hours.

When you're far away and you meet people you like, you stay friends forever. Distance speaks volumes. We walked around the art opening a bit more to see the rest of the pieces. We still had a soccer game to go to and then out for dinner later. Crazy how my adrenaline had kicked in and, surprisingly, I wasn't tired at all. The soccer game was being held at a stadium where all the soccer games for the Olympics were going to be. I'm glad I was there before the Olympics started because I'm sure the crowds would have been insane.

As we drove to the stadium in another death cab, I noticed that construction crews were covering people's homes. I asked Peikwen what was that was all about. He explained: "The government here doesn't want the tourists or the athletes who are coming for the Olympics to see any poverty or trashy looking homes, so they are just covering the people's houses that don't look nice."

I thought: "That's pretty fucked up," I jokingly asked him: "What do they do with the homeless people? Kill them?" Wow, that jokey comment pretty much bombed as Peikwein didn't respond. Neither did his girl. That was the only time I felt uncomfortable with them. I guess there are some things that are better not to know about.

We arrived at the stadium and I noticed the front was packed with people smoking cigarettes. The Chinese fucking love their cigarettes! Peikwen told me that, because you're not allowed to smoke in the stands, you have to smoke out front or in the bathrooms. The rules here were so backwards! These people were smoking like it was their last cigarette. Literally inhaling like they were smoking joints. Like they were hookers sucking the last dick they would ever get to suck. It was hysterical. I'm so glad I don't smoke.

We walked into the stadium and took our seats. I was amazed to see how many people from other countries were there. People from all over. Brazil, Canada and The United States. I had no idea how many people liked to visit China. I'm not even a soccer fan, but I was excited to see the game.

It was a girls' soccer match featuring Brazil against China. As the game began, I noticed that the

Chinese would root for whoever was winning. I asked Peikwen why that was? He said: "The Chinese don't really have loyalty to a certain team. They will get behind any team that is winning. Plus, the Chinese are huge gamblers, so they will place bets against their own country." I guess at the end of the day money talks.

Halfway through the game I had to take a piss, so I told them I would be right back. I walked into the men's restroom only to find it packed with Chinese men smoking their heads off and waiting in line to use the urinals. I couldn't believe my eyes with what I was witnessing. In the States, when you enter the men's restroom, we wait a few feet back from the urinals until it is our turn, then we walk up to it when the person before us leaves.

Not in China! They actually wait behind each other all the way up to the urinal. So, if I was peeing, I had ten guys behind me waiting to go. And I mean right behind me, like inches behind me. The guy behind me could've reached out and patted me on the shoulder while I was doing my business!

Then on top of that you have guys trying to cut in front of you in your face. The men would literally line-hop into different lines to get ahead as if you were invisible. Talk about no personal space. I had to body check three guys who tried to get ahead of me as I got closer to my turn.

Dirty little fuckers too, picking their noses and cutting in line while they smoked their cigarettes. The way they acted you would think I was on another planet. A real dirty one, that is. It was one of the most disgusting, public restrooms I had ever been in. I finished my business and muscled my way out of there and back to my seat.

I told Pekwein about my experience and he just laughed: "Oh yeah. I should have told you about that." They both turned and laughed at me like they just played a cruel joke on me. I smiled as I drank my Diet Coke. At least I hoped this was a Diet Coke and not some Chinese manufactured chemical drink.

The game went on and the Brazilians won. As they scored the final goal to wrap up the game, you could see all the Chinese people clap for them as if they were Brazilian, too. So strange! We left the game and headed back to my hotel to drop me off. The photo shoot was going to be early in the morning, so I needed to get some rest, even though I could've stayed up all night.

It was time to be responsible. I mean, hello, I am here to work! We got to the hotel and we said our goodbyes. Peikwen said: "We're going to a club tomorrow night. You should come with us. You'll love it. My friend is the DJ, so we'll get right in." I responded with: "Sounds great, I'll let you know when I get done." I walked back into the hotel, got to my room and crashed. What a day. It was pretty fun being on the other side of the planet.

The next morning came faster than a high school kid getting his first lay. The jet-lag was kicking in and my body was really feeling it! As I dragged myself into the nice hot shower in the beautiful hotel room, I started to run the next few hours through my mind. I was saying to myself: "OK, Brandon, you have a big day today! This is a huge opportunity to shine as a celebrity hair stylist and it's days like today that allow you to have that title."

I dried myself off, gathered up my gear and headed to the suite where we would be shooting. The photo shoot was actually being shot right there in the Grand Hyatt, in one of the master suites, way at the top of the hotel. Cosmopolitan magazine in China is like Vogue magazine here in the States. Vogue magazine in China isn't as popular there as it is here. Cosmopolitan was the bigger name in China.

I headed up to the suite and Sandy was already there with this really cute, Chinese girl who appeared to be the stylist. Sandy greeted me and said: "Brandon, this is Tian Tian." Tian Tian was this really pretty Chinese fashion stylist who worked for the magazine. Being a stylist, she had amazing style! I remember she was wearing these kick-ass boots that most girls would give their left tit for! On top was a leather motorcycle jacket with a small skirt. She looked like someone who I would want to be my girlfriend. I'd always wanted to date a girl who was somewhat in the fashion business because if they were cute, then the style was there to match.

I said: "Hello," to her and began to unload my gear. As I was plugging in my curling irons and blow dryer, I could see Tian Tian was checking me out any chance she could get. I have to admit that I was really attracted to her from the first moment I saw her. I'm not usually into Asian girls, but this one was definitely an exception. While I was getting unpacked, this older woman walked in with an assistant and a photographer behind her.

This woman's name was Vera. Vera was the 'Anna Wintour' of China. For those of you that don't know - and I can't imagine that many of you don't - Anna Wintour is a legend in fashion circles. She's the Queen Bee in the fashion world and has been the editor of Vogue since 1988. If you're a designer and she even looks at you the wrong way, your career is over. If you still don't know who she is, then you're obviously not into fashion or magazines! Just watch Meryl Streep in *The Devil Wears Prada* movie. Her ice-queen character Miranda Priestly was supposedly based on Wintour!

Anyway, Vera basically was the head of all fashion for mainland China. Not quite in Wintour's league, but still a huge deal in Asia. I remember that when I introduced myself to her, she wasn't very friendly. She just kind of gave me a quick handshake, like I was contagious or something. I might have gotten a tiny, brief smile but that was it. Later, I found out that she actually really liked me, but that was the extent of her emotional range.

The fashion business is a tough one and I'm sure, being a female in a Communist country like China has to have its obstacles! I could tell that Vera demanded respect and wasn't fucking around! I could only imagine how many people she screamed at on a daily basis. But what stood out for me the most with Vera was that she didn't shave her armpits.

This really threw me off because she not only wasn't shaven, but she was fucking owning it! She flailed her arms around, directing people on the shoot. She raised her arms whenever she felt like it. It was like she was setting a trend with the hairy armpits and she didn't give a fuck about it.

It sort of bugged me out because, as an American, I'm not used to seeing a woman in such a position like Vera, rolling around with hair under her arms. In the States, women who don't shave their armpits are usually hippie type chicks, or lesbians really. Maybe Vera was a lesbian? I doubt it. This woman didn't give a fuck and everybody on the shoot minus Sandy and myself, was afraid of her.

The photographer that was working this gig was also very famous in China. He was like a Mario Testino or an Annie Leibovitz. I have to be honest, most of the major photographers I had ever worked with were kind of assholes! The two I mentioned above, I had never worked with, so I can't say anything about them, but I have worked with other, reputable photographers in the States and from what I witnessed, they were slightly abusive to their assistants and the crew. I've always felt that most, not all, but most photographers take themselves a bit too seriously.

This also goes for hair stylists and make-up artists who work on big photo shoots. I always hated this kind of attitude and, really, it's a big reason why I'm not too fond of doing photo shoots, unless it was like this kind of situation, where I'd been flown in by a powerful socialite like Sandy. It's difficult for me to take these people seriously because after all, we're creating art! Creating art should be enjoyable, not scary. This photographer was like the ones I just described. He took himself a little too serious and then, when we started shooting, he wouldn't allow me to look at the monitor to see how Sandy's hair was looking!

All photographers, even the assholes, want the hair people to see what's going on, in case there's a hair out of place. When a hair is out of place in photographs, it stands out like a pink elephant. He was just being a dick, like most of them are and was trying make himself feel like he was in charge. He quickly learned that I didn't give a crap who he was and as far as I was concerned, he was no different to me than my Chinese food delivery guy. He was just holding a camera instead of a to-go bag!

I snapped at him to let me look at the monitor and he could tell by my tone that I wasn't playing around. I had come a long way for this job and my reputation was on the line just as much as his. Tian Tian translated what I was saying to him and he lightened up a bit and gave me the opportunity to look at the monitor.

After about an hour of shooting, everyone started to relax and actually enjoy the process. Sandy looked amazing! Between the magic that Tian Tian had done with the wardrobe and my virtuoso hairstyling, she looked like one of the most beautiful women in the world! Sandy is tall, thin and has a beautiful face that could make any mogul turn into a little boy. Her skin was soft and flawless! It was better than porcelain! As the saying goes: "Black don't crack." Well I'm telling you right now: "Asian don't raisin!" Sandy didn't have one fucking wrinkle on that gorgeous face and she has the brains to back it up.

She was devastatingly beautiful and for a glam squad, Sandy made our job really easy. As the shoot continued, Sandy was working the camera like she was the supermodel Gisele Bundchen! I had no idea that she could model like that. Even though she's beautiful, I always fancied her as a smart person who used her brains. When you have the beauty to match the brains, you're pretty much unstoppable! My respect for her was growing by the second. Looking back at my career, Sandy was really the one that made it happen for me. No-one brought me the jobs like she did and no-one - and I mean no-one - had friends like Sandy's friends.

Every person she knew was more famous and powerful than the next and she is so classy and elegant that it would be tough for any one woman to match that type of energy. Sandy was one-of-a-kind and to this day she holds the title for getting me the best jobs on earth!

I also have to give Sandy credit for getting me laid! I already owed her for the Google wedding, which the yoga instructor story got back to Sandy really fast. I think Sandy got a kick out my promiscuity on the road. She was already telling Tian Tian to hang out with me and take me out later. Being in Tian Tian's shoes, when a woman like Sandy tells you to do something, you do it!

But Sandy wasn't without haters, that's for sure! When you're really successful, there will always be a group of people who are going to hate on you. When you have haters, it's a sign that you're doing something right. I will never say anything negative about Sandy because she did nothing but try to help me. She was like a very powerful agent who was in my corner, no matter what. Remember that she stopped being friends with Jane when Jane tried to sabotage our relationship. Like I said, haters are a good thing and Jane was a huge hater!

Here I was in China, with Sandy, on a huge photo shoot and what was she trying to do? She was trying to get me laid with Tian Tian the stylist. Talk about not being selfish! If Sandy was just an actress, it would be the other way around. I would have had to be kissing her ass left and right on the entire trip because most actors are insecure and require all the attention. But Sandy was the poster child for security and beauty and she didn't give a fuck what anyone thought of her. If she did care, she hid it well.

Sandy's persistence paid off with Tian Tian because before the shoot ended, Tian Tian asked me for my phone number and said she wanted to show me around later on that night.

After the shoot, I retired back to my room for a quick, disco nap. I felt like the shoot was a huge success and I was finally able to relax a bit. I still had another two days in Beijing and it looked like I was going to have a date tonight with Tian Tian. Tian Tian, by the way, meant Sweet, Sweet in English. Talk about a sign from the universe as far as what was going to happen later on that evening. With a name like that and a hot little body to match, fireworks were definitely in the cards for later on. Chinese fireworks!

I was also supposed to hook up with Peikwen and his wife later on to go to this club called Suzie Wong, in downtown Beijing. I had set up a time to meet

Peikwen and wife for dinner and I told him that the stylist from the shoot might be joining us later at Suzie Wong.

As I headed out the hotel lobby and into the streets of Beijing to meet Peikwen, I get a text message from Tian Tian. Thank God she spoke English! She said that she wanted to meet up with me later and wanted to know where I was staying.

I texted her back telling her that I was having dinner first, then I would be heading to Suzie Wong afterwards. I asked her if she wanted to meet us there. She responded right away and said: "Yes!" and to text her after dinner.

So now that I had a date locked down for later, I was on the way to dinner with Peikwen and his wife, and after the awesome shoot we had done earlier in the day, this was looking like it was going to be an amazing evening! I met up with Peikwen and his wife and off we went to the restaurant. I couldn't remember the name of the restaurant, nor could I pronounce it, so sorry if I can't give you the recommendation when you're in Beijing!

We sat down to order and I let Peikwen order for the table. One thing I noticed right away about the menu was the way they showcased the meat - it was shown raw on the menu! I nervously asked Peikwen: "They are going to cook the food, right? Especially the chicken?"

He just laughed at me and said: "Yeah, that's just how they design the menus here in China. Chinese people like to see the meat raw on the menu for some reason." I would also see this in other restaurants I would go to while I was there.

The food started coming out to the table and each dish looked stranger than the last. The Peking duck still had the head attached, things looked like they were still moving and the smells were so different from anything I had ever smelled in Chinese restaurants in the States. But, I'm an adventurous guy, so I just went for it!

I looked down at my phone and I saw that Tian Tian had sent me a text. I responded quickly and told her to come join us at Suzie Wong nightclub. As we ate, Peikwen's wife asked: "Brandon, do you have a date?" I just gave a devilish grin and continued eating whatever I was eating. I couldn't really tell what I was eating but, damn, it was really good. It could've been chopped up Chinese babies for all I knew, but it was fucking delicious!

We wrapped up dinner and headed to the club. Tian Tian was going to show up at any moment, but as we entered the club, I noticed so many beautiful Chinese girls. It seemed like there were more girls than guys. I said to myself: "I hope I'm not bringing sand to the beach!" Tian Tian was already on her way so no point in worrying about that!

The club started to get crowded and we met up with the DJ, who is actually Peikwen's friend. I was so lucky to have been able to hook up with Peikwen. I call myself the 'Mayor of Brentwood' here in LA, but Peikwen was the 'Mayor of Beijing'! There's nothing worse than traveling to a new country, and not knowing anybody or anything. I was fortunate to not have been caught up in the tourist trap.

The DJ's name was DJ Chaussie. He gave himself the name Chaussie, because he was half Chinese and half Australian. He was super cool and bought us shots to get the night going. I was already getting wasted from the drinks at dinner.

The shots took me over the edge. Suzie Wong was decorated in a 'Ming Dynasty' style. There was red everywhere and pictures of the actual Suzie Wong all over the place. Think of the nightclub Tao, mixed with the movies, Chinatown and The Blade Runner, all rolled into one.

As I was starting to get a little blurry, Tian Tian showed up. I stood up to greet her and kissed her on the cheek. I took this opportunity to grab her tiny waist and cop a feel. I was pretty wasted by this point, so any fear I had was completely gone! I did the introductions and immediately ordered her a shot. She had some catching up to do!

Peikwen was able to speak to her in Chinese and introduced her to his wife and the other girl we were with. Next thing you know, we were all ordering another round and were all chatting away like college kids. The shots kept coming and Tian Tian was nudging herself closer to me. The music was so loud that it was hard to understand each other. Most of the conversation was happening through our eyes. She asked me about myself and how long I had been doing hair, but between the liquor, the music, and her thick Chinese accent, it was hard to make conversation without saying: "Huh?" every two seconds.

At this point her legs were stuck to mine underneath the table and more people had joined us who knew Peikwen and his wife, so we were forced to be super close to each other. Another round of shots came and I was feeding Tian Tian liquor like she was an alcoholic baby!

At this point, anything coming out of Tian Tian's mouth sounded like baby talk and I was ready to make my tongue her 'binky!' She must have been reading my mind because she laid a kiss right on me and we didn't come up for air for another 10 minutes. Tian Tian and I had no regard for the people at our table. We were making out hard and completely forgot about anyone else.

Finally, after about 10 minutes of tongue swashing, Tian Tian said: "Take me to your hotel!" There wasn't any language barrier with that request! I gave a look to Peikwen. By this time he knew what was up. He gave me that male, universal look of: "Go get it buddy!" Tian Tian and I ran out of Suzie Wong like marathon runners!

She hailed a cab and we locked lips again all the way back to the Grand Hyatt. We got to my room and she threw me on the bed like I'm her bitch! Wow, these quiet, Chinese girls were aggressive! She ripped off my clothes as I was pulling her top off, exposing her skinny, little body. No hairy armpits! Thank God!

I pulled down her skirt and panties and go down her like she was a plate of Dim Sum. Her body was so hot and she tasted amazing. She was moaning and quivering as my head was buried between her legs. Every girl has her own scent down below and I'm not talking about smelling fishy or anything like that! Yes, some women can have an unpleasant smell, but what

I'm talking about is every woman has her own, hormonal smell that turns men on when they're going down on them. It's an individual thing as I'm sure men have their own smell as well.

Her pussy was so wet and her smell, which was really good, was coming off her body in waves of intensity. Her hands were clinging on to my hair, which was a sign that I was doing something right. She tugged on my head as a signal that she wanted to go down on me. We 69'd for about a half an hour before we started to fuck.

I barely knew this person and we were doing things that married couples don't even do! She turned herself around and put me inside of her. No lube, no condom, nothing! I wasn't about to stop to call down for a condom and I had a safe feeling that she was disease free.

How wild and crazy could this girl be compared to my previous sexual encounters? Her hair was so long it went past her butt so her hair was everywhere. I remember twisting her hair into a ponytail and holding it out of the way while we were fucking.

Her thin, pale white body was moving and gyrating in all directions as I was bending her and stretching her like she was the Asian Gumby! There's nothing hotter to me than a girl moaning and groaning in another language. It was all so different from the women back at home and I could see why American men come to China and never want to leave!

Being American, with tattoos, in a strange land like China, you automatically become like a rock star. Tian Tian was completely losing control of herself with me! She was powerless and I had no idea what I was doing to make that happen. I wasn't about to question it and wasn't about to stop her.

The room was getting really muggy from the sex while the sheets were soaking wet with our sweat! There was no sign of stopping with this girl! She kept wanting more and more and I was doing everything I could to keep going. It was like she hadn't had sex in a long time and she was treating me like I was her last cigarette.

After about three hours, we finally gave ourselves a break and laid on our backs on the bed looking up at the hotel room ceiling. She confided to me that she had never done anything like this before. I have been told that before by other women, but for some reason I believed her. She told me: "You're so hot, Brandon, I have never been with a guy who looked like you before!" I have never had sex like that before with anyone!" That I believed.

Just from being in Beijing for a couple days, the men here didn't really strike me as being aggressive and passionate and I was just speculating, but it seemed like Asian men weren't really known for heavy packages in their pants. I'm not saying I'm hung like the brothers, but it's no thimble either!

She grabbed me again mid-conversation and put me inside of her! This girl was on fire! We fucked a few more times and when I looked at the clock I realized it was getting close to 4am in the morning. She was treating me like her drug and she was getting her last couple hits before she would hit the road.

After we finished, she abruptly got up and started to put her clothes back on. Still in a daze, I sat up slowly and rested my head on my hand as I was watching her zip up her boots. Now all of sudden, she seemed in a hurry to leave. She'd had her wicked way with me and she couldn't get out the door quick enough!

I was surprised. I thought we'd make some kind of connection. You don't fuck someone four times in one night and not feel anything! I asked her: "Tian Tian, what's wrong? Do you have to get up early for work? I'm sorry if I kept you too long." She looked down at me still lying on the bed.

She shook her head and smiled as she headed for the door but not before telling me: "No, I have to go home because my boyfriend is probably worried about me!"

Well, that was like being hit over the head with a wok!

Fucking Chinese girls!

HAYDEN'S PLACE

In life, things change. Nothing really ever stays the same, does it? Sometimes things change for the better and sometimes they change for the worse. And sometimes the change is beyond your control.

Sandy and her husband Mortimer got a divorce. Once that happened, Sandy stopped coming to Los Angeles. She no longer had a house in LA and once my schedule picked up, going back and forth to New York became a thing of the past.

After Sandy got divorced, I thought that the New York connection would dissipate. The divorce affected me as well because all of the events like the Oscars, the Golden Globes and every other event she attended suddenly disappeared! It seemed like that situation changed for the worse.

On the flip side, and lucky for me, Hayden and her husband ended up moving here to Los Angeles. Shortly after they moved here, they were also divorced! I would like to say that I felt bad about that, but I would be lying. I obviously felt bad for her and her children as divorce is always a stressful situation.

But all of a sudden, Hayden was living here and now she was single. Hayden, being really beautiful and the sweetheart that she is, had men coming at her left and right. When someone like Hayden gets divorced, word gets out quickly! I still was keeping my feelings quiet because Hayden never really gave me any hint that she was interested in me.

We had maintained the hairdresser and client relationship and rightly so because a client like Hayden, who would have me do her hair at least twice a week, plus her kids, was a meal ticket and then some!

Now that's a total of four clients, plus her ex-husband who had also remained my client through all of this and had been unaware of my feelings for Hayden. So, between all of them, that was five clients I would be risking if I breathed a word about my true feelings for her. I kept my mouth shut and really just did everything I could to let those feelings go. Hayden was used to a certain type of lifestyle – a lifestyle that I couldn't provide right at that time.

As a hairstylist and now a young hair care, product owner in the beginnings of building my business, what did I really have to offer Hayden other than really good sex? Our relationship had grown into a great friendship and I wasn't willing to risk all of that. As new boyfriends would appear, I would work through the pain. I remember the first guy she dated seemed like it would move into something serious. I had to be happy for her!

She was my best client and the rule is, you fuck your client, you lose your client. I kept my feelings from her and remained the supportive, friendly hairstylist who would always be there for her with whatever she needed. I don't know if her boyfriend sensed any feelings from me.

I'm sure he was a bit surprised that I was always at her house doing her hair. I guess if I had the tables turned and I was Hayden's boyfriend, the last person I would want doing her hair would be me. I was like that bad penny that always turns up!

I always remained polite to any guy that she would date, not that there were a lot of them. But I would always strive to be nice and courteous to them. At this point, I had also changed from the young, wild, alcohol infused hairstylist, to a more mature, sober business owner who was growing his new hair care brand, throughout the United States, landing big accounts like Neiman Marcus and Walgreens.

Although Hayden seemed impressed with my ability to close these types of accounts, she never gave me any inclination that she was interested in me. As far I was concerned, I was the one who had the feelings and as I have said a few times already, I tried everything I could to keep them buried. The one crazy thing about your feelings, it's impossible to run from them! As time went on my feelings were starting to grow even more.

When you spend a lot of time with someone, and you already love them, it's virtually impossible to keep them at bay! The more time I spent with Hayden, the worse it got for me. Now that she was living here, I would see her as much as I would see my friends. She even invited me to the house to have dinner with her family. She would come to the salon to get her hair done and we would walk together to get coffee and just talk about stuff.

Hayden not only became my number one client, she was becoming a real, true friend. I have seen her in vulnerable moments where she would be crying and really upset and all I wanted to do was to hold her and love her and tell her it would be okay. It would take all my strength not to take her in my arms and hold her like a lover would.

I would pray at night to God and I would ask him to please make me rich so I could have her! I felt like that was the only thing that was in my way. I believed it was the only thing that was holding me back. She would comment on how handsome I was and how sweet I was to her and she was taking notice of the wisdom I had developed over the last few years. She would compliment me and tell me all these things and I would just say to myself: "Just get the money Brandon and your life will be complete! Just get rich and she'll be yours!"

Now you're probably thinking, why didn't you just call this book *Sex, Hair & Hayden?* Since the beginning of time, everybody is driven by something. Prehistoric people were driven by hunger. If they didn't want to be hungry, they had to go out and hunt for food. Every billionaire out there was driven by something whether, it was the desire to not be poor, or maybe they wanted to get attention from someone. According to the romanticized Hollywood version of events in the movie *The Social Network*, even Mark Zuckerberg started Facebook because he wanted to date women!

Well, it was that simple for me, too. Over the last 10 years of my life, what's driven me to be the most successful person I can be is Hayden. Now that I've known her for over 10 years, she's still a driving force in my life, whether I like it or not!

Now I know that most people are going to say that money isn't everything and that love and money are two completely different entities. I'll be honest, only poor people think this way. I'll admit that money can't buy you love, but it sure can increase your options! In my world and in Hayden's world, money talks and bullshit walks! I have to give her credit for indirectly making me more ambitious in my career. I truly believe I would not have been so driven or ambitious if she hadn't come into my life.

I would always be telling myself: "When you get the money, then maybe you can get Hayden." Of course, my feelings for Hayden didn't stop me from dating or having sex - a man's still got needs! But every girlfriend that I have had since I met Hayden, has been - whether rightly or wrongly - unfavorably compared to her. I always kept her at the top of my list of things I wanted in my life. As time went on and boyfriends would come and go, I became less and less afraid of showing her my feelings.

It all started around my birthday.

Before I moved to Brentwood, I was living in an apartment in West Hollywood and on my fucking birthday, I was attacked by a neighbor's dog! Literally, the morning of my birthday, I got to the elevator to head out to work and this fucking dog jumped out of the elevator and attacked me! It was such a shock, that I tripped over myself and fell to the ground. The dog's owner, some screenwriter in Hollywood, never compensated me for my phone that was broken and never really apologized for the incident.

I called animal control over the attack, as they had three dogs in their apartment, which then made living in the building very uncomfortable for me. Despite various attempts to get the guy to pay for the phone, I realized he was never going to pay up – or get rid of the dogs. I'm not really a person who's interested in suing people, so I decided to move out and look for an apartment in Brentwood.

I was able to get out of my lease because of the dog attack and I asked Hayden if I could stay with her for a week or two until I found an apartment in Brentwood. Hayden was more than accommodating to me and said: "Of course you can, no problem."

Hayden's house is fucking huge and because I had known her for so long, it was a comfortable transition for me. While I stayed in her house for those two weeks, I was like part of her family. I would see her first thing in the morning over coffee, when most women don't want to be seen by anyone.

But even with her hair all messy, no make-up and in a bathrobe, I knew that this was the woman I wanted to spend the rest of my life with. I loved spending that time with her in the mornings. It was almost like that fucking dog did me a favor because I was now temporarily under Hayden's roof, which was a dream come true!

I would be standing next to her in the morning making coffee and I would smell her morning breath and it made me want her more. I wished that I was the one that was waking up next to her and I would have no problem kissing her with morning breath. Her morning breath smelled good to me! I would see her in the raw and her true beauty gave her this glow that I had never seen in a woman before. I knew that I could love this woman under any circumstance and under any condition!

When you're living with someone for any amount of time, you really get to know them. You see them when they're vulnerable, you see them cry, you see them happy and upset. Every emotion that I would see Hayden go through made me love her even more. It's an unconditional love, like the way a parent loves their children. This is how much I was in love with Hayden!

Believe me, I fought these emotions. I fought them hard. It was a tough situation to be in when you're so in love with someone and it seems almost impossible to have them. Especially when they're right there in front of you! Plus, Hayden, as a client, meant a lot of money for me. We were talking about my number one client!

Also, her now ex-husband is also a really good client and powerful as fuck, so I definitely did not want him to know how I felt about her, even though they were divorced. How was that conversation going to go down? "Hey man, I'm glad you love your hair, by the way, I'm in love with your ex-wife. That will be $200 please!"

I was in a fucking pickle!

There were nights when we were both alone in her house and I so badly wanted her to come downstairs and take advantage of me. I was staying on the bottom floor so I was really separated from the rest of the house. I even had my own entrance so I wouldn't bother anybody as I came and went.

As much as I loved staying in Hayden's ridiculously large mansion, I was on an aggressive mission to find an apartment. I didn't want to take advantage of her kindness for much longer and I also wanted her to see that I could afford an apartment in Brentwood without any help.

I finally landed a great spot in Brentwood, just down the street from my salon. I stayed at Hayden's for a total of 14 days, which was so generous of her but finding my own apartment didn't come a moment too soon. I was catching myself staring at her whenever she was near me. My feelings were really starting to get the best of me and moving out as fast as I could was the only way to ease the pain! I moved into my new spot in Brentwood and tried to keep myself as busy as possible.

Moving into a new apartment in a new neighborhood allowed me to keep my mind occupied in hopes of shaking off these feelings that were hijacking my life. I was still doing her hair a few times a week, but I work fast and I made sure that I kept it all business when I was around her. The problem was she was so damn beautiful that it was impossible not to compliment her and tell her how pretty she was or how great she would look or how sweet she was.

She would fucking sneeze and I would think it was the cutest thing I had ever seen. Her energy was like a powerful magnet that kept drawing me in! When she would talk to me she would always be so engaged in what I was saying. I knew it was because she really cared about me – what I didn't want to admit was that she cared about me like a best friend or a brother, not a potential boyfriend.

Just knowing that she was interested in my life made it hard for me to let go of these feelings. As much as I loved the money she was spending on getting her hair done, sometimes I wished that she would stop so I could give my heart a break!

It was Halloween and The Colony in Malibu had closed off the street for a big street party, so the really rich could take their kids trick or treating to other rich people's homes. A few days before this, Hayden had wanted me to come to the house to do her hair for her weekly blow dry.

As I was leaving, she asked what I was doing for Halloween. I cautiously told her: "Nothing in particular, maybe a house party if something good pops up." She then asked me if I wanted to come to the Colony party with her.

She had a friend that had a house there and she was invited. She said: "If you're not doing anything you can come with us." Us meant her and her son. I jumped at the chance and answered right away: "Yes, I would love to!" She gave me the time that she wanted to leave and the plan would be that I would meet her at her house, then we would all drive together. "Sounds perfect," I said, "I want to come for sure!"

Wow, I couldn't believe she was inviting me out. Was this my chance? Was she giving me a sign? I needed to look extra hot if she was bringing me around her friends. I didn't sleep a wink the night before Halloween! I was so excited to just be with her. I guess this was all I'd ever wanted. To just be part of her life in some way other than just doing her hair. Just to be able to be out with her in public, where we could be seen together.

In my mind, I was going to be the perfect date for her even though to her it was just as friends. I arrived at her house right on time and off we went to Malibu. As we drove to Malibu, I stared at her arms and that beautiful skin that I was so attracted to. She had that beautiful scent that had me in a trance while I was driving us up the coast.

As I was driving we were talking about each other's day. I so badly wanted to hold her hand as the sun was setting in the distance. This felt so right to me. I felt like her husband and we were going to see friends together.

I knew that I wanted to be this woman's husband, or at least I could be if she would let me. I finally had gotten myself into the position I have always dreamed of. Finally, I was driving to a social event with Hayden and there was not a blow dryer in sight. She finally wanted to be around me without her getting her hair done!

This was a huge moment in my life. Imagine you're a guy, you're looking through a Victoria's Secret catalogue and all of sudden, your favorite model from the catalogue is now in the car with you and you're off to meet her friends. It was a surreal moment and I already didn't want it to end.

We arrived in Malibu and we started to walk up the private street known as The Colony. It was Halloween so most people were dressed in a fancy costume, but the majority of the people invited to this street party were either really famous or just really rich!

Within five minutes I had spotted one of the Beastie Boys, Elon Musk (the guy who owns Tesla!) and Robert Downey Jr. And as I said, that was just in the first five minutes! All of the homes on this street were worth at least $10 million, with many of them even more expensive.

We started to walk towards her friend's house and were swept up in the crowd of hundreds of kids trick or treating and running around like crazy from their sugar rushes. Once we started walking up the street her son disappeared with his friends and we were now alone together. All I wanted to do was grab her and make out with her. Every time I looked right into her eyes, my heart and stomach felt like they were in my throat, but I hoped I was keeping it cool so she wouldn't notice.

I was hanging on every word she said and every time she turned her head to look at something I would just continue to stare at her beautiful profile. Her face, her hair, her smell, her skin, all of it was just calling my name.

We arrived at her friend's house, which was half way up The Colony. The house was sick! We walked in and we were greeted by her friends as a lot of them were already there. When she introduced me, she introduced me as her friend, not her hair stylist! My heart was beating so loud, I was afraid she'd hear it!

While she was mingling with her friends I went to grab us a drink and started mingling with people on my own. I started talking to people that were near the appetizers and started conversing with them. I could see Hayden out of the corner of my eye and she was busy talking to her friends. I wanted her to see me talking to other people, so that she would know that I was self-sufficient. I wanted her to see that I could hold my own with this crowd.

After about 15 minutes I walked over to her to make sure she was good. I asked her if I could get her something to drink and if she needed anything. She said:

"Brandon, do you know those people over there?" I quickly responded with: "No, but I do now!" I then walked off to grab us a drink. I had no idea what she was telling her friends as far as who I was.

At the end of the day, because I knew how these friends of hers were, I knew that they were probably suspicious about what was happening. All of a sudden, Hayden had rolled into the party with this younger guy who's her 'friend'. I loved it! I'm sure most of her friends were probably like: "Yeah, they're fucking for sure!"

She had friends at the party whose kids went to school with her kids, so they would see each other every day. All of sudden, I had appeared out of nowhere and I was not easy to hide. I was standing out at this party and, I have to admit, Hayden and I looked like a beautiful couple!

The night was coming to an end and it was time to leave. I had so much fun just being with her and even if I wasn't really her boyfriend yet, she definitely treated me like I was. It wasn't that she was being affectionate in any way but she seemed so comfortable around me, like the two us being together was so natural! When we parted, I hugged her tightly so I could smell her neck and just feel her for a few seconds. I wanted to kiss her so badly but I stopped myself and headed out.

I basically floated all the way home. I could smell her on my clothes and, I must admit, I went to sleep in the shirt I was wearing because it smelled like her. I don't care if that sounds weird because after that night, I was full-blown in love with her! If I thought I had been in love before, I was kidding myself. Before it had been like a schoolboy crush. Now it was the real deal!

When I got home, I tried to sleep, but it just wasn't happening for me. It had been one of the most exciting nights of my life and our lips hadn't even touched. That's how strong of a hold she had on me!

I had known Hayden now for about 10 years. For 10 years I had wanted this woman! I don't think I'd ever wanted anything more than her. I had to say something. Maybe she wanted me too? Maybe that was the sign. I had convinced myself that I had to be the man and be the one to make a move! So ,what if I lost her as a client?

I kept telling myself that this was much more important than money. Money wasn't everything, there were far more important things in life. This was love and I knew after the party on Halloween night that I was not going to be able hold in my feelings anymore!

A few days went by and we had been texting back and forth. It was just random stuff we were texting about, not lovey-dovey stuff but nevertheless, we were now communicating almost daily like friends. Hayden loved music as I did and I started sending her songs that I liked. She would tell me about bands that she liked and because I would hang on her every word, I took every opportunity to reach out to her.

After a couple days of texting back and forth I decided to go for it! I began telling her how I felt! It all came bubbling to the surface and I was unable to hold it in anymore! I figured that music would be my way in. She seemed to really respond to the music I liked so I figured that was the way. She had text messaged me about something, I think it was to do her hair and I had found this beautiful song by Ray LaMontagne called *Hold You In My Arms*. If you don't know this song, it's really romantic and beautiful.

I decided that I was going to send her the song and I was going to say something really beautiful to her so that maybe she would get the hint. I attached the song to my text and I typed these words to her: "Hayden, here is an incredibly soulful song, for an incredibly soulful person. If I had written this song, I would have written it for you." I double-checked my grammar so I didn't look like an idiot, I took a deep breath and I hit send!

Holy shit! I couldn't believe I had just done it! There was no going back now and I didn't want to take it back either. I gave it a few minutes as I had no idea what she was doing at that precise moment. My heart was racing a mile a minute. Five minutes went by and nothing. It was like tumbleweeds! I was getting a little nervous but, in reality, five minutes was nothing even though it seemed like a lifetime!

Then I heard my phone buzz from a new text coming in and it was her! I couldn't believe my eyes. She responded with: "Oh my God, Brandon, that's such a beautiful song. You have me in tears right now!"

Oh my God. I couldn't believe it. It was working! She was responding! Then without hesitating I texted her right back and I said: "I'm having a difficult time hiding my feelings for you Hayden."

Right away she responded with: "What???" It never occurred to me that she might be shocked. In my mind, she was as elated as I was. So, I kept on going, like a bull in a china shop there was no stopping me now!

I answered with: "I can't hold back my feelings for you anymore. I've tried, but I can't hold it in any longer! I want you to know how I feel about you!" As I pressed send that time, it finally dawned on me that she was probably shocked that I was telling her this.

She texted me back right away and said: "Well I was coming to see you tomorrow anyway for my hair, let's have lunch because we need to talk about this. I'll come an hour early so we can sit and talk, OK?"

Crestfallen? I didn't know how to feel right then. She hadn't declared her love right back and I couldn't tell if she was into it or if she wasn't. I replied: "Yes, of course. I'll be at the salon waiting for you. We can have lunch near the salon."

The next day seemed like an eternity from the day before. Of course, I didn't sleep a wink. Being in love with Hayden had been killing my sleeping pattern! I got to the salon and my palms were sweaty and clammy.

I found myself pacing up and down the salon until she showed. Then, like an angel, she appeared. She walked up to the door to the salon and said, all business like: "Let's go have our talk now OK?" Seemed like she didn't want to wait either.

We walked to the restaurant that was right in front of the salon. The restaurant was called Baltaire Steakhouse. It's a beautiful, high-end steak house that is probably one of the most expensive restaurants in

Brentwood. I wasn't going to tell her how I felt about her at a Chipotle!

So, we walked into the restaurant and grabbed a booth in the back of the bar area so we could have some privacy. We didn't really say much to each other before we sat down. It was like we were both saving it. We sat down and the bartender came from around the bar to take our order. I think we both ordered coffees to start. My heart was pumping on overtime and I could see in her face that she was nervous as well.

I took a deep breath and told her everything I had ever wanted to say to her. Ten years of feelings just poured out of me. Once I started, it was like the floodgates were open and they couldn't be closed again. I told her: "Hayden, I'm so in love with you! I have been for so long. I can't stop thinking about you. You have been running in my thoughts ever since we have met and for the life of me, I cannot hold it in anymore! All I do is think about you and I want you so much it hurts!"

She started to say something and before the words came out of her mouth I went for it! I kissed Hayden so fast that one wrong move from either side could have caused an unintentional head butt.

Fortunately, she opened her mouth at the same time I did. Finally, my lips were touching hers! All this time, all these years, and it was finally happening! It felt like I was imagining it. It was like I had risen above my body and I was looking down at the both of us.

It was everything that I thought it would be. I put my hands around her arms so I could feel her skin that I had always dreamt of. I could feel my leg trembling with excitement and my stomach felt like I had a butterfly commune living inside of it.

As I touched her body and ran my hands up and down her arms, I could feel that she was frozen! As our lips were locked, I grabbed her arms and threw them around my body so she could feel me as I was slightly shaking!

I was scared, I was excited and I never wanted it to end! I felt like I had died and gone to Heaven. If I did nothing else in my life, this moment would see me through to the end.

Right then and there, as we were kissing, I told God: "Please, take me now Lord, I'm ready! I want to remember it just like this!"

THE END